PRAISE FOR HEIDI MCLAUGHLIN

The Art of Starting Over

"Pulls you in with one hard yank, and, while your heart is in shreds, you can't put it down. It's not your average small-town, second-chance romance. The pain is worth it, because when the pleasure hits—it comes in strong."

—Abbi Glines, #1 *New York Times* bestselling author of the Rosemary Beach series

"Second chance romances are my love language, and this one did not disappoint. A beautifully rendered emotional slow burn complete with crackling chemistry, a charming setting, and a cast of characters to fall for completely. Nostalgic, hopeful, and full of heart!"

—Marissa Stapley, author of *Lucky*

"A big, beautiful story about the power of love to heal and grow our very human hearts. Get the tissues ready for this one!"

—Jennifer Probst, author of *To Sicily with Love*

"*The Art of Starting Over* is a fantastic story of second chances and starting over. The residents of small-town Oyster Bay add great found-family elements into the story. A definite must read!

—Taylor Delong, author of *Pucked Up Plans*

Heartbreak Hill

"*Heartbreak Hill* is a heartbreakingly beautiful novel. Grayson and Reid's journey to love is emotional until the very last page. You don't want to miss this read."

—A. M. Guilliams, author of *Bring Me Back Here*

"*Heartbreak Hill* is a beautiful, heart-stirring, stick-with-you-for-days story of several lives that are intertwined through loss and an extraordinary act of giving."

—M. E. Montgomery, author of *Call It Fate*

"*Heartbreak Hill* took me on a roller coaster of emotions. Heidi has a remarkable talent for creating characters that leave a mark on you."

—J. C. Hannigan, author of *Riverside Reverie*

"In *Heartbreak Hill*, McLaughlin weaves a poignant tale of love, loss, and second chances. Grab your tissues . . . You're going to need them!"

—Taylor Delong, author of *Waiting on Forever*

Before I'm Gone

"Palmer's ability to find the beauty of life in the face of death makes her an admirable heroine. Readers should have tissues ready."

—*Publishers Weekly*

"*Before I'm Gone* is a heartbreakingly beautiful love story about finding your soulmate against all odds."

—*USA Today* bestselling author Ashley Cade

"This book is absolutely gut-wrenching and broke my heart into a million pieces, but their story hit me in such a beautiful way."

—Vanessa Valencia, Goodreads

"Beautiful and emotional, cried buckets."

—*AC Book Blog*

"I am not okay. And that's okay. Damn, this book wrecked me with all the feels. Such a cathartic cry I hadn't realized I needed."

—Courtney, Goodreads

Cape Harbor

"I love a good second-chance romance, and Heidi McLaughlin did NOT disappoint."

—*New York Times* bestselling author L. P. Dover

"This is a story that will stay with me for a long, long time."

—Sara, Goodreads

"A beautifully written story that will pull you in and tug at your heartstrings."

—Nikki, *Crazy Cajun Book Addicts*

"The reader will instantly fall in love with Cape Harbor."

—Nicki, *The Overflowing Bookcase*

"McLaughlin knows how to put a person in touch with their emotions."

—Isha, *Hopeless Romantic*

The Beaumont Series

"If you want to read a book that is all heart—full of characters you will instantly connect with and love from the first page to the last—then *Forever My Girl* is the book for you."

—Jenny, *Totally Booked Blog*

"*Forever My Girl* is a sweet, loving, all-around adorable read. If you, like me, have a thing for musicians and reconnections, then this read is for you."

—*Jacqueline's Reads*

"This is an utterly moving story of second chances in life, of redemption, remorse, forgiveness, of loves lost and found again, of trust regained. Through alternating points of view, we feel both Liam's and Josie's emotions, fears, and sorrow. These are well-developed characters whose love for each other survives time and distance."

—*Natasha Is a Book Junkie*, on *Forever My Girl*

"*My Unexpected Forever* completely outdid my expectations and blew *Forever My Girl* out of the water. *My Unexpected Forever* is without a doubt a book that I would recommend, and Harrison is officially my new book boyfriend!"

—*Holly's Hot Reads*

Maybe It's Fate

ALSO BY HEIDI MCLAUGHLIN

STAND-ALONE NOVELS

The Art of Starting Over

Heartbreak Hill

Before I'm Gone

CAPE HARBOR SERIES

After All

Until Then

THE BEAUMONT SERIES

Forever My Girl

My Everything

My Unexpected Forever

Finding My Forever

Finding My Way

12 Days of Forever

My Kind of Forever

Forever Our Boys

Forever Mason

Forever My Boy

THE BEAUMONT SERIES: NEXT GENERATION

Holding Onto Forever

My Unexpected Love

Chasing My Forever

Peyton & Noah

Fighting for Our Forever

A Beaumont Family Christmas

Give Me Forever

Everything for Love

The Beginning of Forever

The Road to Forever

THE SEAPORT SERIES

The Lobster Trap

The Love in Sunsets

Sail Away with Me

THE ARCHER BROTHERS

Here with Me

Choose Me

Save Me

Here with Us

Choose Us

NASHVILLE NIGHTS

Sangria

Rye

HOLIDAY NOVELS

Santa's Secret

It's a Wonderful Holiday

Stranded with the One

Love in Print

This Christmas

Maybe It's Fate

HEIDI
MCLAUGHLIN

Published by Montlake, Seattle

www.apub.com

EU product safety contact:
Amazon Media EU S. à r.l.
38, avenue John F. Kennedy, L-1855 Luxembourg
amazonpublishing-gpsr@amazon.com

ISBN-13: 9781662537363 (paperback)
ISBN-13: 9781662537356 (digital)

Cover design by Ploy Siripant
Cover image: © Jung Getty, © goinyk / Getty

Printed in the United States of America

For Erik:

You're my person.

Prologue

At seventeen, you thought you had your entire world figured out. Your parents were wrong about everything, and the boy you were in love with—the one everyone had warned you about—was the love of your life. Deep down, a part of you knew he was going to hurt you, destroy your faith in men, in the world. But you didn't care because, at that moment, he was your whole world, and he'd told you there wasn't anything he wouldn't do for you.

Except stick around when the line on the stick turned pink or blue or appeared twice. And while you were happy because a baby meant you'd be with him forever, he had other ideas.

As did your parents. They were deeply religious and didn't understand why you'd insisted on disobeying them. Why would you throw your life away for a boy who didn't care about anyone but himself?

I love him, Daddy.

Love wasn't enough. At least not to him.

Love meant something else to him, and as long as everything was just the two of you, there weren't any issues.

Three of you became a problem.

I lay back and stared at the blue sky. I tried to imagine the clouds forming those shapes everyone saw when they gazed upward, but all I saw were mounds of cotton balls floating off to someplace better than where we were.

My best friend, Antonia, lay beside me, her hand in mine, staring at the same sky, the same clouds, the same nothingness.

"Maybe I should do what my parents want and give the baby up for adoption." Instinctively, my hand covered my lower abdomen, where my little pea nestled.

"I can go with you, if you want to speak to someone about it."

Antonia had always been by my side since we were three. Although I didn't remember us at three, four, or five, I did remember us starting kindergarten together. Our teachers called us "inseparable busybodies," and they wanted us in different classes. The joke was on them. The powers that be, thanks to Antonia's aunt being the registrar at school, put us in the same class every single year. It wasn't until junior high that we had different classes.

Different likes.

Always best friends.

"What if I keep her?"

"Is it a girl?"

I lifted one shoulder in a shrug. "I guess it could be a boy."

"Or twins."

I groaned at the thought and covered my face as a fresh wave of tears began to fall. "What have I done?"

Antonia let go of my hand and propped herself up on her elbow. "Nothing that any of our classmates haven't done. We're graduating soon, Miriam. Things will be okay. You can still go to college if you want."

I did want to, but I knew my parents wouldn't foot the bill if I had this baby. I'd heard about some programs, though. The government gave a lot of financial aid to single moms, and I could take out a school loan.

"If I keep this baby, we won't be able to go to school together." Going away to a big school like the University of Arizona had been our dream. Now it was just Antonia's unless I made the right decision. Or the wrong decision. It was hard to know which decision fell into the right category.

"If you keep this baby, you'll be a mom, Miri."

"I know." My words were barely above a whisper. Being a mom was something I'd always said I'd do. Sure, I wanted a career, but I wanted children too. I just never thought I'd be a mom at eighteen.

"When do you have to decide?"

Without asking, I knew what she meant. I supposed when you were early in your pregnancy, everything was on the table.

"Soon." I already knew I wouldn't be able to do it, to follow through with ending my pregnancy. The father—the boy—I had considered the love of my life didn't want anything to do with me or his child. He'd walked out on me, saying he had bigger dreams and aspirations than working some nine-to-five job so he could buy diapers and formula. This was news to me, since he'd already dropped out of high school and had a part-time gig at the auto shop.

Antonia lay back down, scooching closer to me. We tilted our heads toward one another, both sighing.

"Maybe my parents can help?"

She had the best parents. Renzo and Carmela Bernardi were kind and gentle, and they let Antonia and her siblings, Rocco and Isabella, do anything they wanted, as long as they obeyed the law.

"Renzo would hunt . . . *him* . . . down." I couldn't even bring myself to say his name. Anyone who walked out on their pregnant girlfriend didn't deserve a name.

"He would." Antonia squeezed my hand. "So would Rocco."

The thought of her family helping me this way brought more tears to my eyes. Why couldn't my parents feel the same way?

"If I don't do what my parents want, they're going to ask me to leave. They won't tolerate me showing up at church with a protruding belly and no band on my finger."

"You don't want to marry him, Miri."

I coughed out a strangled sob. "You know, when I saw the lines on the test, I thought he'd get down on his knee and ask me to marry him. The moment was so vivid in my mind. Him sweeping me off my feet, twirling me around, and telling me how much he loved me. How we were going to be a family."

"Just because he didn't, doesn't mean someone won't. He wasn't the one for you, Miriam."

"I wish I'd listened to everyone."

"This is one of those hindsight moments. We can't change what happened because, if you want to get technical, I encouraged you to date him. I saw how your eyes sparkled when he came near. He's hot, but unfortunately, he knows it and uses it to his advantage."

"Don't I know it."

I lost track of how long we lay there, watching the clouds move overhead, letting time pass us by, the tall grass tickling us with each gust of wind. I was content because nothing mattered here. Antonia would never judge me for my decisions, and she was the only person to have vowed her unconditional support.

She must've sensed I needed a little reassurance, because she reached for my hand. "Are you getting hungry?"

My shoulder lifted in a weak attempt at a half shrug. "Do you think eating for two is a real thing?"

"We learned about cravings in health class, remember?"

I nodded. "I wish we'd learned more about the consequences of the bad-boy attraction and sex."

Antonia laughed. I knew it was in good fun, and not mocking. "The teachers would never. Parents would throw a fit. Can you imagine what the school board meeting would be like?"

I laughed with her. She was right. "My mother would've lost it, demanding to know why her daughter had learned how to put on a condom." I covered my face with my hand. "If only."

"It's not just your responsibility." Antonia's voice was soft, kind. She was right. I was not the only one to blame. "Things happen."

"Things?" I turned to look at her, only to find her staring at me.

Antonia shrugged as best she could while being prone. "I didn't want to call the baby an accident, because if you decide to keep him or her, then they definitely weren't an accident, ya know?"

I wanted to hug her and strangle her at the same time. Why did she have to say things to make me question my already-questioning mind?

"If I keep this baby, will you still be my friend?"

"Always and forever, Miri."

"And if something ever happens to me, you'll take care of them for me?"

Antonia nodded.

"Do you promise?"

"With my whole heart, Miriam. I'll treat your son or daughter like they're my family. I'll be Auntie Toni." She smiled brightly. "Besides, nothing will ever happen. We're going to grow old together. Remember?"

"Yes, spinsters. The two of us sitting on a porch in our creaking rocking chairs, yelling at the teens racing down the dirt road."

Antonia chuckled. "Why do we live on a dirt road?"

I gave her another half shrug. "Because we bought and restored an old farmhouse."

"We did?"

I nodded. "We have chickens for fresh eggs every morning, and a goat because they like to eat grass, and we wouldn't have to mow."

"No cats, though, because I'm allergic."

"Barn cats are a must because they keep the mice away."

Antonia shuddered. "Our home sounds magical."

"It will be because we'll be together." I held up our clasped hands. "Best friends forever."

"The future spinsters of America."

We both laughed until our sides hurt, and then everything turned serious again.

"I'm scared."

"I know you are. Let's go talk to my mom, Miri. She'll help you."

"Okay."

Antonia drove her Ford Escort at a snail's pace, telling me I had precious cargo, and she wasn't going to be the one at fault if we got into an accident. As much as I appreciated her efforts, I wanted to go to her house and get this over with.

I wasn't afraid of what Carmela would say. I was afraid of the look she'd give me. It didn't matter how hard someone tried; you couldn't mask initial disappointment. Even though I wasn't her daughter, I'd grown up in her home, and she treated me like I was.

There wasn't a parent alive who would be excited to hear that their son or daughter was having a child at seventeen. Well, I'd be eighteen when the baby came, which I guess made me an adult.

We pulled up in front of the two-story colonial. My heart jumped into my throat when I saw Renzo and Rocco throwing a football out front, while Carmela was on the front step, watching her husband and son.

To me, Antonia's family was perfect. They never fought, they were always laughing, and they genuinely seemed to love each other. It was the kind of family I wanted and strived for. Carmela was the kind of mother I wanted to be.

Antonia got out of her car and met me at the passenger side. We walked together up the pathway, until we reached her mom.

"Hey, girls. Did you enjoy your outing?"

Antonia nodded. "Mama, can we go inside and talk?"

Carmela looked from her daughter to me, and as soon as I diverted my eyes, she knew I could feel the disappointment coursing between us.

"Come on. I just took some cookies out of the oven."

We followed her into the house, taking off our shoes as we entered. The Bernardis had mauve carpet in every room, with a white-and-floral-patterned couch. Rarely would I ever sit on it, out of fear I'd spill my drink or something. Antonia and I would always put pillows on the floor when we watched TV with her family. To the right, after you entered the home, was the dining room. Their family table was large, seating up to eight people. The thinly crocheted tablecloth that draped over it had been made by Antonia's great-grandmother back in Italy. If you sat at the table, you moved the tablecloth. That was the rule.

Off the dining room was the kitchen and breakfast nook. Carmela motioned for us to go sit. We did and then waited.

Antonia reached for my hand under the table. She held it tightly. I fought back the onslaught of tears waiting to spill over. Carmela came to the table with a tray of cookies and three glasses of milk.

She pulled her chair out and sat, the silence among the three of us palpable.

"Did you girls do something illegal?"

"No, Mama."

Carmela nodded and looked directly at me. Her hand covered mine. "Are you in . . ." She didn't finish before I started nodding. She was up and out of her chair, and I was in her arms before the tears spilled over.

"I'm scared."

She cradled me. Unlike my mother, who'd told me to get out of her sight. Maybe the difference was because I wasn't Carmela's daughter. I probably wouldn't ever know.

It felt like an eternity before she let me go. When I sat down again and looked at Antonia, I saw that she'd been crying as well, but she managed to give me a smile.

"Do your parents know?"

"Yes, ma'am."

"I imagine they aren't happy."

"No, ma'am."

Carmela nodded.

"Do you need a place to stay?"

I nodded, unable to find the words.

"Do you need to see a doctor?"

Again, another nod.

"Very well. I'm going to go see your mom and let her know you're here. And then we'll figure everything else out." She placed her hand on mine and squeezed it reassuringly. "No matter which road you choose, it's going to be hard."

"I know."

We sat for another moment until she cleared her throat. "Let's eat these cookies before the guys come in. We need the pick-me-up more than they do."

For the first time since I'd taken and failed the only test that would ever matter, I felt like things would be okay.

Chapter 1

Antonia

My footsteps were heavy, clunky, as I speed-walked toward the conference room, my business phone pressed against my ear and my personal phone vibrating wildly in my pocket. At the first cubicle I saw, I set down the dozen or so manila file folders I was carrying and reached into my pocket for my phone. The caller ID told me it was my best friend, Miriam.

"Not a good time, Miri. I'm about to head into a huge meeting. Can I call you back?" I scooped the folders up again, sent a silent apology to the man sitting at the desk I'd dumped them on, and continued down the hall.

Miriam and I had been best friends our entire lives. Our relationship wasn't one of those where you lost track of each other and found one another again on social media. We had the spend-your-birthdays-and-holidays-together type of relationship. For all intents and purposes, Miriam was my soul sister, or whatever you'd consider to be more than a sister. And even though I had a real-life sister who shared the same parents, my relationship with Isabella didn't hold a candle to the one I had with Miri.

"I know. I'm sorry."

"You're gonna have to listen to me huff and puff. I'm late for this meeting, and my shoes are killing me." I hung up my business line when the client put me on hold. I didn't have time to wait for them to figure out what they needed from me. They should've been ready when they called. "Miri?"

She cleared her throat. "Can you come to Grove Hill?"

Grove Hill was a smallish town a little over two hours north of Boston, in New Hampshire's White Mountains. Miriam and her kids, Cutter and Nova, lived on the outskirts of town, in an old farmhouse on a dirt road. The house was a money pit, but she was determined to restore it to all its glory. Mostly because it had been her dream when we were seventeen.

"I don't have my calendar in front of me, but as far as I know, I'm not doing anything this weekend. I'll come after work on Friday."

Miriam and I grew up in a tight community in Boston, went to private school, and lived together while I went to college. It was because of her that I stayed behind and went to Boston University instead of the University of Arizona, our original dream school before she got pregnant.

She needed me more than I needed to be a Wildcat.

After I graduated, I thought we'd continue to be roomies, but she wanted to raise her son where he could have a yard to play in, while I wanted to live in a high-rise, which wouldn't exactly have been ideal for a toddler.

Miriam worked as an accountant in Grove Hill and did the mom thing, while I stayed in Boston and landed a job as a senior consultant with a focus on corporate restructuring at Caldwell & Crest, a corporate consulting firm specializing in mergers, acquisitions, and strategic business planning. Miriam teased that I was like Richard Gere's character in *Pretty Woman*, buying, dismantling, and selling off struggling companies. Only, unlike Edward Lewis, it wasn't my money that was being spent, and I had bosses to report to.

Bosses who'd expected me in a meeting five minutes ago.

"Toni, I need you to come today." Miri's voice was quiet, almost hard to hear.

"Why? What's wrong? Are the kids okay?"

"They're fine, at school. I-I need you."

I stopped in front of the all-glass conference room and raised my finger when my boss, Brendan Caldwell, stood and gave me a "What the fuck are you doing?" look and tapped his watch. If he hadn't also been my boyfriend of four years, I would've been worried about my job after telling the boss to wait.

"Miri, you're scaring me. What's wrong?"

"I'm sick, Toni. I need you to come."

My heart fell to the floor and my mouth went dry. I stared through the glass, knowing Brendan and our clients were sitting around the large, ornate conference table, but I couldn't see them. My vision blurred, and everything around me seemed to move in slow motion.

"Miri?"

"Please." Her voice broke and I nodded, despite her not being able to see me.

"I'm on my way."

It took me a moment to regain my composure. Once I had, I opened the door and asked to speak to Brendan outside.

"We're in the middle of something, Toni, and we're waiting on you." Brendan's lips were stretched tightly across his mouth.

I forced a smile as all the others looked at me. "Yes, but this is important." I didn't leave him a choice. I stepped out, let the door shut behind me, and walked down the hall toward the break room. Thankfully, it was empty, so I wouldn't have to ask anyone to leave.

"What on earth could be so important that it can't wait until after this meeting?" Brendan huffed as he came in and shut the door behind him.

"Miriam is sick, and I need to go to her."

"Now?" His eyes widened.

"Yes, now. She called. She needs me."

Brendan rolled his eyes. If he wasn't so damn gorgeous, his dismissiveness would've pissed me off. He didn't have the type of relationship that I had with Miri with any of his friends. Sure, he'd meet his buddies for golf or to play squash at the courts, and he played in charity games with them, but he wasn't close enough with any of his friends to drop everything.

I was.

Brendan was senior partner at Caldwell & Crest—a company his grandfather had founded—and he also worked in mergers and acquisitions. He was one of the best negotiators in the business and could sweet-talk candy from a baby.

Brendan was tall, lean, and athletic, with neatly trimmed sandy blond hair that he parted on the side and a clean-shaven face. He was the picture-perfect preppy boy, always model-ready, and exactly the type of guy you'd find in a Black Dog or Vineyard Vines catalog. He used to row at Harvard, and he often reminded me how his team had beaten BU one year in some regatta.

He leaned against the wall and stuffed his hands in his pockets, looking dashing and pissed off at the same time, but he was definitely unimpressed with me, and I was wasting his time. We were both headstrong and determined, and neither of us were willing to back down if we strongly believed we were right.

"When doesn't she need you?"

I knew the question was rhetorical. He would never tell me, but I suspected he wasn't a fan of Miriam's, which didn't bode well for my relationship with Brendan. Miri wasn't going anywhere. Not only was she my soul sister, but I was also "Auntie Toni" to her two kids. There wasn't a thing in this world I wouldn't do for her or them.

"I don't know, Brendan. I'm not in the business of keeping track of when Miriam needs me. But she said she's sick, and I need to go. I'm sorry, but I'm confident you can handle the meeting."

"What is it?"

"What do you mean?" I looked at him with confusion.

"A sniffle? A cough?"

Now, I rolled my eyes. "Oh, please."

"What?" He shrugged. "This isn't the first time she's interrupted our plans."

"A meeting isn't a plan." I kept my voice low and pointed to the door.

Brendan smirked and pushed away from the wall. With his hand on the doorknob, he looked over his shoulder. "When will you be back?"

"I don't know, maybe tonight. Probably tomorrow morning. I won't know until I'm there and can see Miri."

He nodded, but the gesture felt dismissive. "Don't forget we have dinner with my parents Saturday night."

Shit. Shit. Shit.

"I won't."

Brendan shook his head and walked out of the room. His voice boomed as he greeted our clients but dimmed quickly as the door shut. I gave myself a minute to center myself before leaving the break room and heading toward my office.

On my way, I kept my head down and my phone pressed to my ear as I called the garage attendant and asked him to bring my car around. Most of the time, I left it parked in the garage at the office. It was easier than driving the car to my apartment every night and paying for parking elsewhere. I could park at the office for free and not worry about it. Honestly, Miriam and the kids were the only reason I even had a car. If I had to go see a client, we used a car service.

While I waited for my car, I packed my laptop into the bag the kids had bought me for Christmas last year. Seven-year-old Nova had picked it out, while her teenage brother had wanted to give me the newest electronic gaming something or other. I suspected his gift would've been for his own benefit and not so much mine.

With my calls being forwarded to my cell phone, I shut off the lights and headed toward the bank of elevators after letting my assistant, Amaya, know I would be out for the rest of the day but available via phone and email. I didn't have to worry about her doing her job while

I was gone. She'd been with me for three years now and was a complete asset, taking on more responsibility than she needed, and, in doing so, she took a little bit off my plate.

By the time I'd made it to the lobby, my car was idling out front. The valet saw me walking toward him and ran to open my door for me. He took my bags and set them in the back and told me to have a good day.

Working for Caldwell & Crest was my dream job. I had interned for them during my senior year of college and gladly accepted an entry-level position while I finished grad school. Upon graduation, I was given a raise and had steadily worked my way up the ladder since then.

Brendan and I were able to date for a year before anyone figured it out. We got a little too handsy at one of the company's Christmas parties, and the cat was out of the bag. No one seemed to care, and we promised to always keep things professional at work. And while I would've loved a little office hanky-panky, Brendan would never consider it. He was afraid his father or grandfather would find out and shame him. I told him this was why there were locks on the door and couches in the offices, but what did I know.

I stopped quickly at my apartment, leaving my car double-parked with its flashers on while I ran in to grab an overnight bag, just in case. This wasn't the first emergency trip I'd made north to Miriam's, and it wouldn't be the last, but I knew well enough to bring a change of clothes. Once Nova found out I was in town, she would want a sleepover and breakfast, and denying her anything was near impossible.

Nova was my mini me, despite having zero blood relation. She was inquisitive and had a vivid imagination, creating the most elaborate stories for us to act out. I used to do the same thing and had an imaginary friend when I was younger. A friend Miri hated because they never got along—according to me. Nova was my hugger, attached to my side like glue, and I wouldn't have changed our relationship for anything. Except when she grilled Brendan and me on when we were going to have a baby. She wanted a baby cousin and wanted one now.

At times, I wondered the same thing and often brought it up with Brendan when we were sitting around on a lazy Sunday morning. His answer was always, "Soon."

What did "soon" actually mean? Did it have a timeline? I wasn't getting any younger, and I'd always thought I'd be married for a year before we had children. My clock was still ticking, but not as loudly as it once had.

Two hours later, I arrived in Grove Hill. I asked the AI system in my car to call Miriam. When she answered, I said, "I'll be there in fifteen. I just pulled onto Main Street, and there's a tractor in front of me. Slow mooooving." I said "moving" so it sounded like a cow mooing—something Nova would've appreciated.

"I'm in the hospital, Toni."

I slammed on the brakes and signaled to pull over. In a small town like Grove Hill, there always seemed to be a parking spot along the curb.

"What did you say?"

Miri coughed. "You heard me."

"Why didn't you tell me this when you called earlier?"

"Because I didn't want you to worry. I know how you get when your mind is elsewhere, and I needed you to get here in one piece."

Miri wasn't wrong. I hated driving because my mind was often preoccupied with work. "I'll be there in a minute." We hung up, and I turned around and headed toward the other end of Main Street, where the hospital was. I had no idea what I was about to walk into, but my gut told me it wouldn't be good.

Chapter 2

Weston

I stood in the middle of the gym and scanned the kids along each wall. They had their toes on the line, waiting for me to blow the whistle. Along the half-court line, rubber balls stretched out in a neat row.

"Are you ready?" I called out.

The kids mumbled a halfhearted, "Yay."

"I can't hear you, Timberwolves. I asked, Are you ready?"

This time, their response was louder. One kid might have even roared, but it was hard to tell because I had several linebackers from the football team in my PE class.

I gave them one last look before heading to the sideline. No way was I standing in the middle of the court during a game of dodgeball. The last thing I wanted was to get pelted with a rubber ball.

As soon as I'd stepped over the black sideline, I blew my whistle. Both sides raced to grab a ball, and I watched their strategies unfold. Some kids hurled the balls as hard as they could, while others teamed up, throwing simultaneously to catch their targets off guard.

The first kid out was Cutter Vaughn. I'd never admit it if anyone asked, but Cutter was one of my favorite students. Coaching him in basketball and baseball was a privilege. He was the kind of athlete every coach dreamed about—dedicated, hardworking, and never one to complain. Baseball was his golden ticket, and I planned to call some old major league buddies and Division I and II coaches once the season started about getting him signed. With their help, maybe I could get Cutter some looks. Otherwise, I doubted he'd go to college; I knew his mom probably couldn't afford it.

The Vaughns lived two houses down from me on a dirt road just outside town. Every day, I drove past their house and wondered how it was still standing. Miriam Vaughn was always outside fixing something, whether it was spring, summer, or fall. I'd lost count of how many times I'd stopped to offer help, only for her to politely decline.

She needed it, though she'd never admit it.

And every time I passed by, Cutter was outside, too, shooting hoops or throwing his baseball against the pitch-back net. His determination and work ethic never failed to impress me.

"What happened?" I asked Cutter when he walked over the court to stand next to me.

He shrugged. "I saved Eleni."

Eleni was his girlfriend, according to the Grove Hill rumor mill. From what I'd seen in the hallways between classes, it was easy to believe the rumors were true. But that wasn't something I could ask my student or player. As his teacher and coach, I had to keep my boundaries—unless he came to me for advice.

One by one, more students joined us on the sidelines, some panting and out of breath, others fuming about getting out.

"Are we playing again, Mr. Schmidt?" Malik Carter asked, his tone eager.

"Do you think you can stay in the game longer this time?"

Malik gave me the "Come on, Coach, are you serious?" smirk and nodded confidently. He was our basketball team's point guard—a smart, strategic player who always thought two steps ahead and saw the floor better than anyone in the state. He played on a travel team during the spring and summer and already had a select number of colleges recruiting him. Malik had a bright future and was a great kid to coach.

When one last student stood victorious, I blew the whistle before he had a chance to celebrate and told everyone to get on the line. They did so quickly.

"Count off: one, two, three, four." Unfortunately, I had to watch each of the kids yell out their numbers, because you'd be shocked at who couldn't follow directions or forgot which number came after three. "All right, if you are a one or three, stay here; twos and fours, go to the other end."

"Coach, really?" Cutter groaned. "Now I can't protect Eleni."

"Very noble of you," I told him, but I didn't remind him that she'd lasted longer than he had in the last round. "Line up."

For the most part, my classes went smoothly. The kids followed instructions and enjoyed coming to class. They used this time to burn off pent-up energy or let out some frustration. School wasn't easy—not even when I was a student. Teachers could be tough, and classes were often challenging. Since graduating with my degree in physical education, I'd made it my goal to create a safe space where students could express themselves.

Like last time, I lined the rubber balls up along the mid-court line, walked off to the side, and blew my whistle. I watched, my head moving back and forth, as kids aimed for their classmates.

They jumped, ducked, and dodged flying balls, hollering excitedly when they got one of their classmates out, and groaning when they didn't see the round orb coming toward them from the side. It was usually the smaller, sneakier kids who prevailed. They tended to be quicker and often used the taller students to hide behind until they were the last ones standing.

Jayden Torres threw his arms up in victory when he was the last one remaining. With him standing five foot nine, he'd completely shot down my theory of the smaller, faster student. His speed and agility played a factor, though. Jayden was one of the fastest kids in the state, having won the state title in the one hundred, two hundred, and four hundred. He'd told me once that he ran track for fun, but basketball was where his heart was.

He came to the sideline and was congratulated by his classmates. I knew that outside of here, the students didn't always get along, but during gym class, I stressed the importance of teamwork. I never wanted anyone to feel as if they didn't belong or didn't have a partner in class. There was nothing worse than seeing a kid struggle in PE.

With five minutes to go before the bell rang, I excused the kids to go and get changed. My other counterparts often kept their classes until a minute before, but I never saw the reasoning. I never wanted the kids to feel rushed to change and make it to their next class.

After I'd excused them, I went out into the hall and stood between the two locker room doors. I'd asked the kids many times to wait in the locker room until the bell had sounded, and while most did as I asked, a few of them didn't.

The door to the boys' locker room opened, and Cutter appeared. I gave him a quizzical look. He smiled sheepishly.

"What can I do for you, Mr. Vaughn?"

"What time do we have to be at the game?"

Cutter tried to be subtle as he looked over his shoulder at the other door. My guess was that Eleni would be coming out shortly so they could do what teenagers did at this age—make out.

I bit the inside of my cheek to keep from smiling or laughing, needing to maintain a straight face. This boy knew exactly what time he needed to be at the gym tonight for the game. And when the door to the girls' locker room opened and Eleni stuck her head out, I knew I was right in my assumption.

"Ms. Chen," I said, giving her a nod. She blushed, ducked back inside, and closed the door.

I glanced at Cutter, who suddenly had a fascination with the floor. I didn't know much about the Vaughn household, but I suspected Cutter's father wasn't in the picture. Being a meddler had never been my forte because I respected people's privacy. I feared, though, that

Cutter needed a male role model, someone to guide him through these building hormones.

"If you ever need to talk, my office door is always open," I told him. "You can also text me."

He nodded. "Thanks, Coach."

The bell rang, saving us both from any awkwardness. I watched as the kids filed out of the locker rooms, but I mostly kept my attention on Cutter and Eleni. High school was already hard enough, but adding in teenage hormones made life seem like hell. I remembered, all too well, my first girlfriend, who eventually became my wife. I shuddered to think what our children would've been like if we'd had any. We would've ended up being the kind of parents who said, "Do as we say, not as we do."

I continued to stand in the hall, monitoring the students as they made their way to their next classes. Locker doors slapped, voices carried, and current and former kids said hi as they walked by. I had to issue a few warnings about roughhousing in the hall, but overall, the transition from one class to another was easy.

Generally, I gave the kids three minutes to get changed and be on the court for class. This was the time I stopped in my office, checked my phone for any important texts, and used the teachers-only bathroom. If all went as planned, my next class would be in the gym when I came out.

Class after class went off without any issues. Everyone enjoyed a relaxing day of dodgeball. Did the game have any purpose? Not really, but the students enjoyed it, and it was one of those games that allowed you to let out a ton of energy. It was better than running, in my opinion. And it was nice to break away from the curriculum every now and again.

I finished up my attendance reports for the day, late as usual, and shut my light off. I would be back in a couple of hours for tonight's basketball game.

This was my third year coaching varsity basketball, and the only reason I had the job was that the former coach had walked off the court, mid-game, three years ago. I was the assistant at the time, filling space during the winter months while I waited for baseball season to start.

My first year as head coach was rocky, and we lost all but three or four games. The next year had been marginally better, but this year had been vastly different.

The Grove Hill Timberwolves were undefeated.

At the core, this team had heart and determination. They played well together, worked as a team, and were never hard on one another. If one boy struggled, the others stepped up.

Tonight, they faced a crosstown rival. Between the two teams, most of the boys knew each other because they all played travel ball together. They were friends until they stepped onto the court.

In hours, the stands would be filled with parents, friends, and family, and the student section would come to life. Cheerleaders would guide their classmates in cheers while the Timberwolves played to packed stands.

It was games like tonight that electrified me as a coach and them as players. The gym would be loud, with students standing up the entire game. Nothing excited me more than looking into the stands to see the signs people had made or those fat heads that parents had printed off. Although some of them were rather scary looking.

As I headed out of my office and toward the parking lot, I saw my favorite student with his arm leaning against a pole with his girlfriend next to him. Cutter was smooth, I'd give him that, but I feared he'd find himself in a situation he wasn't ready to be in.

"See you tonight, Mr. Vaughn. Five thirty," I reminded him as I walked by. He had a ton of potential to take his game to the next level, and I wasn't about to see him throw it away.

I was in a damned-if-you-do, damned-if-you-don't situation. As much as I wanted Cutter, along with my other students, to succeed, it wasn't my business. The last thing I wanted was to be told I was overstepping. All I could do was offer an ear and some sage advice if he asked.

I hoped like hell he'd ask.

Chapter 3

Antonia

My stomach clenched as I pulled into the hospital parking lot. I told myself there was nothing seriously wrong with Miri because this wasn't some state-of-the-art hospital. Honestly, it was nothing compared to the medical facilities we had in Boston. If Miri was truly sick, I would have packed her things and moved her and the kids to my place.

I walked through the lobby with my phone pressed to my ear, acting like I owned the place. My ankle-length peacoat flowed behind me as I undid my scarf. "Hey, what floor and what room?" I asked as soon as Miri answered.

"Five," she said, her voice hoarse. I prayed it was just from lack of sleep and nothing more.

It couldn't possibly be anything else.

I jabbed my finger repeatedly against the elevator button, knowing full well it wouldn't make the car arrive any faster. Still, it felt satisfying to do it.

"Okay, I'm on my way," I said before hanging up just as the elevator door opened. I stepped inside, pushed the button for the fifth floor, and then pressed the door-hold button for someone shouting, "Hold the door!"

A doctor stepped in, slightly out of breath. He smiled kindly at me but didn't press a button for a floor. "Thank you," he said with a nod. "Sometimes these elevators are so slow."

"Yeah," I replied, unsure of what else to say.

He rocked back on his heels and whistled quietly. Here I was, my heart threatening to beat right out of my chest, and this man, who was probably tasked with saving people's lives, didn't seem to have a care in the world.

"Are those comfortable?" I nodded toward his blue scrubs. "I've always wondered."

He smiled, and I wondered if it was his normal, everyday smile or a practiced one. "They are. I tend to wear them even when I'm not doing my rounds."

I nodded, remembering what rounds were from the *Grey's Anatomy* marathons Miri and I would watch. Of course, as soon as I thought back to the many nights we'd sat on the couch, eating popcorn or ice cream, I instantly wanted to ask the fine doctor next to me if what we'd seen on the show was accurate. Was he hooking up with his coworkers in the break rooms?

Instead, I asked, "What's on the fifth floor?"

He met my gaze, and his demeanor changed. Gone was the sweet smile, replaced by sadness. Before he could tell me what I faced, the doors opened. He nodded and stepped off, leaving me no choice but to follow.

My feet moved slowly as my eyes scanned each room number, studying the three digits as if I couldn't comprehend them on sight. When I came to Miri's room, I stood in the hallway, staring at the curtain surrounding her bed. My best friend was in there, waiting on me. She would give me news that my gut told me wouldn't be good.

With a deep breath, I cleared my throat, stepped in, and walked around the curtain with my brightest smile on my face. I had a role to play, an expectation. I was the happy-go-lucky bestie who didn't stress about anything but work.

Miri was on her side in a half-fetal position, hooked up to monitors. I ignored them and set my purse on the table before sitting down on the edge of the bed.

"Hey, bish. What's up? Flu bug?"

Miri's eyes watered instantly, and what was left of my heart fell to the ground. I scooted closer to her and ran my fingers over her light-brown hair. Her hazel eyes never left mine. Miri and I had the same eye color, with mine being a smidge darker.

"What's wrong?" I kept my voice low and barely above a whisper, afraid it would crack.

"I have cancer," she said, matching my tone.

I nodded and bit my lower lip, and I didn't even bother trying to fight the tears. "Okay." It took me a minute or two to get my thoughts together. "We can fight this. Right? We're a strong team."

Miri reached for my hand and held it tightly. "I can fight this."

"And win," I added. If anything, we had to remain positive. "I guess the first thing we need to do is get you transferred to Boston. I'll make some calls."

"I can't go to Boston."

"What, why not? Don't be silly. Boston has the best doctors. You're not staying here."

"The kids have school, Toni. I can't take them out of school."

Shit.

I nodded. I hadn't forgotten about them, but I'd definitely forgotten about the logistics of schooling. "I'll figure it out, Miri. But you have to know I won't stop at anything to get you the absolute best care. You and I both know it's not here."

"I know," she said quietly.

"Are you in pain?"

"Not really."

"Scoot over," I told her as I maneuvered my way onto her bed and held her in my arms. This was better for both of us. She didn't have to see my tears or the fear I was certain my eyes held. "How'd you find out?"

"I had my annual exam last week, and my doctor found a couple of lumps. She sent me for an MRI, and the radiologist didn't like what he saw, so they admitted me while they ran more tests. I didn't want to do anything until I knew more."

I leaned back. "So, you may not even have cancer?"

She gave me a slight shrug.

"Bish, can you be any more dramatic?"

"I could try," she said, laughing.

We were quiet for a moment, the situation heavily weighing on us. If they wanted to run more tests, then something was wrong. I felt this deeply.

"Are the kids at school?"

"Yeah," she said quietly.

"Do they know you're here?"

She shook her head. "Cutter has a game tonight."

I looked at my watch and saw the time. He was probably on his way home from school.

"How long do you have to stay?"

"They said overnight."

"Okay."

Overnight. I wasn't a doctor, but even I knew that staying overnight for tests was rarely a good sign.

I held her tighter as my mind shifted back and forth from saving her to protecting her kids. The only family Miri and the kids had was me and mine. Her family had kicked her out of the house when they found out she was pregnant at seventeen.

"I'm going to call my mom and have her drive up," I told Miri. "This way I can be with you, and she can help with Cutter and Nova."

Miri nodded against my chest. I felt her tears wet my shirt.

"Everything's going to be okay, Miri. I'll make sure of it."

Reluctantly, I had to leave Miri at the hospital. It was the last thing I wanted to do, but she needed me to get Nova off the bus, or the driver wouldn't let her off, and they'd start calling Miri, asking where she was.

We agreed I wouldn't tell the kids their mother was in the hospital, at least for tonight. The ruse would be that Miri had an out-of-town client she had to help with their books. I told her it was unlikely the kids would buy the lousy excuse, but since it was the middle of January, Miri felt they would, since tax season was right around the corner.

While I sat in the car and waited, I pressed my mother's name on my phone and waited for the video chat to connect. Before my mom came on the screen, my emotions got the best of me.

"What's wrong and why are you in the car?"

"I'm at Miri's," I managed to squeeze out as my throat seized. "She's sick, Mom. I don't know how sick but sick enough they're keeping her overnight in the hospital and . . ." I couldn't bring myself to say the *C* word. Deep down, I figured if I never had to say it, then it wouldn't come true. I wouldn't be putting it out there in the universe for it to be real.

I glanced out the window, at the snow-covered yard, and took a deep shuddering breath. "Mom."

"I'll be up tomorrow," she said without hesitation.

I nodded, unable to find my voice as tears streamed down my face. My reflection in the camera had me wiping angrily at my cheeks, removing my streaked and smeared makeup before the kids saw me.

"I love you, Mom."

"And I love you. Whatever this is with Miriam, we'll make sure she's taken care of."

We hung up, and those final words from my mom lingered in my mind. My parents were one of a kind and had the biggest hearts. From the time Miri was seventeen, my parents had made sure she knew they always had her back.

The rumble of the yellow school bus, caked with mud from the road, caught my attention as it pulled up in front of the dirt driveway.

I got out and walked briskly to the edge of the driveway, waving to the driver. She opened the door cautiously.

"Who are you?" She was blunt, which I appreciated. I wouldn't want any kid getting off the bus with a stranger.

"I'm Nova Vaughn's aunt," I told her as I tried to look in the bus for Nova. "I'm on the pickup list." The driver turned slightly as Nova approached. Her face lit up when she saw me.

"Stay there, Nova. I need to call this in."

I smiled at her. "How was school?"

Nova shrugged and tossed me her backpack. It was light, except for the metal lunch box she insisted on carrying. Last summer, when we went school shopping, Miri and I pointed out all these cool insulated lunch bags, but Nova wouldn't have it. She wanted to use Miri's Wonder Woman lunch box. Miri and I had the same one in first grade, but mine was long gone. How she'd managed to keep hers all these years was beyond me.

The driver received permission to release Nova into my care, and Miri's seven-year-old daughter launched herself into my arms when she reached the bottom step of the bus. Compared to her friends, Nova was petite, with a wiry frame. She was a carbon copy of Miri with the same light-brown hair that fell in soft waves down her back. Her hazel eyes always held a hint of mischief.

"Cute pigtails," I told her as I set her down. I held her hand and slung her backpack over my shoulder.

"Thanks, Mama did them this morning." Nova skipped the length of their driveway.

We walked up the stairs of the white, two-story home with black shutters to the wide farmer's porch. At the other end, in front of the large picture window, were two white rockers. They faced the road because that was where we could see the sunset every night.

I opened the screen door and pushed down on the lever to unlatch the door. Inside, Nova hung her coat on the set of hooks in what New Englanders called the mudroom, and then we walked into the front area of the house. I sighed heavily and glanced toward the top of the staircase while Nova groaned. Loud music blasted from upstairs.

"Cutter's home," Nova said with a sigh. "He's in loooove," she said with so much sass it reminded me of when I was younger.

"You'll be there someday."

"Nope. No way." She shook her head. "Boys have cooties."

Funny, I used to think the same thing.

"Go get a snack and start your homework. Cutter has a game tonight."

"Toni, where's my mama?"

And there it was, the question I hoped we'd avoid because her uber-cool aunt was there, but I knew I'd never be able to.

"Your mom had to go out of town for the night."

"How come she didn't tell us this morning?"

"It was a last-minute thing." I hated how the lie came so easily.

"And you had to come here?"

"Nah, kiddo. I was already on my way for Cutter's game." Another lie. I rarely made it to any of his games unless they were on a Saturday or in a town closer to Boston.

Nova gave me a suspicious look. I deserved it and couldn't handle the scrutiny, so I used the excuse to go check on her brother to get away. The staircase leading to the three bedrooms and bathrooms was painted black to contrast with the white railing. Two or three summers ago, Miri had sent the kids to Boston for a week while she sanded and repainted the stairs. According to her, she'd rather clean gutters than have to paint.

At the top of the stairs and to the immediate left was the shared bathroom. Along the wall were built-in cabinets, with an old-fashioned laundry chute leading to the basement. On the right side of the railing, Nova's room was first, then Cutter's, and at the end of the L-shaped hallway was Miri's room, where she had her own bathroom.

At Cutter's door, I rapped my knuckles against the wood, hoping it wouldn't take much to get his attention.

The door swung open, and he stared, dumbfounded. "Why are you here?"

"Nice to see you too." I reached out to ruffle his hair, but he leaned away from me. I tried not to let this hurt my ego, but it did. We used to be close, inseparable when he was younger, and then he became a teenager, and everything changed.

"Mom had to go out of town to see a client," I told him. "I'll take you to your game."

"I can walk."

I shook my head. "We'll leave at five." I turned and walked toward the stairs, where I stopped and glanced at him standing in the doorway. Every moment he and I had shared flashed in my mind, from the moment he was born, and I held him for the first time, to him learning his first word—"Mama"—to him crawling, walking, and trying to give us heart attacks when he began hanging from everything. And then there was his first day of kindergarten, with Miri and me holding back tears as he confidently walked in to meet his new friends, and the day he officially turned into a teenager and suddenly grew taller than either of us. I smiled softly before heading downstairs.

Miri had to be okay. No, she had to be more than okay. These kids depended on her. They were all she had.

Thirty minutes before we had to leave, Cutter came downstairs, dressed in khaki slacks and a red polo shirt. He only dressed up for special occasions and for game days. I knew the latter was a rule his coach had put in place. If Cutter had his way, he'd wear sweatpants, T-shirts, and sneakers everywhere.

He stepped into the living room, looked at us briefly, and then turned toward the kitchen. I got up from the couch, where Nova and I had been sitting while she practiced her reading, and went into the kitchen.

"Do you need dinner?" I asked, knowing full well I wasn't the best at the home-cooking thing. Brendan and I rarely cooked. We either got something out, ate leftovers, or had one of those already-made meals we just had to heat up.

Cutter grimaced.

I didn't fault him one bit for the look.

"Right. How about something from the snack bar at the game?" Something told me this wouldn't be enough for him.

"There's a sub shop in town. If we leave now, I'll still make it to school on time." Cutter sounded hopeful.

I nodded, fully in agreement. "Nova, grab your coat and make sure you have all your stuff for the game." I spoke loudly enough for her to hear me in the other room. She let out a resounding "Yes."

"Where's Brendan?" Cutter asked. The two of them had an okay relationship, especially when it came to sports. For Cutter's fourteenth birthday, Brendan had taken him to see the Celtics. They had courtside seats, and I think LeBron James was there or something.

"He's working. It didn't make much sense for him to come up if this is just a quick trip for me."

Cutter nodded. "It's too bad he isn't here. We're playing our rival tonight. It's going to be a good game."

"I'll send him some videos and your stats. Come on, let's go get some food and head to your game." He let me put my arm around him for a brief moment. It was something, at least.

Chapter 4

Weston

The varsity team needed to be in the stands, supporting the junior varsity team, by tip-off. I also expected my boys to come to the game dressed in a professional but casual way. I believed appearances were important and hoped to set a standard for those boys when they were older. I'd noticed that a few of the boys couldn't afford the luxury of a nice pair of slacks or a button-down shirt, and I made concessions.

Never excuses.

It was my duty as their coach, teacher, and role model to set an example. During the baseball season, I wore a full uniform. This was standard among all coaches in every league. But during basketball season, I opted for slacks and a pullover, or something equally comfortable. The team got off lucky. They were only dressed up during a bus ride to the game or until halftime, when they left the JV game to get ready for their own, and then it was uniform time. I, on the other hand, had to wear this getup the entire night.

During the JV game, I stood along the wall next to the admission table, which afforded me the ability to acknowledge each player who walked in. I enjoyed greeting the parents and shooting the shit with some of the dads.

I had never taken the stance as a coach that I should be unapproachable or that my time was off limits. The one thing I wouldn't discuss with parents was their sons' playing time. If it was a question, it was something the players needed to discuss with me after practice or during my office hours. Never before or after a game. Emotions ran much too high to have a serious conversation about playing time, especially after a game.

Most of the parents respected my decision, but there was always one in the group who thought their son was the next Michael Jordan. All I could do most days was nod, listen, and store the conversation for later.

Every sport had the parents who scouted other teams for you, whether you'd asked them to or not. It made them feel useful, when in reality, they were living out the dream they'd had when they'd started coaching their sons in rec league.

In the end, it was all good. Anytime a parent came forth with information on another team or player, I took it. I'd be remiss not to.

I nodded at the players as they entered the gym. Some came over to chat, but most went and sat with their team and classmates. When Cutter came in, I was momentarily stunned by the woman who followed behind him. He said something to her and then went to the stands to sit down. The woman stood at the table to pay and then walked to the end of the gym, which was the visitors' section, and sat on the bottom bleacher with Cutter's little sister.

Something about this woman made me lose focus for a moment. I tried to recall if I'd seen her before, but my mind came up blank. I watched the doorway for Cutter's mom, knowing she'd stop over to say hi and thank me for always looking out for her son.

Throughout the JV game, I found myself watching the woman. Cutter's sister seemed very fond of her, and instead of watching the action on the court, they were coloring together.

After halftime, my team made their way to the locker room. I used this time to walk to the other end of the gym to talk to the athletic director about absolutely nothing. In hindsight, I wished I hadn't.

"Hi, Coach," Cutter's sister called out. She gave me a little wave, and when I smiled, her cheeks blushed. I hated that I didn't know her name, or I would've stopped and chatted, asked her how school was, and found out who was with her.

But instead, I made eye contact with the woman and then stumbled over my feet, almost falling face-first onto the court. If people saw, they said nothing, and I didn't hear any audible laughing. I was afraid to look behind me, though, out of genuine fear she . . . this woman . . . had seen everything.

From my new vantage point, I could stare without getting caught. She sat there, with her legs crossed, wearing jeans and a sweater. Half her dark-brown hair was pinned up, exposing her high cheekbones, while the rest flowed down her back in soft waves. She was polished and more put together than most of the parents in the stands, and she definitely stood out as someone who wasn't from Grove Hill.

Every so often, she pulled her phone from her purse, typed, and then either put it away or brought the little girl toward her and snapped a photo. It made me wonder who she'd sent the picture to. Was it to Cutter's mom?

Was it for her husband?

I angled myself to see if I could spot a ring and then chided myself for doing so. What did I care? Why did I care?

Every answer failed me because I was attracted to her and didn't even know her.

It was like she'd heard my thoughts and looked up. Our gazes met and held. We were maybe two or three feet from each other, and it was like no one else existed around us. There was something raw and real about her presence. It was like we were meant to meet in this moment, and yet I had to maintain my professionalism. I couldn't ask her what her name was, and there wasn't a chance in hell I could ask Cutter.

This woman, someone who had my thoughts jumbled and my heart doing things I hadn't felt in years, smiled. My knees knocked together, and I forced myself to rest against the wall for stability.

"You okay?" the athletic director asked.

"Yeah, a little lightheaded." This wasn't exactly a lie, but it also wasn't the truth. It was more like I had lost the ability to think or function like a human.

"Do you need some water?"

I nodded and accepted the bottle from him. After twisting the cap, I took a big swig, drinking most of it down.

In a flash, the buzzer sounded, and the JV game was over. I shook my head to clear my stupor and made my way toward the locker room, already late for the pregame pep talk. How could I preach to my team about punctuality when I couldn't even hold myself to the same standard?

When I reached the boys, they were all sitting in their chairs, waiting for me. "Sorry I'm late, gentlemen." I proceeded to go over the game plan, which honestly hadn't changed from the previous games. We discussed our defensive strategy and reminded ourselves to block out the fans and to have fun. At the end of the night, it was a game. Someone had to win, and someone had to lose.

As a team, we walked together and waited for the warm-up music to start. Once it did, Malik led the team out and into formation. Before I'd even entered the gym again, I told myself I wasn't going to look across the court and into the stands. Yet, as soon as I made it through the doorway, I did, and she was still there. Only now, she had her phone out, and it looked like she was taking videos of Cutter.

It struck me then that I couldn't recall a time when Cutter's mom, Miriam, had ever missed a game. She was his number one fan, always in the stands, cheering for him. Cheering for all the boys. Most of the parents were like that, which I appreciated. As a coach, it was important for the boys to see sportsmanship among the parents. When they won, we all won.

"Wes, are you good, man?" my assistant coach and coworker, Jerome Levy, asked.

I nodded and ran my hand over my face, letting out a shallow groan. "Yeah, just . . ." What was I doing? I glanced across the court again and saw Cutter's sister cheering, even though the boys were still in warm-ups. "Yeah, just thinking," I told him.

Jerome and I were good friends outside of work. We rarely ever disagreed on game strategy, whether on the court or the field, and we often balanced each other out. Where Jerome preferred structure, I was more laid back. Our styles complemented each other and never confused the kids.

The horn sounded at the one-minute mark, and the boys ran toward the sideline. Jerome and I high-fived each of the guys. Our starters sat on the bench while I crouched in front of them with my whiteboard, where I'd listed who each of them would guard, and went over my half-assed game plan.

When our announcer began introducing the visitors, I handed my board to Jerome, left the rest of the pregame chat to him, and went to greet each player at half-court.

And then it was our turn. While the fans were loud for our opponent, the noise reached a body-vibrating decibel level when our announcer said, "And now your starting lineup for the Grove Hill Timberwoooooooolves."

The boys made two lines—a tunnel of sorts—for their five teammates. Jerome and I stood at the front of the line and held our hands out for each of the boys to slap as they ran by. One by one, each player was announced. They ran through our line, met one of their teammates at the end for a choreographed celebration dance, and then shook hands with the officials and the opposing coach.

After the starting lineup was announced, we all stood for the national anthem, and then it was time for the tip-off. Before I sent the guys out there, we huddled up. "This is a big game with big emotions. We're going up against our friends, and regardless of the outcome, we'll still be friends. Go out, play your game the way you know how." We raised our fists.

"Timberwolves on three. One, two, three," Malik said before the five of them walked onto the court.

I sat and set my clipboard on the bench next to me. After tip-off, I would stand and pace the length of the coach's box, guiding the boys. There wasn't a doubt in my mind they knew the plays and the defensive schemes, but they were kids, and they forgot sometimes. It was my job as their coach to give them reminders.

The whistle blew, and the official walked to center court and tossed the ball in the air. Cutter jumped, his fingertips knocking the ball back to Malik. The game was underway, and while my focus should have been on the boys, my eyes drifted across the court to where the woman with Cutter's sister was. She had her camera up, her hand moving along with the action of the game.

Jerome elbowed me. I looked at him, and he motioned toward the other end of the court. The official jogged toward the center, where the reporting table was, and reported the foul. I groaned when he displayed Malik's number on his fingers.

I stood and clapped. "Let's go. Hands off and slide your feet." I had no idea what Malik had done because my attention was elsewhere. "No more," I muttered to myself. If anyone heard me, my statement could easily have been for the team as well. But mostly, it was for me. Whoever was here for Cutter shouldn't have been any of my concern.

Despite the wild thumping my heart did each time I looked over at her, I could easily chalk the sensation up to the excitement of game night.

Yep, that's exactly what it was.

Chapter 5

Antonia

I kept Miri updated throughout the game, each time Cutter scored or did something I thought was good. I didn't know crap about basketball, but almost everyone cheered for Grove Hill. And each time I texted Brendan with a video or the score, he said the game was close. All I knew was Cutter scored a lot, and Nova and I clapped a lot.

After the game, we waited in the gym for Cutter to come out from the locker room. When he did, Nova ran toward him. He scooped her up and lifted her toward the basketball rim. She hung there for a second, sending my heart to the floor and back up again.

"You look scared," he said when he approached me.

"I was afraid you were going to drop her."

"Nah, I do it all the time. Did you take any videos?"

I nodded and considered handing my phone over so he could look through them, but I didn't want him to inadvertently see any texts from his mom. I hated lying to him, but he and Nova didn't need to worry about their mom right now. I was doing enough of that for everyone.

"Come on, let's go home." I put my arm through the crook of his.

"Everyone's going out for ice cream," Cutter said as we walked out of the gym. "Do you think I could go?"

I was positive Miriam would let him go, but she knew the kids and their parents and knew who to trust. I didn't.

"What time would I have to pick you up?" I worried about Nova. She needed her sleep. Cutter did as well, but being nine years older than her, he could manage.

"Coach Schmidt could bring me home," Cutter said. "He lives down the street from us."

Cutter's face fell when he saw me grimace. I wanted to say yes but felt uncomfortable doing so. I didn't know his coach, and Miri had never mentioned him. That didn't mean she wasn't a fan; he just wasn't someone we'd ever chatted about.

Nova tugged on the corner of my jacket. I looked down at her. Her wide, expressive hazel eyes bored into mine. She waggled her index finger at me. I bent and listened.

She cupped my ear and whispered, "Can I go for ice cream?"

I did the same. "Why are you whispering?"

"Because Cutter gets pissy if I go."

I rolled my eyes. "Don't say 'pissy,' and yes, we'll go for ice cream." I rose to my full height and nodded at Cutter. "How about we all go, but Nova and I will sit far away from you and the team?"

Cutter smirked. "It's not that serious."

Brat.

Miri had mentioned his attitude and that he was at times defiant and snarky. I'd reminded her that I'd been the same way with my parents, and this was a stage most of us went through. Everyone but her. She never would've dared to cross her parents. The repercussions would have been far too grave, evident by the fact that she hadn't seen them since she was seventeen.

Nova and I followed Cutter out of the gym and to my car. As we approached, he turned to me with a glint in his eyes, which immediately put me on alert.

"Can I drive?"

I shook my head. "No, thanks."

He sighed dramatically and threw his head back. "Come on, Toni."

"Nope, not with Nova in the car." I pressed the fob to unlock the doors. Nova followed me around to the driver's side and got in behind me, while Cutter dumped his bag in the back seat and then sat in the front.

"Brendan would let me drive."

"Brendan isn't here," I reminded him as I started the car and pulled out of the parking spot. "Where is the ice cream place?"

"On Main," he muttered, pressing his head to the window.

"You played well." I hoped to break whatever the tension was between us.

"Thanks. Coach says I have a shot at playing in college."

"Really? That's great."

"Yep," Cutter said, a little perkier this time. "This summer will be a good test. We're going to travel south for some big tournaments."

"Who's 'we'?" I turned onto Main Street and began looking for a place to park. Cutter pointed to a spot, which I effortlessly paralleled into.

"You have to teach me how to parallel park," he said as he unbuckled his seat belt. "Mom refuses to park on the street unless she can pull in."

"I'll teach you," I said as I put my car into park and shut it off. I glanced at Nova through my rearview mirror. She looked tired but had unbuckled. Honestly, she deserved ice cream. We all did. Once we were on the sidewalk, I asked Cutter again what he'd meant by "we."

"My travel team," he said as he held the door to the ice cream parlor open. Despite it being winter, the place was packed, mostly with teens from the basketball game. We took our place in line and waited.

"Go on."

"Oh, right." Cutter shook his head. "I played with them over the summer. Do you remember when you and Brendan came to my games in Boston?"

I nodded.

"That's the team. We did really well, and Coach is going to take us farther south, where we'll find better competition and more scouts."

"What are the scouts for?"

"College," Cutter said as we moved forward. "The tournaments give scouts a chance to see a ton of players at the same time."

"So this summer travel is for basketball?"

"It's for baseball too," he said. "Coach has the schedule down to a science—at least that's what he says. He makes sure there isn't any overlap."

"Overlap?"

"You know, for those of us who play two sports. Like I'll never have a basketball tournament on the same weekend there's a baseball tournament."

"Ah," I said, pretending to understand. If it wasn't for Cutter, I probably wouldn't have ever seen a game of any kind. Whenever Brendan went to one of the many sporting events in Boston, I tended to stay home, where it was quiet and not crowded.

Cutter, Nova, and I ordered. Once we had our ice creams, he went to sit with his team while Nova and I found a spot for the two of us. She ordered vanilla with sprinkles, while I went with my favorite: black raspberry and chocolate.

"Do you want a bite?"

She shook her head no. "Do you want a bite of mine?"

I nodded and leaned forward, taking the spoonful from her. "So good," I muttered with my mouth full. "Do you want to try mine?" I asked her again. Nova was a fussy eater. Miri tried to get her to try everything, but Nova often refused.

She scrunched her nose and shook her head. "No, thanks."

I shrugged. "Oh well, more for me."

Nova and I finished and then colored on the place mats for a bit while we waited for Cutter. In hindsight, I should've texted Miri and asked her if it was okay for Cutter's coach to bring him home. It was cold out, Nova and I were both tired, and my mind was elsewhere.

When she began rubbing her eyes, I told her I'd be right back and went to get Cutter, knowing full well I could face his teenage wrath, making me miss the sweet little boy he'd been.

As I approached the group of kids, I gave Cutter a soft but apologetic smile. He rolled his eyes and groaned audibly. "Sorry," I said when he came near. "It is a school night, and Nova needs to get to bed."

Cutter, in all his teenage angst, walked past me and out the door without waiting for me and his sister. I sighed heavily and went back to Nova to gather our things. "Come on, kiddo. Let's go home."

"How come Cutter is a butthead?"

"He's salty because I won't let him stay out later."

"Mommy would be sooo mad at him right now."

Well, this is good to know.

"Yeah . . ."

The ride home was quiet. When we got to the house, Cutter slammed the car door twice and stomped up the stairs. I ignored him. It was the only way to deal with a sullen teenager, according to the wise words of my mother.

After Nova's bath and a bedtime story, I tucked her in and left her door ajar. Bracing for attitude, I then knocked on Cutter's door.

"Yeah?"

I cracked it open a bit. "Do you take the bus in the morning?"

"Mom usually takes me."

"Okay, what time do we need to leave?"

Cutter gave me the time and told me to drop Nova off after him.

"Okay, good night, Cutter."

"Toni?"

He said my name as I began closing the door. There had been a time when I was "Ant Toni," making a play on my name, but he hadn't called me that since he'd turned thirteen. I missed those days.

"What's up?"

"Is Mom okay?"

"Yeah, why?"

Cutter shrugged. "The last couple of months, she hasn't been feeling well. She had a cough and said it was nothing, but she seemed very tired."

I let his words sink in and worked hard to mask my facial expressions. "When she gets home tomorrow, I'll ask her."

He stared, long and hard. No doubt trying to figure out if I was lying or not. I hated lying to him. When he was little, I promised to always tell him the truth. But I'd also promised Miri. Besides, his mother wasn't home because she was having testing done, and if it turned out she was sick, that would be something Miriam would have to tell her children.

"Good night," I said after a long silence. Cutter gave me a half smile and turned in his swivel chair toward his desk. Slowly, I closed the door and stood there for a moment with my fist poised to knock again. I remembered being a teen and how hard life seemed then, and that was when life was easy. Of course, I could only say that because being an adult with bills and responsibilities wasn't all that fun.

I walked down the hall to Miri's room and went in. It was better for me to believe she was away at work than lying in the hospital. As I crawled into her bed, I thought about calling her but didn't want to wake her. Knowing her, though, she was likely staring out the window, looking at the stars. I got up, opened her blinds, and then texted her: I'm looking at the stars.

Me too, she texted back right away.

This would be enough for the night.

The next morning, after dropping the kids off at school, I called Brendan to check in and told him I should be back by dinner. I was that optimistic about Miri's test results. On my way to the hospital, I stopped and got us both coffees and doughnuts, even though the latter wasn't on any approved list. Hers or mine.

"Knock knock," I said as I pushed my way into her room. I had forgotten she was technically in a shared room, but she was the only one in there at the moment. When I came around the curtain, Miri's face lit up when she saw the muted grayish-brown recyclable tray in my hands. "I'm probably going to get into trouble for bringing junk food."

"I don't care." Miri sat up in bed and reached for her coffee. She took a sip and sighed. "The nurse brought some this morning, bless her heart. It was trash. I don't know how they survive on that sludge."

"That's probably what keeps them functioning."

Miri reached for the bag and took out the fresh Boston cream doughnut. "Did you get these at the Cozy Cup Café?"

"I did. Cutter said you liked their pastries."

"Samira has become a good friend."

I popped an eyebrow at my lifelong friend. "Are you replacing me?"

Miri didn't miss a beat and nodded. "Samira lives here. You don't."

"Ouch. That hurts."

Miri shrugged. "Such is life."

"When do your results come back?" I took a drink of the coffee, looked at the cup, and nodded my approval. "This is good."

Miri looked at me smugly, as if I was a fool to doubt her.

"This morning. The nurse said a doctor would be by before they started their rounds."

"You haven't met with a doctor yet?" I was confused. Who had she been seeing since they'd admitted her?

"No, just the assistants or whatever they're called. Medical assistant, I think?"

I didn't know whether to agree or not, so I filled her in on my elevator trip from the day before and how I'd been tempted to ask the doctor I'd ridden up with if any of the romantic stuff in *Grey's Anatomy* was accurate but had held my tongue.

"I'm sure it's fictionalized," she said.

"Really? You don't think doctors and nurses get heated or overly emotional and need a release?"

Miri shook her head. "You need to read a book."

"I read last night, thank you very much. Speaking of which, Cutter's attitude gave me whiplash."

She nodded and sighed heavily. "He has a girlfriend and her parents are strict, which I appreciate. I'm trying to give him leeway, but then I think about me and . . ."

I reached for her hand and held it. "Kids have sex, Miri. You can't stop them. You can just teach them about protection and the consequences of the action. Educate him."

Miri scoffed. "Easier said than done. I might talk to his coach. I don't know. Cutter needs a male role model."

"I'll have Brendan talk to him. They seem to get along."

There was a knock on the door, and Croc shoes squeaked on the linoleum. When the curtain moved and the doctor came into view, I was surprised to see the same one from the elevator ride.

"Hello, Miriam," he said as he looked at her chart and then to her, and finally to me. "I'm Dr. Niall Frederick."

"It's nice to meet you," Miri said as they shook hands.

"I'm Antonia," I said and shook his hand as well.

"Nice to see you again," he said.

"Again?" Miri asked.

I motioned toward him. "Elevator ride, yesterday."

Miri mouthed "Oh," and then her eyes widened. Let's just say I was happy I didn't embarrass myself and ask him the inappropriate questions.

"Is now a good time to talk?" he asked, looking at Miri. She nodded, and he pulled a chair from the next space over. He sat, set his file on the table near Miri's bed, and crossed his legs. I fully expected him to clasp his hands, but he didn't.

"We have your results back, Miriam."

Right away, I knew this wasn't going to be good. I stood and took her hand in mine.

"Is it cancer?" Miri asked.

Dr. Frederick nodded. "The findings show cancer in multiple parts of your body, including the pancreas, breast, and colon." He leaned forward slightly. "Based on the imaging and blood work, the cancer originated in your pancreas and has metastasized to your liver, lungs, and breast tissue. Pancreatic cancer is particularly aggressive and often goes undetected until it's advanced, which explains why you didn't feel significantly ill until recently."

Miri's hand turned cold in mine as he spoke.

"It started in the pancreas?" Miri's voice was quiet, barely above a whisper, yet it echoed in the sterile hospital room.

He cleared his throat and then continued. "Yes. Unfortunately, pancreatic cancer is known as the 'silent killer' because symptoms don't typically appear until the disease has progressed. The fatigue and discomfort you've been experiencing are common early indicators, but they're easily mistaken for stress or normal life pressures. The blood test confirmed the findings from the MRI. Certain cancers release specific proteins into your bloodstream. Between what we saw on your images and the elevated levels, this condition is what we call metastatic cancer."

"Oh God," I mumbled at the sound of his words. Tears fell instantly. There was no way to stop or combat them. This wasn't something Miri could've prevented with a monthly self-exam or a yearly mammogram. It wasn't like she could've stood in the mirror and examined the organ for bumps, lesions, or any abnormalities.

"With the cancer spreading to several organs, it becomes more complex to treat because one site might react positively to the treatment, while another may not respond at all. This doesn't mean we don't have options, though. We will find a way to treat you. At this stage, our primary goal is to manage the cancer and slow its progression while mitigating any symptoms that arise."

"Is there a cure?" Miri asked quietly.

"It's not likely we'll be able to cure the cancers, but we can focus on treatments that might help extend your life."

"What about a second opinion?" I asked. "I live in Boston. The hospitals are better there. More equipped. I'll take her there."

Dr. Frederick nodded. "Please do," he said. "I'll tell the charge nurse to send Miriam's file there."

"How long?" Miri asked.

"With the right treatment—"

"How long?" Miri asked again, this time more forcefully. "Am I going to see my son graduate? My daughter? Will I see my son get married? My daughter become a mother?"

Dr. Frederick took a measured breath. His eyes were soft, kind . . . practiced. I could tell he'd given more bad news in his years as a doctor than he had good. My heart sank, even further than before. I held Miri's hand, willing her to feel the comfort I couldn't put into words.

"With aggressive chemotherapy, we're typically looking at six to twelve months. Without treatment, significantly less. I want to be clear, we're not fighting to cure this cancer, Miriam. We're fighting to give you as much quality time as possible with your children."

Miri's face crumpled. "So I won't see Cutter graduate. Nova's only seven."

"The treatment we're recommending is aggressive precisely because every day, every week, and every month matters. Some patients exceed our expectations, but I believe in being honest about what we're facing."

The door clicked closed softly, and Miri let out the most gut-wrenching sob I'd ever heard from anyone. I held her as tightly as possible while rubbing her back.

"We'll get a second opinion," I told her, trying to give her a small semblance of hope. "Boston has the best doctors. We'll pack up the kids and leave right away."

Miri said nothing. She held on to my arms, clutching them to bring me closer, and sobbed. Her tears matched my fear and heartbreak. There wasn't a time in my life when she hadn't existed, and I wasn't sure I could exist in a world where she didn't.

Chapter 6

Antonia

Nothing about what I'd heard, about what the doctor had said, made any sense to me. Miri was sick, and in my heart of hearts, I knew there would be no magical cure for what she had. My brain said otherwise while also screaming, Why and how?

Why was this happening to her? She was the kindest, nicest, loveliest person I knew. She didn't wish harm on anyone, even if they'd scorned her. Miri never said a bad thing about those types to anyone, except to me, but I was her best friend, her confidant. I'd never betray her, and people should be allowed to vent their frustrations.

How was this happening to her? How had her system gotten so horribly bad, without her or her doctors noticing?

Cutter's voice rang out in my mind . . . *The last couple of months, she hasn't been feeling well. She had a cough and said it was nothing, but she seemed very tired.*

Was it only the last couple of months that she hadn't been feeling well? Did she not prioritize her health? Of course she had. Miri would never do anything to put her babies in harm's way or to not be with them. They were her life.

Miri quieted in my arms. I was afraid to move out of fear she would start up again, and rightly so. She had the right to cry, to sob, to scream if she wanted. I suspected the anger would come next, and then the denial.

I held Miri tighter, wishing like hell I had the right words. Everything failed to make sense in my mind except my need to fight. To fight for Miri, for Cutter, for Nova. Even for myself. I had to be the one to step up and make sure Miri got the care she deserved. And believe me, she deserved the best there was.

I needed to call Brendan—there was no way I was leaving Miri—and he'd have to accept that I was going to be working from home. Regardless of whether it was from Grove Hill or Boston, I wasn't leaving her side.

After a knock at the door, a nurse entered Miri's cubicle. "Hi, Miriam. I'm going to run an IV and take some blood."

"What's the IV for?" I asked as Miri sat up and gave her arm willingly.

"Pain meds, if needed. And fluids. We want to keep her as hydrated as possible. Over the next hour or so, others will come in to talk about your options. Dr. Frederick will be here shortly to meet with you and go over a treatment plan."

"Are you in pain?" I asked Miri.

She shrugged. "I don't know."

"Wouldn't her illness cause her a lot of pain?" I asked the nurse.

"Yes, but sometimes the brain blocks the pain receptors. It's not uncommon or unheard of, but now that she knows . . ." The nurse trailed off.

This wasn't happening.

"I need to go call work," I told Miri. "Be back in a minute." I excused myself while the nurse inserted the IV, then walked out of the room and went to the end of the hallway, barely able to keep my tears at bay. Biting the inside of my cheek, I pressed my mom's name on my phone and held it to my ear.

"Hey, honey."

"Mama . . ." It dawned on me that I only ever called her "mama" when something was wrong.

"It's cancer, isn't it?"

I couldn't keep it in and let the gut-wrenching, heartbreaking sob loose. I couldn't inhale enough air to keep from hyperventilating. My howls were loud and matched my mother yelling my name on the other end. Finally, I rested against the wall and slid to the ground.

"She has cancer." I finally said the word through a barrage of hiccups.

"Okay," she said. "Cancer is treatable, Antonia. I know it's hard to hear, but it's something people can and do survive these days. They'll take her into surgery and remove the cells, and then she'll start treatment. Miriam is a fighter. She'll come out on top."

If only it were this easy.

"It's all over, Mama. Everywhere. In her colon, breasts, and pancreas."

"Wh-what? How?"

"I don't know. Most of this is a blur . . ."

"The kids."

"They don't know. I . . ." I cleared my throat, not that it did much to remove the rock that had formed there. "I drove up yesterday when she called to tell me she was sick, and stayed with the kids last night. Cutter knows something's up, though."

"Wait, did she know?"

Did she?

"No, I don't think so. I don't know."

Now, I didn't know what to believe. Would Miri lie to me? To the kids?

I couldn't fathom it.

"I can't lose her, Mom."

"I know. You won't. I'm on my way. I was going to wait until after rush hour to leave, but I'll leave now."

"We're at the hospital. Fifth floor."

"Where are the kids?"

"At school. I'll be here until Nova's out of school. Cutter has basketball practice, so I have a little time there."

"Call your sister."

I closed my eyes and nodded. "I am. I know oncology isn't her department, but she'll know what to do. I want to bring Miri to Boston for treatment."

"That's smart. I'll have your dad reach out to some friends too. He must know someone at Dana-Farber."

My father was a retired firefighter and was well known among most of the emergency services in Boston. He had friends everywhere, and it was likely someone owed him a favor or two.

"Call Isabella. Make sure I'm on Miriam's visitor list. I'll be there shortly." Mom hung up, and I sat there, as if I expected her to call back immediately, which was silly. I knew she'd be leaving as soon as she spoke to my dad.

I pulled my phone away from my ear and sent a text to my sister, who was a nurse: I need you to call me when you have a chance. It's not urgent, but it is. Miri's sick, and I need advice.

My next call went to Brendan.

"Hey, please tell me you're on your way back."

"Miri has cancer, Brendan."

I was met with silence.

"Brendan?"

"Yeah, I'm here. I'm just . . . 'sorry' doesn't seem like the right thing to say. What can I do?"

"I'm going to need time off," I told him. "At least until I can figure out how we're going to proceed."

"Well, it's obvious she'll start treatment right away."

"It's all over, Brendan. Her blood work showed metastatic cancer in multiple organs."

"How the fuck? How did we not know this? Wouldn't she have been in pain? Sick for months?"

"I don't know."

Brendan groaned, and I imagined him running his hand over his face. "I'll cancel dinner with my parents this weekend and come up."

"Thank you, but hold off. My mom's on her way, and we need to tell the kids and figure out our next steps."

"You don't want me there?"

His tone caught me off guard. I frowned and closed my eyes. "It's not that, I just need a couple days, Brendan. Thank you for offering."

Brendan sighed deeply before replying. "Yeah, okay. Let me know."

"I will—"

Brendan hung up before I had a chance to finish my sentence. I chalked his dismissive attitude up to being busy and feeling unwanted. His love language was . . . well, I wasn't sure. It could be he didn't have just one and genuinely embodied all five of them.

On my way back to Miri's room, I stopped at the nurses' station and gave them my mom's name: Carmela Bernardi. Once she arrived, she would take over. That was her nature.

I stood outside Miri's door and battled my inner turmoil. I needed to go in there and be her happy-go-lucky best friend who grabbed life by the horns and didn't back down from anything, instead of the best friend who was dying on the inside at the thought of losing her.

Miri needed me to be strong, to be her rock.

Before I crossed the threshold, Dr. Frederick walked toward me. "Can we speak for a moment?" I asked him as he neared. He nodded, and I motioned for him to cross the hall, away from Miri's room.

"Give it to me straight," I said bluntly. "Is she going to survive this?"

His expression told me everything I needed to know. He couldn't mask the inevitable.

"How long?"

"It's impossible to predict exact timings," he said. "It could be weeks or months. It all depends on the treatment plan. I've given her the options. Aggressive is the way to go, and we'll monitor the response."

I nodded and wiped my fallen tears. "I want to take her to Boston. It's where I live, and the hospital there—"

"I remember," he said. "There isn't a doubt it's the best in the world. I had my staff send her records to my colleague there for a second opinion, per your earlier request. As soon as she calls, I'll let you know."

"Oh. Okay, thank you." His statement caught me off guard.

"You're welcome."

"She's my life," I told him before he could walk away. "We've been friends since we were three, so almost our entire lives."

"She's lucky to have you."

I shook my head. "You don't get it. I'm lucky to have her, and I can't lose her. Miri's my constant. I can't tell you the last time I bought something, like shoes or a suit, that she didn't approve of. Everything I do has her stamp of approval."

"I do understand and know this is going to be a challenging hill to climb. She or you should probably call her family."

"Wait, why? Can't she go home?"

He looked over his shoulder. "The chemotherapy protocol we're recommending is extremely aggressive. It will compromise her immune system significantly, and we need to monitor her closely."

"She can't stay here!" I snapped. "Miri has two kids. They need her."

I need her.

"I understand. Once we see how she responds and establish her baseline, she can receive treatments as an outpatient and be home with her children between sessions."

"How long would she need to stay here?" I asked.

"Initially, a week to ten days. Then treatments every two weeks as an outpatient, assuming no complications."

"Right. I'm sorry for snapping. I'm frustrated and—"

"I get it. Go be with your friend," he said. "As soon as I hear from my colleague, I'll be in to talk with Miriam."

"Thanks."

Dr. Frederick nodded and continued down the hall. I supposed it was best he didn't tell me what the fifth floor was for when I asked. But Miri had to have known.

I went into her room without knocking. She was on her side, staring out the window.

"Did you know?"

"What?" she asked as she looked at me.

"Did you know you were sick?"

She shook her head and closed her eyes.

"Cutter said you hadn't been feeling good and were tired a lot. Did you know you were sick, Miriam?" I hadn't meant to raise my voice, but the anger, hurt, and fear I felt came out in a rush.

"I didn't know, but I thought something was wrong."

"Why didn't you go to the doctor sooner?" I asked as I sat down by her bed. I reached for her hand and held it tightly in mine.

"I had the appointment scheduled and didn't think . . ." She trailed off. "I didn't know I had a lump in my breast," Miri said quietly. "I checked all the time and didn't know."

"It's not your fault. This isn't something you could have prevented or caught earlier," I said, nodding. "We'll figure it out. We need to talk about your treatment. Dr. Frederick says it's going to be an aggressive plan, and you'll likely have to stay in the hospital. I'll take as much time off as I have to, and my mom is on her way. He also sent your paperwork to Boston for a second opinion. Miri," I said softly, "we have to tell the kids. This isn't something we can hide from them."

Miri nodded as tears filled her eyes.

My own tears flowed.

"I think you should start your treatment now, even while we wait for the second opinion. The faster we fight, the better the chance, right?" I hated suggesting she stay in the hospital, but there wasn't another choice.

"Okay," she said weakly, almost like she'd already given up.

I looked around her room. "We need to get you a private room. Somewhere where Nova can hang her artwork, and the kids won't worry about interrupting anyone else if they put another patient in here."

"I don't know how to tell them."

I smiled softly. "I don't think there's an easy way. Cutter's smart; he's going to know something's up when he comes home from practice and you're not there. When my mom gets here, I'll leave her with you, and I'll go get the kids."

Miri nodded.

"We've got this," I whispered to her. "We're the strongest team out there, right?"

She nodded again, but her eyes looked empty. I prayed Miri hadn't given up the fight before she had even started.

Chapter 7

Weston

Jerome and I stood on the sideline, watching the boys run through their plays during their scrimmage. We allowed them to play basketball without the adults interrupting and telling them what to do or calling fouls. This was their time to work on their game-time skills and teamwork. While I tried to make sure every boy played in every game, there were times when some teammates didn't play alongside the starting five. Scrimmaging gave me an opportunity to see the boys differently.

The buzzer sounded, and Cutter finished the play, even though his last two points wouldn't count. Everyone huddled at center court, gathering around Jerome and me.

"Tomorrow night we have another tough one," I said in the circle. "Each game from here on out is going to be a battle. Our undefeated record puts a target on our backs. Other teams want to beat us. It's bragging rights. Each time we step out onto the court, we need to be at our best. If you're not feeling it, there's nothing wrong with saying so." I paused and looked at each of the boys.

"Yes, Coach," they all said.

"All right, bring it in. Timberwolves on three." I counted down, and we all yelled. The boys ambled off toward the locker room, while Jerome and I started toward my office. The door to the gym opened and closed, grabbing my attention. I turned and saw her . . . the woman who was at the game for Cutter last night. As much as I wanted to think she was there because we'd had some kind of crosscourt connection, I knew better.

With my best coach face in place, I walked toward her. "Can I help you?"

Immediately, she stuck her hand out. "I'm Antonia Bernardi, Cutter Vaughn's aunt. Are you his coach?"

"That's me, Weston Schmidt, and that's Jerome Levy, my assistant." I pointed toward Jerome, who stopped picking up the cones we had out to wave. "What can I do for you?"

"Is there a place we can talk?"

"Sure, my office is this way."

I looked at Jerome and wondered if I should motion for him to join us or not. Selfishly, I wanted to sit in my cramped space with her. The instant attraction I'd felt last night was back, but tenfold. None of this made sense. Sure, she was beautiful, but so were a lot of women.

We entered my office, and I waited for her to cross the threshold before I closed the door behind her. She sat in the chair across from my desk and clasped her hands in her lap.

I sat across from her and inhaled sharply when my heart twisted. She wasn't just beautiful.

Antonia was striking.

Her deep-brown, shoulder-length hair framed her face in loose waves, and though the fluorescent lighting wasn't forgiving, she seemed to glow. Not in a way that came from makeup or careful grooming but from something deeper, something raw and untouchable. A quiet strength.

Then there were her wide-set hazel eyes, a mix of deep green and rich gold that shifted with the light. They were red-rimmed, shadowed with exhaustion. Even so, they held me captive. There was something unguarded about them, as if she wasn't just looking at me, but through me, like she was searching for something she couldn't quite name. And for the first time in a long time, I wanted to be that something.

And her mouth.

Christ, her lips were full and looked velvety soft. They were slightly parted, as if she had a million words she wanted to say but didn't know where to start. My gaze lingered there a second too long before I forced myself to meet her eyes again.

I cleared my throat and shook my mind clear. She took my cue, which I was thankful for because I had no idea how to proceed.

"I need to make this quick," she started. "I don't want Cutter to know I'm in here." Antonia cleared her throat and adjusted in the chair. "We've had some bad news; his mom is dying. She's going to tell him tonight, and I suspect he'll need someone to talk to that isn't me. Miri said the two of you are close—"

"Wait, what?" I tried to process what Antonia had said but couldn't, for the life of me, accept that Miriam was dying. She'd been a fixture in my life ever since I moved to Grove Hill and was one of my most dedicated parents, always first to volunteer.

My stomach dropped, the air in the room suddenly feeling too thick, too heavy to breathe. This community couldn't afford to lose someone like Miriam. My chest tightened, a sharp, noticeable ache in my heart.

How could this world be so damn cruel?

My jaw clenched and my palms grew sweaty, a sure sign of impending tears. I refused to cry in front of Antonia. Not because I was afraid to express myself, but because she didn't know me, and I had already imagined her as part of my future. Something told me crying might scare her off.

"Sorry, Miri said you're close—"

"No, not that part, and I'm sorry for interrupting you. Ms. Vaughn is dying?"

Antonia looked away, but not before I saw her eyes fill with tears. She inhaled deeply and cleared her throat again. "Yes, cancer. I'll be taking care of the kids for the time being. My name and number are on Cutter's file if you need anything." She stood and turned toward the door.

I stood as well. "If you need anything, please don't hesitate to call. I live a couple houses down from them. Please . . ." I paused, needing to take a deep inhale to keep my emotions in check. "Whatever Cutter needs, I'm available."

Antonia partially looked over her shoulder and gave me a half something. It wasn't a smile or grimace, but more like acceptance. She opened the door and disappeared from my office. I sat back down and let what she'd told me run on repeat through my mind.

Jerome came in and sat in the previously occupied chair. "What was that about?"

I glanced at the open door and heard the boys coming out of the locker room. "I'll have to tell you later, but it isn't good." I got up from my desk and went out to the hall. It was my job to make sure the boys didn't do anything that would get them into trouble with the school.

Antonia stood in the hall with a few other parents. I tried not to look at her but failed. Last night at the game, I'd seen some life in her, especially when she'd interacted with Cutter and his sister. Tonight, I knew it had been an act. She was saving face for the benefit of the children.

Cutter came out of the locker room laughing, until he saw Antonia. I stepped back and watched their interaction.

"Hey," she said as she pasted a smile across her lips. "How was practice?"

"Fine," he said plainly. "You didn't have to come in."

"I didn't know if you'd see my car outside."

He stood there, with his teammates walking past him. "Where's my mom?"

Miriam was such a strong presence in his life, and the way his shoulder stiffened, I could tell he knew something was wrong. I stepped forward, thinking I could help, but then I realized I had nothing to offer. This was something between them, and it didn't involve me.

"Grandma's in the car with Nova."

Cutter stood there with his fist clenched around the strap of his bag. "Is my mom home?"

She smiled and gave him a slight nod. "Come on. It's cold, and my car's running." She moved toward the door.

"Can I drive?"

I saw her shake her head and Cutter's head fall back. He let out a loud groan. The trials and tribulations of a teenage boy were an ever-revolving story. I'd heard countless stories from the team and students about how they hadn't gotten into driver's ed and how private driving lessons were too expensive. I kindly reminded them of where they lived and how there wasn't anywhere to drive. Not to mention, kids needed to slow down and not try to grow up so fast.

After the last boy had left, Jerome and I went back to my office. I filled him in and then sent an email to all of Cutter's teachers, letting them know of the situation and promising to keep them apprised once I'd found out more information. It was important for his teachers to know and show him grace if he needed it.

Something told me he would.

Chapter 8

Cutter

As soon as I came out of the locker room and saw Toni standing there among the other parents, I knew something was wrong. It wasn't like my aunt didn't come to visit. She spent Christmas with us, along with some other holidays, and we went to her place in Boston during the summer. I liked going to visit her. Being in the city was nice, and Toni lived at the top of an apartment complex with a view overlooking the harbor and downtown.

Toni being here now was different, though. My mom always told Nova and me when Toni was coming to visit—mostly so we'd help her clean or make sure our rooms didn't look like disaster pits. She was always worried about how Toni saw us, for some reason, which didn't make much sense to me, considering they were best friends.

My best friend was Flinn Langston, and we were nothing alike, which worked for us because we never had to compete against each other. He was into skateboarding and snowboarding, while I was into basketball and baseball. For whatever reason, our friendship worked well.

Though I was close with most of my teammates, I only confided in Flinn. I trusted him to keep my secrets and not steal my girlfriend, Eleni. A couple of my teammates liked to flirt with her, which pissed me off. My mom said as long as Eleni didn't flirt back, I should ignore the other guys for the sake of the team. I didn't always agree with my mom, but I did listen.

I followed Toni out of the gym, staying a couple steps behind her. There had been a time in my life when I called her "Ant Toni" instead of "Aunt Toni" because I thought it was funny since her name was Antonia. I didn't remember when I started calling her just "Toni," but I knew it had hurt her feelings. She wasn't really my aunt. And the grandma she'd referred to earlier was her mom—no relation to me whatsoever.

Nova and I didn't have any family except for our mother, and now I was pretty sure something was wrong with her.

As we approached the car, the back window went down, and my little sister stuck her head out. "Cutter!" She waved like we hadn't seen each other this morning.

"Hey," I said as I opened the back door.

"Do you want to put your bag in the trunk?" Toni asked. Without giving me the option, she pressed the key fob and opened the trunk. I walked over, put my bag in there, and then slammed the lid shut. Nova opened the back door and moved over for me.

"Grandma's here," she said as she pointed to the front seat. Toni's mom turned and smiled at me.

"Such a handsome young man," Carmela said.

I rolled my eyes but gave her the crooked smile I knew she loved. With her here, I thought I'd play it to my advantage. "Grandma, Toni won't let me drive."

Grandma's eyebrows went up, but Toni shook her head. The tension in the car was thick, and I'd probably made it worse.

"Not tonight, Cutter." Toni sighed heavily as she shut her door.

Yep, something was definitely wrong. There was no snark from her. No promise of being able to drive later or Brendan coming up to take me driving. "Where are we going?"

"To see Mommy. She has a boo-boo."

I rolled my eyes at Nova's baby speak. "Talk like a big girl, okay?"

Nova nodded.

"What's wrong with our mom?"

"Cutter, you were right. Your mom hasn't been feeling good, so she's in the hospital for the night. We're going to go see her. She misses you and Nova," Toni said as she put her car into drive and pulled out of the parking spot. Through the side mirror, I watched my high school fade into the dark abyss of nothingness and wondered if I would be back tomorrow or the next day.

Toni turned the volume up on the stereo, and Nova sang along to some pop song. I knew the words but couldn't recall who sang it. My phone vibrated, and I took it out of my pocket to see a text message from Eleni asking me how practice was. I told her it was fine and put my phone away. I would call her later, after I did my homework.

"Can I take pictures on your phone?" Nova asked. I wanted to tell her no but didn't want to upset her. I took it out of my pocket again and checked my notifications to make sure there wasn't anything inappropriate on there from one of the guys. They liked to send ridiculous memes that my mom wouldn't approve of.

Nova took my phone and opened the photo-sharing app. She took a picture and sent it to my contacts. I didn't mind. My friends were used to Nova sending them photos. Most of them were funny. After each picture, she changed the filter and took more pics. Notifications came in from friends that Nova knew she could answer. Eleni and Flinn would send back funny pictures to Nova. She showed them to me, and I laughed with her and posed for some.

My mood shifted when Toni pulled into the hospital parking lot. She parked, and the four of us got out of the car. Grandma held Nova's hand, and we followed Toni into the hospital. We waited for the elevator in silence and then rode up to the fifth floor. We didn't have to stop to check in or ask what room my mom was in. My suspicion grew. My mom was definitely here yesterday, which was why Toni had come up unexpectedly. Which also meant Toni had lied to us.

The door we stopped at was slightly ajar. Toni pushed it open, and we followed. The TV was on, but the volume was low. My mom sat on the bed, wearing her favorite ratty sweatshirt with a faded Boston University logo on it. I looked around and realized I hadn't ever been in a hospital room before. Were they all the same, with white walls, tan bedding, and brown chairs? Or did each hospital decide on an assorted color scheme?

Two years ago, Mom let us paint our bedrooms as part of the remodeling job she was doing that was also never ending. Nova's room was pink, with a dark-purple-and-blue wall meant to look like outer space. The solar system was also painted on her wall.

My room was mostly white, except for the green wall I'd painted to look like grass. Mom helped me paint a baseball diamond on the wall, which I thought was pretty neat. It was something she'd seen on a do-it-yourself show.

Nova ran toward our mom and hopped up onto her bed. They hugged each other tightly. My mom watched me for a bunch of seconds before she closed her eyes and gave her attention to my sister. I tried to step forward, but my eyes landed on one of the machines near the bed. I followed the tubing, and my heart lurched when it ended in my mom's hand. How sick was she?

"Are you going to just stand there?" she said, her voice breaking through my thoughts. "You had a good game last night," she stated. "I read the paper this morning, and Toni sent me a ton of videos."

"Thanks." I moved forward an inch or so and then stopped. Grandma and Toni were on the other side of the room. Grandma sat in the ugly brown chair, while Toni perched on the windowsill. She wasn't looking at us but outside.

"How come you haven't texted me?"

"I've been trying to rest so I can get better," she said, but I suspected this was a lie. "And my hand hurts." She lifted the hand where her IV was. I nodded, but I didn't buy her excuse for a second.

"Come here." I did as she'd asked and fell into her outstretched arms. For the longest time, it was me and her against the world, and then Nova joined us. We were all each other had.

After she released me, she kept her hand in mine. She looked at us, her children that she often referred to as the best thing to ever happen to her, and smiled a watery-eyed smile.

"Mommy, why are you crying?" Nova asked, her voice reverting to the soft baby tone she still sometimes used.

"I'm sad, my sweet girl."

"How sick are you?" I finally asked, unable and unwilling to keep sitting here without knowing.

She let her tears fall. I wiped one cheek clear for her, and she whispered a thank-you.

"I have cancer."

I didn't need to ask her to repeat herself or to clarify. I'd heard her loud and clear. Her hand squeezed mine, and my gaze dropped as my own tears began clouding my vision. Behind me, Toni sobbed.

"What does that mean?" Nova asked. She was so innocent and not damaged by the world. At sixteen I shouldn't have been, either, but I had friends who'd lost their grandparents to cancer and other diseases. Flinn lost his grandfather last year to stomach cancer, and he still told me all the time about how much he missed him.

"Mom is really sick, Nova."

My mom's eyes met mine, and then she looked at her little girl. "There are some bad things growing in my body, and I'm going to take a lot of medicine to fight them."

"And you'll get better?"

Mom nodded. "But I'm going to be sick sometimes and very tired."

"Who's going to get me off the bus?"

"Aunt Toni is going to stay with us for a while, and Grandma will be here all the time."

"Grandpa too?" Nova asked.

Mom nodded. "Why don't you go with Grandma to the cafeteria and get some pie? It's really delicious." She brought Nova into her arms and hugged her tightly. Nova crawled off the bed and went with Toni's mom, leaving us alone.

"Why can't I go get pie?"

"Because I wanted to talk to you without Nova in the room."

A lump formed in my throat. "Are you . . ." I paused and fought back the emotion bubbling within me. "Dying?"

Another sob came from Toni, but my eyes were solely on my mom. Tears streamed down her face, wetting her sweatshirt. She reached for me, but I kept my distance, needing her to answer me first.

"Are you?"

My mom nodded. The simple gesture broke something inside me, and I couldn't hold back any longer. I cried as a big wave of anguish engulfed me. Mom didn't hesitate and wrapped her arms around me. I wanted to fight her off, to push her away, but I didn't have any strength in my body. She tightened her hold as I collapsed against her, my own tears soaking the back of her sweatshirt while our sobs kept pace with one another. I was going to lose my mom. It wasn't a matter of if, but when.

We stayed like this for minutes, or maybe hours (time seemed insignificant in our grief), holding each other and rocking back and forth, crying into each other's necks. I bubbled incoherent sentences filled with questions that she didn't have answers to, all while she apologized and told me how much she loved me. I didn't want to let go, out of fear that once I did, she'd slip away and be gone forever.

We finally parted, and she cupped my cheeks with her hands. Our hazel eyes matched until I was being moody, according to my mom. Then mine turned dark and intense.

"I'm going to fight," she told me. "I'm going to be strong as long as I can and fight for every single day I can get with you and your sister. The doctors can't cure this, but they can give us more time together. That's what I'm fighting for. More time."

I nodded, not trusting my voice.

"Leaving you and Nova is not an option for me. I'm not done being your mom."

She ran her hand through my wavy hair and reminded me I needed to get it cut. She was right. My mom was always right.

We heard Nova before the door opened. I stood and walked over to the sink and wet a paper towel. After dabbing my face, I turned toward everyone. Nova smiled brightly as she pointed to a piece of pie and one of those small cartons of chocolate milk.

"I got this for you," she said in her happy, singsong tone. It was like she'd forgotten our mother had told her she was sick, and maybe that was for the best.

The five of us gathered around my mom's bed and ate hospital cafeteria apple pie, drank chocolate milk, and acted like this was an ordinary occurrence for our family.

It was anything but, and something told me we'd have many more moments like this. Toni would make sure of it.

Chapter 9

Antonia

The day after Miri told the kids about her diagnosis, I brought her home. We'd heard from Dr. Frederick's Boston colleague, whose assessment was the same. Dr. Patricia from Dana-Farber had reviewed Miri's scans and confirmed the diagnosis: stage IV pancreatic adenocarcinoma with metastases to liver, lungs, and breast tissue. She agreed with the aggressive chemotherapy approach and estimated the same timeline of six to twelve months with treatment.

This wasn't the news either of us wanted to hear, and with it, Miri decided she would do her treatment in Grove Hill, where she could stay with her kids. I didn't blame her, but I was also angry.

At her. Health care. The world.

I was going to lose my best friend. Her kids were going to lose their mom. None of this was fair, and yet I had to paste on a happy face each time someone entered the room because reality was depressing enough.

"Even the best doctors in the world can't change what this is," I said to myself as I stared out the kitchen window.

My fingers tapped the countertop while I waited for the coffee to finish brewing. Miri was asleep, my mom had taken Nova to the mall, and Cutter was at his friend Flinn's house. The quietness was unnerving, unwanted, and oddly needed.

The bean water stopped filling the pot, and I poured myself a cup, added cream, and then made my way outside to the porch. After turning on the portable heater, I sat in one of the rockers, sipped my coffee, and let my mind wander.

I needed to make a list of things that had to be done in preparation for Miri's passing. Approaching the inevitable, though, seemed like such a crass thing to do. How would I sit my friend down and ask the important questions? There was so much to do, with many of them being urgent. It was all stuff I didn't want to think about, yet I didn't have a choice.

My eyes closed as my foot moved the rocker back and forth. This was where Miri and I liked to sit and watch the sunset. She'd always said she would buy an old farmhouse with a porch because this was exactly what she wanted: the peace and quiet of the country, but not so far away that she didn't have services. Miri wanted land: a place for her kids to run free and where she could grow her own vegetables. The only thing she didn't have, thankfully, was animals. Although Nova desperately wanted a puppy.

As if I had conjured up a dog, a yellow one came onto the porch and headed right up to me.

"Scout!"

The dog barked and wagged its tail. Its owner appeared and gave me a wave. I waved back, recognizing him as Cutter's coach.

"Sorry about my dog. We were out walking, and I usually let him run along the road. Miriam gives him treats when she's out."

"He's not bothering me." I scratched him behind his ear. He rested his head on my lap, and for a brief second, all my worries dissipated. How could an animal I didn't even know ease my mind so easily?

Weston stepped onto the porch and leaned against the column. I'd meant to ask Miri more about him, but I hadn't found the time. I got the sense she was fond of him, and maybe there was something there she hadn't told me about yet.

"Can I get you some coffee?" The thought quickly became a question.

"Sure, I'd love some."

I motioned for him to sit in the other rocker and excused myself. Pausing in the hall, I listened for Miri moving around upstairs. Dr. Frederick already had her on some medicine, and early next week they'd install a PICC line to administer her chemo.

In the kitchen, I pulled a tray out from under the counter and added cream and sugar containers to it. I refilled my cup and poured a mug for Weston. I searched high and low for dog treats and couldn't find anything but took a carrot out of the refrigerator, hoping Scout liked them.

Weston was near the steps, bent over and inspecting the rotting boards. There wasn't a part of the house that didn't have an issue that needed to be addressed. I mentally added it to the long list growing in my mind. The smartest thing would be to sell the house and put the money into a trust for the kids—if it even made a profit.

"Just another thing falling apart around me," I said as I carried the tray to the small table between the two chairs.

"I can fix it," he said as he sat down. Scout followed, sitting obediently next to him. The dog looked out over the yard, watching for some hidden danger only he could sense. "I've loaned Miriam some of my tools when she's fixing stuff. She'll never accept my help, though."

"She's stubborn. Me, not so much," I told him. "I'll take all the help I can get."

"Duly noted." He held his cup up. "Thank you."

"My pleasure. I didn't know what you liked and forgot to ask, so I brought cream and sugar out."

"Black is perfect for me."

After we sat there for a minute, drinking our coffee, I broke the silence. "Thank you for not benching Cutter. He was rather upset with me when I told him I'd spoken with you."

"He would have to do something drastic to get benched. Not only is he one of my best players, but he's also one of my leaders. The other players look up to him. Cutter understands the game. I depend on him a lot."

I nodded, even though I didn't understand any of it. All I knew was Cutter had yelled at me, telling me I had no right to tell his coach about his mom. There was no point in arguing with him. Cutter was going to be an angry teen for a very long time.

"Is there anything I can help with?"

What an open-ended question that was. I shook my head. "I don't know whether I'm coming or going right now. Miri will start treatment next week, and then I guess I'll figure it out from there."

"Miri . . ." He paused after saying her nickname. "When we first met, she introduced herself as Miriam, and I've never heard of anyone calling her Miri. Not even her friends in town."

"It's my nickname for her. I had trouble saying her name when I was younger and have always called her Miri."

"It suits her. She never mentioned that she had a sister."

"We're not related," I told him. "We've been best friends since we were little."

"Ah." He nodded and took a sip of his coffee.

"Oh, I almost forgot." I took the carrot off the tray and showed it to Weston. "Can Scout have this?"

He laughed. "I was wondering if that was for him but didn't want to assume. Scout would love it."

I called Scout over, and without me asking, he sat and held up his paw for me to shake. I held the vegetable out in front of him, and he took it gently from me. "He's such a good boy."

"That he is. I wasn't looking for a dog until I met him. It was love at first sight."

"Nova wants a dog," I said for no other reason than to continue the conversation.

"Having one might help her cope with what's going on."

"Yeah, but everything's so up in the air."

"Can I ask what happens to the kids when . . ." Weston trailed off.

I sighed heavily and took a sip of my coffee. "I don't know. Miri and I need to sit down and make a plan for them, her house . . . everything." I wiped at my fallen tears. "She's young. This shouldn't be happening. Those kids are her life, and they need her. I need her."

"I know I'm going to sound like a broken record here, but if there's anything I can do to help, please let me know."

"Be there for Cutter," I stated. "My dad and brother are in his life, but they don't live here. He's going to need someone close that he can confide in. Guide him." I glanced at Weston, who met my gaze. His eyes were a warm brown and full of empathy, making me wonder if he'd gone through something like this. Had he lost someone he loved dearly? I continued to stare, which he didn't seem to care about because he kept his eyes on me the entire time.

And then Brendan popped into my mind, as if I was doing something wrong. I turned away, heat rising to my cheeks, and I cleared my throat.

Weston did as well. "What do you do for work?"

"I find corporations that are on the brink of financial despair and offer to buy them out to save them from bankruptcy."

"You're a pirate."

I looked at him sharply, and he shrugged. "Sorry, slip of the tongue."

"No, it's fine." I didn't have the energy to argue. "People either think I'm a savior or someone hell-bent on ruining others."

"Which one are you?"

"It depends on the company." I looked into my empty cup and sighed. "Sometimes companies need a complete overhaul. You can't replace the CEO or CFO without replacing other members of management because their ideologies on business all align. If they failed once, they'll fail again. In this aspect, I guess I am a pirate."

I added, "But also, if you have a family company that's struggling and I come in to help and they can get on board with the business plan, what's the point in breaking them up?"

"So, you don't go in and tear apart companies for shits and giggles?"

For whatever reason, his question made me laugh. "Definitely not. Honestly, I don't remember the last time I laughed at work."

Weston chuckled. "That's a shame. I laugh all the time. It's really the best way to lift your spirits."

He had a point. "Do you like working with kids?"

He shrugged. "The alternative was to stay home all day and stare at the wall. I suppose there are times when I'd prefer the wall because it doesn't talk back, but yeah, I love my job."

"Have you always wanted to be a teacher?"

Weston laughed. "Nope, but getting my degree in physical education was the easier path in college, and it made for a nice retirement."

Retirement?

"Wait, what?"

He chuckled again, and I found that I liked the sound of it. I wasn't wrong when I'd said I didn't laugh at work. No one did. Work was always so damn serious. We were always straight-faced, no nonsense. The idea of work filled me with dread. I hadn't looked at my emails since I arrived, nor had I returned any of Brendan's messages. He was angry with me, and rightly so; I dumped a lot on him, but he could handle it for a few days while I figured things out.

"Teaching and coaching is my retirement job," Weston said.

"What did you do beforehand?"

Weston's cheeks blushed. He looked at the yard and tried to hide the small smile spreading across his lips. I knew I was missing the punchline of whatever his career used to be.

"You honestly don't know?"

I shook my head slowly.

He glanced my way, his smile still in place. For a moment I wondered if he was one of those male models who used to grace our TV with their underwear ads.

"In my other life, I was a professional baseball pitcher until I had a career-ending injury."

"Wow." I shook my head. "Sorry, Cutter never said a thing. I mean, I knew he liked his baseball coach, but I didn't know you played professionally."

"It's not something I talk about, but yeah. I mean, it's not a secret. Everyone in town knows, and during the annual summer parade, the town makes a big deal about it. And there are times when the league will ask me to do appearances and other things." He shrugged as if what he used to do wasn't a big deal.

"I don't know shit about sports," I told him. "I go to Cutter's games when he's playing near my home, but that's about it."

"Where's home?"

"Boston."

His face fell at the mention of the city I lived in, and I wanted to ask him why, but he masked his expression quickly by looking away. Before either of us could continue, the screen door opened, and Miri stepped out. She looked like her old self. Not sick. Not someone facing the biggest battle of her life. Scout ran up to her, and sure enough, she slipped him a dog treat and then crouched down to hug him.

As much as I wanted to watch her, absorb her energy, I found myself watching Weston instead. There was something about him that I couldn't quite put my finger on. From our brief interactions I knew he was a good guy, and I liked that about him. Especially if Cutter was going to need someone to talk to.

Chapter 10

Weston

Miriam smiled softly at me after she finished petting Scout. He loved her. But he also loved anyone who would rub his belly and feed him snacks. She walked down the stairs and into her yard, tilting her head back. I never took my eyes off her, watching and wondering what she was doing.

The sun shone down, and Miriam sighed. "It's a gorgeous day."

We said nothing. It *was* a nice day, but not something I would've considered gorgeous. The sun was out and melting the snow, which would make the ground soft and the roads turn to mud. I supposed in the grand scheme of life, winter turning to spring could be considered gorgeous—if spring were coming in March, like in Boston. But here, spring could arrive in June, if Mother Nature didn't take pity on the people of Grove Hill.

Miriam came back onto the porch. Antonia and I both stood, and Miriam chuckled. "Rolling out the red carpet for the dying."

Antonia took a quick inhale, and I pondered how to reply. Do you say yes to something like this? Meet humor with humor or let the comment go by the wayside?

Miriam shook her head and eyed her friend. "If I can't joke, then I'm not going to make it very long, am I?"

"You dying isn't something I care to joke about." Antonia stepped aside and directed Miriam to sit in the rocker. "Would you like coffee? Tea?"

"Tea would be fine."

Antonia looked at me. "Can I get you anything else? A refill?"

"I'm fine. Thank you."

She nodded softly and then disappeared into the house. I sat back down and looked at my dog, who sat expectantly next to Miriam. She slipped her hand into her pocket and handed him a treat. She patted Scout's head and leaned down to kiss his nose.

"You're such a good boy," she said to him. "Do you think he knows?"

What a loaded question. I laughed and directed my answer to be about my dog being a good boy and not sensing Miriam was sick. "Yes, I tell him every day, and I believe Antonia told him as well. He's going to get an inflated ego if we keep complimenting him."

Miriam huffed. "Toni."

"Toni?"

She nodded. "Her friends call her Toni."

"I'm not sure we're friends, at least not yet."

"You will be," she said as she continued to make lovey faces at my dog. "Aside from my kids and the staff at the hospital, you're the only one that knows."

I swallowed hard. Was this a burden? I didn't think it was. "I did tell Jerome. He won't say anything, but it was important for him to know as well, since he also teaches and coaches Cutter."

"That's fine. It's only a matter of time before everyone will know." Miriam sat back and began rocking. "My son is going to need you: someone to talk to."

Her words tore at my heart. She was going to be in the fight of her life, and she was worried about her son. "He'll have me," I said and then cleared my throat. "Cutter will have the whole town to lean on."

Miriam looked down at her hands, and I saw her lips move into a fine line. I knew I shouldn't stare but couldn't help it. I wondered if this moment would be one I recalled in the future. Maybe when Nova was older, in ten years . . . a thought struck me then: Would I even know her in ten years? Would they go live with Antonia in Boston? Or Miriam's parents?

They were the missing piece in all of this. I'd never seen them at a game or heard Cutter ever mention them.

The screen door opened, and Antonia returned. She handed Miriam a teacup and set the saucer down on the tray, then wiggled a bottle of water at me.

"Thanks," I said as I stood and took it from her. I motioned for her to sit in the rocker while I leaned against the pillar. We sat in awkward silence for a minute, and I considered leaving. I supposed it was one thing to sit and talk to either of them, but both made me feel like a third wheel. Not to mention, there was an obvious worry between them.

After chugging half the bottle, I righted myself. "I'm going to head to the hardware store, and then I'll be back to fix the loose boards."

Miriam met my gaze. "You don't have to do that, Wes."

"I know, but I want to."

I nodded to them and then took my leave, calling for Scout to follow me. I half expected him to stay back and milk the two ladies for more snacks, but he sauntered behind me.

As I walked home, I thought about what I'd need from the hardware store besides wood and realized I should've inspected the porch better. For all I knew, the columns needed repairing, along with the roof, the screen door, and the wood trim. The house would also fare better if it had siding instead of clapboard.

You're getting ahead of yourself. It wasn't my house, and I didn't have a vested interest in it. Nor had Miriam asked me to fix anything. Still, I wanted to. It was one less thing she or Antonia would need to worry about.

I opened the truck door, and Scout hopped in. He sat in the passenger seat and liked to stick his head out the window, which meant I had to keep the heat cranked this time of year, or I'd freeze.

He wagged his tail in excitement when we drove past Miriam's, and he continued to watch her house until it was out of sight.

"Don't worry, we'll go back so you can get more treats."

At the mention of treats, Scout's ears perked up, but since I didn't hand him anything, he went back to looking out the window, with his tongue hanging out of his mouth.

When we came to the first stoplight, someone called his name. He was like the town mayor, only everyone loved Scout. He would happily accept any pets if people were willing to stop and give him some.

Luck was on my side when the Rusty Nail hardware store came into view: I found a spot out front that didn't require me to parallel park. Scout was allowed inside, but I left him in the truck since I wouldn't be gone terribly long.

The door chimed as I walked in, and I followed the voices toward the register. Rusty, the owner and a friend of mine, waved when he saw me and went back to talking with the lady at the counter. I made my way to the back, where he kept his lumber, and began gathering the necessary pieces.

"Whatcha making?" Rusty asked moments later.

"Fixing the Vaughns' porch," I told him as I held a two-by-four out, checking to see if the piece of wood was warped.

"Ah, I've talked to Miriam about replacing the wood with Trex, but I'm not sure she can afford it."

Trex decking was a high-performance material engineered to resist fading. It didn't splinter and shouldn't warp if installed correctly. It was also pricey upfront but would last at least twenty years, if not up to fifty.

The thought crossed my mind to buy a handful of boards and slowly replace each one, but I quickly dismissed it. "Enticing," I said to Rusty and shook my head. "As is, she'll be mad I'm even doing this much."

"Ain't that the truth. I swear every time she's in here, she's talking about some project she found on Pinterest. I never think to ask if she's actually done any of the jobs she's told me about."

I laughed. Cutter had mentioned the same thing a time or two. "Yeah, I'm not sure. I've never been past the porch. I was over there this morning and noticed the boards needed to be replaced. I figured I could at least get that started for her, especially since it's nice out."

I wasn't about to tell him what was going on with her or how she wouldn't fight me on helping her out now. How sad was it that it took her dying to accept help? I shook my head and added another board to my flatbed cart.

Where I failed in this project was not measuring the deck beforehand or inspecting each piece of board. Right now, I had to guesstimate the size since, at some point, I'd decided to replace the entire front portion.

"You taking the whole thing down?" Rusty asked.

I shook my head. "I think it might be best if I go board by board. I hadn't planned on replacing any joists or jacking the roof up. Might just piecemeal it for right now."

He slapped me on the shoulder. "Holler if you need some equipment."

"Will do." After I finished loading the wood, I stopped by the nail section and picked out what I thought I'd need. It didn't escape me that I was doing all of this in haste, and I knew why.

Antonia.

As much as I didn't want to think about her, I was. Her standing there on the porch, with the sun shining down on her. She glowed and took my breath away.

If this had been any other morning, one not marred by the news of a friend and parent being terminally ill, I would've been thrilled about Scout running up to her. I'd be the first to admit I would totally use my dog to flirt with someone, especially if that someone was Antonia.

My heart may have skipped a beat or two when she invited me to stay for coffee. Sitting there and watching the day come to life was peaceful, despite the heaviness that surrounded her. I'd lost people in my life, but never like this. I'd never had to be someone's caretaker.

I took my supplies to the counter, where Rusty stood chatting to another local. The name of the fellow escaped me, but we greeted each other like long-lost friends anyway. More people knew me than I did them because of my former career and my current one as a coach.

When I'd first moved to Grove Hill, I was treated like a celebrity. It didn't matter where I went; someone was asking for my autograph or a picture. This lasted for about a year and now only happened when a tourist came to town and I just happened to show up where they were, or when I was asked to make an appearance. I didn't mind any of the fanfare. It made me feel loved and appreciated.

Rusty rang up my purchase and helped me load everything into the back of my truck. After he'd showered Scout with some attention, he reminded me about our standing trivia game at the local pub. Rusty, Jerome, me, and whoever we could rope in as our fourth usually dominated trivia night. Rusty had a knack for knowing the most obscure things, while I tended to get most of the sports questions correct, and Jerome rocked geography. We made the best team.

I drove straight to Miriam's. She and Antonia weren't sitting in the rockers anymore when I pulled in. I sat there for a moment and imagined what it would be like to have someone sitting on my porch and waiting for me to come home again. I had that once with my high school sweetheart, turned wife, turned ex-wife. There had been a time when we couldn't get enough of each other, and then I got hurt.

It wasn't my injury that drove her away or the fact that I wanted to retire instead of being demoted from a starting pitcher to someone who came in to relieve the starter or the reliever. It was that we didn't see eye to eye on life, on living in a small mountain town, or having children.

Brianna wanted different.

I wanted more.

I shook my thoughts clear and shut off my truck. As soon as I opened the door to let Scout out, Antonia and Nova came outside. Another woman followed, who sat down and pulled Nova onto her lap.

Antonia came toward me. "How much do I owe you?"

"For what?" I asked as I dropped the tailgate.

"For the supplies? Labor?"

"If you help, not a thing," I said, winking. It was a lame attempt at flirting, but her cheeks pinked slightly, and that was enough for me.

She laughed lightly. "And if I don't?"

"Still nothing," I told her as I pulled a couple of the boards from the back. "I'm not doing this for payment or anything."

"Then why?"

I nodded toward the house. "Because this town cares about the Vaughns. Because I care."

Antonia looked over her shoulder, and I tried not to stare but couldn't help myself. She wore jeans, a collared shirt with a sweater over the top, and, while the ground was soft and in parts muddy, she had on a pair of loafers. Not exactly winter shoes.

She looked back at me and held my gaze. I wanted to ask her out to dinner or tell her I'd bring some steaks over, and I'd grill for her, Miriam, and the kids. Anything so I could spend more time trying to get to know her.

"Well, I feel bad you're doing this because it's Saturday and you've worked all week. If you need help, let me know. I don't know squat about construction, but my dad does, and so does my boyfriend. I can call them if you need me to."

At the mention of a boyfriend, my heart sank. That would be my luck. I finally felt a spark toward someone, and she had a boyfriend.

"I'll be fine." I grabbed three boards, lifted them onto my shoulder, and walked toward the house. As I got closer, I changed my frown into a smile for Nova's sake, because it definitely wasn't for me.

Chapter 11

Cutter

I lay on the ground, with my basketball under my head. Nothing about this was comfortable, but the aches and pains I had in my neck reminded me that I had the ability to feel something.

Anything.

Beside me, Flinn did the same. Only he used his skateboard to prop up his head.

We'd come to the park first thing this morning. He rebounded for me while I got some shots up, and I took videos of him skateboarding. We were the most unlikely duo, but our friendship worked for us. Neither of us had any expectations of one another. He was my best friend and the only one who knew about my mom.

"What's gonna happen?"

I lifted one shoulder in a half shrug to his open-ended question. He could've been asking about my mom, her death, or our final in our global studies class. It didn't matter because I didn't have an answer for either question.

"Where are you going to live?"

"Dunno."

"Do you think your dad will come back?"

Flinn was the only one who knew about my dad and what a loser he was. None of the guys on the basketball team or baseball team knew about him. When asked, I always said I didn't have one, which for the most part was true. I let them all believe my mom used a donor or had one of those immaculate conception pregnancies.

Twice.

The truth of the matter was, I did have a dad. Nova did as well. I supposed luck was on our side that we'd had the same "donor." But that was where I'd run out of luck. I'd had the dubious honor of meeting my father. He'd spent about six weeks of my life living with us, acting like a dad, telling me he loved me, tucking me in at night. The same shit my friends all had when they were growing up. He even tried to tell me I was throwing the ball wrong. It was a damn good thing I didn't listen to him because he didn't know shit.

The only thing my dad knew—and he was a master at it—was leaving. His extended stay into our lives ended on a Saturday morning, after breakfast, when he needed to go into town to get a part for his bike. Since he didn't tell us which town, it would make sense that the one he needed to go to was seven years away.

That was how long he'd been gone.

Or was it eight years now?

I didn't have to be a rocket scientist to deduce that he left when my mom told him they were going to have another bundle of joy.

Strike that . . . *unwanted* joy, at least in his book.

Nine months later, Nova was born.

At first, I was mad at her. At my mom. They took—no, they drove—my dad away. I finally had a dad, and we had a real shot at happiness, until Nova. I held a grudge for about a year or maybe longer.

While my mom was pregnant and for Nova's first year, she stressed the importance of me being a big brother, a role model, and the man my little sister could look up to. I didn't understand what any of that meant until her sweet voice said my name. She didn't have a care in the world other than she wanted me to play with her, cuddle with her, and read to her, and to be something she could climb on.

It was when Nova said my name that everything changed for me. She became my biggest cheerleader at my games. I could hear her screaming for me above all the parents. She was the first person to run up to me, hug me, and give me a high five, but most importantly, she never told me I sucked or that I was doing something wrong. For that reason, I would always be in her life and make her my priority. Now more than ever.

"I hope not," I said to Flinn after processing his question. "What would he even do? Tell us we had to go live with him? Nova doesn't know him."

"Neither do you," Flinn said.

"I know enough."

I knew what I'd learned in those six weeks. He was a loser. He wasn't a man, but a child who—when he didn't get his way—bailed. I had a better relationship with Rocco, Toni's brother, or Coach Schmidt and Flinn's dad. Even Brendan, although I hadn't known him that long. If I needed anything, I could call them.

I pulled the basketball out from under my head and shot it toward the sky. This was a great way for me to work on my form. Flinn changed his position as well and sat on his board.

"You can come live with me," he said.

I shook my head. "Nova's afraid of your dog."

"Don't you think your aunt Toni will take Nova?"

And not me?

My hand slipped, and the ball almost hit me in the face. I moved my head just in time; my thoughts ran wild. Would Toni take Nova and leave me behind? They were close, and Toni definitely favored my sister.

She used to favor you as well.

What was going to happen to me when my mom died?

Would I go into foster care?

I was forced to bite my tongue to ward off the impending tears from coming to the surface. I didn't want to cry in front of Flinn. At least, not again. I had already done so when I showed up at his house this morning.

"I mean . . ." I shrugged. "I guess my mom will have to talk to your parents."

"Yeah, there's probably a bunch of legal shit that has to happen."

And we're out of time.

I sat up abruptly and looked away. The tears clouded my vision whether I wanted them to or not. Flinn's hand rested on my shoulder.

"You know you can stay with me anytime."

I nodded and bit my lower lip to keep from crying. How had this become my life—where I cried at the park because my mom was dying, and I had no idea where I was going to live?

"I'll talk to my parents tonight and see what's what."

I shook my head. "I don't think my mom wants anyone to know just yet. She said something about waiting for the treatment and whatnot."

"All right. I'll wait."

Deep down, I knew I could trust him not to say anything to his mom. Chances were, she'd find out from someone else who'd found out from someone else. That was how all the rumors were spread around town.

My stomach growled. I pulled my phone out of my pocket to check the time and saw a slew of text messages, most of them from Eleni, asking me if I was okay. I hadn't told her yet and really hadn't planned on it.

The last one from her made me smile: I love you.

I may have only been sixteen, but I was in love with her. The guidance counselor once caught us kissing in the hallway. We'd skipped class, thinking we knew the best place to hide, and wouldn't you know it—busted. He took me to his office and called my mom, who had to come and sit in a meeting. My mom said she was going to ground me for breaking school rules but didn't see the point. Eleni and I would see each other at school, and the school wouldn't do anything to keep us from seeing each other in or during class or at lunch.

My mom did sit me down every day after school and teach me about the birds and the bees. The entire week was awkward and uncomfortable for both of us. I understood, though. She wanted a different life for me because being a teenage mom had been hard for her.

I saw a text from my mom. Seeing her name on my phone made my heart lurch. How many more messages would I get before they stopped altogether?

Mom: I love you. I hope you're having a great time with Flinn.

My throat tightened, and I could no longer hold back the tears. Flinn sat next to me, being there without saying anything.

I read and reread her message and finally took a screenshot so I could save it. I had no idea what happened to a person's phone after they died, but I never wanted to lose her messages. Even the ones where she yelled at me to get my ass home.

"Do you think the phone store can show me how to download my texts?"

Flinn shrugged. "Not sure. I guess we should go ask them."

I wanted to do it now, versus later, because later never came. Or it did, and then it was too late. We left the park and walked toward our downtown area. People honked and called out our names. We waved. People stopped us on the street, and we chatted. To everyone, we didn't have a care in the world. It was a lazy Saturday, the sun was shining even though it was cold, and we were two teens strolling the streets.

I imagined that once the news spread about my mom, these same people would stop me and tell me how sorry they were to hear the news and ask if I needed anything. That's what people did. They cared.

Flinn and I entered the phone store and waited for one of the clerks to come over and chat with us. It took a bit, which we figured was because neither of us was old enough to buy our own phones, and we didn't have our parents with us.

"What can I do for you?" the clerk asked. He kept his hands behind his back and jutted his chin out, which I thought was odd. It was almost like we bored him.

"Is there a way to download all of my text messages?"

"Yes, of course."

I waited.

So did Flinn.

"Okay. Can you tell me how?"

The clerk began to roll his eyes but turned away before I could see him do it fully. Flinn shook his head and muttered under his breath that this guy was an asshat. Part of me understood because we weren't buying anything or changing our plan, but the other side of me wondered if this guy was being a jerk because of how we were dressed. Flinn was in all black, with a chain hanging from his belt loops, while I wore some ratty sweats and an oversize sweatshirt. Besides the fact we were completely opposite from one another, we didn't look great.

We followed the clerk to the counter, and he angrily tapped the keyboard while huffing every few seconds. If I didn't want the information, I would've made a scene. Having the text messages from my mom was important. There was a good chance I'd never go back and read them, but I also didn't want to lose them.

When the clerk sighed heavily, Flinn spoke up. "Is your dad dying?"

"Excuse me?"

"I didn't mumble or slip up," Flinn said. "Is your dad dying?"

"No." He looked from Flinn to me.

"His is, and he wants to keep the messages he has. If you can't get the instructions, maybe someone else can."

Again, the clerk looked at us and then pressed one button. The printer behind him came to life. He took the few sheets of paper, stapled them, and handed them to me.

"I'm sorry about your dad."

It didn't even bother me that Flinn had said what he said or used my dad instead of my mom. I wished it was my dad dying. Hell, for all I knew, he was already dead. If he was, I'd dig him up and find a way for him to die all over again, as long as my mom could stay.

Outside, I folded the sheets of paper and put them in my pocket.

"Thank you."

"He was pissing me off. I had to say something."

"I appreciate it."

Flinn nodded.

We walked the rest of the way back to his house, and then I walked the last half mile to mine. Once I was alone, I talked to myself. I yelled, screamed, kicked rocks, and let my tears flow. Life was unfair.

The whole lack-of-dad thing had really messed me up, but not having my mom would destroy me. I would never admit this to her, but she was my best friend, and I didn't want to live in a world where my mom didn't exist. Especially not when I was only sixteen. Even Nova deserved better.

I turned into our long dirt driveway and paused when I heard a bark. Scout, my coach's dog, ran toward me, with Nova following behind. We met halfway, and I gave the dog some good behind-the-ear scratches.

"Cutter, guess what?" Nova bounced anxiously.

"What?"

She held her hand up, with her index finger pointed toward the sky. "One, Grandma bought you some new sweatpants. Two, Mommy says we can have pizza for dinner. Three, Coach is building us a new porch." The last one, she jumped up and down at, while I frowned. Nova couldn't say Coach's last name, so she called him "Coach."

"Why is Coach building us a porch?"

Nova shrugged and reached for my hand. She held it tightly while she skipped along to my stride. When the house came into view, sure enough, Coach Schmidt wore a work belt and a ball cap, and he had a table saw out.

"Hey, Cutter," he said as he looked up from marking a line on a piece of wood.

"What are you doing?"

He nodded toward the hole in the front porch. "Getting those boards replaced before someone falls through. Do you want to help?"

I didn't. I wanted to go up to my room and bury my face in my pillow. Instead, I nodded and told him I'd be right back. Inside, I went upstairs, stared at the pillow I'd intended to soak with my tears, and changed my clothes. It looked like I was going to learn how to repair a porch instead of wallowing in self-pity.

Chapter 12

Antonia

Cutter came thundering down the stairs, wearing a pair of jeans and a flannel. Miri sat next to me, wrapped in an afghan blanket my mother had crocheted for her before Cutter was born. Miri set her book down and smiled at her son.

"Are you going outside to help?"

He nodded. "Coach asked me to. I didn't think I should say no."

"That's very nice of you."

Cutter shrugged, which was the way all teens played things off. Cutter helping his coach was huge. It would not only teach him how to repair what was broken but would also give him some time with Weston, away from school and the team.

"Nova said we're having pizza for dinner?"

"We are," Miri said as she reached for his hand. When he didn't move to take hers, she dropped her hand back into her lap. Despite her trying to hide her feelings about being rejected, I saw it, and I wondered if her son had as well.

"Cool. Can Eleni come over for dinner?"

Miri nodded. "The rules remain."

Cutter sighed loudly.

"Which are?" I asked. His little teenage temperament put me on edge. I didn't want to think he would take advantage of his mother right now, but those hormones wreaked havoc on young, impressionable minds.

"Eleni isn't allowed upstairs," Miri said as she kept her eyes on her son.

"What if I keep my door open?"

I had to give Cutter credit, because I would've asked the same thing. Any alone time I could've gotten with any of my boyfriends would've been a disaster. Thankfully, my parents had known of my wily ways. My siblings and I had strict rules in the house, although those rules didn't apply when I was at someone else's house. Honestly, I was lucky I hadn't found myself in the same situation as Miri, especially since we both gravitated toward the "bad" guys.

Miri shook her head, and while I couldn't see her eyes, I imagined they rolled. "Not allowed upstairs means not allowed upstairs."

Cutter did, in fact, roll his eyes. Oh, to be sixteen again. He and his girlfriend had already gotten into trouble at school, and Miri had mentioned that Eleni's parents were strict, which told me if these two wanted to get into trouble, they'd find a way.

"Fine. But she can come over for dinner?"

Miri nodded.

"Thanks, Mom." Cutter bolted from the room, slamming the door on his way out. Miri jumped, the loud bang startling her. She stared at the space where her son had stood. I couldn't even begin to imagine what was going through her mind. How would someone start to process the fact that they were dying and might not live to see the milestones every parent looked forward to seeing?

"Do you want some tea?"

Miri shook her head. "Tea can't fix this."

True, but it would be nice if it could. This was how our school nurse would fix whatever ailed us—with herbal tea, which was her answer for everything. It didn't matter if we had a nosebleed, cramps, or a broken arm; she offered us tea.

My phone beeped with a text from Brendan: How are things going?

The question made me want to laugh. I knew he was being sincere, but how did he think things were going? There was a giant elephant in the room, with a blinking neon sign, telling me my best friend was dying and there wasn't jack shit I could do about it. Nor could he. To make matters worse, Miri and I needed to have the talk about what would happen after she was gone.

I felt bad for telling him to stay home, because I knew he wanted to help, but with my mom here, things were crowded. Plus, Brendan preferred for us to stay in a hotel or a bed-and-breakfast, and there was no way I'd leave Miri.

I typed back: Things are . . . sad.

I looked at my words and fought back my tears before I sent the message.

Brendan responded right away: Will you be in the office on Monday?

The question gave me pause. I glanced at Miri, who held a book in her hand, but I couldn't tell if she was reading or not. Could I leave her? Could I go back to my life and leave my mom to take care of her?

No, I couldn't.

I typed back: No. I'll call you later to discuss.

"Brendan's going to want to come visit," I told Miri as I put my phone down. "He's already tried, and I told him to wait."

"Do you love him?"

Her question caught me off guard. "Yes," I said after a brief pause. "Why?"

Miri shrugged. "I don't know. Sometimes, I see you, I see him, and then I see the two of you together, and you're different when he's around. On edge."

I'd been with Brendan for years, and she had never mentioned anything.

"Do you not like him?"

I don't know why I asked. It wasn't like I could change the situation now.

Miri looked at me. Her eyes were wet and shimmering with tears. Ever since she'd been given the news, she'd done nothing but cry. Not that I blamed her. In private, it was all I was doing as well. The shower took the brunt of my anger, sadness, and frustration.

"He's not who I would've chosen for you," she said as she reached for my hand. "But I see why you're with him."

"Why's that?"

"Because he's in your world."

I pondered her answer and had to agree with her. If I didn't work at Caldwell & Crest or did what I did for a job, Brendan wouldn't have been my first choice. He was what others referred to as a bro. His boys came first, after the dollars in his billfold. Yes, he said he loved me, and we spent quality time together. He was generous, flirtatious, and a catch. But if one of his frat brothers called with a tee time in Miami, Brendan was on the next plane out of Logan.

Although, I'd done the same thing for Miriam.

Friendships were important, but so were relationships, and Brendan had never done me wrong. So, yes, he was in my world, and we fit.

"He's a great guy, Miri."

She smiled softly and turned toward the window. Outside, Nova laughed, and my mom rocked in the chair. Every so often, we heard the power saw, followed by hammering and the nail gun.

"How come you never pursued things with Weston?"

Miri chuckled. "Never even gave him a thought."

"Really? Why the hell not? Have you looked at him? Clearly, he likes you."

"Because it's not me he's interested in," she said as she gave me a pointed look. I shook my head slightly, and she nodded. "I can see it in the way he looks at you."

There was no way he liked me. We'd just met.

As if on cue, Weston stood in the front window with his back to us. I had to admit, he had a nice backside and was ruggedly handsome.

"I was shocked to find out he used to be a professional baseball player. You never told me."

Miri lifted one shoulder. "I didn't think it mattered. He rarely talks about it, and no one in town really bothers him about it. Unless it's during baseball season, and then everyone will go on and on about how Wes played in the majors."

"Wes?"

She nodded. "That's what he goes by."

"Huh, he introduced himself to me as Weston." I stood and went to the window. As soon as Nova saw me, she waved and motioned for me to come outside.

"Sort of how you didn't tell him to call you Toni." Miri smirked.

Hadn't I? I kind of liked how Weston called me Antonia.

"Do you want to go outside?" I asked Miri, needing to change the subject, although going outside to where Weston was working was exactly the way to accomplish the task.

She shook her head no. "I'm comfortable and enjoying the quiet."

I laughed because things definitely weren't quiet. Not with the table saw and hammering. "All right. I'll be back in a minute." I opened the door and carefully stepped outside. If my mom and Nova were still on the porch, it must have been safe.

I glanced toward Cutter and Weston (or Wes, whatever he preferred to be called), who had their heads together, and Weston pointed to something on the wood. He'd taken off his long-sleeved flannel, and each time his arm moved, his bicep flexed. I should've looked away and put everything Miri said out of my mind because it seemed like nonsense.

"He's teaching him the basics," Mom said as she motioned toward them when I glanced her way. Had she caught me staring? "What he's learning now, he'll be able to use in the future. This was very kind of Wes to come do this."

So, he'd introduced himself as Wes to my mom as well. I wasn't sure why this bothered me, but for some reason, it did. Unless there was a more intimate meaning behind it?

I sat down next to my mom, and Nova switched laps. She leaned back against me and rested her head on my collarbone.

"Do you have to go home tomorrow?" she asked, used to me leaving on Sundays whenever I came to visit.

"No, I'm not going home for a bit."

"Because Mommy is sick?"

Hearing Miri's daughter say those words made my throat seize. I nodded, unable to find my voice.

"Are you going to live with us?"

With what little voice I had, I said, "I don't know."

My mom reached for my hand and squeezed it. I didn't have the courage to bring this up to Miri, to ask her what would happen to her kids when she was gone. To her house? Her possessions? I would rather die than let her babies go into foster care, but what say would I even have? We weren't related, and the last time I'd checked, the best friend didn't have any rights.

"Does Miriam have a will?" my mom asked as we rocked there.

I glanced at my mom, needing her now more than ever, and so thankful she'd dropped everything to come to Miri's. "I don't know. I know it's something we need to talk about and get taken care of. The conversation probably should've happened today, but I'm afraid to put it out there, where the universe can run with it."

"It has to be done," Mom said. "I can do it if you'd like."

"No, it needs to be me, I think." Even though it was the last thing I wanted. Doing so made it feel like Miri's death was inevitable, that it would be here sooner than anticipated. I didn't want that. I wasn't ready and never would be. One, five, or ten years wouldn't be long enough. I needed her in my life forever.

My arms tightened around Nova as she snuggled deeper into me. My mom got up, disappeared into the house, and then came back with a blanket. She draped it over us and tucked Nova in.

"I thought you were a big girl who didn't nap?"

"Sometimes, I'm tired," she said into the crook of my neck. It amazed me that she could fall asleep anywhere. As much as I wanted to keep her for myself, Miri shouldn't miss out on these moments.

"Come on, let's go find your mom. I bet she needs some snuggles." I carried Nova into the house and found Miri where I'd left her. She brightened at the sight of her daughter. "I think this lug belongs to you."

Nova laughed as I set her down.

"She's ready for a nap."

"Me too," Miri said as Nova rested her head on Miri's leg.

Instead of watching them, and burning the image into my mind, I stepped back and took a picture of them. Nova would need it for later.

Back outside, I sat next to my mom again and held her hand while we watched Weston and Cutter work. When they needed us to move, we did, and set the rockers up in the yard.

"I'll stay as long as you and Miri need me."

"Thanks. I will have to run back to Boston sometime this week and get some things. Maybe I'll take Miri with me, just so she can get away for the day."

"Your dad will be up next weekend. I told him about Wes rebuilding the porch, and now he's concerned with whatever else might be wrong."

"Everything," I muttered. "This house is a money pit."

"We'll get it fixed up."

"Yep, just in time for her to die and not enjoy the house she loved so much. Just in time for us to sell. What a fucked-up situation."

"Indeed, it is."

In between cutting and hammering, Cutter came over to me. "Eleni said she can come for dinner."

"That's great. Do I need to go pick her up?"

Cutter shook his head. "Her mom will bring her, and then maybe we can take her home."

"That works."

He ran his hand through his hair. "I didn't tell her about my mom yet."

"No one says you have to tell anyone anything," I told him. "It's your news to share when you feel comfortable."

He nodded. "I also invited Coach for dinner since he's doing all this work."

I glanced at his coach. His arms flexed each time he lifted a board. He met my gaze and smiled, which normally I would have appreciated. Except what Miri had said earlier echoed through my mind, and I couldn't get past it. Was he here because he liked me or because of Miri? Was it a little of both?

Cutter cleared his throat, and I looked at him. "I'll make sure to get enough pizza for everyone."

"Thanks, Toni."

"You're welcome."

Cutter went back to work, and once he was out of earshot, my mom leaned over. "He's going to take it the hardest, and he's going to take it out on you because you're the closest person to his mom."

"Yep." Fun times ahead. I sat back and sighed. Maybe I could get Miri to say something to Cutter, like some deathbed promise, anything to save mine and Cutter's relationship.

Chapter 13

Weston

When I'd set out to fix the porch, I had no idea it would be with Cutter. Until I saw him walking toward me, asking him to help had never crossed my mind.

I was glad it had.

"I've never built anything," he said after he'd gone in and changed his clothes. "I'm not sure what to do."

"I'll teach you." I handed him the measuring tape and laughed. We were both in for a treat. This was how my dad had taught me to build. Our first build was a birdhouse. I had won a kit at some fundraiser and wanted to give it to my mom for Mother's Day. Only, I'd never used a hammer, so my dad taught me. Our next project was a doghouse. From there, I would do odds and ends around the house, but nothing major.

We walked to the porch, where his grandma and sister sat in the rocking chair.

"Hi, Coach," Nova said happily.

"Hey, Nova."

"Cutter, can I play with that thing?" she asked, pointing to the tape measure.

"Later," he said. "I'll measure you and write your height on the wall."

Nova beamed.

"Do you need us to move?" Carmela asked.

"No, ma'am. For right now, you'll be okay."

Carmela had introduced herself as soon as I came back from the hardware store. I learned she was Antonia's mom, but the kids referred to her as their grandma. There was a story there, I was sure, but it was none of my business.

Facing the porch, I pointed to the boards that needed to be replaced. Some were rotted, while others had split down the middle.

"What we're going to do is replace the damaged ones to prevent any injuries or further deterioration."

"Where did you learn how to do this?"

I pointed to the first board we were going to replace and had Cutter put the tape measure down. We stretched it across the board and wrote the measurements on a sheet of paper.

"My dad," I told him. "He was in construction and taught me how to repair most things. I'm not sure I could build anything substantial, but repairs I can do."

"Huh, I figured you played baseball every day."

"I did." I huffed. "After. Don't get me wrong, I appreciate everything my dad did for me," I said as we walked toward the makeshift workstation I'd set up. "But he was strict and rode my ass. I didn't have a lot of freedom as a teen. Work and baseball, on top of keeping straight A's because my parents couldn't afford to send me to college without a scholarship."

"But you were drafted right out of high school?"

I nodded and showed Cutter the rumpled sheet of paper with the measurements and then demonstrated how to measure the numbers out on the new board. Once it was marked, we went over how to properly use the saw.

"Being drafted out of high school isn't always the best or smartest thing for a naive eighteen-year-old."

"Really? Isn't that like a dream come true?"

"Sure is, and the money is nice, until it's all broken down for you, and you realize how much you have to pay an agent, taxes, rent, and living expenses. Then you see that your mid-six-figure deal isn't a lot when it comes down to it."

I added, "And on the other end, you have a scholarship to a top-notch college, which means a guaranteed education and some life skills, all for the price of playing the game you love."

"You chose college?"

"I did, for the first three years. At the end of my junior year, I was drafted again. This time around, I went higher in the draft and had a much better contract."

"So you won regardless."

I nodded again. "I did. My parents were happy, and so was my wife."

Cutter's mouth dropped open. "You're married? How come Mrs. Schmidt isn't at our games?"

This was what happened when I got carried away in a conversation. I'd never had any intention of telling him about my wife or that part of my life. People tended to define you by your marriage and subsequent divorce, which was something I didn't want to happen.

"My ex-wife lives in New York."

"Oh, sorry."

"Don't be. Here, put these on." I handed Cutter a pair of safety glasses and asked him to recite the safety rules on the saw. He did so effectively.

"Okay, are you ready to cut?"

He nodded but looked apprehensive.

"Do you want me to show you?"

"No, I think I got it."

I put my safety glasses on and nodded for him to continue. Step by step, he followed the instructions I'd taught him. When the saw went effortlessly through the wood, I applauded.

"Nice cut."

"Thanks. That was sort of fun."

I patted him on the back. "Now for the really fun part. We need to pull up the old one and pray the brackets underneath are stable and don't need to be replaced."

"Because that would be hard?"

"And time-consuming." I didn't want to tell him I was concerned about his mom's mobility. While she could walk today, with her diagnosis, which Carmela had filled me in on, who knew how long it would be until her legs gave out on her?

"Now, we're going to lift that board," I said as I picked up the crowbar. "Normally, we'd dismantle everything."

"But not today."

"Nope." I held the crowbar up. "Do you want to do this part?" If I were in his shoes, I would absolutely want to do some damage to whatever I could.

"Yeah, for sure."

"Don't break the window, Cutter," Nova said from her perch on Carmela's lap.

"Ha ha," he said as he stuck his tongue out at her. I gave him a short lesson and let him go to work on getting the board up while I measured a few more. Once he had it up, we pulled old nails, and I checked the bracket for any wood rot. With everything looking and feeling solid, we hammered the new board in place.

"It doesn't match," Nova pointed out.

"Nope, we'll stain it to match in a few days."

"Grandma, you like to paint. Are you going to do it?" Nova asked Carmela.

"Yes, of course," Carmela said. "You can help me."

I looked up in time to see Nova nod excitedly.

Board by board, Cutter and I cut and replaced the damaged boards. At least no one would fall through any rotted boards, which I was proud of, but mostly, being able to teach Cutter how to measure, use the table saw, and build something with his hands made me feel like I had a different purpose in his life.

Antonia had asked me to be there for him, and if this was one of the ways I could, then so be it. I'd rebuild the entire house if that was what it took.

At some point, she'd come outside and sat next to her mom, with Nova now on her lap. I tried not to watch her, especially knowing she had a boyfriend. Any attraction I felt needed to subside because nothing would ever come from it, except the pang in my heart at knowing she wasn't available.

When it came time for us to work where the rockers were, I was relieved when Cutter asked Antonia and Carmela to move. For some reason, the thought of having to talk to Antonia put a lump in my throat. Pretty asinine when I thought about it. We'd spoken before without any issues.

"Do you want to have dinner with us tonight?" Cutter's question pulled me from my thoughts. "Toni is getting us pizza."

"Um . . ."

"I know my mom can't pay you for this work, so this would be like a payment."

I nodded and accepted his invitation. The last thing I wanted was for Cutter or Miriam to think they owed me anything. As soon as I said I would join his family for dinner, he went over to Toni. He looked excited while talking to her, even though I tried not to stare.

"Everything okay?" I asked when he came back.

"Yep. Eleni is coming for dinner, too, so I was just giving Toni an update."

"If you need me to go get the pizza, let me know."

"Coach, you've done a lot. Toni will get it."

"Okay, this is the last one, I think." I handed the board to Cutter. "Once we get this one nailed down, we'll check the others, mark them, and then do them next weekend, weather permitting."

"We have a game on Saturday," he reminded me.

"Sunday it is then."

Antonia had taken Nova into the house and came back out with her purse over her shoulder. "Be right back, Mom," she hollered and then walked toward us. "I'm going to get the pizza," she said. "I also ordered two large salads and cheesy bread, and I'll pick up a couple of bottles of soda. Anything else?"

I looked from Antonia to Cutter. We both shook our heads. "I think that about covers it."

"Thanks, Toni," Cutter said.

"Yes, thank you."

She held my gaze for a second and then looked away. As much as I wanted to watch her walk to her car, I refrained. I was going to need a good night out with the guys to get over this infatuation.

Cutter and I finished, and I told him to go in and clean up while I took care of everything outside. I knew exactly how much he would freak out if he didn't look his best for Eleni. When I was his age, I had Brianna, who was always dressed up for school or anytime she'd come over to my house. She made me feel like I needed to look the same, but I couldn't bring myself to dress like I was going to work. I think, in my senior year of high school, I wore sweatpants to school every day.

Antonia pulled back into the driveway just as I was closing the tailgate of my truck. I walked to the car and waited for her to shut it off before I opened her door.

"Thank you." She smiled. Her eyes held mine for a long beat, and my knees threatened to buckle.

"My pleasure." Antonia moved to the side and opened the back door. I shut the driver's side and held my hands out for the food. "Smells good."

"Gio's has such amazing food. It's my favorite."

"You've had it before?"

Antonia nodded. "Usually, every time I'm here."

I looked to the sky and pursed my lips. "Why did I think this was your first time here?"

"I'm not sure," she said. "I was here during Christmas, but when I do come, it's usually for a weekend, and we tend to stay in."

"Ah, makes sense. Honestly, I'm either at home or school, especially during the season."

She smiled kindly, as in one of those "Cool stories but leave me alone" gestures. Antonia walked ahead of me, which allowed me to roll my eyes. Hard. Was I trying to flirt? I didn't even know, except I shouldn't flirt because she was off limits.

"Dinner!" Antonia yelled as we walked in. I followed her to the kitchen, where Nova, Carmela, and Miriam were putting out plates, bowls, and glasses.

The doorbell rang, and Cutter yelled that he would get it before thundering down the stairs to the front door. Seconds later, Eleni came into the kitchen.

"Hey, Mr. Schmidt."

"Eleni, it's nice to see you."

This was one of the things I didn't like about living in a small town: It was hard to escape the students. But on the other hand, I was happy to be with the Vaughns. It was hard to find balance sometimes.

I set the pizza boxes down on the counter, opening each one, and then I stepped back and watched this family. What surprised me the most was Cutter. He guided his mom to sit and then brought her a plate of food. She cupped his cheek, and I thought she was going to kiss him but instead said, "I'm not an invalid yet."

Miriam laughed, but the rest of us didn't. Antonia muttered a string of obscenities. Cutter stared at his mom and shook his head. Maybe in this case, laughter was the best medicine.

Cutter caught me watching him. I smiled and wanted to tell him how proud I was of him, but that would be for another day.

Antonia approached and handed me a plate. "You're eating, right?"

"Yes, of course."

"Thank you for what you did out there."

"It was really nothing."

Antonia looked around the busy kitchen and then back at me. "No, it was everything. Watching you teach Cutter was important. He doesn't know it now, but someday, he will, and he'll appreciate how patient you were with him. So, thank you. Like I said, he does need a role model, and Miri really values your relationship with him."

She put her hand on my forearm and rested it there for a moment. Our gazes met, and we smiled at each other longer than what acquaintances would do. Her hand dropped slowly, brushing the side of my pants. I wasn't sure if she realized what she'd done or if I was thinking too deeply, but she inhaled and then stepped to the boxes of pizza.

"Coach, you gonna eat?"

Once again, Cutter's voice brought me back to reality and the family before me. They all looked happy despite everything that was going on.

Chapter 14

Antonia

All night, I had my phone in my hand, snapping pictures and taking videos of Miri with the kids, with me, with my mom, and of her smiling. I even captured moments between Cutter and Eleni, and Cutter with Weston. I wanted to remember this night. The laughter, the smiles, the overall feeling of love flowed from everyone, even Weston and Eleni. It was such a warm evening, everyone gathered around the small table.

At the end of the night, I drove Eleni home. She and Cutter sat in the back seat, two lovestruck teenagers with their futures brightly in front of them. Every so often, I glanced in the rearview mirror at Cutter, who was being strong and determined to mask his emotions with his girlfriend.

I didn't blame him for not telling her, but then again, I questioned why he hadn't. Surely, she'd be someone he could lean on for support. He was going to need it.

Hell, I was going to need it.

I didn't have the first clue how to handle grief. I'd lost my grandparents, and while their passing had saddened me, my heart didn't feel anything like it did now. It was so hard to breathe, and I felt like there were a thousand pinpricks jabbing into me. It didn't matter how many times I rubbed my chest, or closed my eyes to inhale and exhale, the pain was there because my heart was breaking.

It was breaking for me, knowing that I would wake up one day and Miri would be gone. I wouldn't be able to call her, hug her, or bask in her presence. I wouldn't be able to tell her I was getting married or have her stand next to me when I said "I do." She wouldn't be there for the little things, the everyday things that I had learned to count on throughout my life.

It was breaking for Cutter, knowing he wouldn't come home to his mom after school or find her in the stands, cheering him on. He wouldn't get to tell her he had met the love of his life or have her hold him after his first breakup.

It was breaking for Nova, knowing she was going to grow up without her mom. She was never going to look out and see her mom in the audience at her dance recital. She was never going to be able to tell her mom she was going to be a mom herself.

It was breaking for Miri, knowing she wouldn't watch her babies grow up to do amazing things. She would never see her son graduate and follow his dream of playing professional baseball. She would never see her baby girl go to prom or walk down the aisle. Those were the simple things she had wished for her children.

A tear fell, and I glanced at Cutter. Eleni sat in the middle of the back seat, with her head resting on his chest and his arm around her. He caught me looking at him and didn't smile. Even she wasn't enough to keep his thoughts far away from the nightmare.

I signaled and turned down her road, driving slowly to give them a few more seconds of this bliss. When I pulled into her driveway, I put the car into park and pressed the button to unlock the doors.

Cutter exited and held his hand out for his girlfriend. I loved how much of a gentleman he was with her. I knew not to stare but couldn't help it. He walked her to the front door. She rose on her tippy-toes, kissed him, and ducked inside.

I looked down at my hands when he walked toward the car. The passenger side opened, and he got in, sinking into the seat with a heavy sigh.

"She's very nice," I told him as I reversed out of the driveway. "I'm glad I got to meet her."

"I like her a lot."

"That's good." We got to the corner and stopped. The silence between us filled the car. I glanced at Cutter, who looked out the window.

"I don't want my mom to die," he said so quietly I barely registered his words.

"She's going to fight and hang on as long as she can. The last thing she wants is to leave you and Nova."

"Why didn't she go to the doctors earlier?"

I'm asking the same question.

"I don't know, Cutter. I imagine if she didn't feel well, she pushed it aside because there were other things going on. It's part of being a mom, I guess. You take care of kids, jobs, house, before you take care of yourself. It's not like our bodies tell us the good, the bad, and the ugly of what's going on inside of us. How many times have you ignored an ache or a tightness, telling yourself it's going to go away? Lord knows, I've been exhausted at work, sometimes for weeks, and then I bounce back. I think it's human nature to push aside the 'I don't feel well' notion and go about our day because going to the doctor or the walk-in is a hassle."

"And now it's too late."

I didn't want to agree with him, at least not verbally, so I said nothing because yes, it was too late. Miri would need a miracle or an act of God to survive this. Even with treatment, it would have to be so aggressive and work immediately for her to have a fighting chance, and her doctor said that was unlikely. Too many cells to fight all at once.

"Cutter, don't let these days, weeks, and months be filled with anger. Your mom doesn't deserve to see it. Not on your face or mine. In private, we'll rage."

I pulled forward and drove back to the house slowly. As soon as I put the car in park, Cutter bolted from the car and ran toward the garage. I watched for him until he emerged. He started shooting baskets on the basketball hoop Miri had installed a couple of years ago. I left my headlights on for him.

"When you're done, can you shut the lights off?"

"Sure," he said as he took another shot. Either he would or I'd wake up to a dead battery. Looking back at my car, I sighed heavily. We hadn't gone to pick up Miri's car from the hospital yet and would need to do that tomorrow.

It didn't escape my notice that he didn't thank me. Honestly, I didn't expect him to. He was already hurting, and at sixteen, there were enough emotions going on in his body; he didn't need me to harp on him.

I paused on the porch and listened to the thud of the basketball when it hit the backboard and the swish of the net with each basket he made. Sports would be his outlet and hopefully help him grieve and heal. He would be surrounded by a coach who clearly cared for him and teammates who, I hoped, would have his back.

Inside, the earlier excitement in the house was gone, and left in its wake was the knowledge that someone we loved with our whole hearts was dying.

I leaned against the entrance from the hallway to the living room and watched Miri as she sat on the couch. She had the television on, but if I had to bet, she wasn't watching it. I couldn't imagine what was going through her mind. Hearing from a medical professional that you're dying has to do something to your psyche. Every day, we wake up and live to die. It's a matter of time for all of us. But for Miri, finding out she had an impending end date must have been screwing her up even more.

Clearing my throat, I made my way into the room, smiling at her as I drew closer. She tucked her legs underneath her, giving me the space to sit beside her.

"Dinner was fun," she said, to which I nodded.

"It was. I'm glad Eleni could come over. She makes Cutter smile."

"Among other things," Miri said with a smirk.

I shook my head. "You were lovestruck once upon a time. I'm sorry, I mean twice."

"And look where that got me."

My eyes looked toward the ceiling, where I assumed my mom and Nova were.

"I believe I said something philosophical back then when you found out you were pregnant with Cutter."

"Something about how he wasn't an accident?"

I nodded. "Those were wise words back then." We both laughed because, accident or not, she'd fallen into the same trap and had ended up with Nova.

"Do you remember the promise you made to me that day?"

I thought for a minute and then shook my head. In our three-decade-long friendship, I'd made her a lot of promises. I certainly didn't want to think about one, only to find out I hadn't fulfilled my end of things.

"That day, when we lay there under the clouds, I asked if you would take care of them if something ever happened to me. Only at the time, there was one. Now I have two."

It took a moment, but everything came back to me. That day changed us both. My best friend was going to be a mom and within days would move into our house, while her parents would lose their ever-loving minds. I'd never seen people go batshit crazy before, threatening my parents with baseball bats, all while reciting sermons from their church.

"I remember," I told her. "But I also distinctly remember me saying nothing would ever happen to you." Tears pricked the corners of my eyes. I sniffed hard and swallowed the lump in my throat.

Miri reached for my hand. "You and I both know that isn't true anymore, and I don't have much time to get everything figured out, but this one is important." She took a deep, shuddering breath. I didn't want to look at her, out of fear I would lose it, so I kept my eyes forward and my hand in hers.

"The kids love you, Toni. You've been in their lives from day one. I can't be there for them anymore . . ." She trailed off as I looked at her. I could finish her sentence for her, but even words failed me.

She wiped at her tears, but to no avail. They fell like a stream, leaving streaks of wetness on her face.

"Will you take my babies after I'm gone? Will you be their person? Their guardian? Their mother?" She choked out the last word, which shattered my already-broken heart.

I nodded and pulled her into a hug. We both cried. Being Cutter and Nova's guardian was a no-brainer. I would've fought for them, regardless. Miri naming me legally would make things easier for us.

When we parted, I wiped the tears from her face. "You know I love them with my whole heart. Of course I'll take them."

"I don't want to disrupt your life."

"Don't worry about me," I told her. "Everything will work out." I was lying to myself. When Miri left us, we'd grieve, hard. When she passed, we'd be broken.

"We do have a list of things we need to figure out, Miri. Like the house, your possessions, and your finances. And we'll need to make sure you have a will, so no one comes knocking on my door to take the kids away."

I didn't want to say it out loud, but their father worried me. No one had any idea where he was, and he'd already popped back into Miri's life on one occasion. Granted, that was eight years ago, but still. News of her passing wouldn't take long to spread, especially if he was keeping tabs on her from afar. But he was for another day, another time.

I only wanted to think about Miri, the kids, and the uphill battle we faced.

"I have some life insurance through work," Miri said, pulling me from my thoughts. "It won't be much, but . . ."

"If the kids are the beneficiaries, I'll move the money into a trust for them," I told her. "That'll give them a little something when they're older."

Miri nodded. "I'm not sure what to do about the house."

"I'm not sure, either, but we'll ask the bank. It might be as simple as adding me to the deed, although that can take time." I patted her leg. "Either way, tomorrow we'll do as much as we can before you start treatment. I do need to go to the office on Tuesday, so while you're at the hospital, Mom will be here for you and the kids. I'll be back either late Tuesday night or first thing Wednesday morning."

"This would all be easier if I had stayed in Boston."

"Miri, this would never be easy, no matter where we were. Losing you is going to destroy me, whether it happens here or there. I don't know my life without you in it."

"I don't know my life without you in it," she said, repeating my words to me. We hugged again until she snuggled into my arms. I rested my chin on the top of her head and stared into the nothingness.

I had an unpleasant suspicion our time with Miri would be very limited.

Chapter 15

Antonia

After making sure the kids were at school and Miri was settled at the hospital with my mom for treatment, I got on the interstate and headed toward Boston with tears in my eyes. I'd cried, but nothing like now. The sobs came hard and fast, squeezing my throat as I gasped for air. I white-knuckled the drive and entered the city with glassy, red-rimmed eyes, not caring what people thought when we were stuck side by side in traffic. This would be my greatest loss, and I didn't even know how to begin the process of being okay with what lay in front of me.

I went right to the office, not caring what people might think of my tearstained face. I needed to see Brendan. No, seeing wouldn't be enough. I needed to feel his arms wrapped around me and wanted to hear him tell me everything was going to be okay.

Thankfully, his secretary wasn't at her desk, but Brendan was at his. I walked in, shut the door, and rushed toward him. He pushed back from his desk and took me into his fold. At first, he was rigid, and then he relaxed. I imagined I'd scared the shit out of him.

"Did something happen?"

I shook my head as best I could while trying to combat the flow of tears. He would understand the tearstains on his shirt but wouldn't appreciate them.

"I'm going to lose her."

"I'm sorry," he said as he held me tighter. "I wish there was something I could do."

I relaxed a bit and leaned back enough to look at him. "There has to be someone you know," I said. "Or some experimental study going on?"

He shook his head slowly. "None that I know of."

A sudden rush of anger came over me. I stood and began pacing his office. "Are you kidding me right now? You have so many friends, and not even one of them is working in the medical field or doing some lifesaving experiment?"

"It's not something we talk about, Toni."

"Call them," I said, pointing to the phone. "Pick it up and fucking call them. You know someone who can fix all of this."

Brendan came toward me, catching me before I collapsed onto the ground. His office door opened, and he barked out, "Not now."

He picked me up and carried me to the brown leather sofa he kept in his office for entertaining, although he took naps on it often, and preferred any entertaining to happen in the boardroom.

I curled into him and continued to sob while he held me, stroked his hand up and down my back, and whispered that everything was going to be okay. The last part was nothing more than a coping mechanism, because nothing was going to be okay. It wasn't now and it would never be.

He held me until my tears stopped and my breathing leveled out. I finally extricated myself from his hold and excused myself to use his en suite bathroom.

The person who stared back was not me. Until last week, I was this put-together businesswoman, dressed in designer clothes and shoes, with not a hair out of place—no nonsense, looking like I'd stepped out of a magazine spread.

Now, I looked haggard. Tired beyond recognition. My hair had dulled, my eyes were constantly bloodshot, and I couldn't remember the last time I'd washed my face properly. I'd never done a one-eighty so fast in my life.

I didn't like the person in the mirror. That wasn't me, and whoever it was wouldn't be strong enough to help Miri through what seemed impossible.

If I needed her, then she needed me one hundred times over. I needed to get my shit together and be strong for her.

I turned on the cold water, cupped my hands, filled the bowl I'd made, and then bent over to cover my face. The coldness stung at first but quickly became refreshing. I did this a few times before I felt refreshed enough to face Brendan as my boss and not my lover.

Patting my face dry, I glanced at myself in the mirror. I was somewhat better, but not quite there. After finger-combing my hair, I pulled it back into a ponytail, bringing some of my sides down to give myself a semidecent polished look.

With my hand on the doorknob, I twisted and walked out with my shoulders square and an expression meant for business.

"Better?"

His question or statement caught me off guard. He didn't ask if I was better or how I was feeling; he stated the word as if I'd had some momentary issue.

"Unlikely," I told him with petulance. The lack of thoughtfulness in his question irritated me.

Clearly unfazed, Brendan handed me a stack of folders. I didn't reach for them, instead staring at the tricolor stack with contempt and confusion.

"What's this?" I hesitantly took the folders from him.

"The projects I've been working on, on your behalf." Brendan sat down and swiveled toward his computer. "I've taken the liberty of setting up the necessary client meetings. When you sit down to go through them, you'll see which ones I've marked as priority. Those are the ones that need your utmost attention."

As much as I wanted to devote every waking second to Miri and the kids, I had to work. My job paid extremely well, and it wasn't something I could give up. But it was something I could do from home if necessary.

"I'll look at the schedule," I told him. "And adjust as necessary."

"No need. I looked at your calendar."

I pinched the bridge of my nose and worked to keep my breathing level. "Thank you, but I need to have some flexibility right now, Brendan. Miri needs my full attention. I'm going to take my files with me and set up an office at her house."

"I need you here," he said. And while I wished he meant it in a romantic way, he didn't. Business first.

"Everything I need to do can be done via video conference. If I must fly to a location, I'll work those details out later, but for right now I need to work remotely or come into the office twice a week."

Brendan sighed and leaned back in his chair. He steepled his fingers and pretended to be in deep contemplation. This was his go-to business move, and it was meant to keep his clients on edge, wondering which way he was going to go.

Normally, I agreed with his pensive nature, but right now it pissed me off.

"Here at Caldwell & Crest, we're not big proponents of work from home. We offer our staff state-of-the-art facilities, a gym, cafeteria, and top-of-the-line computers. I'm not—"

"Stop," I said forcefully. "Whatever you're doing, just stop. I don't need this bullshit right now. If you don't want me working from home, fine. I won't."

He smiled, and it made me want to punch him.

"So, I'll be taking a sabbatical. I don't know when I'll be back." I turned to leave, to take myself down to human resources to see what needed to be done to make this happen, because I wouldn't be treated like a low-level employee who didn't want to come to work every day.

"Antonia, wait."

I refrained from turning around, giving him my back to speak to.

"If I didn't do the spiel, someone would complain."

"Who? The bookshelf? Your bottle of scotch?" I finally turned to face him.

Brendan stood and came toward me, enveloping me in his arms when I was within reach. "I love you, and I'm sorry I had to go into boss mode."

"You almost went home single," I told him.

His deep chuckle reverberated against my chest. "That would not be favorable." Brendan stood tall and cupped my cheeks with his hands. "I'm sorry. I was being unreasonable. The last thing I want is for you to leave, and while I don't like the idea of you working remotely, I understand it needs to be done until things level out and are under control."

What in the hell did that even mean? I thought about asking, but frankly, I was too exhausted to care.

Brendan's hands went to my shoulders, and he started massaging. I rolled my neck and melted into the kneading.

"This feels amazing."

"I'm sure you're not sleeping well."

I shook my head. "'Well' doesn't exist in my vocabulary right now."

"I'm sorry," he said as he continued to push his fingers into my flesh. "What can I do?"

As much as I wanted to think he could fix everything, he couldn't. I couldn't. "Give me grace," I said. "I need to be there for Miri and the kids."

Brendan nodded.

"Come up this weekend? Cutter has a game on Saturday, and he'd like to see you."

"I have a tee time in Miami on Saturday."

I stared.

Hard.

And narrowed my eyes at him. Did he really put his stupid golf game in front of being there for a sixteen-year-old boy who was losing his mom?

I stepped back and shrugged his hands off my shoulders. "I have to go."

"Wait," he said as he reached for my hand. "I can let them know I won't be there."

"Oh, you can?" My tone was laced with sarcasm.

He nodded, and I fought the urge to roll my eyes. "I'll book us the bed-and-breakfast we like in town."

I didn't like it. He did.

"I'm staying with Miri, Brendan. You can't expect me to leave her."

It took a moment for my words to sink in. He nodded and blinked a couple of times. "No, you're right."

I closed my eyes and rolled my neck; the long-standing tension had built to an almost unbearable throb. "I gotta go." I stepped forward to kiss him but pulled up short. Giving him affection felt off. A sensation was gnawing, telling me now was not the time.

"I'll be there for Cutter's game."

"Thanks." I left his office and went to mine with the folders Brendan had so kindly given me. I grabbed what I needed and made my way to my car without stopping to talk to anyone else. An email to the staff would suffice, letting them know I would be working remotely for the foreseeable future. The only time I could see myself leaving Miri's side would be to go see a client's facility and observe how they operated. Other than that, everything could be done via email or video conference.

At my apartment, I met with the property manager and told him I would be gone for a bit and that my apartment would be empty. We made an agreement: He would go in once a week and make sure everything was in working order. The last thing I needed was for a pipe to burst.

I packed more clothes, cleaned out the refrigerator, and grabbed all my essentials. After a quick trip to the garbage bin, I headed to my car and made my way north.

At this time of the day, traffic in the city was minimal. The highlight of this drive was the snowcapped mountains in the distance. They looked beautiful with the way the sun bounced off them. They were nice to look at while driving, but you'd never catch me on one. Snow wasn't my thing. Despite Boston being in New England, its annual snow accumulation wasn't as much as people thought it was, and while it did snow, it melted quickly.

As I drove, my mind drifted to the conversation Miri and I had had about me taking the kids. It was what I wanted, but I wasn't sure how they were going to react to moving. Nova would be fine, but Cutter . . . he was a whole different story. I couldn't even pretend to understand what it was like to move during the teen years because my parents had lived in the same house since they'd gotten married.

How do you sit a teen down and say, "Sorry your mom died, but now you have to move"? It didn't matter how I tried to form the statement in my head; it felt wrong and hurtful.

I couldn't conceivably take Cutter away from his last two years of high school, but I also couldn't stay in Grove Hill. Not if I wanted to keep my job, and I was going to need my job if I was to take on two children and raise them as their mother had.

I banged my hand on the steering wheel, and my tears returned. Everything was so fucked up, and there wasn't one easy solution to fixing any of this.

Chapter 16

Antonia

By Saturday, everyone knew Miri had cancer. It didn't take long for word to spread, and it took even less time for people to start showing up at her door or saying something to me in the local grocery store. I found out quickly why so many people loved living in a small town. It was the closeness, the camaraderie, and the overall feeling that everyone was family.

The parents of Nova's best friend, Mara Blanchard, had volunteered for anything and everything one could think of. One of my biggest concerns was being there when Nova got off the bus. The driver wasn't allowed to let children off the bus unless a parent or guardian was available, and with my mom not able to uproot her entire life, we needed another plan. Thankfully, Miri could call in, instead of having to go into the school, to add Mara's parents to the approved-pickup list.

Cutter was a bit easier. Most of the time, I would pick him up from school, and I talked to Miri about teaching him how to drive. While I hadn't figured most of anything out, one thing I did know was I wouldn't take the kids out of school until the end of the school year. Their mother was dying, and the last thing they needed was to lose their friends. But, I knew if I needed anything, Flinn Langston's parents would step up, or Weston.

While Miri slept, I snuck out for a walk. My plan was to walk the mile into town and grab coffee from the Cozy Cup Café, which was owned by one of Miri's friends, Samira. I'd get some doughnuts and take them back for Miri and Nova. Cutter had a game today and preferred not to load up on sugary snacks.

At the end of the driveway, I started at the sound of movement. Looking to my left, I saw Scout running toward me. Crouching, I braced myself for the lick attack that was about to happen. I'd never been a huge fan of dogs, but this guy oddly brought me a sense of calm, and I needed as much of that as I could get right now.

"Good morning," Weston said as he ran toward us. He grinned, and my heart raced a smidge. My heart shouldn't have been doing anything.

"Sorry, we were working on commands, and he saw you."

"It's okay. I don't mind." I gave Scout a few more pets and then stood. "How was Cutter this week?"

"He was good," Weston said, nodding. "I think he has a good support system around him."

"Did he tell his friends?" I asked.

"I think kids just found out." Weston shrugged. "I haven't heard anyone come out and ask him, so I think they're just in the know and hanging out like normal."

"Well, that's good, I guess." I looked down the road and motioned. "I'm heading into town to get breakfast. I need the exercise, so I thought I'd walk."

Weston tilted his head slightly, and if I wasn't mistaken, there was a slight smirk playing on his lips, making me wonder what he was thinking.

"Mind if Scout and I come with you?"

I shook my head. "Not at all."

Weston hooked Scout's leash to his collar, and we started down the road. I regretted saying yes because I wasn't sure there was anything for us to talk about, but I didn't want to be rude. He was free to walk up and down the road whenever he wanted and didn't need my permission to go into town.

We walked for a few minutes in silence until Weston cleared his throat. "Can I ask you something?"

"Sure, although I may not have the answer."

He huffed a little and smiled. "What happens to the kids when Miriam . . . you know," he asked sheepishly.

"I'll take them. Long before Cutter was born, she asked me to take care of her baby if she couldn't. I promised." I shrugged. "I've known them since before they were born. I was there when she had them and was the second one to hold them. It makes sense for them to go to me, and if it wasn't me, it'd be my parents."

"That'll be nice for the kids. To be with someone they know."

I let out a small groan. "Remind me of this when Cutter wants to yell and scream at me."

"He's going to go through a lot," Weston said. "Not only are his hormones all over the place, but he's losing his mom, and his dad—"

"Doesn't exist," I said, interrupting him. "Their dad isn't in the picture. Never has been. I'm not even sure he knows he has a daughter."

"Wait, so he left when Miriam was pregnant? Just up and left his son?"

I grimaced. "Sort of. He wasn't around for Cutter until he showed up randomly. It was like he had an oat to sow, did, and bailed when Miri told him they were having another child."

"Bastard."

The one-word statement made me chuckle. "Among other things. I don't want to say he ruined Miri's life, but . . ."

"No, I get it."

"Yeah . . ."

"What about Miriam's family? Will they fight you for the kids?"

This time I let out something that sounded like a half cough, half laugh. "She's an only child, and her parents disowned her when she wouldn't give Cutter up."

Weston opened his mouth to say something but quickly closed it. I half grinned and continued walking toward the crosswalk.

"Wow. I wasn't expecting you to say that."

"It's something that doesn't come up, ya know? People don't ask at games where the grandparents are. My parents show up. They fill the holes left by Miriam's family."

"I like your mom," he said as we crossed the street. He held the door for the Cozy Cup Café and waited for me to enter.

"Is Scout allowed inside?"

"Yeah, Samira loves all dogs."

The Cozy Cup Café was a vibrant place. As soon as you walked in, the yellow walls welcomed you. Small tables lined one wall, with booths along the other. In the center, round tables were available for bigger parties. Toward the back, where patrons placed their orders, was a large display case with fresh pastries, cakes, and muffins. I wanted to buy the whole lot and eat it all in one sitting.

We walked to the counter and waited in line, which moved fairly fast for a Saturday morning. I placed my order and motioned for Weston to place his, as I intended to buy his breakfast since he'd repaired the porch.

He had his phone on the tap-to-pay before I could maneuver around him and Scout.

"I was going to pay," I told him as we walked to one of the empty tables.

"I figured, but that wouldn't be very gentlemanly of me."

"Well, thank you. Next weekend is on me."

His eyebrows popped up. "Are we doing this again next weekend?"

I shrugged. "I'm going to need friends. I know I can count on my mom, but she has her own life. Nova has a friend whose parents will help with pickup if I'm stuck in a meeting or at the hospital."

"I'll be your friend," he said.

"Me too," Samira said as she approached with our coffees and the order of doughnuts I'd placed for Nova and Miri. "You just have to let us know what you need."

"Us?"

Samira smiled. "I know you're not here a lot, but Miriam has a nice little friend group. Usually, we get together once a week to gossip. It's our 'book club,'" she said, using air quotes around "book club."

"Do you actually read?" Weston asked.

Samira shook her head, smiled brightly, and placed her hand on his shoulder. "We bring books, but we also bring wine, and let me tell you, loose lips sink ships."

"Oh, lovely," I said, trying not to laugh. "So what time is book club next week?"

Samira paled. "It was Miriam's turn to host."

"And she'll host," I said. "Her last however many weeks she has need to be normal. It's better for the kids to see her living her life."

"Are you sure?"

I nodded. "Tell me when and what time, and Miriam will host."

Samira beamed. "Edith and Vera will be so happy. We really want to help out where we can."

"Believe me, I'll take all the help I can," I told her as I handed her my phone. "Put your number in there and text yourself."

She did and handed it back to me.

"Please let me know what Miriam usually does when hosting."

"I will. This will be fun."

"That's the goal, to make things fun for her."

Samira excused herself to help another customer. I watched her walk away, lost in thought.

"You're an amazing friend," Weston said.

I shook my head slightly. "I don't know about that. Miri would do the same thing for me. There's a good chance she doesn't want anyone at the house, but I refuse to watch her sit there and wither away."

"Is she going to the game?"

"She is. It's important for Cutter to see her out there. She already missed one game and doesn't need to miss any more."

I reached into the bag and took out one of the doughnuts. They were fresh and still warm. My mouth watered at the thought of eating it. I held it up to Weston; he smiled and politely declined.

"I shouldn't eat this, but I tend to eat my feelings."

"I have a home gym in my garage if you ever want to work out."

"Really?"

Weston leaned forward and held my gaze. His dark, slightly wavy hair had some hints of gray around his temples. It made him look distinguished and charming. His eyes were a warm brown and full of kindness and empathy. He smiled, and the corners crinkled.

"The gym here is very expensive," he said quietly. "Even with my status, they wouldn't give me a discount."

"Your status?"

He looked taken aback by me questioning him. "Remember, I told you I was a former professional baseball player?"

I mouthed "Oh" and nodded.

"Early in my career, people rolled out the proverbial red carpet for me, but then I retired, and I thought they'd do the same, especially here, but nope."

"Are you on social media?"

He nodded.

"Okay, so the next time you want something, you tell them you'll post about using their facility or drinking in their coffee shop. It takes some negotiating, and you don't do it before you walk up to the counter. You set a meeting."

Weston sat back and grinned. "Or you make friends with the café owner and get her to love you, and build your own home gym so you don't have to watch the gym bros take selfies or videotape their workouts."

I leaned back and matched his grin. "Okay, very valid." I paused and then said, "Why do men do that?"

Weston laughed. "I have no idea. Anytime I ever worked out, I had state-of-the-art facilities, either in high school, college, and then the pros. I went into the place here and wondered what I had walked in on."

"Well, I might take you up on the offer."

"Gym's open twenty-four seven."

"Wow, such great hours."

"I even have a sauna," he said, waggling his eyebrows.

I hid my laughter behind my hand and cleared my throat. "Thank you."

"For what?" he asked as he took a drink of his coffee.

"For making me laugh, for being an ear."

Weston winked, and I tried not to think anything of it or look too deeply into his facial expressions. He was just being friendly.

My phone vibrated, and Miri's name popped up on my screen. I read her text, told her where I was, and said that I would be there soon. "Miri's awake; I should get back."

"Let's go." He stood, reached for Scout's leash, and then hollered to Samira that we were leaving.

On our walk back, I asked, "Is there anything I need to know about Cutter's basketball or baseball schedule?"

Weston thought for a moment. "I don't believe so, but I'll go through the emails I've sent to the parents and make sure you get a copy."

"Thanks."

"Has he mentioned the travel teams?"

"I know of them because he's been in Boston playing before, but that's about it."

"It's fairly convoluted, so how about I come over tonight and explain everything? I think that might be the best way instead of asking him and reading it all in an email."

"Okay, yeah, that'll work. We don't have any plans later."

We stopped in front of the driveway.

"I'll see you at the game," he said and continued toward his house. His words caught me off guard. He would see all of us at the game, but he'd singled me out. Why?

Chapter 17

Cutter

It was game day, and normally, I felt stoked about playing. Nothing compared to the exhilaration of being out on the court, knowing the other team had to do whatever they could to stop us.

To stop me.

I wanted twenty-five points today—a career high. I had come close twice but never managed to break past twenty-four. Maybe if I had taken one more three or driven harder to the basket for an and-one, I could've made it.

Although all of that depended on how I played and whether Coach pulled me out early.

If we ran up the score, some of us would have to sit. I hated the bench. It made me antsy. My legs bounced while I sat there, watching my teammates. I wanted to be out there with them all the time. How fun would it be if basketball were an eight- or ten-man sport?

"It'd be wild," I muttered, tossing the basketball in the air. I always practiced my form in my bedroom before I'd head downstairs for my power breakfast.

My mind drifted to my mom. She always made my Saturday morning game day breakfast, but who would do it when she was gone? My stomach twisted at the thought of her not being here. She was all

I knew. All I had ever known. Sure, Toni had been around forever, but she wasn't my mom and never would be.

I knew I was supposed to love Toni, but why? Because she was my mom's best friend? My honorary aunt?

"When did you stop liking her?" I asked my empty bedroom, hoping the walls might answer. I wished I remembered when I woke up and decided Toni wasn't my friend anymore. She had always been there for us—at my games when they were close to her, here for the holidays, letting us stay at her place in Boston for a week of fun.

"So why?"

I couldn't think of a valid reason other than the fact that she felt like another mother figure, and I didn't want one.

My thoughts spun in circles, from my mom to Toni, back to my mom, and then to Eleni.

I sighed at the image that formed in my mind. The two of us spending as much time after school as we could before practice. I counted down the days until we could be alone together. We wanted privacy and hated looking over our shoulders to see who was trying to sneak up on us or who was lurking. The last thing I wanted was for one of my friends to see Eleni and me touching each other. If rumors started about her, I'd lose my shit on everyone.

Her parents were strict when I was there. We weren't allowed to leave the living room, where one of her grandfathers kept a watchful eye on us. At my house, we had a little more privacy, but not by much. If we left the house, Nova followed. And Eleni wasn't allowed upstairs.

It was like my mom was punishing me for her mistake when she was a teenager, even though she'd never admit I was a mistake. At least she hadn't ever treated me like I'd ruined her life.

Right now, I felt like Eleni was the only good thing in my life. She knew about my mom because everyone in town knew about my mom but hadn't said anything to me yet. I loved that she was waiting for me to tell her when I was ready.

What if I was never ready? Even thinking that my mom was going to die sooner than forty or fifty years from now made me nauseous. She couldn't leave me and Nova.

There was a knock on my door, and then it opened. "Hey," my mom said as she leaned against the doorjamb. She didn't look sick, other than the bandage I could see peeking out of her shirt. She must have had some IV type of thing put into her body, so the doctors wouldn't have to put one in her hand every day she went in for treatment.

"Hey," I said as I continued to toss the ball in the air.

"Can I come in?"

I nodded, with my head against my pillow, and then said, "Sure." I tossed the ball a couple more times before stopping.

Mom walked in and went to the corkboard she'd put up after we redid my room. I didn't want one, but she said she'd had one when she was younger. That she had saved all her mementos and wished she could look at them every now and again.

Now, I didn't mind it because Eleni often printed pictures of us, or the newspaper put me on the front page, and I definitely wanted to keep those things.

"Big game today?"

I shrugged. Technically, Coach wanted us to consider every game a big game, but sometimes they were just games you were expected to win easily. This was one of those games. However, with that mindset, we'd lose.

"Yeah," I said. "You're coming, right?"

Mom smiled, and my heart stopped for a moment. Would I forget her smile? The one she just had for me? Tears pricked, and I pushed them away. She didn't need to see me crying.

"Of course I am. You know I would've been there last week . . ." She sighed and moved toward me.

I sat up, and before I could motion for her to sit next to me, she did. "You know I didn't want to miss the game last week."

I nodded.

"And you know I don't want to miss any of your games. Ever."

Again, I nodded and held my breath. I didn't want to cry in front of her.

My mom reached for my hand. Our fingers linked, and she squeezed. "There is going to come a time when I may not look my best, so if you think I'm going to embarrass you, then you tell me to stay home, and I will."

The tears I didn't want to show her spilled over. I stared at the wall instead of looking at her. I was the man of the house. I was supposed to be strong for her.

Her fingers touched my chin and tugged me to look at her. She had tears as well.

"I'm scared," I whispered.

She nodded. "I know. Me too."

"What are we going to do?"

My mom smiled softly. "You're going to grow up to be an amazing man who thrives at life, who doesn't let anyone or anything hold him back from what he wants."

"But you won't be here to guide me."

Her head moved back and forth, as if she was admitting it all repeatedly. "But I believe I'll see all. I'll be here." She placed her hand over my heart. "And here." And then put her fingers on my temple.

"It's not going to be the same."

"I know," she said, and more tears fell from her eyes. "I need you to do me a favor."

"What's that?"

"Continue to be the best big brother to Nova. She's so young and won't understand any of this."

I scoffed. "I don't understand any of this, Mom. How come you didn't go to the doctor sooner? Why did you wait until you were so sick that death is the only answer?" I stood up and began pacing.

"Cutter." She said my name softly. "I only started not feeling good a couple of weeks ago. Sure, I was tired, but I thought it was from the long hours at work. It didn't occur to me that something so horrible could be wrong."

She stood and came toward me, placed her hands on my cheeks, and held me in place. "Leaving you and your sister is worse than knowing I'm not going to be here someday. Knowing I won't be here to watch you . . ." She paused, because her list of what she was going to miss was long.

"Knowing you're hurting fills me with regret because what if there was something I could have done this year? Last year? Where did I go wrong?"

As much as I wanted to step away from her, I couldn't. I looked in her eyes—eyes that matched mine and Nova's—hoping I could remember everything in the way she looked at me.

"I love you, Mom."

"You're the love of my life, Cutter Vaughn. Don't you ever forget it."

I nodded and fell into her arms. Her hold was still as tight as it was before we knew she was sick.

"Come on," she said as she motioned toward the door. "I need to make your breakfast, and then we gotta get you to the gym."

"I need a minute."

She wiped what was left of my tears away with her thumbs. "Okay, my son. Eggs, bacon, and hash browns?"

"Yes, please."

"Home fries or shreds?"

I thought for a minute and remembered how Nova loved home fries. "Home fries, please."

Mom brought me forward until she could press her lips to my forehead. "Love you," she said as she turned toward the door.

"Mom?"

She looked over her shoulder.

"What's going to happen to us?"

My mom smiled softly and tilted her head. "Antonia will be your guardian. She's going to take care of you and Nova."

Deep down, I knew this, but I needed to hear it. Toni was better than foster care, but I also wondered if we would go live with our grandparents.

Now that my mom had confirmed we'd stay with Toni, I had more questions. Would I have to leave school? Would Toni move to Grove Hill? Would we stay in this house?

"Toni is going to teach you to drive as well," Mom said. "Please listen to her."

I couldn't help the smile that spread across my face. I'd wanted to learn to drive since I turned fifteen, but for some reason my mom always put it off.

"I will. Thank you for asking her."

Mom smiled again. "It wasn't me, Cutter. This was Toni's idea." She closed the door to give me the time I needed to regain my composure. When I saw Toni this morning, I would have to thank her. She didn't have to ask my mom, but she had, and now because of her, I'd get to learn how to drive.

I took some deep breaths, fist-pumped the air, and went into the bathroom to splash some water on my face. When I opened the door, Nova was standing there in her mini Grove Hill Timberwolves jersey. It had my number and last name on the back.

She held out her hand for a high five, which I happily tapped. "Can I have a piggyback ride?"

I rolled my eyes and pretended like this was a big deal. It wasn't. Crouching down, she hopped onto my back and locked her hands over her wrists once they were around my neck.

"Aunt Toni went and got us doughnuts."

"It's game day."

"I know, dork," she said, laughing. "Why do you think I have this jersey on?"

I shrugged. "Because I'm your awesome big brother and you want the world to know how much you love me."

"You wish, but I do love you. Thank you for the ride." I set her down in the hall, and she ran toward the kitchen. I followed, hearing voices.

When I entered, I took in the scene and worked to commit it to memory because I doubted I'd see this again. My mom stood at the stove, cooking. Toni moved around the small table we sat at often, setting dishes down. Nova rummaged through the bag of doughnuts from the Cozy Cup Café. And Brendan, Toni's boyfriend, smiled when he saw me.

"Brendan!" I wasn't sure why I was so excited to see him, but I was. He was a cool guy and fun to be around.

"What's up, my guy?" He came over and gave me one of those strong hand-clasped bro-hug things. I had yet to master it but had tried working it out with a couple of the guys on the team.

"Are you here for my game?"

"Of course, and then I hear we're going for a drive later."

"No, you're teaching him the basics," Toni said.

Brendan rolled his eyes and mouthed, "You can drive."

I appreciated him but owed a huge thanks to Toni. After chatting with Brendan for a few more minutes, I made my way over to her, now sitting at the table.

"Thank you for saying something to my mom."

"You're welcome," she said without looking at me. I knew it was because I'd been a jerk to her, and yet she'd still spoken up on my behalf.

After breakfast, we climbed into my mom's Tucson, which was a bit cramped with all five of us, especially with Brendan and me being so tall, and headed to the school. I almost told them to stay home until my game, but I wanted my mom to drive me and suspected Toni wouldn't allow her to drive by herself, which left Nova with Brendan, which probably wasn't a great idea.

Although, if we were going to be a big family soon, he would probably need to spend some quality time with her.

Chapter 18

Antonia

For an hour and a half, cancer didn't exist. In that time span, we cheered, ate popcorn, and shimmied to music. We hooted, hollered, and stomped our feet each time the Timberwolves made a basket.

Each shot Cutter took, we held our breath.

On the drive over, Cutter told Brendan he wanted to score twenty-five today, so Brendan kept his stats. Every made "bucket," Miri checked to see where her son was.

When Cutter hit his goal, Miri stood and clapped for her son. I had no idea what the significance of the points meant, but I was proud of Cutter for creating a goal and achieving it.

At the end of the third quarter, the game was tied. In the fourth, Cutter went off, according to Brendan. I pretended to understand what he meant, but honestly I had no clue. I knew Cutter was good at his sports—basketball and baseball—but that was it.

During the game, I looked over at Brendan and watched him as his eyes followed the flow of the game. He was like the proud uncle he didn't know he was about to be. I would tell him later, after everyone had gone to bed. Maybe we'd sit on the porch and light the propane lantern for some heat. Maybe he'd make things easy and suggest we move in together.

I would need his help in telling the kids they'd be moving before school started in the fall. That wasn't going to be an easy or comfortable conversation, and I expected Cutter to object, and rightly so. Maybe this was the time for Brendan and me to buy a house and take our relationship to the next step. We'd raise the kids together and finally give Cutter and Nova the father figure they'd missed out on.

No one ever wanted to switch high schools in the middle of their four years. Lord knew I wouldn't have wanted to if something had happened to my parents.

At the final buzzer, the teammates hugged and then shook hands with the other team.

"How come they don't storm the court like I've seen on TV?" I asked Brendan.

"That's mostly college and usually when the school has beaten their rival, a highly ranked team, or they've won a championship."

I nodded in understanding.

"That reminds me," Miri said as she touched my arm. "The basketball championship will be the first weekend of March."

I pulled my phone out and grimaced when I saw that Brendan and I were supposed to be in Aruba. I added the dates and put my phone away.

"We're in Aruba that weekend," he said without missing a beat.

"We'll have to postpone," I said under my breath. This wasn't the place to have this conversation, especially with Miri sitting in front of us. The last thing she needed was for her impending death or her children to feel like a burden on me. They weren't. I didn't care if I had a wedding date booked; I'd cancel it at this point.

Brendan stood and walked down the bleachers until he was on the court. I watched him throw our garbage away and focus his attention on Nova. I was willing to bet that if he had his car there, he would've left.

"I can find someone else," Miri said quietly. "If taking the kids is too much."

I blanched at her words and mentally cursed Brendan out for having the gall to bring up that trip in front of her.

"Miri, I may have been seventeen when I made that promise, but I meant it wholeheartedly. Your babies are my babies, and it'd be a cold day in hell before I allowed anyone to raise them but me." I pushed her hair behind her ear and smiled.

"Ignore Brendan. He doesn't understand our friendship because he doesn't have one like ours. He wasn't there from the beginning of us or even Cutter. He's new to this and doesn't have anyone he'd drop everything for."

"Not even you?"

Sadly, I shook my head. "Sometimes I wonder, but he means well, and we'll figure it out. Never know, maybe the kids will have a much-needed vacation."

She smiled at that, and so did I. The kids would need some peace after all of this, and Aruba sounded amazing for them. I ran my fingers through her hair and prayed she wouldn't lose it all before the end.

"Cutter!" Nova yelled her brother's name as he came out of the locker room. She launched herself into his arms, and he carried her to the rim so she could hang from it.

"He's a good brother," I said to Miri as we sat there.

"He's the best son a mother could ask for."

"On Monday, we need to sit down and finalize some things. Okay?"

Miri nodded but never took her eyes off her kids. Couldn't say I blamed her; they were pretty fantastic.

We finally stood and met Cutter on the court. He immediately went to his mom and hugged her. I took my phone out and videoed the moment. He'd want it later.

And so would I.

Weston came out of the locker room. I smiled and expected him to come toward us, since I had invited him over for dinner. When he didn't, I called out his name and walked toward him.

"Oh, sorry. I didn't see you. What's up?"

"Uh . . ." I glanced over my shoulder at our group and frowned before turning back to him. "I wanted to remind you about dinner."

"Dinner?"

I nodded slowly. "This morning, I invited you to dinner with us." And then I remembered I hadn't, but maybe I'd thought about it. "Actually, it wasn't dinner, but you were going to come over and fill me in on the travel stuff. I think we're getting sandwiches. What can I get you?"

Weston looked off into the distance and then at me. "Maybe some other time." He turned away before I could form any type of rebuttal.

I stood there for a moment, wondering about his very visible shift in disposition. He'd acted like we weren't friends, even though he said he would be one.

Miri, Brendan, and the kids joined me, and we walked out of the gym.

"What's for dinner?" Nova asked while still being carried by Cutter.

"I was thinking subs from the deli," I said as we reached Miri's SUV. Everyone piled in, with me in the driver's seat.

"Actually, I was thinking of cooking tonight," Miri said as I closed the door.

"If you're up for it," I said, driving through the parking lot. We passed a row of vehicles, one of which was Weston's. For some reason, I strained to see if he was standing there or sitting behind the steering wheel.

He wasn't.

For some reason, I was a little put off by the cold shoulder. I thought he was someone I would be able to count on. If the boys had lost, I could understand, but they'd won, and it looked like they'd played well. But what did I know?

After we finished a dinner of roasted chicken, potatoes, and vegetables, along with some homemade dinner rolls, Miri, Brendan, and I sat in the living room. Nova went to Mara's for a sleepover, and Cutter was upstairs, probably making Saturday night plans with his friends and Eleni.

"Dinner was amazing," I said as I handed Miri the glass of wine she wasn't supposed to have. She wanted one, and there was no way I'd ever tell her no. If her treatment stood a chance at extending her life, I'd be all for it, but it didn't. At best, she had months, and that was only if every nasty cluster responded to treatment.

"It felt good to cook and not dwell," Miri said as she took a sip. "I don't want to dwell."

"That's good because I told Samira you'd host book club soon."

Miri smiled and laughed. "Book club where very little reading takes place."

"Then why do you call it 'book club'?" Brendan asked. "Why not call it what it is?"

"Well," Miri said as she put her glass on the coffee table. I watched her every move for any sign that she might be tired or in pain. The doctor had her on a boatload of painkillers, and she could lose some of her functions, but she hadn't as of yet. Still, I waited.

"It started out as a book club. We used to read a book a week and talk about it, but then it became more. Like when Vera's husband asked for a divorce. She needed someone to talk to, so she talked to us." Miri shrugged. "We still pick a book and read. We just allow ourselves longer than a week on most."

"Kind of like when you go golfing," I said to Brendan. "It's not like you golf and then come back. You stay around, shoot the shit with your buddies, get drunk, and miss your flight."

Brendan smirked. "Touché."

Miri yawned, and I looked at the time. It was close to eight. "Are you tired?"

She nodded. "I think I'm going to go up and take a bath, and then crawl into bed with the book." Miri winked at Brendan as she stood.

He chuckled.

I went upstairs to make sure Miri was okay and checked on Cutter. He was in his room, on the phone with Eleni. His door was ajar. I knocked and waited for him to tell me to come in.

"Hey, I just wanted to see what your plans are this evening."

"A bunch of us are going to Malik's to hang out."

"Are his parents home?" I already sounded like a mother and not a cool aunt.

Cutter rolled his eyes. "Yes. His house and parents' cell phone numbers are on the refrigerator."

"Great. Do you need me to give you a ride?"

He shook his head. "Jayden is picking me up, and yes, before you ask, Mom lets me ride with Jayden, and he has a graduated driver's license."

I opened my mouth to ask about Jayden's number, but Cutter beat me to it. "His number is on the refrigerator as well."

"Wow, this was easy. Let me know when you're leaving. I'll be downstairs. Your mom is taking a bath, and then she's going to bed."

"Thanks, Toni."

"You're welcome."

As I walked back downstairs, I wondered when Miri and I would sit the kids down and talk about the future. I would need to have some kind of answer for Cutter, mostly, about our future. The thing was, I had no idea what was going to be right. My job was in Boston, and while I was in Grove Hill now, I couldn't stay forever. At some point, Brendan's dad would want me back in the office.

Brendan was in the kitchen doing the dishes when I walked in. I poured myself another glass of wine and sipped slowly. "You don't have to do those."

"I figured if they were done, you could come back to the bed-and-breakfast with me."

"You know I can't."

"No, I don't know that you can't." He shut the water off and dried his hands. "Miriam's going to bed. Nova's at a friend's house. Cutter's going out. What on earth would keep you here?"

"They keep me here," I told him. "Something could happen. The kids could need me."

"Nothing's going to happen." Brendan placed his hands on the counter, one on each side of me. "Come back with me."

I shook my head. "You're going to have to get used to this."

"Used to what?"

"Us, with kids."

He stood straight up. "What are you talking about?"

"The kids aren't going anywhere, Brendan. I'm their guardian."

He took a step back and then another. "Wow . . . um, I'm not sure what to say." He ran a hand through his hair and blew out his breath.

"There's nothing to say," I told him. "I'm not letting some strangers raise my best friend's kids."

"They have other family, Toni."

"No, they don't. You know this. Other than my parents and siblings, I'm their family." I pointed to my chest and strained to keep my voice low.

"So, what? We're going to completely change our lives to accommodate two kids?"

"Yes, we are."

Brendan gripped the back of the chair and looked at me. "We never talked about kids, Toni. I thought we were on the same page here with careers, marriage, travel. Kids were never part of the plan."

"That's not true, Brendan. Anytime I've brought up us having kids, you've said soon. Maybe that's been your 'plan,'" I said, adding air quotes for emphasis. "We have no plan. We've been together for what, four years now?" I held my left hand up. "Do you see a ring here? Are we sharing an address? No, we're not, so again, I ask what plans?"

"We talked about taking things slow."

"When we started dating, Brendan. You move slow then. Not years later."

"I think it's a bit irresponsible to tell someone you're going to take care of their kids."

I scoffed and pinched the bridge of my nose.

"I don't want kids, Toni."

"Well, I don't know what to tell you, Brendan."

He paced while I drank my wine.

"This is stupid to fight over."

"I agree, but I'm not changing my mind. My best friend is dying; she doesn't need to worry about where her kids are going. They're going to me, and that's final."

"Fine."

"Fine, what?"

"We'll send them to boarding school. It'll be good for Cutter. He can go to the one I went to. He'll excel there and will be able to get into Harvard. As for Nova, my mom will know of a good one."

I stared at him in horror. "You've got—"

My soon-to-be diatribe was interrupted when the front door slammed. I walked into the hallway and toward the door in time to see Cutter running down the driveway.

"That's fucking great," I muttered as I stomped back to the kitchen. With my finger raised, I squared up to Brendan. "No, absolutely not. I am not sending them away to be raised by people who don't know them. Nova's a baby. She needs nurturing. They're losing their mom, and you think it's okay to send them away to school because their mother dying isn't in your plan."

He stared.

"That's your plan, Brendan. Not mine."

"I don't want kids, Toni."

"Then I guess you don't want me." I stepped away from him and went to grab my coat. He followed.

"Are you really going to choose them over me?"

"The fact that you're so in your own head right now and only thinking about yourself should give you the answer. But in case you need a verbal, yes, I am and always will."

I walked toward the door, opened it, and held it for him to walk in front of me.

"So, this is it?"

"Yeah, it is. I'm sorry, but we don't want the same things in life."

"What about your job?"

I scoffed. "I'm pretty damn sure my job is safe, and if it isn't, you'll hear from my attorney."

Brendan stood there for a second, with his coat hanging from his hand and his head shaking. He finally stepped off the porch and walked to his car. I didn't care if he looked back or regretted what he'd said. I had others to care about now.

There wasn't a doubt in my mind that Cutter had heard what Brendan said. Before I left to go look for him, I called his phone and was sent right to voicemail. I sent him a text, letting him know I wanted to talk.

I went back to the kitchen and pulled the contact list from the phone. My first call was to Jayden, asking if Cutter was with him.

"No, ma'am."

"If you pick him up, please let me know. Okay?" He said he would.

I got in my car and began driving without having a clue as to where I was going. I kept calling Cutter's phone, but nothing. Up and down the road I went, driving into town and through various neighborhoods.

Two hours later, I pulled into the driveway and resigned myself to waking Miri to tell her I'd lost her son.

Chapter 19

Weston

I thought I had waited long enough before returning to the gym to see Antonia and her boyfriend. When I opened the door, our gazes met, and there was no turning back. I saw avoidance, though, and I remembered how, when my relationship with Brianna had started to fall apart, I'd mastered the art of avoiding everything.

Antonia came toward me, completely unaware of what I was feeling, which was my fault. I needed some time to take the sting out of what I'd seen tonight.

I had hoped, when I looked across the gym to see her, that she'd be there and maybe wave at me. It was stupid of me to think she would even be interested in me. I probably had ten years on her, and I was a teacher. There was no way I could compete with the big corporate men in Boston.

Except, financially I could. Although I suspected Antonia didn't believe me when I'd told her I used to be a professional baseball pitcher. If I wasn't a sports fan, which she clearly wasn't, I doubted I'd believe me either.

I shook my head and chided myself for even having those thoughts. We'd known each other for a week, and loosely at that. There was no reason for me to think Antonia was even interested in me. I was the one who was attracted to her.

She called my name, and my heart sang happily at the sound of her voice, but my mind screamed to keep walking. I couldn't. My emotions were mine, and not at all her fault.

"Oh, sorry. I didn't see you. What's up?" I hated lying, but I couldn't think of anything else to say. Even this felt wrong, when I wanted to point at the man she was clearly with and ask who he was, even though I knew. Cutter had told me before the game started that Toni's boyfriend was going to keep his stats for the game.

Wasn't that special?

"Uh . . ." She looked back at the Vaughns before looking at me. I could see it in her hazel eyes, the confusion. My sour attitude came off me in waves. I was sure of it. "I wanted to remind you about dinner."

"Dinner?" Hell yes, I wanted to have dinner with her, but not with her boyfriend there.

"This morning, I invited you to dinner with us. Actually, it wasn't dinner, but you were going to come over and fill me in on the travel stuff. I think we're getting sandwiches. What can I get you?"

I couldn't stand there and look at her, not without being pissed. She was the first woman I had met since Brianna, and I liked her. It was a schoolboy crush, the same I warned my boys about, and yet I had fallen quickly. Her boyfriend walked toward us, and I had zero desire to meet him.

"Maybe some other time."

I greeted parents in the hall, and instead of leaving, I went toward my office. In there, I kept the lights off and the blinds pulled, needing some space to clear my thoughts.

Of course, they were about Antonia. From the first time I'd seen her across the gym, I'd had this wild attraction to her. It had only increased when she came into my office the next day and told me about Miriam.

This woman was putting her life on hold to take care of her friend's kids and planned to raise them after her friend died, which only increased my attraction to her. I really thought that after breakfast this morning, I would be in the clear to ask her to lunch or dinner, or just spend time with her at the house.

When I invited her to use my home gym, I meant it and hoped she would take me up on my offer. It was there for her to use whenever she needed to get away or wanted to exercise without the gym bros staring at her.

I needed to heed my own invitation and hit the weights or the heavy bag when I got home. My gym was the perfect place to let go of whatever was building inside.

An hour after the game, I finally left my office. The coast was clear; all the players and parents had gone home, and I was certain I wouldn't run into Antonia. I assumed she'd be at Miri's, eating the sandwich she said they were going to get for dinner.

On my way home, I stopped at the Ridgeview Diner, one of our most popular places and the bar I liked to hang out at. I walked in and headed to the left where the bar was, then sat down at the first empty stool.

"Coach, what can I get for ya?" Lee Waters, the owner, said.

"Working tonight, huh?"

"Yep, short staffed," he huffed.

"Sorry to hear that. I'll get the fish and chips dinner and a water."

"Sounds good." He walked away, only to return a minute later with a tall glass of ice water.

"Thanks." I drank most of it down, wishing it were something stronger, but that would have to wait until I was home. When I started teaching, I vowed not to drink in town where my students could see me. A lot of the parents and some of the kids, when they were younger, used to watch me play, and they saw me as a role model. To me, role models didn't drink and drive, even if it was just one. Sometimes, that was all it took.

My dinner came, and I ate in relative peace. A few people I knew came in, said hi, and congratulated me on the win before moving on to their table.

While I ate, I watched a college game on one of the TVs in the bar and chatted with Lee whenever he refilled my water. I paid my tab and drove home, taking the long way around so I wouldn't have to drive by the Vaughns' house. It was petty, but for my own good.

As soon as I got home, I let Scout out in the back. Normally, I'd take him for a walk, but it wasn't in me tonight. He deserved better from me, and I would have to make it up to him tomorrow. I stayed out with him, mostly out of fear of coyotes or bears. Regardless of my backyard being fenced, hungry wildlife would find a way to a food source.

After changing into some shorts, Scout and I went into the garage. I turned on some music and began working the heavy bag. With each punch, I told myself my feelings for Antonia were ridiculous. I knew love at first sight didn't exist, and anything I'd imagined was nothing more than seeing a beautiful woman across the court after being alone for so long.

Maybe that was a sign I needed to put myself out there, join a dating app or two, or finally let the ladies in town set me up with someone. The problem there was I knew everyone in town, and none of them ever sparked any type of response from me. Not like Antonia had. That had to be something.

The side door to my garage opened in a burst, startling the shit out of me. I purposely kept it unlocked so my friends could use my gym whenever they wanted. I was startled to find Cutter standing there, his face red and his chest heaving.

I went to the counter and pressed pause on my phone, silencing the music. "You okay?" I asked as I put my T-shirt on.

He shook his head slowly.

"Come on in." I unwrapped my hands and grabbed two bottles of water, handing him one.

"Wanna talk?"

Cutter didn't say anything as he held the bottle. I had hoped he'd come to me when it finally hit him that his mom was dying. Since he'd gotten the news, he'd been resigned. I didn't want to push him into having to talk to me or Jerome, but I also didn't want him to lose his shit in the middle of a game because his emotional cup had tipped over.

"We're moving," he said dully.

I sighed and ran my hand over my damp hair. This was something I had expected, and I immediately wished I had gone over there tonight to discuss Cutter's summer plans. The basketball team could manage without him, but not the baseball team. He was an integral part of the rotation.

"When I spoke to Antonia this morning, she said she hadn't made a decision on where you'd live."

Cutter looked at me. "You knew?"

I nodded. "We had breakfast this morning and talked about it."

"How did she seem?"

I tilted my head and looked at him oddly. "I'm not sure what you mean."

Cutter huffed and began pacing. "Did she seem like she wants us, or did she act like we're nothing but a fucking burden to her?"

I held my hand up but then dropped it quickly. Cutter had earned the right to cuss. His life was imploding, and a little colorful language wasn't going to change that.

How had Antonia seemed?

Resigned?

Accepting?

It wasn't going to matter what I said, because Cutter was going to take whatever I said the wrong way.

"Why don't you tell me what happened, and I'll see what I can do to help?" I motioned for Cutter to sit on the bench, but he shook his head and continued pacing.

"I came downstairs to get something to drink. Toni and Brendan were in the kitchen. I could tell they were arguing, so I sort of just waited for a moment to interrupt them."

In other words, he was eavesdropping like any other teenager would do.

"I heard Brendan say he's sending us to boarding school, that it'll help me get into Harvard." He ran his hand through his hair. "I don't want to go to Harvard, Coach. And he said Nova will go to one, too, but she's just a little kid and . . ." He looked at me with tears streaming down his face. "Do you think we could go to the same boarding school so she can stay with me? Who's going to protect her if I'm not there?"

My heart broke for Cutter.

"Like, my mom's dying, and now I gotta leave my friends and team . . . and my sister because my mom's dying . . ."

I went to him and pulled him into my arms. He sobbed against my chest, his fists gripping my T-shirt. Cutter's knees gave out, and I managed to get him to the bench before he crumpled to the ground. There were no words to comfort him, because nothing was going to be okay in his world. It was one thing to move—moving happened all the time; it was a fact of life—but losing your only parent wasn't part of the deal.

Scout came over and rested his head on Cutter's leg, knowing he needed a bit more attention. He hiccupped as his sobs eased, and angrily wiped at his wet cheeks.

"I'm sorry."

"You have nothing to be sorry for, Cutter. I can't even imagine what you're going through right now."

"I hope my mom makes it through the summer."

"Me too." I did, but not for the reason Cutter wanted her to. He knew how important the travel season was when it came to recruiting, especially this summer and next.

I put my arm around his shoulders and gave him a little shake. "I'll talk to Antonia and see if we can work something out for the summer."

"I thought Brendan liked me," Cutter said quietly. "Guess not."

"I'm sure Antonia's husband likes you. This was probably just a shock to him, that's all."

Cutter shook his head. "They're not married, and according to my mom, he needs to shit or get off the pot. Whatever that means," he said, mumbling the last part.

She had said "boyfriend," hadn't she? Why did I say "husband"?

"Eavesdropping again?"

He shrugged, which was all the admittance I needed.

"Does your mom or Antonia know you're here?"

Cutter shook his head. "I ran out when I heard what Brendan said."

"Understandable." I stood and made my way to the counter to grab my phone. "I'm going to go change, and then I'll take you home. It's too dark for you to walk on the road."

"Coach?" Cutter called as I reached the door leading into my house. I glanced at him. "If Toni says we have to move, can I live with you? At least until I graduate and go to college."

His question gave me pause, and I found myself nodding before I could stop myself. "If it comes to that, yes, we'll figure something out."

"Thanks."

"Anytime, Cutter." I left him and Scout in my gym and ran inside to put some sweats on. While we didn't have any snow on the pavement, the nighttime temperatures were still dipping into the twenties.

I'd never disliked someone I hadn't met before, but I really couldn't stand Brendan. At first, it was because he was with Antonia, and I stupidly thought I stood a chance. But now it was more. How does one arbitrarily decide a kid is going to boarding school without even talking to the child? In my book, that was just wrong.

Back in the garage, Cutter and Scout were involved in a rousing game of tug-of-war. Scout would win eventually because he cheated.

"Are you ready?"

At the sound of my voice, Scout dropped the toy and came over to sit by me. I stroked his head and waited for Cutter. At the door, I patted Cutter's shoulder.

The drive to his house was quick and quiet. He got out of the truck after thanking me. I followed, determined to give Brendan a piece of my mind or at least request a sit-down with Miriam. As Cutter's coach, I had his best interests at heart.

The door flew open, and Antonia came storming out of the house. She flung herself at Cutter, clinging to him.

When she let him go, she cupped his cheek. "Please don't ever leave like that again, and if you do, answer your phone. You scared the shit out of me. Got it?"

Cutter nodded.

"Go inside. I need to speak to your coach and let my emotions settle. We'll talk about you leaving like this in the morning. You should probably call everyone on your contact list because I've spoken to all of them, been to their houses, and they probably think I'm weird."

"You are," he said, smiling. "Sort of."

"Go," she said, pushing him toward the door. She watched him walk toward the house and didn't turn to face me until he was inside and the door was shut.

"I don't get it."

"Get what?" she asked.

"You seem to care so much for him, and yet you're sending him to boarding school? Did you even think to ask him?"

Antonia sighed and muttered something unintelligible under her breath. She pinched the bridge of her nose and groaned. "Cutter isn't going to boarding school."

"But he is next year?"

"Not at all, and if he had stayed, he would've heard the rest of the conversation."

"Well . . ." I was at a loss for words. The last handful of hours could've been avoided if I had picked up the phone, but I was bitter over losing something I'd never had.

I pointed toward the house. "That boy is losing his mind, thinking you and your boyfriend are shipping him off to boarding school. He's hurt, angry, and—"

"I get it," she said, interrupting me. "I don't need a lecture. What Brendan said isn't how I feel. I'm already losing my best friend; I'm not voluntarily sending her kids away. Regardless of what you might think of me, I'm not cruel. I love Cutter and Nova as if they were my own children. I would never do that to them."

Her words sank in. I'd never thought of her as cruel, and I wasn't sure where she would've come up with such a notion.

I stepped forward, intent on wiping a tear from her cheek, but Antonia beat me to it, reminding me that she, in fact, was not single, and I needed to keep my distance.

"Tomorrow," I said, clearing my throat. "I'll stop by after practice, and we can talk about the travel teams."

"Maybe it's just easier if we do it at school since I have to pick Cutter up?"

"I'll bring him home. If that's okay?"

Antonia nodded. "Thanks. I'll make sure he knows." She turned to walk into the house. At her porch, she glanced toward me. "Thank you for being there when he needed someone to talk to."

"You're welcome."

Antonia gave me a small wave, which I returned. I waited for her to go inside and shut the door, wishing like hell I could do more.

Chapter 20

Antonia

Sunday morning, I woke, got dressed, and made my way downstairs. No one was up yet, which was a little reprieve from everything.

As I stood at the kitchen window, I looked out over the backyard. There was a rickety fence that didn't connect to anything else. Miri had planned to replace it and fence in the backyard so the kids could get a dog.

The backyard also had an old dilapidated chicken coop with no chickens, which had been given to Miri at some point. She'd wanted to raise Rhode Island Reds so she'd always have fresh eggs and could offer some to her neighbors. On one particular visit, Miri had taken me to a feed store to look at the chicks. They were cute, but I wasn't on board. I had never given much thought to having pets. My hours didn't really allow for it, and I lived in a penthouse where the outside access was the harbor.

Now, I could visualize some chickens running around out there, picking up bugs and worms from the ground. Having them might be a learning experience for Nova. She could join 4-H and maybe find some solace in having something to do. I had already decided I would sign her up for dance or gymnastics—anything to give her something to look forward to.

"And a dog might comfort them," I said into the empty kitchen.

I heard the creak of the stairs and turned to see who would be coming into the kitchen. Cutter appeared, looking worse for wear. His eyes were red, and he had so much luggage under them, he could've taken a trip around the world. My heart broke for him.

"Morning," I said in a hushed tone, not wanting to wake Nova and Miri.

Cutter shuffled over to me and pulled me into his arms. He held me tightly. "I'm sorry."

My arms wrapped around him, and we stayed like that for a long moment. I didn't want to let him go as a flood of memories surfaced from when he was a little boy, from his kindergarten graduation, when we went to Myrtle Beach and he found a shark tooth, to when I took him to work with me a couple of years back. I didn't know how Brendan couldn't see how much this boy meant to me. I'd never hidden my feelings for Miri and her children. His attitude made zero sense to me, and I felt like his outburst about not wanting children had been his way of saying he didn't want me.

Oddly, I was okay with it.

Cutter stepped back and pressed his fingers into his eyes. He sniffed hard and then let out a low groan. "I hate crying."

"It's supposed to be cathartic, but yeah, I'm with you there. I think there's a permanent tearstain on my pillow."

"Can you promise me something?"

"Promises are something I'm very good at," I told him as I leaned against the counter. "What's up?"

"If the doctor tells her she's out of time, you'll let us know, right? So we can be with her as much as possible?"

My heart twisted, and I felt like I'd been punched in the gut by a heavyweight boxer. I nodded, unable to find my voice.

"Thanks." He turned and started walking out of the kitchen.

"Are you going back to bed?"

"Nah, I thought I'd walk over to the school and shoot some hoops. I'd do it outside, but I don't want to wake my mom."

"Do you mind if I go with you?"

"I don't mind."

"Great. Go get dressed. We'll leave in five. I'll drive us over, and then we'll stop and get everyone breakfast on the way back."

Cutter nodded and stepped out of the kitchen, only to return right away. "I'm glad it's you."

"What do you mean?"

"That Nova and I will live with. I'm glad it's you because we'll be together, and you know us. I was worried we'd have to go into foster care."

I gave him a soft smile. "I'd never let that happen, and neither would Grandma or Grandpa. If it's not going to be me, it'll be them. You'll be with family."

Cutter smiled and left again. I waited until he was upstairs before I turned on the water to drown out the onslaught of emotions coming from me.

Dealing with my own grief would be hard enough, but dealing with Cutter's and Nova's was going to be unbearable. The three of us were going to need an outlet—one as a family and then an activity of our own.

When I heard Cutter coming down the stairs, I grabbed my purse and met him at the door. I put on my parka and saw that he was wearing a sweatshirt. I figured he'd work up a sweat and wouldn't need a coat since we were driving over.

"Crap, I forgot to start my car," I said as we got outside. Thankfully, the sun was shining, and the temperature felt halfway decent.

"Can I drive?"

My automatic response to his asking before had been no, but he needed to learn, and I was going to be the one to teach him.

"Have you driven your mom's car at all?"

Cutter nodded. "Around town. Mostly to and from school."

"All right." I unlocked the doors, and Cutter got in, tossing his basketball into the back seat. I sat in the passenger seat and mentally ran through the basics.

"Press the brake and push the start button."

He did as instructed after he'd put his seat belt on and then kindly reminded me to put mine on. Then he surprised me by checking and adjusting the mirrors and seat to accommodate his height.

I may not have taught him that, but I was proud and couldn't hold back a smile.

Cutter backed out of the driveway slowly, using the rear reverse camera.

"Do you know if you'll be allowed to have the camera on during your test?"

"I'm not sure," he said. "I think Coach will know. I'll ask him."

"Okay." At the mention of his coach, I thought about last night and how he'd brought a very distraught Cutter home. He was so protective of him, being his ally, which was exactly what I wanted Cutter to have. He needed to have someone, besides me, fighting for him.

At the end of the driveway, he pulled out onto the quiet road, put the car into drive, and slowly pressed the gas pedal. By the time the stop sign came into view, he was going over fifty in a posted thirty-five.

"Cutter, please slow down."

"Oh crap," he said as he looked at the speedometer. "I'm sorry, it didn't feel like I was going that fast."

"Yeah, this car has some go to it."

He slowed and came to a full stop, then looked right and left. "I think I need to lighten up on the gas pedal." Cutter looked a bit scared, and I welcomed it. It'd be best for him to put the fear of God in himself versus me being the bad guy.

"I think that would be a good idea." I laughed, hoping to lighten the mood.

He moved forward until he had to turn to get to the main road. He stayed there longer than normal. I placed my hand on his forearm and gave him a reassuring squeeze.

"Is this your first time on the main road?"

"No, just lost in thought," he said as he pulled onto the road.

"I do that often."

"It's easy to do these days."

He wasn't lying. My thoughts moved so fast I had a hard time keeping up.

There was minimal traffic on the road this early, which made a driving lesson a bit less stressful. Still, my anxiety spiked as we drove. I kept my head on a swivel, looking for potential issues he might not see.

"Do you know how to get to the school?"

He thought for a moment. "Uh . . ." A look of horror masked his face.

"Are you being serious with me?"

Cutter laughed. "Yes, I know how to get to school."

A laugh bellowed from me. "When Grandpa taught me how to drive, I couldn't even find my way home. I could give anyone directions to my house, school, or wherever, but when I was driving, I had no idea how to get anywhere."

At the stoplight, Cutter scratched his head. "I think I turn at the next light?"

"The second light," I told him, and then I realized he was pulling my leg again. I rolled my eyes and nudged his shoulder.

Cutter groaned. "Oh boy."

Cutter managed to make it to the school and parked easily. I didn't understand why Miri wasn't letting him drive more. We got out and walked toward the court.

"We should talk about yesterday," I said when we reached the court.

"I said I'm sorry."

"It's not about being sorry. It's about what you heard."

Cutter took a shot, and I sent the ball back to him after it had gone through the net.

"I was thinking about that, and Flinn said something about me living with him until we graduate. I don't want to leave Nova, but I also don't want to go to boarding school."

He shot and made another basket.

"I like Brendan, or I did, but now I'm not so sure. I just wish . . ." Cutter bent over and caught his breath. I went to him and put my hand on his back and waited for him to cope with his emotions. He stood and wiped at his eyes. "My mom's not going to be here anymore, and then you want to send me away." His words came out in hiccups.

"Come here." I wrapped my arms around him. He rested his head on my shoulder and sobbed. This was the second time this morning he'd let his emotions flow. I was grateful for it. I didn't want him holding things in and letting them fester.

"Listen," I said as I leaned back so I could look at him. I cupped his cheeks with my hands. "You're not going to boarding school. Not now. Not ever. The three of us will be together for a long time to come." I refrained from saying "forever." Miri had promised them forever, and she wasn't going to be able to keep her promise.

"Brendan was wrong. He spoke as if he knew what was best for you and your sister. Just because he went to one doesn't mean they're for everyone, and they're definitely not for me."

"I thought he liked us."

"He does, Cutter. You and Nova. Me and him, we're not on the same page when it comes to our futures, and I'm okay with that. I'm right where I want to be."

"Are we going to live here?"

I sighed. "This, I don't know yet. I promise you'll stay here until the summer, and then we'll figure things out. I have to figure out my job."

"Brendan will never move here," Cutter said. "He doesn't like it much."

"Well, that's okay. Brendan and I are no longer together, so what he says or thinks doesn't matter to us."

"Wait, what? You and Brendan broke up?"

I nodded.

"Why?"

"Because he gave me an ultimatum, and that is something you never, ever do to someone you're supposed to love."

"Is it because of me and Nova?"

I shook my head. "Absolutely not."

It was because Brendan thought he was more important than Miriam and the kids, when he knew he wasn't. What did that say about me? Why had I stayed with him for so long?

I closed my eyes and let myself really think about our relationship for the first time. When had Brendan ever put anyone before himself? Yes, he'd canceled his tee time in Miami, but only after I'd made a smart-ass comment. When I had food poisoning last year and spent three days barely able to get out of bed, he'd checked on me once before going to play golf. The only holidays we'd ever spent together were the ones where his friends had something going on—the Fourth of July, Memorial Day, and Labor Day. Never Christmas and sometimes New Year's.

I'd made excuses for him. He didn't understand close relationships because he wasn't close to his family, at least not in the way I was with mine and Miri. His family was all business—prim and proper—ready to put on a front for anyone staring in from the outside. Whereas mine was about love and compassion, about being there when the people we loved needed us.

The truth slapped me in the face, hard. Brendan put Brendan first. It was so clear now, especially after last night and his insistence that the kids go to boarding school.

"So, no boarding school?"

I shook my head. "But you might have to move, okay? Right now, Grandma and Grandpa are going to help out when I have to be in Boston for meetings or when I have to travel."

"Maybe Rocco can come up?"

I smiled at the mention of my brother. I took the ball from Cutter and tried my hardest to dribble to the hoop. Cutter laughed, which sounded amazing. He allowed me to shoot the ball, which didn't even touch the rim, before he chased it down.

In a weak attempt at defense, I tried to get it back until he held it high above his head. I must've jumped ten times trying to get it before I gave up.

A dog barked, and we both turned to see Scout running toward us. Cutter crouched and accepted the bulldozing the Labrador was intent on giving. It was worth watching Cutter fall on his rear because he laughed, and he laughed loudly. I loved the sound and couldn't wait to tell Miri later.

"Good morning," Weston said when he reached us.

"Morning," I said through some giggles. "Do you walk every morning?"

"Nah," he said with a slight shake of his head. "Only on the weekends. I like to get Scout out to run since he's cooped up a lot with my schedule."

Cutter stood and began dribbling around Scout, who liked it. Every so often he'd bark and try to get the ball from Cutter.

Weston motioned toward the bench. I followed and sat beside him. "How's he doing this morning?"

"He's had a couple of moments, but I think that's expected. My mom will be back today, so I can work. I'll make some calls this week to get the kids into therapy. I'd like to have them talking to someone before . . ." I trailed off and kept my gaze on Cutter. "I think I'm going to get them a dog."

"Yeah? Let me know, and I can help."

"I will."

"You mentioned work. Does that mean you'll be in Boston?"

I shook my head. "No, I'll be here, working between the house and the hospital. They're going to admit Miri for treatment. They want to pump her full of drugs and monitor everything."

My legs swung back and forth, kicking up some dirt with each pass. "Did they say how long?"

"If that's not an open-ended question, I don't know what is. Time . . ." I paused and shook my head. "Six to twelve for the inevitable. This current stay is a week to ten days. It all depends on how she responds, and then it'll be outpatient."

"Damn."

"Yeah. I don't remember if I thanked you for what you did last night for Cutter. I really appreciate you being there for him."

Weston nodded. "He's a great kid. I can't say I've been where he is. My parents are still alive. I have lost friends, though, guys I played ball with. Death hurts when it's a friend. I can't imagine how it feels when it's your mom."

Cutter and Scout walked over to us. "Toni, Mom texted and asked us to bring breakfast back to the house."

"Yep, that's the plan. Are you ready to go?" I stood and brushed off my joggers.

"Can I drive?"

"She let you drive?" Weston said with some flair.

"Coach, I'm going to be a great driver."

"Of course he is because I'm teaching him." I gave Cutter a wink and then looked at Weston. "Can we offer you and Scout a ride home?"

"Thanks, but we're going to run for a bit."

"Have a good day, Weston."

"You too, Antonia."

Cutter and I walked toward the car. He got in on the driver's side and looked a little too comfortable in my car.

"Don't get any ideas," I told him.

"But it's so nice."

"Yeah, yeah. Come on, let's stop at the Cozy Cup Café and get breakfast, and then we'll go home and do nothing all day but love on your mom."

That was how I wanted to spend the day, on the couch with Miri, watching mindless TV and just being with her. Tomorrow would be hard enough.

Chapter 21

Weston

We were a week away from playoffs, and the boys were getting antsy. Our last game hadn't gone as planned, despite us coming away with the victory. Malik and Cutter were off. They were in early foul trouble, they had problems knocking down their shots, and they were in a funk.

I had noticed it earlier in the day, during class, and tried to pinpoint the issue before the game. Both swore nothing was wrong, but I suspected they weren't being truthful. The only thing I couldn't figure out was whether the boys had a problem with each other or if Malik was also having some family matters.

Even now, the boys seemed to be lost in their own worlds.

I suspected Cutter's shift was due to his mom being in the hospital all week. Antonia at least had brought her to our game last night, which had surprised me. Although, by looking at Miriam or speaking with her, you wouldn't know she was sick. She was always smiling and, when at the games, cheering her heart out. As a teacher and coach, I knew she'd be sorely missed at the games.

Before I dismissed the class to go get changed, I called Malik over and asked him to help me put the cones away. We were finishing a unit on scooter hockey, which the kids absolutely loved. Thankfully, we hadn't had any accidents. There was nothing worse than a scooter rolling over a finger.

Malik picked up the cones nearest him and brought them over. He put them in the bag and then started to walk away.

"Malik, can we talk?" Without him turning around to face me, I could already sense the eye roll. It was the way he tilted his head slightly and the visible tension in his shoulders.

He turned, and I saw so much anguish in his eyes. Malik shook his head.

"Do you want to go to my office and talk?"

"Can't, I got class next."

"I'll write you a note, excusing you."

Malik gave my offer some thought and finally stepped toward me. I walked side by side with him because I didn't want any of his classmates to think he was in trouble. Besides, I didn't want him to see me as someone in power, but as his friend. Someone he could confide in.

When we got to my office, Jerome was in there, working on his computer.

"Coach, I'm going to need the room for a minute," I said as we entered.

"He can stay," Malik said.

"All right. Let's sit over here." For the office of a physical education teacher, mine was a decent size, but it was because I was a coach and the head of the department. The other PE teachers' office spaces were the size of closets, since they didn't spend a ton of time in there.

My office, besides my desk, had a two-person sofa and some oversize throw pillows that the athletes liked to sit on when they came in here. I had direct access to the locker room and a door that went out to the fields, making it easy for me to get to the baseball field.

Malik opted for one of the chairs near my desk. I took the other one, moving it to the side of him, and Jerome sat on the couch.

"Coach Levy and I noticed a shift in you this week. We want you to know that you can talk to us if something's bothering you. You're a valuable part of our school, team, and community, and we want to be there when you need us."

Malik leaned over, covered his face with his hands, and groaned. "I'm in trouble."

"Is it legal trouble? Do you need an attorney?" Jerome asked.

"No, sir," Malik said as he sat back in the chair. He looked around the office but never at me or Jerome, shaking his head. "Ugh . . . Janelle's pregnant."

The news hit me square in the chest. Malik wasn't the first student of ours to experience a teenage pregnancy, but he was the first one of my players in my coaching experience.

Malik was my thinker, the brains behind my offense. As far as I knew, he'd been with Janelle Canson for a few months. She was a year behind him in school.

"Malik, there are a whole list of things Coach and I could say right now, but none of them are going to mean squat to you," Jerome said. "So, let's start here: Do you and Janelle have a plan?"

He shook his head. "She hasn't told her parents yet."

"Have you told yours?" I asked.

"No, I don't know how to look my dad in the face and tell him I messed up, that I threw my chances of going to school to play ball down the drain."

Malik was from a single-parent family and had a dad who worked two jobs to give his son every opportunity. I liked his father a lot, and he was determined to help his son succeed. I couldn't imagine how this was going to go.

Malik had colleges looking at him, and rightly so. He was one of the most talented kids in the state by far and deserved a shot at a scholarship.

Even with a child on the way.

Malik ran his hands down his shorts. It struck me then that he hadn't changed back into his usual dress pants and polo shirt. He always came to school dressed in what I would call business attire because his dad told him to treat school like a job.

A straight-A student, Malik was tall, slim, and extremely athletic. He kept his dark hair neat with a tapered cut, wore glasses, and flirted up a storm with the staff. There wasn't a teacher here who didn't like having him in their classes.

"Have you and Janelle talked about options?" I asked.

Malik nodded. "She wants to keep it."

I glanced at Jerome and let out an exhale. "What can we do to help?" We were way beyond the responsibility talk about safe sex, condoms, and what would happen if you didn't use one. Malik didn't need a lecture from us because he'd get that at home.

"I don't know." His voice broke before he could finish the sentence. "This isn't what I want. I want to go to college and turn pro, and now I can't."

"No one is saying you can't, Malik. It'll just be harder," I told him.

"Janelle said once colleges find out I have a kid, they won't want me."

I didn't know if that was true or not, but it wasn't something I was willing to gamble on.

Jerome got up, went to Malik, and pulled him into a hug. "We'll figure the college stuff out," he said. "Right now, we want to make sure you're okay. That Janelle's okay. The road ahead is going to be tough to navigate, but you have a support system, and you need to use it."

"Coach is right, Malik. We're not going to turn our backs on you. You're not the only one who's ever gone through this. If you don't want to go to class, you can stay in here," I told him. "I'll get you excused for the rest of the day and see if we can get your work sent down."

Malik nodded. "Thanks, Coach."

"Why don't you go get changed, grab your stuff, and get comfortable?"

Malik got up and left, closing the door behind him. Thankfully, I didn't have another class to be at.

"What in the . . ." Jerome didn't need to finish his sentence. Any colorful word would've fit perfectly there.

"I don't even know what to do for him," I said as I leaned back in the chair. "How does this even happen? Aren't there condoms in the health center?"

Jerome nodded. "Just because they're free doesn't mean they're going to use them."

I groaned loudly and pounded my fist on my desk. "His dad is going to force him to quit playing and get a job. Doing that is a surefire way to lose any chance at a scholarship."

"He could have a job and still play," Jerome said. "There are places on Main Street that'll work around his schedule."

"Really? Like who?"

"The grocery store for one. And I bet Lee would give him a job at the diner. Hell, that's the place to work, if he can start waiting tables."

Nodding, I got up and went to my desk to write some establishments down on a sheet of paper. "I guess the next step is for him to tell his dad."

"Or Janelle to tell her parents. I don't know them very well."

"No, me neither," I said. "I don't have her in any of my classes."

The door opened, and Malik came back in. He looked sad. There was no other way to describe him. He dropped his backpack onto my small coffee table and took his work out. I sat down and rattled off an email to his teachers, explaining he would be in my office for the rest of the day, and they were to consider this an excused absence. I would probably catch hell for it, but so be it. Malik was more likely to get his work done in here than he was in class.

"You aren't missing any tests today, are you?" I asked.

"No, sir."

Jerome excused himself to go do hall duty for the in-between-classes bell, and I glanced at my lesson plan for my next class. Back to floor hockey for this upcoming period.

"Coach?"

"Yeah, Malik?"

"Do you think you could be with me when I tell my dad?"

"Of course. Do you know when you plan to do that?"

He shook his head. "I'm pretty scared to tell him, honestly."

"I get it. It's been the two of you for a long time, and he works hard to give you everything he didn't have."

"Yep, and now I've gone and messed it up."

"There are two of you in this, Malik. You can't accept all the blame."

He nodded, but I wasn't sure my words were sinking in for him.

"I want you to think about your future."

Malik sat back and scoffed.

"Hear me out. You are talented, and colleges are already looking at you. I don't want to see you give up sports because of this."

He opened his mouth to say something, but I held up my hand to let him know I wasn't finished.

"I'm going to talk to Lee Waters, the owner of the Ridgeview Diner, and see if he has any openings. If he does, I'll ask about flexibility. If you could get a job there and work your way into waiting tables a couple of nights a week, that'll give you a decent paycheck."

"How does that help with college, though?"

"I believe, with the new Name, Image, and Likeness program, you'll be able to market yourself to companies. I'm not well versed on it yet, but I'll do what I can to figure it out."

"Okay."

"The bottom line is, you and Janelle had an error in judgment. Neither of you should be punished for it or lose the future you have planned. I don't know what her plan is for after high school, but I do know yours, and I'd really hate to see you give it all up."

Malik nodded and wiped at his eyes. "I don't have to get married, right?"

I shook my head. "Not unless you want to. Do you want to get married?"

"No, sir."

"All right then." I sighed. "If you're not busy, I want you to write down everything we just talked about so when you sit down to tell your dad, you have detailed notes."

Malik nodded and stood. He came over to me and wrapped me in a hug. "Thank you."

I patted his back and wished I could take all of this away for him. Even for Cutter. These boys didn't deserve their lives to be twisted around the way they were. No one did.

The bell rang, and the current PE class filtered into the hall. Some kids saw Malik in my office and teased him about being in trouble. That was the last thing he needed.

I left him in my office and went to start my next class, hoping like hell nothing else would happen today or this week. I wasn't sure how much more I could take while trying to prepare for the playoffs.

Later that night, after practice, I met Jerome at the pub. He'd somehow managed to snag two stools at the bar, facing the TV. I sat next to him and ordered the local IPA along with a glass of water, and nachos.

"What a freaking week," Jerome said as he took a drink from his pint glass. "Can it get any crazier?"

I thanked the bartender for my beer and took a sip. "Let's see, we have one student athlete whose mom is dying and another student athlete who's going to be a dad. I think that tops it for us."

"All while heading into the playoffs." He shook his head.

"Don't remind me."

"I heard a rumor this morning," Jerome said. "I didn't want to bring it up at school since the walls have ears."

I chuckled. Rumors spread in town like wildfire, and most of them started at the school because the teachers were gossips.

"What did I do this time?"

"Had breakfast with a very pretty woman who's been staying in town, helping her friend."

I huffed as Antonia's face popped into my mind. "Guilty."

"No way!"

"What?" I asked as I looked around, scanning to see what or who had gotten Jerome's attention.

"You like her, don't you?"

I sighed and slumped in my seat. "'Like' is the understatement of the year. I'm infatuated, but she has a boyfriend, so I'm just an admirer from afar."

"No, she doesn't," Jerome said.

"Yes, she does."

He shook his head and took another sip. "Not anymore, according to Samira, and she knows everything."

I let Jerome's statement settle over me and thanked the bartender when he placed my plate of nachos in front of me. If Antonia didn't have a boyfriend, that could be a game changer for me. Although I'd never come out and ask her, nor would I pursue anything with her, given the state of Miriam's health.

It seemed I was no better off than I was when I'd sat down, before knowing that the woman of my thoughts, dreams, and desires was now single.

I picked at my nachos, determined to put her out of mind, at least until I got home and I could stare at my ceiling all night and wonder what she was up to.

Chapter 22

Antonia

Navigating work when all I wanted to do was spend all my time with Miri was the bane of my reality. Luckily, the hospital had a small conference room I could use for my virtual meetings, and thanks to all the modern technology out there, I could keep in constant contact with my admin.

The person I didn't want to talk to was Brendan, but that was unavoidable. He hadn't called since he'd had the nerve to ask if I was choosing the kids over him. Even replaying the conversation in my mind caused my blood pressure to rise. Who in the hell did he think he was? We weren't married, and after being with him for four years, I sensed no advancement toward a proposal.

Still, he was my boss. Well, one of them. His father was the one I reported to and who signed my checks, and I'd made sure to email him and let him know Brendan and I were no longer a couple. I thought it was important to put that out there before Brendan said something to his parents and jeopardized my job. I didn't trust Brendan after he'd made another bullshit comment.

I rolled my eyes as I shut my laptop. Miri snickered, and I glared at her. When I'd told her about Brendan and me breaking up, I'd said it was a long time coming. The last thing I needed her to think was that her children were a burden to me. They weren't.

"What's wrong?"

"Nothing," I told her as I motioned for her to scoot over so I could lie with her. She did and tried not to wince. "What hurts?"

She shook her head and held her breath.

"Breathe," I reminded her as I looked at the bag of Dilaudid hanging from the IV pole and wondered when the machine would administer the next dose. "Do you want me to get the nurse?"

Miri shook her head. "The pain is subsiding."

Instead of climbing in bed with her, I stood there for a moment, holding her hand and stroking her hair. "Better?"

Miri nodded.

A knock sounded, and the lawyer I'd hired, Lydia Hurst, came in. She was local and had come highly recommended by Miri's doctor.

"I'm Antonia," I said, shaking her hand as she entered. "This is Miriam." I smiled at my friend and took in her frail body. Day by day, she was growing weaker, despite her doctor saying things were on track. I didn't believe him. Not when her cheeks looked sunken in and her under-eyes looked bruised.

"Hello, ladies." Lydia set her briefcase down and pulled out a tablet. "I know we have a lot to cover, so let's get started."

Miri cleared her throat. "Everything goes to Antonia," she said hoarsely. She'd complained that the medicines she was on made her throat feel raw, and at times it hurt to speak.

"No," I said firmly as I looked at Lydia. "The house needs to go into a trust, with me as executor until Cutter turns eighteen, and then we'll share the responsibility. Once Nova is of age, they'll share."

Lydia nodded and typed on her tablet.

"And you're taking custody?"

"I am," I said confidently as I looked at Miri and nodded.

"Okay, so what I'll do here is write the will, appointing you as the guardian of the minor children. We'll need a backup."

"Your parents," Miri whispered.

"My parents," I repeated. "Renzo and Carmela Bernardi."

"Has the children's father relinquished parental rights?"

My heart dropped as Miri's eyes widened in horror. I shook my head. "He's not around. He's never met Nova and has only spent a few weeks with Cutter about eight years ago."

"You'll have to petition for legal custody, especially if he comes forward. The court will also appoint a guardian ad litem for the kids."

"A what?" I asked, giving Lydia a blank stare.

"A guardian ad litem is a court-appointed individual, often an attorney or trained professional, who represents the best interests of a person. In this case, Cutter and Nova, because they're minors."

"Okay, so this person protects the kids and not their father?" Miri asked, and I nodded at her question.

"Yes. They will listen to the kids, speak to friends and family, and give their opinion to the courts. Back to their father . . ."

"Like I said, he's not around."

Lydia nodded. "I understand, but the court will require us to reach out to him at his last known."

With my eyes on Miri and my hand firmly in hers, I nodded. "I'll happily fight him for those children. He won't win."

Lydia continued to type.

"Are you able to financially provide for the children?"

"Yes. I have copies of my statements for you. Also, Miri has a small life insurance policy. That'll go into whatever it needs to for the kids. We won't need it."

"Great, thanks."

"After Miriam's passing, the will must go through probate court. This is when it can grant you guardianship."

"How long will this take?"

"The will and trust setup?"

I nodded.

"Normally, a month, but I cleared my schedule to have this done by Monday for you. In the meantime, I'm going to have Miriam sign a document stating she made this will with me today. This document will be binding."

Lydia excused herself and took her tablet out of the room. Again, I combed Miri's hair back and stared into her hazel eyes. She looked so sad, and I wished I could take all of this away from her. No one deserved this, especially her. All she'd ever wanted was to raise her babies in her dream house and just be. Miri was content with the life she had, never asking for anything.

A tear fell, and I dabbed at my face, mindful of the full makeup I'd had to put on this morning for my meeting.

"I'm so sorry," I whispered to her. "This isn't fair."

"You're going to take care of them, right? He won't get them?"

For the second time today, my blood boiled. "He'll never get them, Miri. I will fight until I'm blue in the face to protect your babies from him."

Lydia returned, talking in a high-pitched, happy voice, and bless her heart for her cheerfulness. I turned away and fanned my face to get my emotions under control.

Miri raised her bed as Lydia brought the table closer to her. Miri signed her name, stating the document was her will, and then I signed. This would have to do because time was not our friend.

Before she left, Lydia told us we'd hear from her on Monday. I sat on the edge of the bed and watched my friend.

"Is there anything I need to know?"

She shook her head. "Not that I can think of. Everything's in my address book. All my accounts, passwords, and social security numbers. Other than the house, I only have my credit card, but there isn't a lot on there."

"I should probably go to your office and get your stuff?"

Miri lifted her shoulder. "I think my coworkers there will bring my stuff. It's mostly pictures of us and the kids."

I took her hand in mine again. "I need for you to tell me what you want in regard to the kids. Your hopes, dreams, requirements. For sixteen years, I've been the fun aunt, and while I'd love to keep things that way, we both know things are changing."

Miri took a deep inhale and tried to smile. "I really want Cutter to stick with his sports, even though that might be a burden to you."

"Don't worry about that. I'll work things out with Weston."

She grinned. "He's a good man."

"How come you never dated him?"

Miri shook her head. "Oh no, there is zero spark there. Although I've seen him more outside of games since you came to town."

I rolled my eyes. "I doubt that. He's just coming around to help out."

Miri eyed me, and I shook my head.

"There's absolutely nothing there. Besides, after four years of being with Brendan, I think I'm done."

"You guys never loved each other. At least, not the way you should've after being together that long."

Unfortunately, I think she was right. We dismissed each other easily, and neither of us had bothered to call or text each other since the fateful night in the kitchen. Surprisingly, I didn't miss him.

"Enough about my love life. I want to talk about the kids."

Miri nodded. "I don't want Cutter to miss out on anything, like prom. He's such a good boy. Smart. Respectful."

Moody. But I chalked this up to the fact that his mom was dying, and his teenage emotions were all over the place.

"We've talked about college, so I know he wants to go, and Weston thinks he can get a scholarship, but he'll have to do the travel stuff."

I nodded. "Weston mentioned it. We'll sit down and figure it out."

"It's a financial burden," she said, her voice breaking.

"None of this is a burden, Miri, except that we won't have you."

Tears welled in our eyes. My vision clouded, making it hard to see my best friend.

"And for Nova?"

Miri lifted her shoulder again. "Her personality is just starting to shine. I've been waiting for her to tell me if she wants to take dance classes or play sports. I suspect she wants to follow Cutter, but she should do whatever she wants, ya know?"

I nodded and swallowed the lump in my throat.

"They might need some help."

"I'm already on it, Miri. For all three of us." They were losing their mom, while I was losing a part of me.

Another knock sounded. I stood and this time wiped my tears away, not giving a shit about my makeup. A trio of women walked in. I only recognized Samira.

"Hi," Miri said excitedly. "What are you ladies doing here?"

"Well, Toni told us we'd have book club today, and since you're here, we brought it here," Samira said as she gave Miri a hug.

"Shit. Sorry, I forgot," I said.

Samira waved my apology off. "It's not like you're not busy. Toni, this is Vera; she owns Petal and Vine, and this is Edith; she owns the General Goods store in town."

"It's nice to meet you both," I said as I shook their hands.

"I don't have my book," Miri said.

"When was the last time we actually read a book, cover to cover?" Edith asked.

"Besides, we have more important things to talk about," Vera added.

"Like what flowers I want at my funeral?"

"Miri!" I said, shocked at her statement.

Everyone went silent.

She shrugged. "What? It's not like it's a secret. Why can't I plan things out?"

"You can, honey," Vera said as she patted Miri's leg. "You just left us speechless for a moment. We'll do whatever you want."

Miri eyed me with one of those "Now what are you going to say?" looks. I shook my head slightly and left to get some more chairs. At the nurses' station, I asked for two more because I would just sit or stand by Miri.

When I came back, the four of them were in a fit of giggles, which was nice to see but also broke my heart.

"What's so funny?"

"Oh, nothing," Miri said gruffly.

"Yes, something," Samira said. "She's trying to convince us to set you up with our resident coach."

I found myself rolling my eyes again where Weston was concerned. "Stop." I covered my face as soon as I felt my cheeks heat up.

"See, she's blushing because she knows he's a fine, fine man." Miri laughed and reached for my hand.

"Have you ever seen a picture of him in his younger days?" Edith tapped on her phone and turned it to show everyone. I leaned in closer to take a good look, and Miri was right: Weston was definitely good looking.

"Ah, you're interested," Edith said as she took her phone back.

"He's been a good coach," I pointed out. "Cutter needs that right now."

"Well, I heard from Jerome that Weston has eyes for someone," Samira said.

"See," I said to Miri as I pointed toward Samira. "He likes someone, so whatever you've conjured up in that mind of yours is wrong."

Miri laughed. "I still think it's you," she said and then proceeded to tell the women about him coming over to the house on more than one occasion, when he'd never been over before, other than to pick up or drop Cutter off.

I lost count of how many times I rolled my eyes and had never been more thankful for work interruptions. Having the four of them, three of whom I barely knew, discuss my love life as if I weren't in the room was a bit unnerving. You could easily tell they were all out of the dating game. Weston was being neighborly and hadn't once put it out there that he was interested in me.

Not that I was looking. A week ago, I had a boyfriend. Weston wasn't even on my radar, and I had no intention of putting him there, despite Miri's insistence. This would have to be one of those deathbed requests I'd ignore.

The ladies left when Miri started to fall asleep. We hugged in the hallway, and I thanked them for coming. They each volunteered to bring dinner for us while Miri was in the hospital, but I assured them we were fine since my mother was in town.

While she slept, I did more work and received a reply from Brendan's father to the email I'd sent, assuring me my job was safe, which was a relief. I still had to figure out what the kids and I were going to do.

Cutter wanted to stay in Grove Hill, which I didn't fault him for. His friends, his teams, and his life were there. My job was in Boston, and working remotely was only going to last for so long. It wasn't like my job could be in Grove Hill, and it was sort of late to start a new career.

As I looked at Miri, sleeping in the bed with a machine feeding her drugs to try—and do what, prolong the inevitable?—I didn't know what to do. Staying here was right for the kids, and I'd promised to make them my priority.

Chapter 23

Weston

I stood a few feet from the boys, with the ball on my hip and my wrist draped over it. They were on the baseline, bent over and sucking air after running the snake. This was part of our conditioning and not a punishment, as many might think. Anytime they had to run, it was as if their lives were over. Teenagers were dramatic.

"Tomorrow is our last regular season game," I told them. "We'll have our normal warm-up, and then we'll stop the clock with three minutes to go and have our Senior Day celebration. Each senior will have their name called, and your parents will meet you at half-court for photos. Once we're done, we'll put another five minutes on the clock and warm up. Any questions?"

The boys all mumbled a no. I paced a bit, increasing the anticipation of me blowing my whistle. When I did, they turned and sprinted. Coach Levy timed them with the scoreboard clock so the boys would know their times. Normally, each boy would run individually, but I'd put the fastest boy at the front of the line, and they all had to keep pace with him.

When the last boy touched the end line, I blew my whistle and told them to bring it in. "Great practice, guys. If we take care of business tomorrow, we'll be the number one seed going into playoffs. We'll have a first-round bye. Like last year, you're more than welcome to attend other games with Coach Levy and me. I just need to know so I can tell the other school how many tickets I need. Timberwolves on three."

Malik's voice boomed as he counted the team down, and everyone yelled. Each of the boys took off to the locker room, but Malik stayed.

"Hey, Coach?"

"What can I do for you, Malik?" It'd only been two days since he'd dropped the bomb that his girlfriend was pregnant. I'd told him I'd support him in any way I could and had even reached out to Lee about giving Malik a job.

He looked around, which I assumed was to make sure his teammates were all out of the gym. "Are you free tonight? To talk to my dad with me?"

I nodded. "Of course." I hadn't expected him to be ready to tell his dad so soon.

"I saw Mr. Waters the other day, and he gave me a job. I'm going to learn how to host and bus tables, and then I'll start the training to be a server. I wanted to thank you for reaching out to him."

"It was my pleasure."

"And Janelle . . ." He sighed and took a deep inhale. "She's telling her parents this weekend, and I thought that maybe I should tell my dad first. I hoped she would come with me, but she doesn't want to."

"I understand. This is a hard situation to navigate."

Malik nodded. "It's making me sick to my stomach. She keeps going on and on about how we're going to be a family, and all I can think about is how this was a mistake and we're ruining our lives."

My lips went into a fine line as I tried to find the right words to ease his mind, but the truth was, there weren't any. Malik and Janelle were young, and a baby was going to change their lives, no matter what. For good and bad, but for teens, it was likely the latter, until they figured it all out.

"Anyway, can you come over?"

"Yep. What time?"

"Does now work? My dad didn't work today, so he won't be overly tired, and he'll be happy you've stopped by. At least for a few minutes." Malik's face turned grim. "I'm really afraid he's going to kick me out."

I put my hand on his shoulder. "Even if he does, my door's open. You'll have a place to stay."

"Thanks, Coach." Malik ran toward the locker room, leaving me with my thoughts.

At this point, I should've considered opening a home for my players. I'd already told Cutter he could live with me, although I wasn't sure how Antonia would feel about that. She'd said she and the kids were here, at least until the start of next year. And then what?

"And then nothing," I muttered to myself as I walked toward my office. Antonia had a life away from Grove Hill. She had a boyfriend and a job, and she didn't need the likes of me trying to intervene.

Lust was a tricky emotion to navigate, evident by what Malik was going through, although we were in completely different situations. I hadn't bothered looking twice at a woman until I'd spotted Antonia, and now I couldn't get her off my mind.

In my office, I gathered my things and waited for Malik to come out of the locker room. He tried to look cheerful when, in fact, he looked grim, and his complexion was ashen. I put my hand on his shoulder as we walked out of the gym.

"It's easy for me to say everything will be okay. I don't know if it will be or not, but I do know you can sit down with your dad and accept responsibility."

Malik didn't say anything. I imagined he was probably scared shitless. I would've been.

I followed him over to his house, and as we walked in, his father, Gordon, greeted me like we were old friends. It was shortly after I'd arrived and started my job that Gordon had told me he knew who I was and that he'd been a fan. We'd been friends ever since, but not the type to always hang out. If he wasn't working and was enjoying a beverage at the diner, we'd sit together.

"Coach, glad you could join us," he said as he shook my hand. "I've had the ribs on the cooker since this afternoon, when Malik said he invited you over for dinner. Come in, come in. Can I get you something to drink?"

I gave Malik the side-eye. I didn't like dishonesty, and while it wasn't egregious, he needed to know it wasn't okay to stretch the truth. What would he have said to his dad if I couldn't come over?

"I'm good with water, Gordon. Please don't go to any trouble."

"Nah, no trouble," he said, waving away my comment. "Come on in, the game's on."

I followed Malik into the small living room and sat on the couch, leaving the recliner for Gordon. The sliding glass door opened, and the smell of smoked ribs wafted through the air. My stomach whined in anticipation.

"Malik, set the table, please."

"Yes, sir." Malik went to his room with his bags and then came back empty handed. I stood and went to help, needing something to do because, honestly, I felt awkward.

Gordon went in and out, returning with a plate of ribs and tinfoil-wrapped baked potatoes.

"What can I do?"

"Please, just sit. You're our guest." No, I was going to be a mediator and support system for one of my students. I asked Malik what he and his father would drink with dinner and busied myself gathering their beverages.

"Okay, I think that's it," Gordon said. I waited for him to sit down before I took my seat. He asked for our plates and heaped food onto each one. Part of me felt guilty for eating such an expensive meal, knowing Gordon worked two jobs, but not eating what he'd made would be an insult.

Now that I was here, I regretted agreeing. Malik was going to break the news to his father over a home-cooked meal, and it could possibly ruin his night.

While I sat there, the appetite I had was gone. I wanted to support Malik, as promised, but I also wanted this over with. We ate in silence, breaking to talk sports and the upcoming games. Everyone in town expected us to be in the championship game. I had high hopes for my boys but would take each win as they came.

As soon as Gordon pushed his plate away, Malik cleared his throat. "Dad?"

Gordon looked at his son, and it was like he knew. I could see some sense of realization on his face.

"Spit it out."

Malik looked at me, and I nodded, watching as his eyes filled with tears. "I made a mistake."

Gordon nodded.

"Janelle . . . she's . . . uh . . ."

"Pregnant?" Gordon finished for him. He threw his napkin on the table and stormed out of the house.

Malik jumped when something crashed outside. I set my hand on his arm. "I'll go talk to him. You do whatever you're supposed to be doing right now."

I gave Gordon a few more minutes before going outside. I handed him his beer from the counter and stood next to him while the dark sky settled over us.

"He knows better."

"He does," I said in agreement. "We also know what it's like to have out-of-control hormones."

"I've worked so hard to give him a good life and have preached to him about being careful. He had his future in front of him, and now this."

"He can still have the future you guys planned, and he still wants it. Malik is a great student and a strong athlete. I've already spoken to a couple of schools that were interested last year, and they'll be interested this year as well. Malik will go to college, if that's what he still wants."

"Not with a kid. He'll have to pay support."

"With how athletes are treated these days, he'll have funds. He also got a part-time job at the diner to start saving money."

Gordon looked at me. "Did you set that up?"

"I put a feeler out to Lee. He's always looking for help and is willing to work around Malik's schedule."

"How does this affect his status on the team?"

"It doesn't, Gordon. He's not in trouble. He wasn't caught drinking or doing drugs. They're two young kids who made a mistake. We've all been there."

He shook his head and groaned. "Why didn't he just listen to me?"

I let out a small laugh. "Did you listen to your father?"

"Nope, not a single word."

"Me neither. Mine told me not to get married. I did, and look at where that got me."

Gordon laughed, and then his demeanor shifted back. "As much as it pains me to say this, I hope that's not next for Malik."

I put my arm around his shoulders. "Talk to him. Malik is looking for guidance from you. He was afraid to tell you, which is why he invited me over. I'm not here to keep the peace or save him, but here as his coach and your friend."

We stood there for a moment, staring into the nothingness. "Can you let him know I'll be in shortly? I . . ." He sighed. "I need some time."

"Sure will. Thanks again for dinner."

"You're welcome."

Inside, I found Malik at the cleared table, doing his homework. He glanced at me expectantly. I kept my face as stoic as possible. "Give your dad some time," I told him.

"Is he going to kick me out?"

I shook my head. "I didn't get that impression, Malik. I think he's more hurt than anything and scared for you."

Malik looked out the window, where he could see his father's silhouette.

"I'm going to go. Call me if you need anything."

"See you tomorrow, Coach. And thanks."

"Anytime."

As I drove home, I thought about Malik and Cutter. Two of my stars going through something life changing, but for different reasons. Both had such bright futures that something like this could send them down the wrong path.

When the Vaughns' driveway came into view, I slowed and looked down it. Two cars were them, neither them Antonia's. Don't ask me how I'd memorized what her car looked like, but the one with Massachusetts plates in the driveway was not hers.

I continued to my house, pulled into my own driveway, and shut my truck off. I counted to three, and then the barking started. After the day I'd had, it was going to be nice to sit on the couch with Scout and think about nothing for a few minutes.

Chapter 24

Weston

I woke to a text from Malik, thanking me for helping him break the news to his father. They'd spoken for most of the evening, and while this was not the path they'd mapped out, they were on board to try and make it work.

Rereading Malik's text brought me back to the conversation I'd had with Antonia about Miriam and how her parents had kicked her out of the house when she told them she was pregnant. I didn't know if times were changing or if it was the difference in parenting. One never knew how a parent was going to react to news like that, and I was thankful Gordon had done so with Malik's best interest in mind.

I dressed in running gear, leashed Scout, and set off down the road. For some reason, I'd had a lot of pent-up energy these past few days, and while I wanted to think it was because of the playoffs and the expectations of the players and parents, I didn't know if that was it.

Some of it was my lackluster love life, which was solely my fault. Samira had often wanted to set me up with someone, or a mom would flirt heavily during the summer while we were away at a tournament. Neither situation interested me. Dating hadn't interested me until I'd laid eyes on Antonia.

I laughed at the thought. Of course I'd want to spend time with someone who had a boyfriend. If that wasn't bad luck, I didn't know what was. I supposed it was a good thing I hadn't gotten too deep with my feelings for Antonia, especially since her boyfriend would be around town. Not to mention, he'd likely be at the tournaments over the summer.

Jerome's voice echoed in my mind: *Not anymore, according to Samira, and she knows everything.*

Every fiber in my being hoped Jerome was right. Not that I wanted Antonia hurting any more than she was, but I didn't like the idea of this man sending Miriam's kids away.

At least that's what I told myself, because the truth was, I liked Antonia, a lot. And I didn't know how I'd spend all summer seeing her with someone else.

"Great," I muttered when Cutter's house came into view as I recalled the unfamiliar cars in the driveway from the night before. I thought about picking up the pace to speed by the house without anyone noticing. I didn't expect anyone to be outside at this hour, but in my mind, I liked to believe Antonia might've been thinking about me.

I laughed out loud at my thoughts and shook my head. "Get over yourself."

I kept my pace steady for Scout's benefit. Being a Lab, he'd tire out quickly, and there was no way I'd be able to carry the big baby home.

I slowed when I reached the Vaughns' driveway, because I couldn't help but look again to see which cars were parked there. Unlike last night, Antonia's car was there.

A female voice rang out, and a door slammed. Gravel crunched, and my mind screamed at me to start running again, but I stood there, stock still, needing to see if it was Antonia.

When she stepped out onto the porch, dressed like she had been last Saturday morning, I wondered if this would become routine for us—meeting at the end of the driveway—to go get breakfast.

"You could only hope," I muttered.

"Good morning," she said as soon as I'd finished speaking to myself. "Who were you talking to?"

Great.

"Uh . . . Scout."

She smiled at me and crouched to give my dog the attention I sought from her. Maybe if I was as cute as my dog . . . nope, that was just desperation at this point.

"Good morning," I finally said when she stood. She was dressed for winter, with a knit hat on, a parka, and, if I had to guess, thermal pants. "Are you heading to the Cozy Cup Café?"

Her smile beamed, and my heart did this double flip and sank.

"I am." She nodded toward the house. "Miri's determined to make Cutter his game day breakfast, but Nova and I want doughnuts." Antonia turned toward the house briefly. "I also want to give her some private time with her babies. They need it."

Antonia stepped toward the road, forcing me to move back to give her space. She started walking and then looked over her shoulder at me. "Are you coming?"

"Yep." We were now. I tugged Scout's leash, and we fell in step with Antonia. "How's Miriam doing?"

Antonia looked at the ground, her shoulders visibly lifting with her heavy sigh. "It's not good. Her doctor talked to her about her quality of life yesterday. She has to spend most of her time in the hospital. She's home today for the game. The doctor doesn't recommend her even going because of germs, but she insists. I won't tell her otherwise." Antonia shrugged.

"I wish there was something I could do about the game and the germ thing, but there isn't."

"Oh, I know. I offered to have her on video chat, but Miri says it's not the same. She wants to be there, among the fans, immersed in the atmosphere of watching the game and cheering along with everyone else."

"How are you doing?"

Antonia stopped and looked at me for a second and then started walking again. "I have my mom here. She takes the brunt of my anger, tears, and grumpiness. Other than that, I try to remain positive for the kids and just bottle everything up."

"Your boyfriend isn't a sounding board for you?" I blurted out before I could stop the word vomit.

What in the hell is wrong with you? I needed my ass kicked for asking such an asinine question.

Antonia scoffed. "Brendan? No, never. And we broke up."

I wanted to ask her to repeat herself because certainly, I'd heard her incorrectly. Jerome had been right. "Oh?"

She shrugged. "It was a long time coming. We were sort of in this limbo situation. Our relationship wasn't moving forward, and when this shit with Miri started, he thought ultimatums were the best course of action."

We came to the corner and waited for traffic to stop. Once it was clear, we crossed the street.

"Is this where the whole boarding school fiasco came into play?"

She nodded and beat me to the door of the Cozy Cup Café and opened it for Scout and me to go in.

We got in line, standing next to each other. "I'm buying today," she said.

As much as I wanted to be a child and roll my eyes, I didn't. "Fine, but I'm not happy about it."

She laughed a little, and it was nice to hear.

"Anyway, yes. Brendan said the kids would go to boarding school so that they wouldn't interrupt our lives. I said no. That was that."

That was that, and now she was single.

And probably nowhere near ready to date.

We placed our orders, and I reluctantly let her pay. It wasn't in my nature, and when I'd agreed, I didn't think it would be the next weekend. Honestly, I thought last weekend was a one-and-done.

Antonia carried our coffees to the same table we'd sat at on our first visit. We even sat in the same seats, with Scout lying next to my chair.

"Samira, Edith, and Vera came to the hospital to see Miri this week," Antonia said. "I'd forgotten I told Samira that Miri would host their book club meeting, so they brought it to her. They never made her feel like she was dying. They were so gracious. And a bit morbid because Miri said she was going to plan her own funeral, and Vera was on board." She took a sip of her coffee.

"That must've been hard."

"It's all hard. I don't know whether I'm coming or going right now."

"How long until you have to go back to work?" I asked, taking a drink of my coffee.

Antonia pulled a sugar packet from the small ceramic holder. "I haven't stopped working. The nurses set me up in a conference room for when I have virtual meetings, but other than that, I can do most of my work via email."

"That must be nice."

She lifted one shoulder. "I'm not going to be able to continue this way, but I'm not sure I have it in me to move the kids. Miri loves that money pit of hers. It's their home. I don't know if I can be the one to rip it away from them."

I couldn't even imagine the pressure she must have been under. She put the packet back and smiled at Samira as she approached with our food. "I'll have the doughnuts ready for when you leave."

"Thank you," we said at the same time.

After a few bites, she looked at me and said, "So, I googled you while I was on the phone with my dad the other day."

I hung my head in mock horror. As far as professional athletes went, I was pretty tame. I was never in trouble, not with my career or personal life.

"Let me guess: I'm your dad's favorite player, and he's coming to town to take a photo with me?" I leaned back in the chair and grinned widely.

Antonia laughed, and this time the sound went right to my heart. Why was everything so easy with her?

"Actually, he said you had a great career until you had to have surgery, and he wanted me to ask why you didn't return to the game."

I ran my fingers along my cup of coffee. My manager had asked the same question. At the time, the answer had been simple: Brianna.

"If it's too personal, you don't have to answer."

"No, it's not that." I sat up straight and picked at my food. "I thought about returning, but there were things I wanted out of life that I thought my wife wanted. Turns out I was wrong. When I said I wanted to retire, she asked for a divorce. She wanted the glamorous life—the big city, the spotlight, traveling to away games. When I got injured, I realized there was more to life than baseball. I wanted to settle down in a small town, maybe start a family; she realized we wanted completely different things. She didn't want kids or the quiet life I was craving. She wanted a husband who could give her the lifestyle she thought she deserved." I paused, meeting Antonia's eyes. "The ironic thing is, she's now married to a basketball player, living exactly the life she wanted. We just weren't compatible when it came to what really mattered."

"Brianna was your wife's name?"

This time, I laughed. "Thank you, Wiki."

"She's very pretty."

"Ah, yes. Thanks to the internet for storing every image ever posted."

"Did she really leave you because you wanted to retire?"

I nodded and took a bite of my sausage, egg, and cheese burrito. "It took a lot of therapy for me to learn Brianna left because she wasn't happy. Not with me, her life, or the life we shared. She was right for leaving. We're both happier being who we are now than who we were together. We were always better as friends, which is what we are now. We text or call each other occasionally."

My eyes were on Antonia's expressions, waiting to see what she would do or say. At first, Brianna leaving had gutted me, but then I'd woken up and realized I had so much more to offer than baseball.

"Wow, I'm sorry."

I gave her a small shrug. "It was a long time ago, and I'm well over it."

"Well, that's good then. I still have to work with my ex, so there's that."

"Ouch. That might be a tough one."

"Eh. He's probably over it." She scooped a forkful and ate.

"Are you?"

Antonia nodded quickly. "Oddly, I'm not even bothered by it. It was probably for the best."

It was definitely for the best for me.

The rest of the morning and into the afternoon, I sat in my office at school with my thoughts. One might think those thoughts would've been about the upcoming game, but they were all about Antonia. My mom had always said to believe in the signs. Was this a sign?

This one being that Antonia was single, and from my guess, she wasn't heartbroken over it.

She wasn't hard to read, but then again, she could be masking her emotions because of what she was going through with Miriam.

My fingers drummed on my blotter, the rolled edges catching my attention. I moved the scattered papers off the calendar and looked at the date, shocked to see it was exactly three years old. How come I'd never replaced it?

With more observation, I noticed the sentence I had written down: *Start dating again.*

I frowned, not remembering writing those words. The messy scrawl was definitely mine. The date itself didn't mean anything to me, at least not something I could recall. The team would've been heading into playoffs, and my mind would've been on basketball and the upcoming baseball season.

Now my mind was on not only my responsibilities as a coach but my interest in Antonia.

I had to put her out of my mind, at least for right now. We had a game in a couple of hours, and I needed to plan. I brought my computer to life and pulled up game footage and notes Jerome had put together for me, taking my own notes as I watched.

After I finished, I wrote out my game plan: who would guard whom during our man-to-man, what plays we were going to run when they switched their defense. From the video, I was able to ascertain a pattern with their coach, which I could easily work to our advantage.

Voices began filtering in. The boys walked past my office, saying hi as they made their way to the locker room. Within minutes of their arrival, I heard the gym door open, and music began playing.

Jerome came in and dumped his bag on the couch. "Malik's out there and is in a good mood."

"That's refreshing." I leaned back in my chair and tapped my pen against my desk, once again noticing the blotter. I hadn't bothered changing the page and didn't think I would.

"I take it everything went okay with his dad?"

I nodded and gave him a half shrug. "Malik said they talked after I left." I sat up and stood. "It's not an ideal situation for anyone, that's for sure. I just don't want to see him throwing his life away."

"Right."

Jerome and I made our way out to the court, mostly to watch the boys shoot around. I'd always told them that anytime they wanted to use the gym, all they had to do was ask one of us, and we'd come open it for them. I'd rather spend my free time here with them. Anything to keep them out of trouble.

"Coach, wanna shoot?" Malik asked.

"No, thanks. Coach Levy does, though." I gave Jerome a little shove onto the court. Secretly, he loved playing with the kids but was always afraid to show them up. He'd played in college but had never given a professional career a thought.

Game day staff started to arrive. The smell of popcorn and hot dogs wafted through the corridor and into the gym each time the doors opened. Fans began filling the stands, and the school-appropriate music played to entertain the spectators. In the corner, the cheerleaders practiced their routine, and Gordon took it upon himself to sweep the court.

While the boys went to change, I sat on the bench with Jerome and watched the other team filter in. Our athletic director showed them where to go, even though their coach had been here more than a dozen times.

"Who's the tall kid?" I asked Jerome. The boy had to be at least six five.

"Not sure. I've never seen him before."

"Shit," I muttered as I walked toward the admissions table to grab a roster. Sure enough, it listed a new kid. "How'd we miss this?"

Jerome took the flyer from my hand and shook his head. "I watched them on Monday. He wasn't on the roster or the bench."

The state had a rule where players had to have completed ten practices before they could play. Being that Jerome was there at the beginning of the week to scout, and the player wasn't on the bench, one could assume he didn't have his ten practices in. There was no way to tell or even know.

"I hate being unprepared."

"Maybe he'll stay on the bench," Jerome surmised.

He didn't, and by halftime, we were down fifteen.

We gave the boys a minute to get to the locker room. I checked the stats in the home book, and then we were on our way. When I entered the team room, all heads were down. It was clear they weren't in the right mindset.

"Guys, we have seven minutes to talk it out. What do we need to do to turn this around?"

"Execute our plays," Malik said. "Hit the slashers before the defense can adjust."

"We're not helping on defense. Our posts need help because they're just lobbing it into that big kid," another added.

"We need paint touches. If the shot isn't there, we're open on the outside," Cutter said.

"Hard, crisp passes, and they need to be fast," Jayden added. "We need to move their defense."

I made eye contact with each of my players, nodding as they spoke to what they were witnessing on the court and how they were playing.

"The only thing I want to add to what everyone's saying is to play hard, play with confidence, and play the game you know how to play. If you play your game, you'll be victorious. But you can't hang your heads because we're down by fifteen."

We gathered in a huddle and then broke off. Jerome and I followed the boys upstairs and mentally prepared for the second half of the game.

When I came through the door and into the gym, my eyes sought out Antonia. I'd done a damn good job of ignoring her, but now they were homed in on her.

Nova sat on her lap, and they danced in their seat to the music. Antonia directed Nova's arms in every which way while she bopped her legs up and down.

Samira, Edith, and Vera sat around Miriam, almost as if they were creating a barrier around her. It was nice to see and honestly expected. The Grove Hill community took care of their own.

I desperately wanted to go over and visit, but doing so would raise a lot of eyebrows, and my sole focus needed to be on the boys and the game, not the woman across the way whom I wanted to get to know better.

The horn sounded to start the second half, and within three minutes of play, the game was tied. For the rest of the game, I coached my ass off, changing defenses on a whim to throw the other team off. I'd throw on the press, only for them to call a time-out to make the adjustment, and then I'd have my guys pick up at half-court.

For two quarters, the score went back and forth, but the only one that mattered was the one at the final buzzer. Grove Hill won by two.

This evening, when it was time to leave, I didn't hesitate to walk back into the gym, knowing Antonia would be waiting for Cutter.

She smiled at me as I walked toward the exit, even though I fully intended to stop and chat with her.

"Nice win," Miriam said. I wanted to give her a hug but refrained. She had a mask on, and I figured it wouldn't be smart.

"Thanks. Cutter played a great game."

Miriam beamed and walked with Samira to sit down and wait for Cutter to come out of the locker room.

"You won," Antonia said. "Sorry, but that's all I know."

"Fair enough. I could teach you about the game if you want."

She nodded. "That's probably best, considering . . ."

"How about dinner tonight?" I hadn't meant to ask, but now that I had, I felt like a teenager all over again.

Antonia smiled. "In town, right? I don't want to go too far."

"Absolutely. I'll pick you up at six."

"Bring Scout. He can stay at the house while we're out."

Now it was me who was grinning. "He'll love it. See you in a bit." I winked and left her there before I said something stupid like asking her to move in or marry me.

I drove home as fast as I could, showered, fed Scout, and put him in the truck to be on time for my date with Antonia. I didn't care if it was to the diner—we were going out and were going to spend some quality hours in each other's company.

The front door opened as I pulled into the driveway. I didn't bother shutting my truck off as Scout and I made our way to the porch. Scout greeted Nova with a barrage of kisses, causing her to giggle. The sound brought a smile to my face.

Antonia appeared in the doorway, still dressed in the jeans she'd worn earlier. Gone was the Timberwolves shirt, having been replaced by a white collared shirt and burgundy sweater. I held the screen door for her as she stepped onto the porch.

"I left the truck running, so it'll be nice and warm," I said as we walked next to each other. "We aren't going far." I opened the door and waited for her to get in before shutting it and jogging around to the driver's side.

The drive into town was quick. Not that there was ever any traffic unless something special was going on in town. I parked along the curb, and to my surprise, Antonia slid across the seat and got out on my side.

I held the door open as Antonia stepped inside the Ridgeview Diner, the scent of coffee and warm buttered rolls wrapping around us like a familiar embrace. The place buzzed with life. Locals chatting over plates of meatloaf, high school kids huddled in booths, sharing milkshakes. It wasn't fancy, but it was home.

The hostess led us to a corner booth, one of the few spots that still had some privacy. As she slid into the seat across from me, I let my gaze linger for just a second longer than necessary. I still couldn't believe she'd even entertained the idea of going out with me or leaving the house tonight.

"This place is nice," she said. "Miri likes bringing the kids here."

"Have you been before?"

She shook her head. "Prior to now, I'd come up on the weekends. We'd order pizza or drive over to North Conway for dinner."

"Ah, makes sense." Those must've been the trips Cutter had told me about long ago.

"Well, since I dragged you here, I feel like I should at least teach you something useful."

She arched an eyebrow. "Oh? And what exactly am I learning?"

"High school basketball," I said, resting my forearms on the table, keeping my tone casual. "It's the heart of Grove Hill High. That and baseball, but we'll get to that later. You should know the rules if you're going to live here." I let that last part hang in the air, watching to see how she reacted.

Her lips curved slightly, but she didn't bite. "I don't know, Weston. I wasn't exactly a sports girl in high school. But by all means, educate me."

I leaned forward, closing the space between us just enough that her eyes flickered to mine, like she wasn't sure if I was going to talk basketball or something else entirely.

"All right, first lesson," I said, picking up a sugar packet and holding it up like it was part of a play. "You've got five players on the court per team. One of them is the point guard. He's the leader, the one who calls the plays. Think of him as the person who always has a plan."

"So . . . you?" she teased, tilting her head.

I grinned. "I was a shooting guard, actually. Which means I took the shots." I paused, letting my gaze drop to her lips before flicking back up to her eyes. "Made most of them too."

She laughed, shaking her head. "So modest."

"Would you rather I lie?"

Antonia rolled her eyes, but I caught the way her fingers toyed with the napkin in front of her, like she was nervous. Time to push just a little more.

"What about you?" I asked, shifting gears. "What did you do in high school? Besides, you know, prepare to take over the corporate world."

She exhaled, like she hadn't thought about it in a while. "Debate team, yearbook committee. I was busy."

"Of course you were." I smirked. "What about fun? Anything reckless? Snuck out past curfew? Kissed a boy under the bleachers?"

Her cheeks tinted pink, but she narrowed her eyes at me playfully. "That's a very specific question. Did you kiss a girl under the bleachers, Weston?"

I chuckled. "A gentleman doesn't kiss and tell."

She scoffed, but there was a glint in her eye that told me she was enjoying this. Before I could press further, the waiter arrived to take our orders, but we hadn't even looked at the menu.

"Can we have a few more minutes?" The young kid, who I didn't recognize, nodded.

"You didn't deny it. Which means you have a rebellious streak."

She huffed out a laugh. "I plead the Fifth."

I grinned, shaking my head. "You're going to be a terrible basketball student, aren't you?"

"Probably," she admitted. "But I don't need to know the game to cheer for Cutter, do I?"

I shook my head. "No, you definitely don't."

We took a few minutes and looked at the menu. We placed our order when the young man came back and waited for our drinks. Once we had those, I told her more about the ins and outs of the game.

Our food came and we ate, the conversation flowing easily between questions about our lives. She told me about her work at Caldwell & Crest, and I filled her in on my years playing professional ball. We talked about family, her siblings, and how she considered Miri her sister even though she had one. It felt natural, like we'd been sitting in this booth for years instead of just one night.

When we finished, I walked her outside, the winter air crisp around us. She turned to me, wrapping her arms around herself, though I wasn't sure if it was from the cold or something else.

"Thanks for dinner and the adult conversation that didn't revolve around tears and my best friend dying," she said softly.

"Anytime." I reached up, brushing a strand of hair behind her ear before she could react. Then, before she had a chance to step back, I leaned in and pressed a light kiss against her cheek. Just enough to linger, just enough to make her wonder.

When I pulled away, she stared at me for a moment, something unreadable in her eyes. Then, she smiled, a small, knowing smile that told me she wasn't as unaffected as she wanted to be.

Good.

I shoved my hands in my pockets and stepped back. "Next time, I'll teach you how to dribble."

She rolled her eyes and slid over the bench of my pickup truck. "Not if you want to win, Coach."

I definitely wanted to win . . . *her*.

Chapter 25

Antonia

I parked and stared at the hospital. It was five floors, painted in a brownish-yellow color with what I assumed would be colorful landscaping when spring arrived. The main doors and emergency room entrance were around the corner from each other, which should tell people this place was small.

Staff and visitors moved in and out, and an ambulance pulled into the bay. I watched as one paramedic got out and opened the back door, and then a stretcher appeared, along with another medic. They moved slowly, though, not in any rush to get their patient inside, and I wondered why they'd had to bring in whoever it was in the first place.

I finally resigned myself to getting out of the car and going into my temporary office. Miri was already inside, hooked up to whatever she needed so they could pump copious amounts of drugs into her body. What they ought to have done was feed her, since she hadn't eaten a meal in weeks. I got that the medicine made her sick, but not eating was making her fragile body even weaker.

How was she supposed to fight and win if she couldn't keep anything down?

"Because she isn't going to win," I said to the parked cars as I walked past.

It'd been two and a half weeks since Miri had called me in the middle of the day to tell me she was sick and that I needed to come. I'd now done two Monday mornings with groggy kids determined to make me pull my hair out because they couldn't move fast enough, despite being up on time. The constant rush of little humans was exhausting.

And yet, time was moving like molasses.

Every day, eight hours seemed like sixteen. By the time I'd dragged myself back to the house last week, I'd barely eaten dinner before tucking Nova into bed. If it weren't for people like my mom, Weston, and Mara's mom, I didn't know how I'd manage. Whoever said it takes a village to raise a family—they weren't joking. I knew I was going to have to figure things out because my mom couldn't keep coming up to Grove Hill to stay, even though she'd never tell me otherwise. She had a life and a job back home, and as much as I wanted to keep her to myself, my dad missed her.

The elevator ride to Miri's floor was slow, stopping on each floor to let people off and on. By the time we reached the fourth, we were crammed in the small box like a can of sardines. Not that I knew what a can of sardines actually looked like, but if I had to guess, this was it.

I sighed heavily when the number five lit up on the panel above and made my way to the door, barely escaping before they closed. As I walked by the nurses' station, we greeted each other like lifelong friends, and I supposed if I was going to live here, I might as well add them to my list of people.

I didn't know if I could do their job. Not only did they have to memorize all the complex medical words, but they also had to know medical procedures, lifesaving techniques, and which meds could go together, all while maintaining their decency as humans. I'd lost count of how many times I'd wanted to stay in the bathroom and cry. Their scrubs were cute, and they looked wicked comfortable, although I could never get on board with the shoes they wore.

Miri was asleep when I entered her room. I set my stuff down on the extra table the nurses made sure was in here for me and took my laptop out of my bag, only for my phone to ring. Brendan's name showed on my screen. I wanted to send him to voicemail, but it was a workday, and I felt like getting paid.

While rushing out of her room, I slipped my earbuds in and accepted the call. "This is Toni," I said, acting professionally.

"It's Brendan."

"Hi, what's up?"

"Can you do a virtual today, around three?"

This could've been an email. I tapped my screen and looked at my calendar. Cutter had practice after school, so I didn't have to rush home for him, and my mom was still here to get Nova off the bus.

"Yes, that works. My calendar should be updated for you to see."

"It is . . . but I wanted to talk to you."

"About work?"

"No, Toni. About us."

There wasn't an us anymore.

"I know you're upset with me, and I get it. Miriam's important to you, but I want you to think about what you're giving up if you decide to become guardian of her children. Nova's what, five? Do you really want to raise someone for the next thirteen years? And how will you pay for Cutter to go to college? I really want you to think about this because it affects both of us."

I saw red. Was he serious? I didn't know which tidbit to tackle first.

"Brendan, you asked if I was choosing the kids over you, and I said yes. I didn't hesitate or second-guess myself. This is where I want to be, with them, guiding them through life the way their mom would've wanted. Cutter and Nova are a part of my life and always have been. They're not going away. They need me as much as I need them. As far as us . . ." I inhaled deeply and stared out the window, into the parking lot. "My heart isn't broken because you're not in my life, Brendan. I think we haven't loved each other for a long time and were just comfortable in our relationship."

"I do love you."

"I appreciate that, but I don't love you. Not in the way you deserve to be loved, and I honestly don't see a relationship working between us. I'll always want something you can't give and wonder if you're going to bail because we don't see eye to eye on a future together. And you'll always want something I can't give, and that's my undivided attention. The kids will always have that from me. This is where my heart is."

Brendan groaned and then let out a long-exasperated sigh. He wasn't used to women breaking up with him. "See you at three," he said and hung up. I wished we could go back to the days of hearing a dial tone when someone hung up on you because that would've been better than the dead air of a failed relationship.

On my way back to Miri's room, one of the nurses told me we had visitors. I didn't know whether to thank her or cringe that she wasn't considering me a guest.

Chatter emanated from Miri's room, and I heard laughter. I needed to take more videos of her before it was too late. We were almost out of time, and I wasn't even close to being ready. I went in, with a fake smile on my face, and was pleasantly surprised to find Samira and Vera there.

"Good morning," I said to all of them. "How was your nap?" I walked over to Miri and stroked her hair. Some of it had started falling out, but we weren't to worry about that right now.

"The meds make me tired."

And sick, weak, and translucent.

"I know, sweetie." I turned to face the others. "It's nice to see you ladies."

"We're here for the deets," Samira said.

"Deets? About what?"

Vera waggled her finger at me. "Don't you dare play coy with us."

"I'm far from shy, Vera. But I do wish you'd enlighten me on these so-called deets."

"She's worse than you," Samira said to Miri.

Miri laughed, and I had the keen sense of mind to keep up whatever this was just so I could hear her laugh. I raised my eyebrow at her, hoping she could tell me what in the hell her friends were going on about.

"They want to know about your date," Miri said happily.

"What date?"

"The one with Mr. Eligible," Vera said as she fanned herself. "I've tried to set him up with my daughter, but nope. He wasn't interested. But you come to town, and our boy is smitten."

I held my hand up. "Is 'Mr. Eligible' Weston?"

"Of course he is," Vera said.

"We didn't go on a date."

"Yes, you did!" Miri blurted out. "He asked you to dinner, picked you up, and brought you back after curfew."

Vera's and Samira's mouths dropped open. I rolled my eyes and sat down with a huff.

"We went to dinner. It wasn't a date." Or was it? He'd picked me up, treated me like we were on a date, and even kissed me at the end of the night—albeit on my cheek, but still, his lips touched some part of my skin, which was close to my mouth. And I may have covered my cheek with my hand when I stared at myself in the mirror once I got home, asking myself what it meant that I could still feel his lips pressed there.

No, dinner wasn't a date, but maybe I wanted it to be.

Weston intrigued me. He was kind, he had an air of confidence about himself, he listened, and he asked questions. He knew when to show up and when to back off. Mostly, he could have any woman he wanted, and yet he was spending his free time with or around me. And Lord help me, he was sexy, in that ruggedly-handsome-in-a-flannel-but-could-rock-a-suit sort of way.

But it was more than attraction. Weston was everything Brendan wasn't, which felt mean to think. It was clear to me they'd been raised differently, and it wasn't Brendan's fault he'd grown up with entitlement. Although Weston had the same, being a former professional baseball player. His priorities were more focused on his friends, community, and the students he taught and coached. Brendan cared about his tee times and trips to Aruba.

Where Brendan avoided difficult conversations, Weston leaned into them, asking the tough questions that made you stop and think before you blurted out an answer. He listened and didn't gloss over the important things that mattered. Brendan brushed everything aside for a party.

Brendan had always been about the easy parts of life—the elegant dinners, the weekend getaways, the static companionship. But Weston, he wanted the hard stuff. He wanted to sit in hospital waiting rooms, spend his weekends fixing broken houses and hearts, and help teen boys navigate life.

It wasn't fair to compare the two. They were night and day, each with his own attributes and flaws. Weston just was the sun and moon wrapped in a shiny bow.

I swallowed hard to clear my thoughts. My feelings didn't matter because Miri and the kids were my priority. They needed to be my focus. Not the sexy neighbor.

"Did he pay?" Samira asked.

"Yes, but—"

"No buts," Vera interrupted. "That's a date, and he told Jerome, who told Lee."

"Who in the hell are Jerome and Lee?" I snapped.

"Jerome is Weston's assistant coach, and Lee owns the diner you went to the other night," Miri said, her voice growing hoarser. "Lee and Weston are good friends."

"Oh, who are we kidding: Weston is good friends with everyone in town," Samira said.

"Regardless, it wasn't a date. We talked about basketball and . . ." My cheeks flushed. I could feel them burning while these women stared at me with the same raised-eyebrow expression. I rolled my eyes and threw my hands up in the air.

"It wasn't a date," I tried to reiterate, but my voice failed me.

"He likes you," Samira said. "I can see it in his eyes when he's talking to you. He doesn't sit with just anyone at breakfast—mostly Jerome, or he takes his food to go."

"He's being a good friend," I countered.

"Or he's flirting with you," Vera said.

"Oh, he's definitely flirting," Samira said. "I see the way he looks at her during breakfast."

I shook my head and glanced at Miri for some help, but she was almost asleep again. I thought about asking Samira and Vera to leave, but I figured they needed to spend time with her, whether she was awake or not.

It'd been so long since someone had flirted with me. I honestly didn't know what to even look for. Other than Brendan, I hadn't paid attention to another man in a long time.

I bit my lower lip, now wondering how many other signs I had missed.

"He'll ask you out again," Samira said, pulling me from my thoughts.

"The timing isn't good," I told her. "Miri and the kids are my focus right now."

"Weston knows this. He wants to be there for you and the kids."

"As a friend. That's all I can take right now."

The ladies nodded, but they had a little smirk playing on their lips, and something deep down told me this conversation was far from over.

By midweek, the news wasn't good, and even though I'd expected that, it still tore me to pieces on the inside.

"Yesterday's scans show the cancer has spread," Dr. Frederick said. "It was our goal to keep the clusters contained, but we've been unsuccessful." He rested his hand on Miri's leg in what I'd come to see as a comforting gesture. For the little time I'd known this doctor, he'd had an impeccable bedside manner.

Miri and I said nothing after he'd left. What was there to be said? She already knew I was sorry and willing to do whatever I had to fight for her survival, but even the doctors in the best hospital had said there wasn't much to be done.

I crawled into bed and held Miri as she cried. She clutched my blouse, her tears wetting the fabric, while my own fell onto the top of her hair. For a moment, I thought that my tears could save her, that they held the cure she needed. But even in my own fantasy world, I knew that was too far fetched to be believable.

Hope was futile. It no longer existed. Not that it ever did, but in the back of my mind, I hoped for a miracle, for all of this to be a nightmare, for Miri to wake up and be free of this horrible disease that had festered in her body until it was too late to do anything about it.

One of the nurses came in. She smiled softly as she completed her tasks, pressing buttons, reading printouts, and preparing to inject Miri with more drugs.

"No," Miri said croakily. "I'm done."

"Miriam . . ." The nurse trailed off.

"You heard her," I said as I shook my head. "She's done."

The nurse nodded and backed away. I heard the door click closed softly.

"I want to go home," Miri said, pulling me closer. "I want to go home and be with my babies."

"Okay. I'll let them know." How those words had come out of my mouth was beyond me. I bit the inside of my cheek to hold back the body-shaking sob I felt coming on. She wanted to go home. She wanted to die in the house she had always wanted, with her children by her side. I would do whatever it took to make that happen for her, even though it was killing me on the inside.

It took me a handful of minutes to find the strength to move. I knew once I did, this would be final. Before I left her room, I glanced at my lifelong best friend—the woman who had been my one true confidant and the only one who knew absolutely everything about me—and saw her for who and what she was: a warrior.

It took a couple of hours, but Miri was discharged. While staff members got everything ready, I arranged to have someone come to the house every day from the local hospice center. Knowing or seeing Miri in pain wouldn't work for me or the kids, and I wanted her comfortable. I emailed work and told them I was taking a sabbatical. If they wanted to fire me, they could. There was no way I was taking precious time away from Miri. Then, I called my mom and cried.

When we arrived home, a few new cars were in the driveway. We walked in, both of us riddled with sadness, to find Miri's friends there.

"Welcome home," they screamed when she entered the living room. They'd surprised her with a homecoming, treating her as if she weren't coming home to die, but coming home because she was going to live.

While they embraced her, I excused myself to the kitchen, where I found my mom. Her arms wrapped around me tightly. She held me as if she was trying to absorb all my pain.

When we parted, she wiped at my tears and kissed my forehead. "There are no words to ease what you're feeling," she said softly. "But I'm here for you."

"Thanks. I just want to make sure she's comfortable and . . ." I paused when I heard Miriam laughing. "And content. Her friends are making her feel that way right now. I guess I can't be angry they're here."

"Nope, it's how they're going to grieve. While she's your beacon, she's their friend."

I nodded and stepped away. The counters and small table the kids ate breakfast at were full of food. More food than we'd be able to eat.

"Weston said there's a freezer at his house we could use," Mom said as she opened a package of paper plates. "Some of this will need to go there, and some we're going to eat now. Come on, help me put these platters on the dining room table for everyone to munch on."

"How long's this party?"

"Until they want to go home, Antonia."

More people came throughout the day, bringing flowers and gifts, which were mostly nightgowns. At first, I found that odd but then realized how comfortable and easy to maneuver they were when needed. I never would've thought to share Miri this way, but Samira had.

Throughout the day, Samira sat with me and held my hand. She comforted me in a way I didn't think was possible. She would lose a friend, too, a loss that would be felt by the entire community.

When Nova came home, she was delighted to see so many people at her house, especially her mom. I figured she didn't understand, but she'd always remember that one time people had come to her mom's party, and her mom had laughed and smiled. That's what was important.

Weston brought Cutter home, and he, too, was shocked by the number of cars parked in the driveway. I helped him carry the food to his truck.

"Thanks for storing these."

"It's no problem at all," he said as he stacked tin baking dishes in the back of his truck.

"Feel free to eat whatever."

He laughed and said he would. With the last dish settled in his truck, he shut the door and looked at me.

This was the first time I'd seen him since we'd gone out to dinner, in what I was calling a nondate, despite what the ladies had told me.

Weston was handsome; there was no denying that. He also had me by twelve years, which I'd only figured out when I was on the phone with my dad. I used this moment, away from the melee in the house and the prying eyes, to see if the women were right—was he flirting with me?

I stood there with my arms crossed, acting as if I was disinterested so he wouldn't catch me staring as I took him in. It hit me right there and then. He didn't even need to try and be sexy. He just was. He exuded charm. It was like he had it in spades. Tall, rugged, strong, and so masculine without being macho. The other night, he'd shown me he could be playful, patient, intense. This was a man who accepted a challenge and didn't back down from hard work. Weston wasn't the type to ditch out for a tee time in Miami. He was someone who gave up his weekends to help someone in need. My throat tightened as visions of his arms flexing against his tight T-shirt when he'd rebuilt the porch flashed in my mind.

He adjusted his ball cap, showing off the graying at his temples, which, if forced to admit, I found sexy.

The man in front of me exuded kindness and empathy, which showed in his warm brown eyes.

Weston winked, and I blushed, which didn't escape his notice. The smirk, slow and teasing . . . it could melt my resolve if I let it. He tilted his head in question.

I was in trouble if I didn't put my walls up.

"Sorry," I said, shaking my head. "Lost in thought."

"What about?"

If I wasn't mistaken, he stepped a smidge closer to me.

"The other night, when we went to dinner, was that a date?"

Weston's lips lifted into a smile as he tilted his head. "I'd like to consider it one."

I opened my mouth to list the reasons why it wasn't, but he held his hand up.

"I know you just came out of a long-term relationship and you're going through some very heavy stuff right now, but I can't help how I feel. Ever since you walked into the gym—what was it, almost a month ago?—I have done nothing but think about you. You're the first woman since my divorce who has sparked something within me, and that was before I even knew your name."

I didn't know what to say, except, "How'd you know I was single?"

Weston's lips went into a thin line, and then he laughed. "I believe the chain went from Miriam, to Samira, to Jerome, to me."

I rolled my eyes. "You've got to be kidding me."

He smiled and touched my hip lightly, and I found myself stepping a bit closer.

"It seems I've waited for you for this long; I can wait a little longer if you're interested. I don't even need to know if you are, but I intend to come around until you tell me to take a hike."

"I won't do that," I whispered, still unsure of where my head and heart were at.

"That's good." Weston gripped my upper arm, leaned forward, and kissed my forehead while trailing his hand down my arm until his fingers laced with mine. He squeezed my hand before letting go. "I'll see you tomorrow."

Weston hopped into his truck, started it, and backed out of the driveway, but not before giving me a little wave. As soon as he was gone, I turned toward the house and caught Miri in the window. She smiled before turning away.

Before I went in, I turned and looked down the driveway and replayed his words in my mind. Dinner had been a date, and a nice one, and the kiss, while not on my lips and unexpected, left me tingling with anticipation; even though I knew I'd see him tomorrow, my heart was ready for him to come back. Maybe I could call him with a ruse that we had more food to give him. Not that I'd need one to get him to come over.

Later, after everyone had left and the kids had gone to bed and I had Miri settled, we lay on our sides, facing each other.

"Do you want me to call your parents?"

"No, they didn't want me when I needed them, and I don't need them now. Let them read about my death in the paper."

"Okay," I said, nodding.

"Okay," she said as she closed her eyes.

Chapter 26

Cutter

Nothing can prepare you to watch your only parent die. There wasn't a class to take, but according to my guidance counselor, I could read a book. Who in the hell had time to read a book that wasn't assigned as homework? Certainly not me. Not with everything going on in my life. Between school, basketball, and watching my mother disappear from my life, reading was the last thing on my mind.

Ever since Mom decided to stop treatment, each day I woke up, wondering if she was alive or if, by some grace of God, she'd fallen asleep after Nova and I had told her how much we loved her, drifting off peacefully. Because that was what I wanted for her. To just sigh and let go, to stop fighting a winless battle, for my and my sister's sake.

We weren't going to be good after she left us, but we'd get there eventually. Toni would make sure of it, but she wouldn't be our mom, and things wouldn't be the same.

Nothing would ever be the same again.

I'd never come down the stairs and find her in the kitchen, dressed in the ratty robe I'd bought her ten years ago, or look in the stands or bleachers to see her cheering louder than any other parent.

I'd never get to hear her laugh, see her smile, or smell the perfume she loved to wear. If I'd known that this past Christmas was my last one with my mom, I would've tried to make it more special for her, but instead, I'd complained because I couldn't see Eleni.

I'd never get to hear her yell my name to take out the garbage and then tell me she loved me when I came back from doing so. How many times could I say it now so that she'd remember when she was in heaven?

And Nova—would she even remember our mom? Would she remember the way Mom's nose crinkled when she was about to sneeze or how every piece of art Nova brought home, Mom declared a masterpiece?

Would Nova remember how on rainy days, Mom liked to keep the window open just a little bit so we could hear and smell the rain while we were snuggled together on the couch, watching movies?

I knew it would be my job to remind my sister, to bring up funny stories about our mom, but what would happen after I'd forgotten? Who would remind me?

Would it be my job to put Nova's Santa presents under the tree on Christmas Eve?

I had so many unanswered questions that would never have answers because there wasn't a playbook for me to follow.

The clouds overhead didn't move, making time seem as if it were at a standstill. I stared at them from my position on the picnic table. I'd ditched class to come out here. My teacher didn't even bat an eyelash when I got up and left. What are they going to do, ask me what's wrong? Everybody knew.

"Hey," Eleni said as she climbed onto the table and lay next to me. "What are we looking at?"

"Heaven."

She reached for my hand. "My grandpa is there."

"Do you think he likes it?"

"I don't know. I'd like to think so."

"Do you think heaven looks the same for everyone?"

"I think heaven looks the way you want it to. It'll be whatever gives the person comfort."

My lips went into a fine line. I wasn't sure if she was right, but if she was, then I'd bet my mom would want heaven to look like our house, with me and Nova being as loud as possible.

"It's going to be okay, Cutter."

I let her words settle over me and wait for them to make sense. Nothing was ever going to be okay. "You still have your parents, Eleni." The last thing I wanted to do was hold that against her, but she didn't know if things were going to be okay.

"I know."

She seemed sad, and that wasn't my intent. I sighed heavily and lifted my arm so she could rest her head on my chest. "Things are going to be different."

"Is your aunt strict?"

"I don't know, but I'm worried about Nova. Just don't give up on me, okay?"

"Never, Cutter. I love you."

"I love you too."

There were things in my life that I never thought I'd experience: watching my mom fight for every breath, not being able to get up and be with me and Nova and barely able to keep her eyes open.

Each day I wondered if this would be the end, and each night, when I would lie on the air mattress in her room, I wondered if tonight was the night.

I wanted her suffering to stop, but I wanted her better. I longed for her to look at me, smile, and tell me she felt better. Deep down, I knew something like this would only happen in my dreams. That was when everything was perfect.

That was where my mom walked among the wildflowers and the sun always shone brightly.

In my dreams, she wasn't sick and dying. There she was, hugging Nova and me, and dancing barefoot around the kitchen while noodles boiled in water and pasta sauce simmered in a pot.

In my dreams, I never lost my mom. I planned to stay there as long as possible.

In my reality, my mom passed away peacefully, with Toni, Nova, and me telling her it was okay for her to leave, that we'd be okay, even though we knew we'd never be the same.

Toni promised to take care of her babies, while tears streamed down her face. Nova and I promised to love her forever. We told her how much we loved her, how she was the best mom ever, and how we'd never let her down. We had to believe heaven was real and that Mom would be watching over us until we met again.

Grandma came and got us, leaving Toni with our mom. As much as I wanted to stay, I knew Toni needed a moment by herself. They had a relationship I never understood and probably never would. Grandma held us tightly and didn't care that our tears wet her shirt.

The nurse who had been taking care of my mom made some phone calls, and people showed up. Men who I didn't know carried my mom out of our house for the last time ever and put her into the back of some nondescript car. The next time we'd see Mom, she'd be in a coffin, and people would come to visit her and say goodbye. But would she hear them?

Within an hour, people were at our house. Coach Schmidt and Coach Levy, Eleni and Flinn, Samira and Vera, and our grandpa arrived, which was a gift. He gave the best hugs.

For the rest of the day, we sat around, no one really doing anything. Nova cuddled into Grandma's side. Toni talked on the phone with a lot of people, trying to make arrangements for a funeral. Flinn, Eleni, and I sat on the porch. They didn't talk, but just sat there with me. What could they say?

Sorry?

Sorry wasn't what I wanted to hear. The word couldn't fix or change any of what had happened.

After Coach Levy left, Coach Schmidt and my grandpa went and got food for everyone. Not that we could eat, but Grandma insisted there be something for people to munch on.

They returned with food from the diner. Everyone but me and Nova ate a full meal. I picked at some chicken while Nova ate some mashed potatoes. Toni didn't eat at all.

When she left out the back door, Coach Schmidt followed, but Scout stayed with us. He was a comfort for us, and he seemed to know it. We'd talked about getting a dog a few times. It was probably a good thing we didn't because who knew if Toni liked them or not.

So much was up in the air about life now, but one thing was certain: Tonight, when I went to bed, my mom wouldn't be there. She wouldn't be there when I woke, came home from school, or scored my one-thousandth point. She was gone, and there wasn't anything I could've done about it. No amount of love would've kept her here because if that was all it took, she would've lived for an eternity.

My grandpa helped me tie my tie. He'd taught me a couple of years ago, but I'd never had an opportunity to wear one. Things were different now.

Toni explained that Nova and I would stand at the back of the church and greet people as they came in. We'd shake their hands or give them a hug, and we'd thank them for coming. She wouldn't stand with us but would be behind us if we needed her. I didn't want to do this, but according to Grandma and Grandpa, it was important for the people who were coming to pay their respects.

Everyone wore black, except me, Toni, Nova, our grandparents, aunt, and uncle. We wore purple because it was Mom's favorite color.

She wasn't a big fan of black, and I wished the people who'd come to pay their respects had worn a different color.

People shook our hands, offered us hugs, and told us how sorry they were. People lined up to greet us, to offer condolences, and to be there to mourn.

For the most part, Toni stayed where she said she would. Even as people sought her out, she stayed behind. It was like she wanted everyone to see the best of Miriam Vaughn—she wanted them to see us.

And then an older man and woman approached, and Toni was next to me, pushing Nova behind us. I had no idea who these people were, but I sensed nothing good was about to happen. Out of the corner of my eye, I saw my uncle Rocco in the doorway, looking agitated.

The woman smiled the same smile as my mom, and I knew.

"You could've called," the woman said to Toni.

Toni stood tall, and for the first time, I saw a different side of her. Her jaw locked, and she looked pissed; even when she was upset with me, I'd never seen her so rigid before. "I could've, but she didn't want you there, and I will always do as she asks of me."

"She was our daughter," the woman said through tears.

"And you've had seventeen years to apologize."

I swallowed hard as I watched the back-and-forth. While I knew who she was, the word refused to form in my mind. I knew what she had done to my mom when she found out she was pregnant with me.

The woman stepped in front of me. She took my hand in hers. "I'm your grandmother." Instantly, my eyes sought out my grandma Carmela's, and she came forward, her hand rubbing up and down my suit jacket.

"Hello, Victoria. It's been a long time," Grandma said as Uncle Rocco came over and took Nova away.

The woman tried to grin, but it was lifeless. "I just want to say goodbye to my daughter and meet my grandchildren," she said. "Certainly, we're allowed to do that?"

Grandma looked at me and then Toni before looking at the other woman. I couldn't bring myself to give her any other title.

"We'll happily talk after the service."

Grandpa came to me and guided me out of the church with Rocco, Coach Schmidt and Coach Levy, and a couple of men I didn't know who had worked with my mom. I didn't get to hear what Victoria and her husband said to Toni, but I imagined whatever she said in return probably wasn't nice.

The church doors closed, and the reverend stood there while the funeral director guided us in carrying the casket forward. My mom wasn't in there, though. She'd wanted to be cremated. Half her ashes would be buried, and she'd have a marker with her name on it. The other half would be placed in a box for us to decide what to do with. Toni said we could spread her ashes in her favorite places or have jewelry made with some of them.

The doors opened, and the reverend led everyone into the church and down the aisle. I walked behind the casket and reached for Nova's hand as soon as I stepped into the vestibule. Everything about this service was what my mom had wanted, with some additions from me and Nova. I wanted to walk and told Nova she could sit with Toni, but she wanted to walk with me.

Once Mom was placed on the pedestal, we took our seats next to Toni. All around, pictures of my mom were on easels. Nova and I were in most of them. So was Toni. But what caught me was the picture closest to us. Mom wasn't looking at the camera, but the sun. It cast her in an eternal glow, and I imagined this was how she'd gone to heaven.

The reverend spoke, but I wasn't listening. My mom came to church occasionally, but she never forced me to go. Maybe I would start as a way to get closer to her.

"To give the eulogy is Miriam's son, Cutter."

Toni patted my shoulder and gave me a reassuring nod. I stood and took my speech out of my pocket. At the podium, I cleared my throat and began.

"To you, she was Miriam. To her best friend, she was Miri. To us, she was Mom. But mostly, to all of us, she was a friend, a neighbor, 'Cutter or Nova's mom,' and rarely, 'Ms. Vaughn,' because she wanted my friends to feel welcome in our home."

I cleared my throat to fight off the tightening. Crying was something I didn't want to happen in front of these people, but it felt inevitable.

"My mom lived life with her whole heart. Her pride and joy, me and Nova, her words, not mine," I said as everyone laughed. I sought out Toni, who smiled and nodded. "We were her reason for everything. When she wasn't working, driving me to practice or Nova to the library, or coming to one of my games, she loved digging in her garden and sketching plans for the henhouse she planned to rebuild.

"She had a dream to one day own an old farmhouse and was able to make that dream come true five years ago. My mom loved our house and spent her free time remodeling each room. But the porch was her favorite place. If Nova and I couldn't find her in the house, we'd find her in the rocking chair, staring off. Watching the sunset from her porch, regardless of the weather, was something she loved."

I cleared my throat as I looked at the words of my last paragraph. "My mom was my best friend. For a while, it was just the two of us, and then Nova joined our perfect little family. We will never question whether our mom loved us because she told us every day, even on her last day. To our mom, my sister and I would like to say, 'We love you, and every day we'll continue to watch the sunset from the porch you loved so much, knowing that wherever you are, you're watching it with us.'"

I folded my piece of paper and bolted from the podium to my seat. Toni stood and pulled me into her arms for a solid hug, and then she pulled back and cupped my face.

"That was perfect," she said.

A small smile formed, and I said, "She was perfect."

Chapter 27

Antonia

The service for Miri was lovely. I had thought about saying something, telling everyone our story, but in the end, I couldn't bring myself to stand up there and look out at a sea of people dabbing their eyes. Selfishly, I didn't want to share her with people I barely knew.

The reverend finished by inviting everyone over to Miri's house. As soon as her parents had shown up, I wanted to tell him not to say anything, but something told me they'd end up finding us anyway.

While the pallbearers carried the casket toward the back of the church, Cutter, Nova, and my family followed behind. At a later date, the three of us would set Miri into the ground and cover her with the marker the kids had picked out for her. We wanted to say our own goodbyes in private.

Cutter and Nova stood by the black hearse, which would lead a procession to their home. Once the casket had been loaded, I spoke with the funeral director briefly and then sent the kids to my car.

Weston had stepped into a role I didn't know I needed—a friend, a shoulder to cry on, and a protector—and walked next to me with his hand on my lower back until we'd reached my car.

"Do you want me to drive?" he asked, his mouth close to my ear. I nodded, and he guided me around to the passenger side and held the door open for me. He checked on the kids in the back seat and then shut my door.

He slid into the driver's seat, pushed the starter, and then pressed the button for the flashers. The assistant to the funeral director pointed to where my car needed to be. Weston eased forward until he was behind the hearse.

"You did a nice job up there, Cutter," Weston said, breaking the silence.

"That was hard and uncomfortable."

"A eulogy will always be the hardest speech you write or give," I added.

"How come I didn't give one?" Nova asked.

The procession finally started, and I had to look away even though Miri wasn't in the hearse in front of us. Just the fact that we were doing this hurt.

"I'm sorry, sweetie," I said as I cleared my throat. "I didn't think you'd want to stand up there." I turned in my seat to face her. "Would you like to say something at the house when everyone is there?"

Nova nodded, but I suspected she wouldn't want to once she had everyone's attention on her. I reached for her hand and gave it a squeeze. "You did very well in church."

"It was for Mommy."

"I'm sure she was watching."

Nova's eyes roamed around the car and then looked out the window. She hadn't smiled in days, and I missed seeing it. Nova reminded me so much of Miri in the way she looked and in her mannerisms.

I relaxed against the headrest and kept my eyes on my best friend's kids—strong, resilient, and facing the hardest obstacle of their lives. I could only hope I'd live up to her expectations where her children were concerned.

"We're home," Weston said as he turned into the driveway. The hearse parked in the road until the last car of the procession had arrived, and then the director left. What a business death was.

The kids got out of the car and ran up to the house. I sat there with Weston, staring at the garage doors that either needed a great coat of paint or replacing. Either way, something had to change.

"Were those her parents?"

"Yeah," I said, not needing him to specify. "I'm torn because how shitty must it be to find out through an obituary that your only child died, but then again, how shitty do you have to be to kick your only child out of the house because she wanted to keep her baby?" I shook my head. "They never reached out. Not even to my parents to check on Miri. They didn't even know about Nova until today. The way her father looked at me and then at Nova . . . you could see it in his face. She looks identical to Miri, and I'm sure it hurt him to see it."

"Miriam doesn't want her family to have anything to do with the kids?"

I shook my head. "They didn't want her, so there's no need for them to want her children now."

Weston nodded. "I suspect they'll show up today."

"Yeah." I pushed imaginary lint off my dress.

"I don't want you to worry. Between your brother, me, and Jerome, we'll make sure the kids are safe."

I looked at him, and he smiled softly. He'd been my rock ever since Miri came home to die, always there when I needed him and even when I didn't. I didn't know how he managed to do it, but he had a knack for being in the right place at the right moment.

"People are starting to walk in," he said in the quiet. "We can go in or stay in the car. Whatever you want."

"What I want isn't possible."

He nodded, knowing from our past conversations that the only thing I wanted right now was to go back in time and catch the cancer before it got out of control.

"But I guess I need to put on a fake smile and pretend I'm happy to have everyone in her house."

Weston linked his hand with mine. "No one expects you to fake it, Antonia. Go in there and be Miriam's best friend."

That was something I could do easily.

He came around to my side and held the door open for me. Over the past handful of weeks, that was one of the things I'd noticed about Weston: He was a constant gentleman.

Inside, people lingered. They had drinks and made themselves plates of finger foods. While my mom had wanted to make everything, Lee from the Ridgeview Diner had insisted on catering. Samira had provided the family with breakfast every day since Miri passed, and Vera had taken care of the flower arrangements. It was because of Miri and how she treated people that I was able to give her a decent farewell.

I found my sister, Isabella, sitting in the corner with Nova on her lap. "Hey," I said as I approached them. "I'm happy to see you're eating." Nova gave me a one-arm shrug and swirled her celery stick in the ranch.

Isabella was a nurse and had given me valuable advice when I told her Miri was sick. Now, she was taking on the role of another doting aunt.

"Did you see who's here?"

My sister nodded. "She's in the living room. I haven't seen him yet."

A long time ago, my brother, Rocco, had joked one time that Miri's parents didn't deserve names after what they'd done to Miri. We all agreed and had collectively decided to stop referring to them by their first names.

I sighed heavily at what faced me and thanked my sister for watching after Nova. I had zero intention of seeking the Vaughns out. When they were ready to talk, they'd find me. Until then, I mingled, thanked people for coming, listened to their stories about Miri, and kept my eye on Cutter.

Thankfully, he had a strong group of friends surrounding him, but it was mostly Eleni and Flinn by his side. As soon as Cutter told his best friend his mom had died, Flinn was at the door. He'd been at the house every day since, staying by Cutter's side, even at night.

I liked that their friendship was like mine and Miri's. It gave me hope that Cutter would always have someone to talk to about anything.

I wondered if Mara would be the same for Nova or if Nova would shut down. The latter weighed heavily on my mind, and I was thankful we'd gotten into therapy. Not only as a family but individually as well.

Some people stayed for minutes, while others stayed for hours. When the house was almost empty, my mom and Samira worked in the kitchen, packaging up food we didn't need but would keep. Finger foods were great for munching on when your stomach needed something but wasn't ready for a big meal.

The last of the guests were Miri's book club friends. I walked out with them, hugged and thanked them, and told them I'd see them for the next meeting. I would go in Miri's place, at least for a little bit.

When I turned toward the house, I saw Miri's parents lingering in the yard, talking to Weston. I didn't care to know what they were speaking about. I already knew it would be about the kids or Miri.

As much as I didn't want to go over there, I did. This time, I put my hand on Weston's lower back, letting him know I was there. He didn't miss a beat, though, as he cupped my right cheek and leaned down to whisper in my left ear, "They're asking a lot of questions about the kids."

I nodded against his stubbled cheek, and a shiver went through me. There was no denying this man was gorgeous, sexy, and worthy of anyone's attention. But was I worthy of him? If Miri hadn't said anything, I would've been too blind to notice him flirting. He was subtle in his ways, and I appreciated it.

"You wanted to talk," I said very pointedly. "Talk."

"Maybe we can go inside," her father said. I glanced at the house Miri had loved so much and began to shake my head, but having this conversation outside wasn't the smartest idea.

They followed me. I scanned the living room for Nova and then my sister.

"They're napping," my mother said, as if she knew who I was looking for.

Cutter stood when he saw who was behind me. Flinn was still with him, and even he knew the heaviness of the moment.

"We're going to be at the table."

Should I have asked Cutter to go upstairs?

Maybe.

But he was less than two years away from being an adult and deserved to hear what these people had to say.

I sat at the head of the table, and my father sat opposite me, with my mom next to him. Cutter leaned against the wall, with Weston nearby. I didn't care that Weston was there and appreciated that he'd stayed.

Miri's parents took the chairs opposite my mom, which put her mother right next to me. I wanted to move, to go stand far away from them, but I stayed and clasped my hands in my lap.

It was hard to think there was ever a time in my life when I knew these people, but now they were nothing but strangers.

"I guess my first question is, Why you didn't call us?" Kenneth asked. I raised my eyebrow and cocked a look at Victoria.

"As I told your wife, Miri didn't want me to."

She made some audible but indecipherable sound and dabbed at her eyes. "Did she leave us a letter or anything?"

"No, why would she?" I asked, looking at them. "What would she say?"

"The last time we saw her, we both said some things—"

My dad interrupted Kenneth. "I believe the last time I saw you, the day I brought her over to pick up what little clothes you allowed her to take, you told her she wasn't welcome in your home."

"We only wanted what was best for her," Victoria said quietly.

"Cutter was best for her," I said, motioning toward him. "She loved him before he was even here. We all did. He didn't ruin her life. You did. You were so damn worried about your image, you never stopped to think about what you were doing to your only child. You broke her when you told her she had to choose your path. You also lost everything that day," I reminded him. "Miri succeeded despite you."

"Having a child when you're still a child is hard."

"How would you know?" my mother asked Victoria. "Did you do it?"

Victoria gasped as if she was offended. Her mouth opened to say something, but I didn't give her a chance.

"You had years to make amends," I pointed out. "You could've easily gone to my parents and asked them to get word to Miri, but you didn't."

"I was ashamed," Victoria said quietly.

Good. She should've been.

Victoria looked at Cutter and offered him a smile, which he didn't return. I watched him closely to see how he'd react to his other grandparents. He was close with mine, as they were there from the beginning, and my parents doted on him and Nova.

"We'd like to get to know you and your sister," she said to him. I'd suspected that was why they'd shown up.

Cutter said nothing at first and then blurted out, "What would you like to know?"

"We don't have a list of questions, son," Kenneth said.

Cutter turned red. "I'm not your son. Don't ever call me that."

I could swear my father smirked.

Victoria cleared her throat. "We don't live far from the Bernardis. Maybe you could come to our house and get to know us?"

"They're my grandparents," Cutter said. "We're usually pretty busy when we're at their house."

Kenneth and Victoria nodded. I didn't know if they'd expected Miri to keep what they'd done to her a secret or what. One thing was for sure: They'd underestimated Cutter.

"I think you should go." Cutter stood straight up, put his hands in his pockets, and motioned toward the door. Flinn stood right next to his best friend, as did Weston. Rocco appeared in the doorway between the kitchen and dining room. If these people didn't do as Cutter suggested, his family was going to do it for them.

"My aunt has been gracious by allowing you in our home, but I'd like you to leave," Cutter added tersely.

Victoria looked at me with pleading eyes.

"It's his house," I stated.

"We'd like visitation."

And there it was, the bomb and the outlandish request. I wanted to laugh but kept my cool.

"Of? Because Cutter's of age and can decide what he wants to do."

"Of both, obviously. But clearly, he's not amenable, so of Nova."

Nothing but rage coursed through my body as I recalled flashbacks of them yelling, screaming, and throwing things at Miri when she'd told them she was pregnant with Cutter. Their voices, laced with threats, slurs, and nothing but pure hatred for their daughter, echoed through my mind. I remembered it like it was yesterday. They'd kicked her to the curb like yesterday's trash.

These people had had no clue Nova even existed until they'd read Miri's obituary, and now they wanted visitation. To do what—brainwash her? Not on my watch.

My hands clenched into fists under the table. I bit the inside of my cheek. A habit I'd formed to keep me from crying was now keeping me from lashing out.

If they wanted to see Nova, they could prove it.

"If you can tell me Nova's birthday, I'll introduce you right now."

Everyone waited while Victoria's mouth opened and closed, like a fish looking for water.

"That's what I thought." I stood, pushed my chair in, and gripped the back. "All you had to do was apologize and accept her for who she was. That's all she ever wanted from you: acceptance."

I left the room with Weston and Cutter hot on my heels and headed out back. My parents would make sure my message was loud and clear. Cutter wrapped me in his arms, hugging me tightly.

"They can't take us, right?"

I shook my head as best I could. "No, I'll never let that happen."

First thing tomorrow, I'd reach out to the lawyer I'd hired and tell her to get the paperwork for guardianship in front of the judge as fast as possible and pray the Vaughns wouldn't push the issue any further.

If they did, I'd fight.

Chapter 28

Weston

I stayed at Miriam's until shortly after her parents left. I'd dealt with a lot of shitty parents in my time as a teacher; even as a professional athlete, I'd encountered a handful, but none of them compared to the Vaughns. I cringed at having to even refer to them with the same last name as the family I'd grown to love.

In baseball, we used to joke about the brass balls of someone, the audacity. Miriam's parents had the biggest I'd ever encountered. Who waits until their daughter has died to try and form a relationship with their grandchildren?

Kenneth and Victoria, that's who.

Honestly, I shouldn't have been surprised, especially after what Antonia had told me about them. I'd never really expected them to show up. They'd written Miriam off years ago; why care now?

Scout greeted me at the door, hungry and needing to go out. I hadn't spent much time with him today because of the service and wake afterward, but I was grateful to Jerome for coming over to check on him.

I let him out while I made his dinner, and once he'd finished, we went out back and tossed his ball. Each time I threw it, he'd return it and then wait for me to chuck it out into the yard for him. We did this until my arm got tired and Scout's tongue looked like a permanent fixture hanging from the side of his mouth.

While he drank his weight in water, I showered quickly, and then afterward, Scout and I sat on the couch and flipped through the channels.

This past week had been odd, knowing Miriam had passed away but seeing Cutter at school and practice. I had excused him from practice for the week, even though we were getting ready for our first playoff game, but he was there. He put in the time and the effort, and he did what I asked of him without quitting.

I scrolled through the online guide until I found a college game. I turned it on and leaned back, closing my eyes.

The clanging of weights startled me awake. I rubbed my face to clear the sleep away and looked at my watch. It was after eight, and I figured Cutter was in my garage, taking his anger out with some lifting.

"Some guard dog you are," I said to Scout as I stood. He didn't bother to move as I made my way toward my garage. I opened the door, surprised to find Antonia instead of Cutter.

She stood at the heavy bag, punching, slapping, and kicking it. Without saying anything, I went over and held it for her, to give her a solid, unmoving target.

Antonia screamed and hit it again and again. Tears streamed down her face as she whaled on this bag as if it had hurt her somehow.

Each hit had to hurt. She wasn't wearing gloves, and I suspected her knuckles were splitting open. But also, I imagined each blow felt good and was somehow cathartic. This was the perfect way for her to release her anger, the rage she felt inside. Her friend had left her, and no matter how well you prepared for it, the gaping wound left behind would take a lot of time to heal.

Antonia stopped. Her chest heaved, a combination of exertion and crying.

"She's gone," she said, her breathing labored.

"I know." I felt it safe to move, so I stepped out from behind the bag and reached for her hands. Her knuckles were red and likely bruised, but the skin hadn't broken. "I'm going to put some cream on them."

I went to a cabinet where I kept a Bluetooth speaker, a small refrigerator full of water and sports drinks, and every other necessity I needed when I was out there. I found the ointment and took it back to Antonia, who hadn't moved.

She looked utterly defeated. Her shoulders sagged, and she slouched. The hazel eyes that I couldn't get enough of looked lifeless.

I applied the ointment to each knuckle carefully. "You might bruise."

"I don't care."

This much I knew. After I finished, I contemplated throwing the ointment toward the counter because I didn't want to let go of her hands. Sadly, I did the right thing and walked away from her.

My timing was horrible, but that was what I got for staying out of the dating game for so long. Also, my flirting game thoroughly sucked. I'd started the second I could with her, but it had taken Miriam and the others to tell her the dinner we'd had was, in fact, a date.

Short of asking her to be my girlfriend, like the boys at school did, I didn't know what else to do to get my feelings across. She already knew I liked her, but did she understand how much? Did she know I wanted to be there for her?

Was I a fool for thinking she didn't need time to grieve her previous relationship? Probably, but patience had never been my strong suit.

I lingered at the counter, unable to face her with the myriad of thoughts running through my mind. I heard her breath hitch, a choked sob escaping before she could stifle it.

The sound shattered me.

I turned just as her legs gave out, her body crumbling to the floor. I was there before she hit the ground, my arms wrapping around her, pulling her against my chest. She trembled violently, her fingers clutching at my shirt as though she were drowning and I was her only lifeline.

"She's gone," she whispered, her voice breaking, raw with agony. "I don't know how to do this without her. I've never done this life without her."

Her pain was palpable, suffocating. I held her tighter, my fingers threading through her hair as I rocked her gently, murmuring words of comfort that felt hollow even to my own ears. I wanted to take her pain away, to breathe life back into those hazel eyes that still looked so vacant.

She looked up at me, her face streaked with tears, eyes searching mine as if trying to find something to anchor herself with. Her gaze dropped to my mouth, lingering.

Time stood still. I could feel the thud of my heartbeat, heavy and insistent, as she leaned up, her lips brushing mine softly at first, a question, a plea.

And then she kissed me again, harder, her fingers tangling in my hair, pulling me closer. Her desperation was palpable, a storm crashing through her, and I was caught in its wake, powerless to resist.

"Antonia . . ." Her name came out as a rasp, half a plea, half a warning, but she silenced me with her mouth, her lips insistent, bruising. Her body pressed against mine, warm and trembling, her need igniting something fierce and primal inside me.

"Please, Weston. Help me forget."

I lifted her, her legs wrapping around my waist as I carried her to the padded bench, never breaking the kiss. Her fingers slid under my shirt, her touch hot and urgent, her nails dragging across my skin, leaving trails of fire in their wake.

She needed this—needed me. And I was powerless to deny her.

I laid her down, my body pressing against hers, fitting perfectly, like she'd been made for me. Her back arched, a breathless moan escaping her lips as I kissed my way down her neck, tasting the salt of her tears. Her skin was soft, electric. Every touch, every movement a spark that threatened to consume us both.

Her fingers gripped my shoulders, holding on like she was afraid to let go. Her hips moved against mine, a desperate rhythm that shattered my restraint. I groaned, my mouth finding hers again, our kisses fierce and consuming, tongues tangling as we lost ourselves in each other.

She was fire and need, raw and beautiful in her vulnerability, and I wanted to give her everything, to take away her pain, even if only for a moment.

Our clothes fell away, piece by piece, barriers dissolving as skin met skin, hot and slick. Her body arched beneath mine, her breath ragged, her eyes locked on mine, pleading, needing.

I whispered her name, my voice breaking, my hands caressing every curve, every hollow, memorizing the feel of her, the taste of her. She responded with a fierceness that took my breath away, her body moving with mine, meeting every thrust, every touch with an intensity that left me reeling.

We moved together, a perfect, desperate rhythm, her nails digging into my back, her cries muffled against my shoulder. She shattered in my arms, her body trembling, her name a broken whisper on my lips as I followed her over the edge.

For a moment, there was nothing but the sound of our breathing, our hearts pounding in sync, our bodies tangled together. I held her close, my fingers brushing through her hair, whispering words of comfort, of promise.

She buried her face in my neck, her tears dampening my skin as she clung to me, her body shaking with silent sobs. I tightened my hold, vowing to never let go, to be her anchor, her safe place. I could never replace Miriam, but I could be Antonia's next person.

I kissed her forehead, her cheeks, her swollen lips, whispering her name like a prayer. "I've got you, Antonia. I'm not going anywhere."

She sighed, her body softening against mine, her fingers tracing circles on my chest. "I need to go." Antonia moved away and walked across my gym. As much as I wanted to watch her every move, I didn't because I needed to brace myself for what she would tell me next.

Reluctantly, I turned to face her. She was focused on putting the rest of her clothes on.

"Antonia?" Her name came from my lips softly and probably with a hint of desperation.

"I'm sorry, Weston."

I nodded and looked at the ground. "There's nothing to be sorry for. I'm a big boy. I knew the consequences."

Unable to continue to sit there, I stood and grabbed my shorts off the floor. I slipped them on and went to the refrigerator, then grabbed two bottles of water. I took one over to Antonia and then retreated to my corner, giving her space.

She wiped at the tears that still fell. As much as I wanted to comfort her, I couldn't. I didn't think my heart could take the rejection. At least not today. Today, she had been through the wringer, being there for a friend's last life celebration, and now this. From the day I saw Antonia across the court, I'd wanted to be with her. Now that I had, it wasn't enough. I wanted more. I wanted her. I'd known it from the first time I saw her.

I should've said no because she wasn't in the right frame of mind. Because her need for me was out of grief. Having sex with her was a way of helping her forget her pain and not remembering me.

I should've said no.

"Did you drive down?"

"No, I walked," she said as she shook her head.

"I'll drive you back."

"That's not necessary."

I finished the bottle of water and crushed the thin plastic into a ball. "It's not safe at night," I told her. "The kids drive up and down the road at high rates of speed, and there isn't anywhere to step off the side of the road."

She looked at me, and I hoped she understood the message—the kids had already lost their mom; they couldn't lose her too.

Antonia finally nodded. "Thank you."

"I'll grab my keys." I went inside, grabbed a sweatshirt, and went into the kitchen to get my keys. When I came around the corner, Antonia was sitting on my couch, and Scout had his head in her lap. I stood there, resting against the archway.

"Did your wife live here?"

"No. I bought this house after the divorce. She's been here, though, and helped me decorate."

"Are you one of those men who has throw pillows on their bed?"

I couldn't help but laugh. "Nah, although when I was married, we did. It would take five minutes just to crawl into bed. Do you have them?"

She met my gaze and smiled. "Full disclosure, I pile them on the free side of my bed."

"Smart thinking."

This easiness between us was nice, despite the awkward encounter in the garage, and I wished she could see that we had something between us. I also wished she could see how well she fit in my house, even though her ever being here longer than a handful of minutes would be unlikely. She was now a single mom of two.

When she didn't move from the couch, I asked, "Would you like a tour?"

"That would be nice." Antonia stood, and I spread my arms out. "This is the living room."

She laughed, and it was music to my ears.

I showed her the kitchen and the dining room, then walked down the hall to the first bathroom, the spare bedroom, which was used mostly by my parents, and finally my room. I'd never been more thankful that my mom made me clean my room and make my bed every day when I was young. I would've been rather embarrassed if my underwear was on the floor.

"Do you read?"

"I do. Mostly conspiracy-type stuff and wartime books. You?"

"Romance," she said. "I've been meaning to start a library at my place but never got around to it. Maybe I'll do it at Miri's."

"Come here, let me show you something."

We walked down the hall to my office. I opened the door and flipped the light on. Both walls had built-in bookshelves. One side was nothing but novels, while the other side held my trophies, baseball memorabilia, and some news articles I had framed.

"Wow."

"These were here when I bought the house. As soon as I saw the room, I knew I'd buy this house."

"You really were famous," she said as she looked at my baseball collection.

"I was something."

She went to the bookshelves and trailed her finger along the spines.

"Help yourself," I told her. "I have a very easy library system."

"Yeah, what's that?"

I shrugged. "Just tell me which one you're borrowing, and I'll try to remember."

Antonia laughed again. I liked hearing it, but deep down, I knew she didn't want to be here. Not in the way I wanted her here.

I held my keys up. "Are you ready?"

She nodded, and I turned toward the door, only for her to reach for my hand. "What happened—"

"Please don't say it was a mistake."

"Okay, I won't." She took a deep inhale. "But it probably shouldn't happen again for a while."

My heart sang with anticipation. A while wasn't never, and I could live with that.

Chapter 29

Antonia

After dropping a capful of bubble bath into the filling claw-foot tub Miri had in her bathroom, I undressed and stared at my naked body in the mirror.

What I'd initiated with Weston was very out of character for me. I couldn't recall the last time I had done something so brazen and reckless. It was one thing to be impulsive, to live in the moment, but to use a man I knew liked me for sex was something I never should've done.

Except, I enjoyed it and wished the circumstances had been different, because I couldn't tell whether my heart was there with him or if it was my emotions getting the best of me.

Regardless, leading him on wasn't an option.

Neither was forgetting.

We'd crossed a line, and it was going to define us moving forward. I knew we'd have to talk about it, because burying it under the rug and acting like it never happened wasn't the way to live.

My fingers trailed down my neck, ghosting along the marks his stubble had left. I welcomed the sting that came with the roughness, showing me that I was truly alive in the moment and not lost in my grief.

The path of red skin continued over my collarbones and breasts, bringing the vision of him holding me, his head on my heart, while I took advantage of him. He'd let me use him, likely knowing my head wasn't right.

"So get it right, Toni. Nothing is stopping you."

Miri had created a little oasis for herself in her en suite bathroom. She'd painted the walls mauve, added white beadboard halfway up, and wallpapered one wall with pink, yellow, and blue flowers.

She had removed the stand-up shower and replaced it with a claw-foot tub she'd found online or at a resale store. My dad and brother had installed it while Miri put in new tiles.

This was where she'd come to relax at the end of the night. Where she'd soak away the bad and soak in the good.

Before I slipped into the aromatic water, I lit the candles in the corners, turned my music app on, and connected my phone to the speaker.

The hot, bubbly water danced over my skin. I closed my eyes, rested against the cushion, and sighed heavily. A nice bath at the end of the night was something I could easily get used to. My penthouse had a stand-up, two-person shower, and my bathroom lacked life. There was nothing romantic or even friendly about the space, unlike Miri's.

Opening my eyes, I took in the room again. Of all my times in here, I'd never thought of the bathroom as romantic, but it was. This was where you and your lover spent time together, washing away the negativity of the day so you both went to bed with a clean heart and mind.

I closed my eyes again and imagined Brendan at the other end of the tub, but he wasn't there because Brendan would never get into a bath. He would've balked and said soaking in a tub was a waste of time.

Weston was there, though, with his arms resting along the top of the white tub. He had a devilish smile across his lips and his eyes on mine. He'd put his heart on the line for me tonight when he didn't have to. He didn't need to do most of the things he'd done since I arrived in town, but he'd done so because he was a good man.

"A good man who wants to spend time with you, knowing you now have two kids," I said aloud.

"Because he likes you." Miri's words filtered through my mind. I relaxed at the sound of her voice. My tears were instant, falling freely down my cheeks and into the water. My already-broken heart chipped a bit more, knowing I'd never hear her talk to me again or see her smile. How everything between us was nothing but a one-sided memory. There had always been her version and mine, but now I'd only have ours—the way I remembered every moment of our life, friendship, sisterhood.

Promise me you'll find love.

My eyes shot open. Those were the last words from her. Miri always loved making me promise to do things for her and holding me accountable. But this time was different. She wanted me to be happy and knew deep down that Brendan wasn't the one to do that. She could always see he was a temporary fixture in my life. Looking back, I would've liked to see this as well because I probably wouldn't have given him four years of my life.

My last words to her, the ones before she closed her eyes and waited for death to come, were "I promise I will."

Yet another promise I'd made to her and wouldn't be able to bring myself to break.

The ringtone on my phone shrilled, the sound echoing off the bathroom walls, startling me. I reached for a hand towel to dry my hands and then for my phone. Weston's name appeared on my screen, and I froze. This wasn't a text message but a phone call. He wanted to speak to me. My index finger hovered over the screen, waiting for me to make up my mind.

On what was surely the last grating sound, I finally swiped to answer. "Hello?"

"Hi, Antonia. It's me, Weston."

I smiled at the corniness and felt sort of giddy that he would introduce himself.

"Hey. What's up?"

Weston sighed. "I didn't want to go to bed without clearing the air."

"Oh?"

"What happened with us tonight . . ." he started, and I felt my heart drop. In the lack of afterglow, thanks to me moving away from him right away, I wanted to tell him that we shouldn't have done that, but instead I'd told him we couldn't do it again for a while because I wasn't ready to shut the door on him yet. Although I didn't figure that out until after I'd said what I said.

Weston sighed again. "I know you're going through the unthinkable right now, as well as having a recent breakup, but I wanted to be clear about how I feel. Tonight, I should've walked away, but I couldn't. Mostly out of fear I would hurt you. Instead, I took a chance, knowing damn well the odds were not in my favor. I like you, Antonia. A lot. And I don't plan to stop or go away until you tell me to take a hike."

His words, while a bit all over the place, put a grin on my face and gave me a smidge of hope, longing, and desire, but I suspected that was a holdover from earlier.

"Weston, I like you, too, but my thoughts and feelings are jumbled right now. I can't tell if the tears I want to cry now are because of Miri or because, while I should have regrets about what we did—"

"Antonia—"

"No, let me finish. I want to get this out while I have an ounce of courage in me. I don't even know you, not really. I thought I knew Brendan after four years, and I was completely wrong about who he was when things got tough. You've stepped up when you didn't have to. I don't have regrets about what we did, but at the same time, I don't know if it's because I'm broken or because I'm falling for you."

"Definitely the latter," he said, laughing softly, trying to lighten the mood. After a pause, he said, "You can trust that I'm not going anywhere. I'm not Brendan. When things get tough, I don't run. I fix porches and drive kids to tournaments and sit in hospital waiting rooms. That's who I am. I'm not going to pressure you into anything.

That's not the type of person I am. But I will be there, basking in your presence, because while you may not see it right now, being near you is the missing piece to my life."

Honest to goodness, that was probably the best compliment I'd ever received from a person, especially a man.

"I don't know what to say."

"You don't have to say anything, Antonia. They're my words, and I mean every single one. From the moment I saw you, I knew you were going to be someone special in my life. By my side was how I saw you, us standing next to each other as we blaze a path through this world, and if there's one thing I know about myself, it's that when I set my mind to something, I usually achieve it."

"You seem rather sure of yourself."

Weston let out something that sounded like a cocky, self-assured chuckle.

"I'm sure of this," he said. "The way we effortlessly connected. The way we fit together, how we didn't fumble around each other. I'm patient. I'll wait for you to catch up."

"And if I don't?"

"Then you don't, and I'm still your friend. I'm still the guy who will come fix porches and drive kids to tournaments and sit in hospital waiting rooms, because that's what friends do."

"I definitely need friends."

"You have them. Think about what I said. You're not alone in this. Good night, Antonia. Thank you for a very memorable evening."

"Thank you for mine," I said and hung up before I could add anything more embarrassing. I wasn't used to having a man bare his feelings this way. Brendan never told me he liked me without me asking if he did. I told him I loved him first. We rarely compromised on anything. The more I thought about him and our relationship, the more it became clearer that I'd been with him for the wrong reasons, and he'd been with me for . . . who the hell knew.

The water turned cold, and my thoughts never wavered from Weston and our moment together. I finally rinsed off, got out, and, once dressed, I snuck to the kids' rooms to check on them.

At Nova's room, I carefully turned the knob to open her door. She lay in her bed, with my mom's arms wrapped tightly around her. The first couple of nights after Miri's death, Nova had woken up screaming in the middle of the night. While this sleeping situation worked for now, my mom would go home tomorrow. Something told me Nova would end up crawling into my bed.

I walked to Cutter's door, pressed my ear to it, and heard noises coming from his phone. A phone that wasn't allowed in his room. I knocked softly, and the sound muted as I heard him say, "Come in."

"Hey," I said as I motioned toward the phone on his bed. "That's not supposed to be in here."

Cutter stood and handed me his phone. "Do you think we can revisit some of the rules we have in place?"

"Sure, with the understanding I may keep and alter them to my liking, and possibly add my own."

He plopped against his bed. "Okay."

"Can I come in?"

He lifted his head and looked at me, then sat up. "Yeah."

I pushed the door toward the doorjamb but didn't close it. Cutter's desk faced the mural of a baseball field he and Miri had painted on his wall. I pulled out the chair that was tucked under it, removed the pile of clothing, and sat.

"How are you doing?"

He nodded and then shrugged. "I keep telling myself she's on vacation, that she's coming home, but then I remember, she's not."

"I know what you mean. I wanted to talk to you about your grandparents."

"What's wrong with Grandma and Grandpa?" Cutter's eyebrows rose.

"My bad," I said with a heavy sigh. "Kenneth and Victoria."

Cutter rolled his eyes. "I don't know why they showed up."

"Me neither." Except if I had to guess, it was because they wanted to save face with their friends. *We tried,* was what they'd go back and say to their church friends. "But they did, and they'd like to get to know you and Nova."

"What if I don't want to know them?"

"I'm going to say some adult crap that may or may not make sense, but it needs to be said because I don't want how I feel or how your mom felt about them to influence your decisions. If you don't want to know them, then you don't have to. And if you do or if you want Nova to, then we do it on your terms, but I want you to think about it. Right now, we're raw. We're broken, and we're hurting. Sometimes decisions like this, made when we're feeling our worst, aren't made with a full heart."

"What does that even mean?"

I don't freaking know.

"It means, if at some point you or Nova decide you want to, you dictate the time, place, and how much of a relationship you want with them. If it's nothing, then it's nothing. I will support you one hundred percent. If it's something where you want them to come for lunch one day, so be it; we'll have lunch." I leaned forward, closer to him. "What I'm saying is, you set the rules."

"Will they try and take Nova away from us?"

This, I didn't know, but I suspected they might try. "I hired a lawyer before your mom died. Her will states I'm the sole guardian of you and Nova. No one can take you away from me, except the judge, and he's going to see how much we love each other and rule in our favor. He may ask you some questions."

"If he asks if your feet stink, I'm going to say yes."

I lifted my foot and wiggled my toes.

Cutter batted my foot away and laughed. Damn, it sounded nice.

"Can *he* take us away?"

Cutter didn't have to elaborate on who "he" was. I knew. I shook my head. "I'd move heaven and earth for you and Nova. Remember that. Get some sleep. Tomorrow, we'll take it easy because on Monday, you're playing in a very important game."

"I think basketball is the only thing keeping my head straight."

"Well, it's a good thing baseball starts right away; otherwise, someone might have to knock your melon straight."

"Har, har," he said.

"Good night, Cutter," I said when I got to the door. "I know I'm not your mom, and shit's going to get rough at times, but never for a second doubt that I love you as if you were my own." I pulled the door open and stepped into the hallway.

"Toni?"

"Yeah?" I peeked my head in.

"It hurts, knowing my mom is never coming back, but I'm thankful for you, because I couldn't imagine losing my mom and ending up in foster care or with grandparents who never cared to know us. So, thank you for being our person."

Words escaped me. I went back into his room and pulled him into my arms. Before I left, I kissed the top of his head and told him I loved him, and then left before he could see me crying.

I closed Miri's door for the night, not wanting to be in there without her, and made my way to the couch. I could've taken the guest room, but my parents were using it.

The last thought I had before I closed my eyes was about Weston and whether I'd see him in the morning for what had become our weekly walk to the Cozy Cup Café. I hoped I would.

Chapter 30

Weston

As soon as I hooked Scout's leash to his collar, he pulled me toward the Vaughns' house. Did I need to refer to the location differently? What an odd thought to have as I walked down the road. It was still Cutter's residence, and he was a Vaughn. At least for right now.

This morning was a crapshoot. Every weekend since Antonia arrived, we'd ended up walking to the café at the same time. Although the purpose of my walk was to get some exercise, while hers was to eat one of Samira's damn pastries. I couldn't say I blamed her, though. I'd had my fair share and found it extremely hard to deny myself the luxury.

As we neared the house, I felt a little trepidation start to build. What if Antonia wasn't outside? It wasn't like we had a standing reservation to meet each other at the end of the driveway. But I was hoping.

It took a couple of yards before Scout finally fell in step beside me. It wouldn't last long, though, as he'd grown accustomed to hanging out at Cutter and Nova's. I liked that he'd taken on the role of protector and therapist for them—especially for Nova. I was a grown-ass adult, and my parents were still alive. I couldn't even begin to imagine how Nova was feeling.

As we neared, I saw a figure at the end of the driveway, and without a single thought, a smile formed. Scout must've seen her as well because he began to pull on his leash more. I let him go and watched my dog sprint to the woman who had captivated me so easily just by being at the game.

I ran the rest of the way.

When I reached Antonia, she looked up at me and smiled before turning her attention back to Scout. Right then, I knew I would pursue this woman until she told me to back off. She could've stayed home, forgotten about our unspoken Sunday morning breakfast after what had happened, but she hadn't. She was there, putting in the effort in her own way, to show me she wanted to spend the morning with me. The urge to kiss her was overwhelming. It felt like I had a high school crush all over again, with sweaty palms and a palpitating, out-of-control heart.

Still crouched and petting my dog, she looked up at me. "Would you be okay with Scout staying with Nova while we go to breakfast?"

It didn't escape my notice that she considered our Sunday morning trip to the café a date. Although the word "date" probably wasn't what this was called.

"Of course. Is she okay?"

Antonia stood, and as she did, she shrugged one shoulder. "The nights are rough, and my parents are leaving today. I thought if she had someone or something to focus on while they packed their car, she'd be okay."

"I don't think Scout minds as long as I bring him a doughnut."

"We'll bring him two," she said to my dog as she made kissy faces at him. Antonia started toward the house, with Scout following behind. She looked over her shoulder at me.

"Are you coming?"

"Yeah." I couldn't recall the last time I'd moved so damn fast. I was by her side instantly, holding the screen door open for her.

Inside, the house was the same, yet it wasn't. I expected the house to be quiet, filled with mourning, but the television was on, there were voices in the kitchen, and a half-dressed teenage boy thundered down the stairs.

"Morning, Coach."

"Good morning, Cutter."

He walked into the living room and fell onto the sofa. Nova came in seconds later and crawled onto his lap. Behind her, a blanket dragged along the floor, and Scout, with his nose to the ground, looked for a morsel she might've dropped on her way to the couch.

Cutter enveloped her in his arms and brought her blanket up to his chest, tucking it under her head. To my horror, Scout jumped onto the couch and rooted his body right next to Cutter's. Instantly, his arm went around my dog.

"Scout!"

"He can stay," Antonia said as she came into the room. She kissed Nova's forehead and said something to Cutter before turning toward me. "Scout's okay on the couch, unless it's something you don't want him to do."

"No, he gets on mine at home. I don't know where his manners went."

"Mr. Coach, Scout tooted in the kitchen. He doesn't have any manners," Nova said, giggling.

I laughed as well. "Nova, you can call me Weston."

"Did you hear that?" she said as she looked at Cutter. "I get to call him Weston. Not you."

Cutter shook his head. "It's okay. That'll be something special between you and Coach."

His words made my eyes misty. Cutter was such a good boy with a steep hill to climb.

Antonia opened the front door, and I followed her out. We walked side by side, our arms brushing often as we made our way to the café. We made idle chitchat and paused to let the sun warm our faces.

Inside the café, Samira came around to hug Antonia as if she hadn't seen her in months and not hours. "Breakfast is on the house today."

"Absolutely not," we said in unison.

Samira waved our words away. "My place, my rules."

I shook my head as we stepped up to the counter. We ordered our usual, plus a bag of doughnuts to go. We took our coffees to the same table as before and sat down.

"How'd you sleep?"

Antonia blushed.

Was it because of me?

"Honestly, for sleeping on the couch, pretty well. I was oddly relaxed when I fell asleep."

Was she relaxed because of me? I couldn't keep the thought out of my head, even if I tried. I smirked but looked away, hoping she didn't see me.

Suddenly, my coffee cup was really important. I lifted it, took a drink, and then asked, "Why are you sleeping on the couch?"

"My parents were in the guest room and . . ." She took a deep shuddering inhale. "I don't know how I feel about sleeping in Miri's room without her there. Granted, I did use her amazing tub, but that room was her sanctuary, and . . ." Antonia trailed off.

"I get it," I said. "After Brianna left, I couldn't sleep in the bed we'd shared. Everything smelled like her, which made the pain worse."

Antonia's eyes found mine. "Do you think keeping the house is a smart idea?"

I nodded but then wondered if I was being selfish. At first, I hated the thought of losing Cutter. Now, the idea of losing Antonia twisted my guts into a pretzel. She had a life in Boston, likely a much flashier and more entertaining one. The small-town life wasn't for everyone, and I greedily wanted her to stay.

She gazed out the window and sighed. "That's Miri's house. It was her dream. Her blood, sweat, and tears. Not to mention, it's a damn money pit, and I think it needs a new roof." Antonia sighed. "Selling makes sense. It would put money in a college fund for the kids."

"But . . ."

Antonia inhaled and sat up straighter. "But it's their home and their connection to their mom. I have the finances to keep it, do the repairs, and make it into the home she thought it would be. I also have a penthouse in the city. I'm either going to have to sell or rent it out because paying for both seems like a bad financial decision."

"Where's your penthouse?"

"On the wharf. I have amazing views, but the tourists in the summer can be an issue."

"And you live there by yourself?" I hadn't asked much about her relationship—well, previous relationship.

Antonia smiled softly. "Yes, which is why the breakup was so easy. We weren't moving in together anytime soon. I think at most, we have a toothbrush at each other's places."

Phew.

"I imagine you do well at your job, but without prying too much, are you able to afford both?"

She nodded. "I bought my place for a very good deal a few years back, and I went to school on a scholarship, so I was able to double up payments." Antonia sighed. "Maybe I keep it and it's a place for us to stay on the weekends or for vacations. As it is, I need to be in Boston for work at least twice a week and will need a place to stay."

"That'll save on hotel expenses for sure."

"Yeah." She picked her cup up and took a drink.

Samira brought our food over, along with two fresh cups of coffee. "Sorry about the delay. Where's Scout?" she asked.

"He stayed with the kids this morning."

"Well, I put a doughnut hole in the bag for him."

"Thank you. He'll be sure to stop by and thank you later."

Samira left us, and we started eating, our conversation pausing.

"Do you still love your ex-wife?" Antonia asked mid-bite. I choked at her question.

I pounded on my chest with my fist, clearing the clog, and then drank some water to hopefully guide my food down the right pipe.

"Sorry," she said as she took a bite of the applewood-smoked bacon. "I shouldn't have blurted that out while you were eating."

"No, it's fine. It just caught me off guard." I took another sip and cleared my throat. "The answer is yes."

"Oh."

I shook my head. "Not in the way you may think, though. Brianna and I were high school sweethearts, stayed together through college, and married after she graduated. Part of me thinks if I hadn't been injured, we'd still be married. This life"—I spread my arms out—"wasn't for her, but that doesn't mean I stopped loving her. But I'm not in love with her, and I haven't been for quite some time. We're friends. Nothing more."

"Well, that's good to know."

I couldn't help but smile. "Why's that?"

Her right shoulder lifted as she picked at her food. She looked at me with a sneaky little grin on her lips. "I don't make it a habit of spending time with men who are in love with other women."

I held my hands up and shook my head. "I only have my eyes and intentions set on one person, Antonia."

She ducked her head, but not before I saw her smile grow wider. When she finally looked up, she said, "You'll be patient?"

"As a saint," I said, winking.

We finished breakfast and walked back to the house. Cutter, Nova, and Scout were in the same spot on the couch as they were when we'd left. Nova perked up, then scrambled off the couch when Antonia held up the bag of doughnuts.

"Gimme," she said as she took the bag to the kitchen, with Scout following behind to catch any morsel she left for him. Antonia followed her into the kitchen, leaving me in the hall with a conundrum. Go sit with Cutter or trail behind the girls into the kitchen. I heard Carmela in the kitchen and made my choice.

"Mind if I sit?"

Cutter shook his head and adjusted so he wasn't sprawled out. He turned the volume down on the TV.

"What are you watching?"

"Recaps from yesterday's college games."

"Almost time for March Madness."

"Best time leading into spring," he said, laughing. "Outside of baseball season."

I laughed right along with him. "I know we have one basketball game left, but since you brought it up, I'd like to start throwing on Wednesday," I said to him. "This gives you one day to do nothing. I know it's not a lot of downtime, but I'd like to work on your curve before the season starts."

Cutter had a hint of excitement in his eyes. "What about the weight room?"

"Next week. Aside from throwing, we'll give your body a rest."

Cutter nodded toward the other room. "Did you talk to Toni about summer ball?"

"I did. Everything's taken care of for basketball and baseball."

"That's good. I really need to try for a scholarship."

With that statement, I made a mental note to reach out to some of my colleagues and see what I could do to get Cutter some looks. It'd been on my mind for a while, and there was no better time to act than now. Cutter and Malik, regardless of his situation, deserved a shot to play in college, and if I could help in some way, I would.

"You're right," I told him. "With the schedule Coach Levy and I have come up with, you'll be in front of scouts at most of the basketball tournaments. You know I can put you there, but it's up to you to show them what you can do."

"Now more than ever, I need to prove myself," he said. "Thanks, Coach."

"My pleasure. Now, let's watch this recap," I told him. "I need to see where my teams line up."

Cutter turned the volume up, and we sat there watching ESPN replays of NFL recaps.

Chapter 31

Antonia

The small arena where the state championship game was being played was packed shoulder to shoulder with fans, spectators, and family members. My parents, Nova, and I had an in through Weston and were able to have reserved seats.

The mood among us was somber, though. Miri should've been here to see her son in the biggest game of his life. Her absence weighed heavily on me and made me feel like I had failed her somehow, even though I knew I hadn't.

The game came a week after Miri's passing. I'd kept a watchful eye on Cutter, looking for any signs he wouldn't be able to compete tonight, but he seemed solid, which also scared me because I was sure he was hurting.

We were all hurting.

Nova wore her heart and pain on her sleeve. She moped, cried, and barely slept, which meant I'd barely slept. Her bed was tiny, and taking her to the guest room with me was something my mom had advised against. She didn't want Nova to get into the habit of sleeping with me. Each nightmare, I went in, read her a story, and rubbed her back until she fell back asleep. She now had a night-light, something she hadn't had before, and slept with her door open, which meant Cutter had to be extra quiet when he came home or moved about in his room.

My dad had made signs for Cutter and passed one to each of us. We all wore basketball shirts with Cutter's name on them—anything to show our support. Thankfully, in the week since Miri's death, her parents hadn't called, although I was fully expecting them to be a thorn in my side. They'd have to understand that their relationship with Cutter and Nova was strictly up to the kids. I would only intervene when Cutter asked or when I felt lines were being crossed.

Nova and my mom climbed the bleachers to our seats, carrying bags of popcorn and a stack of hot dogs. Nova declared that hot dogs from concession stands were the best; otherwise, she didn't want to eat them. I took her word for it.

The boys came out to begin warm-ups, and my dad was the first one to stand up and start cheering for them. He clapped, pursed his lips in a loud, ear-splitting whistle, and pointed at Cutter. Other parents followed with their own jubilation.

"Cutter!" Nova yelled each time he came somewhat close to the half-court line. According to Weston, we were at the end where the boys would shoot in the second half. All the terminology made me feel a bit out of place. Weston and Cutter had promised to teach me everything I needed to know by next season, but first, they were going to teach me baseball, since that started next week.

According to Cutter, I needed to know when to cheer, when not to throw my popcorn, and when to pace. I'd seen Miri pace a lot during the games where Cutter pitched, and he said I needed to do the same, or he might not be able to get the ball across the plate.

Something told me I was being bamboozled, but whatever. If he needed me to walk back and forth like his mother had, I'd do it. Anything to make this life easier.

Weston came out after the boys, followed by Jerome, whom I'd learned was his best friend. Weston looked across the court, and despite the number of people in the stands, I told myself he was looking for me.

With that thought, my body warmed. Ever since that night in his garage, whenever he was near, my body reacted in the most pleasurable way. The heat his presence brought out in me was unexpected and now welcomed.

I gave him a little wave, in hopes he was looking for me. He waved back, and my cheeks flushed.

"Auntie, Weston is waving!" Nova's little arm went back and forth in rapid succession. He waved again, and she grinned widely. "Can Scout come over later?"

Scout had been a godsend for these kids. And, if I was being honest, for me as well. There was something so soothing about him. It was like he'd been trained to be a therapy dog, when in reality, he was just a caring soul who knew when people needed him.

"We'll see what's going on after the game," I told her.

"I believe Lee is hosting the boys for dinner," my dad said.

"Lee?"

He nodded. "Lee owns the Ridgeview Diner."

"Yeah, I know who Lee is, Dad. How do you know Lee?"

My father looked at me strangely, as if I had three heads. He then tilted his head to the side and shook it slightly. Clearly, I had missed something during my mourning over Miri.

"I worked with him on catering."

My mouth formed into an "Oh," and I looked away, embarrassed. "Yeah, makes sense."

"Anyway, he's having the boys and their families there after the game. So, we're either celebrating a win or taking home second place."

"Regardless of the outcome, as long as he plays well, that's all that matters." I motioned toward Cutter, who was in the middle of the court, stretching. "I really don't want him to go out there and not have his thoughts on the game. He's worked very hard for this."

"He'll be fine," Dad said. "Weston's a good coach. If Cutter isn't playing to his ability, he'll give him a rest. You have to trust Cutter and his coach."

"I know." Except I truly didn't. I didn't know how he was out there, acting like everything was okay. I could barely function or make a decision. Of course, it probably didn't help that Brendan had been pushing for me to come back into the office, despite me taking a sabbatical.

The buzzer sounded, and both teams jogged to their benches. The announcer started and said things about the state, the community, and how parents needed to let the coaches coach, players play, and the referees ref. According to Cutter, most of the refs in the state were blinder than a blind bat, which equated to them missing a lot of calls. I pretended to understand.

The opposing team was announced, and then it was the Timberwolves' turn. My heart began racing, and I was suddenly anxious. Selfishly, I wanted Cutter to have the best game of his career, because I knew Miri was looking down on him, and as soon as I had that thought, I wanted to take it back because then Miri would be here to see her son play in this game. She would've been so damn proud just to hear his name called.

For some reason, I stood as the boys' names were announced. When the announcer said "Cutter Vaughn," I screamed as loud as I could while tears streamed down my face. Miri should've been here to witness this.

Cutter slapped hands with his teammates, then with the three officials, and when he got to the opposing coach, he pulled Cutter into a hug and patted his back. Cutter ran to center court, where the other starters were, and pointed to the ceiling, and then he looked in my direction. I didn't know what to do, so I placed my hand over my heart.

Everyone stood for the national anthem, and then it was game time.

The next thirty-two minutes of playing time were the most anxious and agonizing minutes of my life. I needed the Timberwolves to win because I needed Cutter to have a glimmer of happiness.

I stood most of the game, and as the clock ticked down, my eyes went from Cutter to Weston to the clock. The bench stood in the last ten seconds, and when the buzzer sounded, the entire student body from Grove Hill cheered.

The Timberwolves were state champions.

Despite everything, Cutter had played his heart out and helped his team win.

The students rushed the players, picking the stars up on their shoulders. The pep band continued to play their fight song while the opposing team stood there, waiting. After minutes of celebration, the students were ushered back to their seats, and the awards ceremony started.

I continued to stand, clapping for each member of the other team, but as soon as the announcer said "And now for your state champions, the Grove Hill Timberwolves," I started crying. I couldn't hold the tears back, even if I tried.

The coaches were announced first, and then each of the boys came forward after their names were called and a medal was placed around their necks. The starters were saved for last. That was one thing I noticed: The five who started the game were the same five who ended the game. I was certain it meant something and would ask Weston later about the significance. As Cutter's family, we all appreciated seeing him on the court when the final buzzer sounded.

Parents and fans began filing out. The Timberwolves' family members stayed and waited. One by one, the boys emerged from the locker room to be greeted by their families.

I moved to the bottom row and waited, unsure of what I should do. There wasn't a doubt in my mind he wanted his mom right now, and I knew I'd never fill the void, but I was something to him.

Cutter came through the door, shaking hands with teammates as he passed them. He paused midway and looked at us. I had no idea what he saw, but I hoped he saw a family who loved him, even though we weren't his blood, except for Nova.

"Why don't you go get him," I said to Nova, who took off running. She launched herself into his arms, and like I'd seen him do at the other games, he carried her to the rim and let her hang there.

Slowly, I made my way to him. He held Nova and looked at me.

"You did it."

He nodded. "But she wasn't here to see me."

"I believe she was watching."

Cutter didn't say anything. He reached into his bag and handed me a plastic case with a medal inside and a piece of the net the boys had cut down earlier.

"I want to put this on her marker," he said. "She earned it, too, after all the long hours she put into my career."

"We can put it inside her box if you want. This way it'll be with her forever."

Cutter nodded and then collapsed in my arms, still holding Nova. I wrapped them in the biggest hug I could, praying I could suck all the bad from their lives. I could deal with it. They shouldn't have to.

"Your mom was so damn proud of you."

"I know," he said. "We did this for her."

I stepped back and cupped his cheek.

"Before the game, in the locker room, Malik said we were going to win for Miriam because she was like a mom to everyone. So, we won for her."

Tears flowed, and I didn't bother to wipe them away. There would be a day, somewhere in the future, when I'd think of my best friend and not cry. Until then, I was going to shed every damn tear I could because I was determined to heal.

As soon as Weston came out, he greeted the parents who remained. He walked over to us, and while I was tempted to hug him, I didn't. He'd kept his promise and had shown me he was interested without being pushy, from good-morning texts, to surprising me with coffee and flowers, to telling me I was beautiful while I was doing the dishes. If nothing ever came of us, I'd at least have a really great friend.

He placed his hand on my lower back and then moved it. "Dinner at the Ridgeview?"

"Yes, I'm starving, Coach," Cutter said.

"I don't know. I'm not sure you earned dinner," Weston said, but he looked at Nova, who cracked a smile. "What do you think? Do you think Cutter should get dinner?"

Nova contemplated Weston's question and then shook her head.

"What? Why?" Cutter asked her teasingly.

"Because you missed a lot of shots."

Cutter rolled his eyes. "Oh man, but we won." He pointed to the now-off scoreboard.

Nova thought about it for a minute and nodded. Everyone laughed as we walked out of the gym, state champions.

Chapter 32

Cutter

We were three weeks into the baseball season and about to have our first scrimmage or preseason game tomorrow. These types of games were nice because they didn't count against our record. But then, if we won, it didn't count, either, which sort of sucked.

Despite everything going on in my life, I had a lot to look forward to. Instead of teaching me how to drive, Toni had signed me up for a driver's course, which was mandated by the state. This one wasn't sponsored by the school, so I wasn't limited on driving time. That meant when I was done in a few weeks, I'd be able to take the test to get my license. If all went well, I'd be able to drive myself to school and home from practice.

There were rules I had to follow. Honestly, I'd do anything that Toni or the state told me, as long as I could drive. It sucked, though; I wouldn't be able to drive Eleni or any of my friends around for the first six months. My driver's ed teacher said it had to do with distractions and all that. I'd be able to drive Nova, though, but I wasn't sure how I felt about that. I think I'd be too nervous with her in the car at first.

At least I'd have a car. Toni was going to let me drive my mom's car, which was the one I'd been practicing with anytime she took me out to drive. The scariest thing was that she took me to Boston to learn how to parallel park. I thought I was going to crap my pants a few times, but I mastered it, and when it came time to practice with my instructor, he said I did an amazing job.

While we were in Boston, we stayed at Toni's. Her place overlooked the water and had a view of the city, and for the two days we were there, I sat out on her balcony and people-watched while bundled up in my winter coat, because the wind off the harbor was brutal.

Aside from the parking lesson, Toni took Nova and me to the aquarium and the children's museum. The latter was meant for Nova, but I had fun there, especially with her. I think not having our mom around hurt her more than she was letting on. Each morning, I asked her how she was doing and whether she wanted to talk, but she always told me she was fine. I knew enough to know that "fine" was never a good thing.

Toni took us to her office. No one was there, but it was nice to see where she worked when she came to town. Nova loved Toni's office and spent ten minutes spinning around in our aunt's swivel chair, and we rode up and down the glass elevator. Watching the city come in and out of view was trippy.

One of the mini-vacation events was a tour of Fenway. The team was in Florida for spring training, which was a bummer because I would've loved to see a game. Toni promised we'd come back once the weather was nicer. She knew someone who worked at the stadium and could get us tickets on the Green Monster.

On our way home, Toni let me drive once we were out of the city. The state required we have so many extra hours of drive time, and Toni felt this was a great way to get those in. Plus, it was a Sunday, and there weren't a lot of people on the road.

The sound of my cleats clanking against the concrete had to be my favorite noise. To me, it was a sign that summer was coming. Our nights were getting longer, crocuses and daffodils were beginning to bloom, and on my list of chores for this coming weekend was yard work.

Now that most of the snow had melted, Toni wanted to map out where all the new flowers would go. She intended to spruce up the yard the way my mom would've wanted it. All I knew was there would be a ton more yard work for me.

When I came around the corner of the school, I saw Eleni sitting on the concrete bench surrounding our flagpole. She stood as soon as she saw me, rushed over, and left me no choice but to drop my baseball bag on the ground. The sound of my metal bag sitting on the sidewalk echoed.

I picked her up, and her legs wrapped around my waist as her lips pressed against mine. Neither of us wasted any time deepening the kiss. We rarely had any alone time as it was. Not that we were alone now, but most of my teammates had already left.

Eleni moved her head back and forth. She kept her hands on my cheeks and ground against me. My dick was hard and pressed into her. In the times we'd been alone, we'd touched each other and given each other pleasure. I'd never felt my body get so warm before until Eleni had wrapped her hand around my shaft. She told me she'd read about doing this to me from one of her sister's books, a book her parents would lose their minds over if they knew it was in the house.

The first time she let me touch her between her legs, I thought I was going to jizz in my pants. We'd been at her house in the basement family room. The upstairs door was open, but Eleni didn't care. She straddled my legs and began rubbing against me. I was hard in seconds, but we both wanted more.

My friends always said you gotta risk it for the biscuit. I slipped my hand between her legs and felt her for the first time. It was like my body knew what to do even though my mind was nothing but a haze.

Ever since, we'd been waiting for more alone time so we could go further.

We stopped kissing when a car honked. Someone was always ruining our fun. I set Eleni down and picked up my bag.

"What are you doing here?"

"We had a cheer meeting, so I thought I'd wait until you were done with practice and walk home with you."

"Oh. Coach is giving me a ride."

Her face fell. I hated disappointing her.

"He can give you one too."

Coach would insist whether she wanted one or not. He wouldn't leave her at school or let her fend for herself.

"Did you hear about Malik and Janelle?" she asked as I sat down on the concrete bench to wait for Coach.

"Yeah, it's pretty messed up."

"I guess her parents are pretty pissed off at Malik," Eleni said.

"It's not just Malik's fault," I pointed out.

"No, but . . ."

"There are no buts, Eleni. They decided together to have sex. They're both responsible." Malik had already gotten a job to start saving money for the baby.

"I don't want to fight," she said as she leaned into me. "I'm not even friends with Janelle."

That made two of us.

"Promise me when we do it, we'll use condoms."

"Of course we will," I said. I had already bought a box when I was walking home from school a week or so ago. I wanted to be prepared the first chance we were alone, even if we didn't go all the way. As long as I kept them in a cool, dry place, they'd be fine until the expiration date. The last thing I wanted was to be in Malik's shoes. He'd confided in me about everything. He was scared and also not ready to be a dad.

Coach walked toward us, and we both stood. "Can we give Eleni a ride home?"

"Sure we can."

We held hands and followed Coach to his truck. If I had to guess, I suspected he'd be over for dinner or he'd come by after Nova had gone to bed. I thought he and Toni were dating, but I couldn't be sure. As many times as I had snuck around the house while Coach was there, I hadn't caught them in any awkward embraces.

When I first started playing for Coach Schmidt, I sort of hoped he would fall for my mom. Coach had always treated me well and was a great role model, but my mom had never seemed interested. Neither had Coach.

I climbed in the back and let Eleni sit in front. This wasn't ideal because I couldn't shut the door for her. Maybe I was wrong and should've let her sit in the back? I guess I truly didn't know what to do. My mom had taught me to open the door for people, reminding me it didn't cost me anything to be kind to them. Still, I wasn't sure if I should be in the back or not.

Being back here, though, gave me a chance to touch her hip. I slid my hand under her shirt and touched her skin. She shivered slightly and then turned enough for me to see her smile.

On the way to her house, she spoke to Coach. I listened, but they talked about cheer season and the competitions her team wanted to do over the summer. I wondered how much we'd be able to see each other once school was out. Between my summer league schedule and hers, we might not see each other much.

"This summer, you'll have to come to Boston with us," I said when there was a break in the conversation.

"Do you think your aunt will let me?"

I shrugged. I didn't see why Toni wouldn't let Eleni come with us one weekend. She could stay in the spare bedroom with Nova, and I could sleep on the couch. Although I'd like to crash out on the balcony under the harbor lights and sounds. No one would be able to get to me, that's for sure.

We arrived at Eleni's faster than I wanted. I couldn't wait to drive her home, which wouldn't be until late summer or the start of the school year. Either way, I was looking forward to it.

After she got out, I moved to the front. I couldn't kiss her goodbye, not with her dad standing on the front porch. I watched her house as we pulled away and hoped she wouldn't be in trouble for accepting a ride from Coach.

"Her parents are strict."

"Sometimes that's a good thing, but also a hindrance."

Eleni stretched the rules as far as she could. I was usually the voice of reason because I was pretty miserable when she was grounded from her phone or from me.

I didn't say anything the rest of the way home. Coach pulled into the driveway but didn't shut his truck off. "You're not coming in?"

He shook his head. "Scout's at home."

"Oh, right. Thanks for the ride."

"Maybe I'll see you later."

I got out, gave him a wave, and made my way inside. "I'm home," I yelled as I put my stuff down in the entryway. My mom called it a mudroom. It was far from muddy, especially since Toni made us keep our dirty shoes outside.

"Hello?"

Toni came out of the guest room, which was where she'd slept since my mom died. Before, she would sleep in my mom's room, but no one had really gone in there since.

"Hi, how was practice?" she asked as she rubbed my pitching arm. "All good?"

I nodded and handed her a slip.

"What's this?"

"Prom stuff," I told her. We went into the kitchen. "Where's Nova?"

"Girl Scouts with Mara," she said without looking up from the slip. "So I sign this to give you permission?"

"It's a code of conduct agreement," I told her. "We both sign, and if I break any of the rules, the consequences are there."

Her head moved up and down slowly. "Well, let's talk prom. What color will Eleni wear? We'll get your bow tie to match."

I grimaced and ran my hand through my hair. "I didn't ask her yet."

Toni looked at me confusedly and held the paper up. "What gives?"

I shrugged slightly. "Can we do a promposal thing?"

"What's that?"

I explained what they were, and, to my surprise, Toni seemed on board. "I was wondering if we could take her to Boston for the day and I can do it there. She really likes the penguins."

"And you're going to what, ask the aquarium if the penguins can hold a sign for you?"

Okay, so I hadn't thought it out clearly. I shrugged. She sighed. We both stared awkwardly.

Toni signed the sheet, and then I did. "Put this in your bag so you don't lose it. I'll look some things up and we'll figure out how to do something fun."

"Thanks."

She nodded and sat down at the table with her phone and a pad of paper. I sat across from her and started my homework.

Chapter 33

Antonia

Spring was bananas. Between baseball, Girl Scouts, and having to travel for work, I was exhausted. It'd been two months since Miri passed, and I'd like to say the kids and I were in a decent routine. There were days when I wanted to give up, say fuck it, and haul them back to Boston, where things could be easier.

On those days, I opened Miri's bedroom door and stood in her room, absorbing her essence, smelling her perfume, and imagining her flittering around the room like she had at Christmastime. It was hard to look back at that time and see her sick, with cancer ravaging its way through her body.

Nova trailed behind me as we made our way to yet another baseball field. By now, everyone knew who I was: the loudmouth who screamed the loudest for her nephew and his team. I couldn't help it. Cutter was that good, and I sort of had a crush on the coach.

Weston had given Nova a jersey to wear. It was the smallest one they had in inventory. She didn't care that it went to her knees. She either wore it open and long, or I tied it in a knot for her.

I wore the same shirt as all the other moms. The team had held a fundraiser selling gear, and I may have gone a bit overboard, making sure everyone had something to support Cutter.

We reached the bleachers, and thankfully there was a spot for us on the bottom one. I was worried about Nova not paying attention and getting hit with a foul ball, and I liked to set her up behind me. I'd brought her a backpack full of things to do, most of which were workbooks and coloring books. In keeping with Miri's antitechnology policy, I'd refused to give in and get Nova an iPad, despite the other moms offering her one.

I never thought I'd be the type of person who carried snacks and juice boxes everywhere I went. Half the time, we'd show up at a game and the concession stand would be a mile away or they wouldn't have one. After one too many times of that happening, I'd started bringing the things Nova would need. I'd learned that seven-year-olds were needy, always hungry and bored.

Once I had Nova set up, I sat down and faced the field. I didn't know how Miri did this, day in and day out. It wasn't the games, travel, or time, but the parents from the other teams and what they said about Cutter. Every time one of them opened their mouths, I wanted to put my foot in it. Their nasty remarks about my nephew grated every last nerve I had, and with the number of daggers I'd thrown during games, I should've warned them all by now.

Weston and Cutter said I needed to grow thick skin, which was funny because I was considered fairly ruthless in my daily job. I was never a violent person, but this newly developed mama bear mentality had me seeing red.

The starting lineups were announced, and the opposing parents booed each one of our starters. To show them we were the better team, not only on the field but off, we clapped for each one of theirs. And each of us made sure they knew it. The stare-off was epic.

Today's game was different. Weston had told me earlier to expect some major league scouts and college recruiters to be at the game. He'd reached out to his friends and former colleagues, who in turn had done whatever they needed to throw my nephew and the other boys a bone. According to Cutter and his friends, who had spent lots of time at the house, this was a huge deal, and it was important for them to play to the best of their ability.

I didn't want to ask them why they weren't playing this way all the time and just rolled with it. In the months since I'd become a full-time mom, I'd learned to roll with the punches when it came to teenage boys. Their logic was different and often confusing.

The announcer let everyone know Cutter Vaughn was up to bat with two men on base. I clasped my hands together and kept my eyes focused on Cutter, with the occasional look at Weston. He stood next to third base and did the whole "Here's what I want you to do" secret coded message, which they'd both tried to explain to me, but it went over my head. I just wanted Cutter to smack the crap out of the ball.

He stepped up to bat, and the process started. Pitch after pitch, the ball sailed toward Cutter. Too high. Too low. Too outside.

Cutter lifted his front leg, and I held my breath, waiting to see if he'd swing the bat. The ball came in fast, and if it wasn't for the crack of the bat, I wouldn't have known where the ball was.

I stood as it sailed through the air, landing on the other side of the fence. Our parent section erupted in a loud chorus of cheers and applause as each boy crossed over home plate. I turned to the people behind me, and we all slapped hands, giving each other high fives. The inner child in me wanted to flip the other parents off and stick my tongue out.

By the end, Grove Hill was victorious by ten runs, six of which had come from Cutter. We packed up and waited for Cutter and Weston to join us.

"Great game," I said as Cutter came toward me with a smile on his face. I gave him a high five, which had become a thing for us. At this point, I'd take any "thing" I could as long as it kept a smile on his face. The three of us had been going to therapy, mostly to learn how to deal with our grief. It seemed to be helping, and it gave Cutter and Nova someone to talk to who wasn't me. Although Weston had said Cutter confided in him, which made me happy.

"Thanks," he said as he ran his hand through his hair. It'd gotten longer and shaggier since his mom passed away. I'd asked him about cutting it, but he didn't seem interested.

"What do you say we go out for pizza?" I asked.

"I was wondering if I could go out to dinner with Eleni and her parents?" Cutter asked.

"Yep, of course. Are her parents here?"

Cutter nodded and pointed. They waved, and I told Cutter I'd take his bag home. He dropped it by my feet and ran toward his girlfriend and her family.

"Nova!"

I turned to see Mara running toward us. The two girls hugged as if they hadn't seen each other in weeks instead of hours. They had the cutest giggle, and watching them together reminded me so much of when Miri and I were that age.

A soft yet firm hand found my lower back. I eased into Weston, closing the small gap between us. His comfort was so welcome. It was like he knew when I needed him. I sighed as I watched the girls and smiled as Mara's mom came toward us.

"Is Nova busy the rest of the day?"

I shook my head slowly. "We don't have anything planned."

"Do you mind if she comes over for a bit? We're having some family over, and Mara won't have anyone to play with."

"Not at all. When should I pick her up?"

"We'll bring her back after dinner."

I gave Nova a kiss and told her to have fun, then turned to face Weston. "Please tell me you don't have plans."

He smiled softly. "Just with you and Scout."

I took a deep inhale, thankful I had at least someone to spend the rest of my afternoon with. We started toward the parking lot with our arms full of bags. Weston put Cutter's stuff in his truck and then surprised the hell out of me when he kissed me in the parking lot.

"Oh, wow, um . . ."

He giggled. "I'm going to run home and let Scout out. Then I'll be over."

"With pizza?"

Weston nodded, winked, and headed toward his truck. I climbed into my car and made the drive back to town by myself, listening to a self-help audiobook about moving past grief and growing positively. It had been easy to start with the hate when I'd found out Miri was sick, but after a while, the negativity of it all had weighed so heavily on me that I felt drained.

I followed Weston all the way back to town and to the road we lived on. He honked as he continued toward his house. I pulled into the driveway and stared at the house. Summer was approaching, and a decision needed to be made—not only about here but about my job. The company wasn't going to continue to let me work remotely, even though there hadn't been an interruption in how much business I was bringing in.

The thought of giving up Miri's dream home hurt my heart, and I couldn't imagine parting with the money pit. I got out of the car, took Nova's bag into the house, went to the refrigerator, took out the bottle of wine I had chilling in there, and poured two glasses. I carried them both to the front porch, set one down for Weston, and then sat in the rocking chair.

I looked out over the yard at the blooming flowers Cutter, Nova, and I had planted, and the ones Miri had planted. The flower beds were colorful and full of life, exactly the way she would've wanted. Tomorrow, we'd go visit her at the cemetery and take Miri fresh flowers. Her marker had finally arrived, and the sexton said he'd have it installed today.

Weston's truck turned into the driveway. He got out and sauntered over to the porch. I tilted my head back when he came near; he leaned down to kiss me fully.

"You taste sweet."

"That's a compliment I've never had before."

He laughed and sat in the other rocker. "This for me?"

"No, it's for my other boyfriend." The word slipped through my lips, and I smiled at the sound of it.

"Is that what I am?"

I shrugged. "Do you always stick your tongue in your friends' mouths when you see them?"

Weston cracked up. "No, just yours. I'm good with being your boyfriend." He picked up the glass of wine and took a sip. "I ordered pizza for delivery."

"Ah, I was going to ask where the food is."

He shook his head. "You and your love of pizza."

"It's a talent. I know." I took a sip.

"Boyfriend, huh?" he questioned after a minute.

"Is that okay?" I supposed we should talk about it.

"More than okay," he said. "I know this isn't the time for big declarations, but Antonia . . . when I look at you, I see the woman who dropped everything to fight for her best friend. I see someone who stepped up to raise two kids without hesitation. You don't just love Cutter and Nova; you became their safe harbor. And for the first time in my life, I want to be someone's safe harbor too. I want to be yours."

"Weston . . ." I breathed, my voice barely audible. The words this man had spoken made my knees shake. "If you keep saying things like that, I'm going to fall so hard for you that there's no coming back from it."

"Good," he said with a playful smirk dancing on his lips. "Because I'm already there."

Weston stood with his glass of wine, took my hand in his, and led me into the house. Thankfully, I had the forethought to grab my glass before I was rushed inside.

"What are you doing?"

"This," he said as he kicked the door closed and put our glasses down on the sideboard. His hands were warm against my face, his thumbs brushing over my cheekbones with a tenderness that made my breath hitch. His brown eyes burned into mine, filled with something raw, something fierce, something that sent a shiver racing down my spine.

Then his lips crashed into mine.

The kiss was urgent, hungry—weeks of tension and unspoken desire finally unraveling between us. I fisted his shirt, pulling him closer, needing more, needing everything. His mouth moved over mine, teasing, tasting, taking, and I met him with the same desperation, opening for him, our tongues tangling, stroking, fueling the fire that had been simmering between us for far too long.

His hands slid from my face, one curling around the nape of my neck, the other gripping my waist, fingers pressing into my skin like he never wanted to let go.

One thing was certain: I didn't want him to.

I moaned into his mouth as his hands moved lower, gripping my hips, tugging me flush against him. I felt every hard plane of his body, the undeniable evidence of his need pressing into me, and a pulse of heat shot through me.

I needed to feel more.

My hands slid under his shirt, fingertips skimming over his stomach, feeling the tense ridges of muscle, the heat of his skin. I pushed the fabric up, breaking the kiss just long enough to yank it over his head.

God.

My breath caught at the sight of him—broad shoulders, chiseled chest. This man had twelve years on me and looked better than men my age. He was beautiful, and he was mine. More importantly, he wanted to be mine.

Weston growled low in his throat as he reached for my T-shirt, pulling it up and over my head in one swift motion. His hands roamed over my bare skin, rough palms skimming over my stomach, up my ribs, making me shiver as he traced the curve of my breasts.

"You're so damn gorgeous," he murmured against my lips before his mouth trailed lower, pressing hot, open-mouthed kisses along my jaw, down my throat.

I tilted my head back, giving him more access, my fingers threading into his hair as he kissed his way across my collarbone. His tongue flicked over the sensitive spot just below my ear, and I gasped, my nails digging into his shoulders.

He grinned against my skin, his hands working the clasp of my bra. The second it was free, he pulled it off, tossing it aside before his hands were on me again, mapping every inch of bare skin. His mouth followed, kissing, tasting, until his lips wrapped around one hardened peak, his tongue flicking, teasing, sending a bolt of pleasure straight between my legs.

I arched into him, my head falling back as heat coiled low in my stomach. "Weston . . ."

"Say it again," he rasped, his voice thick with need.

"Weston." I pulled his mouth back to mine, kissing him deep, hard, pouring every ounce of desire into it.

His hands slid to my jeans, unbuttoning them with practiced ease and pushing them down my hips. I kicked them away, barely aware of the cool air against my heated skin, before his hands were on me again, gripping my thighs, lifting me effortlessly into his arms.

I wrapped my legs around his waist, my arms tightening around his shoulders as he carried me down the hall. His mouth never left mine, kissing me like he was starving for me, like he couldn't get enough.

He nudged open my bedroom door with his foot and stepped inside, and then we were on the bed, his weight pressing me into the mattress, solid and warm and everything I'd been craving since the night he'd let me use him.

His hands traced down my body, slipping under the last scrap of lace between us, teasing me, making me tremble. I reached between us, pushing at his waistband, needing him bare, needing him now.

He groaned as I freed him, his body hot and hard against my palm. "Jesus, Antonia."

Then he was kissing me again, swallowing my moans as his fingers teased me, stroked me, knowing exactly how to unravel me.

"I need you," I gasped against his lips, my body arching, aching. "Please."

His breath was ragged, his forehead resting against mine as he positioned himself, his hands framing my face, his gaze locking on to mine.

"I've got you," he murmured. "I'm right here."

Then he pushed inside me, slow and deep, stretching, filling, making me feel every inch of him. My breath caught, my fingers digging into his back, holding on as he moved, setting a rhythm that sent fire licking up my spine.

Weston wasn't just taking me—he was claiming me, worshiping me with every thrust, every kiss, every whispered word against my skin. And I gave him everything, meeting him stroke for stroke, drowning in him, in us.

We moved together, a desperate, fevered dance, until the pleasure built to a breaking point, crashing over us like a tidal wave, pulling us under.

I clung to him as I shattered, my body trembling, my cries muffled against his shoulder. He followed moments later, a deep groan rumbling in his chest as he buried himself inside me, his body shuddering, his hands gripping me like he never wanted to let go.

And I didn't want him to.

For a long moment, we lay tangled together, our breaths mingling, our hearts pounding in sync. Weston brushed damp hair from my face, pressing a lingering kiss to my forehead, his fingers tracing lazy patterns on my back.

"You okay?" he murmured, his voice husky.

I nodded, tilting my head up to meet his gaze. "More than okay."

His lips curved into a slow, satisfied smile. "Good. Not to ruin the moment, but I think I heard the doorbell, which means our dinner is sitting on the porch. Either that or I literally heard bells," Weston laughed.

I sighed, pressing my cheek against his chest, listening to the steady thrum of his heartbeat. He wrapped his arms around me, holding me close, and for the first time in a long time, I felt . . . right.

Whole.

Home.

Chapter 34

Antonia

The next day, we were met with a blazing sun, warm temperatures, and hope. Nova ended up spending the night at her friend's house, and when Cutter came home from Eleni's, he asked if I wanted to watch a movie with him. He put on a romantic comedy; we sat next to each other on the couch, shared popcorn, and laughed. It felt very cathartic to laugh, especially with Cutter.

Weston had left right before Cutter came home. After we shared a pizza in bed, Weston made love to me again. There was nothing rushed, no urgent need; we took things slow and worshipped each other. I hated saying goodbye to him. Even though he was down the street, it seemed like he was miles away.

I stood in the living room, looking out over Miri's flower beds. The sun shone on them perfectly. It was like she was up there, directing its rays to us, knowing we'd need her today.

Nova came downstairs, home from Mara's, wearing a pink-and-yellow dress, and handed me her hairbrush.

"Don't you look beautiful." I took the brush from her.

Nova twirled, and the frilly part of her dress fluttered. "This was Mommy's favorite dress."

"I can see why. It's so pretty." I tapped the tip of her nose with my fingertip. "What would you like to do with your hair?"

"I think pulled up here." She pulled her sides up and showed me. We went into the bathroom, where I kept most of my things. I rummaged through my hair supplies and found two pins.

Nova handed me the spray bottle and stepped onto the stool so she could see herself in the mirror. I wet her hair and then ran the brush through it. Thankfully, Mara's mom had brushed her hair last night before the girls had gone to bed.

"We didn't talk about Mara's. Did you have fun?"

She lifted her left shoulder. "I'm sad there sometimes."

"How come?" I feared I already knew the answer but asked anyway.

"Because she has a mommy, but her mommy is really nice to me and gives me hugs when she thinks I'm sad."

I finished pulling her hair back and then stood behind her, with my hands on the sides of her shoulders. "How's this?"

Nova nodded and turned side to side. "I love it." She looked at me through the mirror again.

"It's okay to be sad, Nova. I'm sad all the time because I miss your mom, but then I remember I have you and Cutter. Being here with you both makes me feel so much better because you're a part of her. I know I'm not the same as your mom, but when you're feeling sad, know that I am too."

Nova turned and wrapped her arms around me. I kissed the top of her head. "I miss her so much."

"I know, sweetie. Me too." There wasn't anything else I could say. I certainly wasn't going to tell her everything would be okay. I didn't know if it would. There was a hole in my heart, a part of me missing, and no amount of therapy or time would fill it.

Nova looked up at me, her watery hazel eyes matching those of her mother. "Can Mommy see me?"

This was the one lie I would tell every single time. I nodded. "Yeah, she can. Even though her body isn't here, her spirit is. She wouldn't want to miss any part of you growing up."

"I just want to hug her one more time."

"Me too. I know I'm not the same, but I do give pretty good hugs."

I waited a beat before holding my arms out. She fell into them, and I squeezed her lovingly with all my might. I thought Cutter would be the one who'd fall apart first. I never thought it would be Nova.

Cutter walked by and stopped at the door. "Lovefest?"

I held my arm out for him and brought him into our fold. "We're having a moment."

"I can use a moment too," he said as his strong arm wrapped around my waist.

The three of us stayed like this for what felt like an hour. While we had somewhere important to be, Miri would be okay with us delaying our arrival.

We freshened up and then piled in the car, with Cutter driving.

"Do you know where you're going?"

He nodded. I couldn't wait for him to take his driver's test. We'd worked hard on all the fundamentals, and he was turning out to be an excellent driver. Of course I worried. There were rules in place, but I was once a teenager and shunned rules. I used to think they didn't apply to me and broke them all the time. Consequences be damned. I wasn't naive in thinking Cutter wouldn't break the rules. It was a rite of passage. I just had to be prepared for it.

There were quite a few cars at the cemetery. I directed Cutter on where to go and reminded him to keep the speed down. With people walking around, I didn't want someone to dart out in front of him and him not be able to stop in time.

The cemetery was tranquil. The company that owned it had put a lot of thought into making it a peaceful place for family and friends to come visit. Tucked away from any traffic and shrouded by tall shrubs for privacy, the space had a welcoming feel. Death surrounded you there, but it was hard to be sad when there was a bubbling fountain, koi fish, ornamental flowers, and benches to sit on.

Cutter parked along the grassy edge. We held hands while we walked along the path until Miri's resting space came into view. The kids had picked her marker and the wording.

We stood there, staring down at the bronze plaque covering Miri's final resting spot. The design had been done flawlessly, and I couldn't have been prouder.

"Wow, I never thought I'd see myself like this," Cutter said as we looked at the raised etching of him, Miri, and Nova. It was one of the last photos of them all together. I had taken it at Christmas, long before we knew she was dying.

"We look funny," Nova said.

"I think you guys look perfect."

Next to the etching was Miri's name, her date of birth, and the date her body had given out on her. The words under all of that were what choked me up the most: "Mommy and best friend."

The craftsman who'd made the plaque was a bit surprised when we didn't go with the standard "daughter," "mother," "aunt," and whatever else others used. The two titles we chose were perfect for our Miri.

"What do we do with the flowers we brought last week?"

"We're going to put them on someone else's grave. Give them a little bit of our happy."

Cutter didn't hesitate. He took the flowers from the metal vase and carried them to two other markers, splitting them up. "Next week, we'll have to remember who I gave them to, so I pick someone different next time."

"I like that." I linked my arm through his and rested my head on his shoulder.

Nova put the bouquet in the vase and fiddled with the flowers. She had picked this week's arrangement of gerbera daisies, pink-and-white carnations, and three white roses to stand for her, Cutter, and Miri, with Cutter choosing last week. Nova finished and stepped back to where we were.

"It's beautiful, just like Mommy," Nova said.

"I think if she had picked this herself, she would agree," Cutter added.

"I think so as well. Who wants to go first?" Ever since we'd put her ashes in the ground, we'd each taken a moment of privacy to speak to her.

"I'd like to," Cutter said.

Nova and I walked toward the car, our joined hands swinging between us. I was surprised to find Cutter not far behind us.

"Everything okay?"

He nodded with a smile. "Yep. I'm good."

"All right, then. Do you want to go next?" I asked Nova.

"Will you come with me?"

We told Cutter we'd be right back. Nova and I walked hand in hand back to Miri's marker. I stepped off to the side but still within distance, so she'd know I was there just in case she needed me. I didn't want to eavesdrop on something that should be private.

When Nova was finished, she hugged me and ran back to Cutter, who waited for her outside the car. He picked her up, spun her in a circle, much to her delight, and then helped her into the back seat.

I stared at the marker as tears welled, hating every second of this. A day would come when I could think of her and the tears would stay away, but I couldn't imagine that day clearly. If ever.

"You were right," I started. "I like him. 'Him' being Weston, in case you didn't know, but something tells me you did know and suspected he'd be the person I needed right now. He's so patient and calm, and the kids love him. But again, you knew this. Scout has been an amazing companion to Nova. I never realized the importance of a dog until now. I'm seriously considering getting them one, but something small so when we travel for sports it can go with us."

I looked behind me to check on the kids and then back at the marker. "The kids are going to be okay, Miri. They're so strong and willing to let me know when they need a little extra love. I never saw myself as a sports mom, but let me tell you, some of those other parents . . ." I shook my head.

"Anyway, Cutter and Nova did an amazing job on your marker. I hope you can see it from wherever you may be."

I crouched down, kissed my fingers, and then placed them on her name. "I love you, Miri." I wiped at my fallen tears, put a smile on my face, and walked back to my kids, who greeted me the same way. And wouldn't you know it, the first thing out of Cutter's mouth was him asking to drive.

I should've known.

The days began flying by. The nicer it was, the faster the day went. If we weren't at baseball, Cutter had basketball practice, which meant we were going in every which direction. Thankfully, I had Weston by my side. Being Cutter's coach helped in that aspect. Although it wasn't until the basketball travel team started that I found out Weston wasn't the coach during the summer; Jerome was. Not that it mattered. Weston would be there, regardless.

On top of me being knee deep in sports and work, the court appointed a guardian ad litem, or GAL, for the kids. I didn't really like her, but she wasn't there for me. It was her job to make sure the kids' needs were being met. Still, I felt like I was under a microscope and really hated being scrutinized. I knew I was a good person who had a job that more than supported Cutter and Nova, but when I told the ad litem I couldn't meet on Mondays or Fridays, I sensed a bit of discord from her. Any other days, except for games, I was home, and she was welcome.

After Miri passed, the attorney filed the paperwork for me to be appointed legal guardian of the kids, which was what we had agreed upon.

Until one rainy day when we were all sitting there, watching a movie. Cutter was in the oversize reading chair, while Nova snuggled next to me. Weston and Scout were also there, but Scout made sure he was next to Nova, pushing his owner to the corner of the couch.

A character on the screen mentioned adoption. I hadn't thought anything of it until Cutter asked if I was going to adopt them. I figured being their guardian was enough.

With their permission, I changed my petition with the court from legal custody to adoption. They would be mine, and no one would be able to take them away. All their forms would have me listed as their parent and not guardian, and somehow knowing this made our bond stronger.

The kids would keep Miri's last name, though, and I was more than okay with that.

As suspected, Miri's parents petitioned the court for visitation. It was something I was against, but ultimately, I left the decision to Cutter. If he wanted a relationship with his other grandparents, I wouldn't stand in the way. But I would also lay some ground rules for Miri's parents. I refused to let Cutter and Nova grow up knowing a mistake could cost them their family, and there was no way in hell I would let them refer to Cutter or even Nova as a mistake.

Weston and I sat on the porch, each of us in a rocking chair, while Nova ran around the front yard trying to catch butterflies with the net Weston had bought her.

I leaned back and closed my eyes, thankful for a quiet moment, when I felt his hand on mine. Peering out of one eye, he leaned toward me.

"I've been thinking."

My heart sank. "Oh?"

He smiled. It was crooked, cocky, and adorable, and not at all reassuring. Sometimes I wondered if we were at two different stages in life. He'd retired from his profession and taken up teaching and coaching because he wanted to give back. I was a mom of two, with two mortgages and a job that took me out of town at least once, if not twice, a month. On paper, I was a train wreck.

"Nothing bad," he said as if he could see the worry in my eyes.

"Nothing bad where you're concerned? Or me? Should I be concerned?"

"Both of us, at least that's what I'm hoping."

"Go on."

"I'm thinking, once the adoption is final, what about you and the kids moving in with me . . ."

My mouth dropped open, and he held his hand up. "Temporarily. This would give us an empty house to do the necessary remodeling. As it is now, if you want to do something, you'll have to live around construction. With everyone out of the house, we can get it all done at once."

While I liked the idea, it wasn't going to be cost-effective. I shook my head lightly. "I'd have to take out a loan, and with two mortgages, I'm not sure the bank would approve. The life insurance the kids received from Miri went into a trust for them, and with the adoption, they won't receive social security benefits. No bank would look at my expenses and hand me a loan right now."

"I would."

I laughed. "When did the Bank of Weston open up?"

"The day I rebuilt this porch," he said.

"I can't take your money. Teachers don't make a lot."

This time Weston howled with laughter. "You still haven't looked me up, have you?"

I shrugged. "A little. Nothing in depth. I think I stopped when it said you were married, but I only looked then after my dad mentioned it. I was preoccupied." I gave him a little poke in his stomach.

"I was very smart with my money during my career, Antonia. I don't need to work but do so because I enjoy coaching. I don't have a problem fronting the money for the house."

"With interest?"

He shook his head, and I raised an eyebrow at him. Weston sighed. "I was thinking more like I move in if all goes well with us living together at my house."

"You? Move in here? With us?"

He nodded the entire time I asked my three-part question.

"That's if you're ready. I know I am." He took my hand. "After being with you and the kids all day, going home to an empty house really sucks, Antonia. I lie awake at night, staring at the ceiling, wondering how long I'll have to wait to ask the three of you to move in with me. Living here, in the home Miriam loved so much, makes sense, but I also know you may not be ready, so I could be putting my cart before the horse, so to speak.

"Antonia, I'm not asking you to move in with me because Scout prefers to be here. I'm asking because I love you. I love Cutter and Nova. You're my family."

As if on cue, Nova squealed in delight as she ran around the yard with Scout. She jumped and moved her net in the air. He'd brought her this little bit of happiness, but it wasn't just this gift. He'd brought Scout into our lives, and he put the kids first every time we planned a night out. Weston never had an issue spending our time with the kids. He wasn't going to be the one to tell me they had to go to boarding school, or that I had to choose between him and them.

Weston knew we were a package deal, and he was the bow to make us complete.

"I know it's fast, and I know you're scared—"

"It's not that, Weston. I worry about the impact something like this would have on the kids. What if this doesn't work out?"

"What if it does and we live happily ever after, raising these two amazing kids?"

I looked at Nova and Scout, best friends already, and then I glanced around the yard and house Miri loved so much . . . *love*. My eyes shot to Weston's.

"Did you say that you loved me?"

He nodded emphatically. "I believe my words were, 'I love you.'"

I smiled, having heard him the first time, but wanting him to say it again so I could absorb the words in this moment. I shook my head, pretending to be confused. "What?"

"Oh, was I not clear?" He paused. "I. Love. You." He enunciated each word.

"That's perfect because I love you too," I said, repeating his words back to him. "Let me talk to them, but I'm definitely a yes on the whole cohabiting thing."

Weston stood and pulled me into his arms. He pressed his lips to mine, and before the kiss could go any deeper, we heard, "Ooh, someone is kissing!"

Thanks, Nova.

Chapter 35

Cutter

Not a day went by when I didn't think about my mom. I missed everything about her, but mostly her presence. Knowing she would always be where she said she would, and now wasn't, was a hard notion to swallow. The ache in my chest was uncomfortable most days, and I'd found that when I didn't think about her, the pain grew.

But thinking about her hurt as well. I was grateful for the text messages and voicemails I'd saved, and for the years of photos and videos Toni had of my mom. She never hesitated to hand her phone to Nova whenever she asked. As much as it broke my heart each time I pressed play—hearing my mom's voice, seeing her happy and healthy instead of sick—knowing that I could hear her tell me she loved me or simply say my name . . . was everything.

My mom was missing milestones in my life, or, as Toni called them, "rites of passage." There was the state championship and now prom. There would be more, like my upcoming college visit. A coach had invited us to campus for a tour and lunch and to see their baseball facility.

Same for Nova. Mom missed Nova earning a badge for selling a lot of Girl Scout cookies, and Nova was going to a horse camp this summer to learn how to ride. Toni was worried, but Weston assured her the camp was safe and highly recommended.

Weston was the other part of our lives my mom was missing. He'd always been my coach, at least since high school, and now he was really part of our lives because he and Toni were dating. I thought I'd miss Brendan, but I didn't. It took me seeing Toni smile at Coach that I knew they were meant for each other. I knew my aunt missed my mom—we all did—but Coach made her days easy. Weston was by far the better choice for Toni and for us. He never acted like he was better than us, and I saw the way he looked at Toni. Sort of like the way I looked at Eleni. Toni said I had stars in my eyes.

Plus, I liked having him around. Ever since my mom got sick, Coach had been someone I could count on, and now he was always there. I'd never had a father figure live with me before, and while it was an adjustment, Coach fit in our family.

One thing my mom wasn't missing were her parents. I decided, for myself and Nova, that we wouldn't pursue a relationship with them, unless ordered by the courts. Even then, Toni said she'd fight a court order with everything she had.

Toni was also going to be our mom—well, officially, on paper. I didn't really care for the "guardian" title because she was so much more than a guardian. She was our mom, aunt, and friend rolled into a fiery, loving, supportive person.

She was our person.

The court-appointed guardian told me and Nova we'd lose the social security benefits if Toni adopted us. We didn't care about money. If we couldn't have our mom, we wanted Toni.

Tonight, Eleni and I were going to prom. Toni and Samira had helped me with my promposal. Samira made me chocolate-covered strawberries and wrote "PROM" on them. Toni and I made a sign that said **I Would Be Berry Lucky if You Went to Prom with Me**. She said it was important to add "Yes" and "No" checkboxes, which I did in strawberry stickers, since they were Eleni's favorite fruit.

Even though we'd been dating for a while, I was nervous about asking her. What if she said no? Or didn't like the way I'd asked? What if her parents told her she couldn't go? I wasn't sure her parents even liked me; I thought they only tolerated me because it was easier than fighting with their daughter about our relationship.

My fears were eased when Eleni said yes before I could even utter the words.

Weston took me to rent my tux. We drove to Manchester, where most of the chain retailers were. He said it would be easier because the selection would be better. Eleni's dress was hot pink or electric pink, and she had provided a swatch—whatever that was—so everything could match.

I wanted to rent a limo, but being a two-sport athlete hadn't left me much time to work. Thankfully, Toni said she would pay for it and encouraged me to ask my friends if they wanted to pitch in. At first, I didn't want to because being alone with Eleni was a priority, but I relented and asked Flinn and Malik if they wanted to share the cost. Flinn asked a girl from a couple of towns over to go with him, and Malik planned to bring Janelle, but she didn't want to go to prom. He was going stag. I didn't think that was fair to him, especially since he and Janelle were no longer a couple. She'd broken things off after word spread that she was pregnant. Malik was confused and hurt but wasn't going to pressure her into anything. He'd been working every chance he could so he could help Janelle with the baby. I was surprised he still wanted to go to prom or be the fifth wheel in the limo. Eleni said Malik might want to ride in the limo for the experience.

Toni was cooking dinner for my friends. We were having roasted chicken and potatoes with a cream sauce, steamed broccoli, and a dinner salad. For dessert, Samira had made these massive cupcakes. They'd arrived earlier in the day and taunted me every time I went into the kitchen to bug Toni.

She slapped my hand when I tried to taste the cream sauce. I couldn't help it. Everything smelled so good, and even though she hated cooking, Toni could cook, now that she'd practiced almost every night. She'd already started teaching me and Nova how to make things from scratch.

Living with Toni was a lot different from my mom. Sometimes they were the same, but they parented differently. Granted, Toni was flying by the seat of her pants. According to her, she had a good support system in place, and since coming to Grove Hill, she'd made friends with Samira, Vera, and Edith. They even kept up their "book club" nights.

Nova and I had the same chores as before, and we had rules. Some were new, like I had to tell Toni where I was at all times. She worried, especially when she was in Boston for work and wouldn't be home until late. Homework had to be done as soon as I got home from school, and we weren't allowed to use the word "fine" when asked how we were doing or how school was. This was something she'd learned from our therapist.

"Everything ready for tonight?" she asked as she gently nudged me away from the stove. "Tux is hanging up?"

"Yep." I went to the cupboard and took out one of the many water tumblers we had. That was another thing that had changed. Toni didn't trust the water in the well since my mom had gotten so sick. We were having a water filtration system put in and had one of those water jug things in the corner. She used the water dispenser for drinking and cooking.

The other thing that had changed was we were moving into Weston's temporarily while the house was being remodeled. We needed new electrical wiring, a roof, and subflooring, and a couple of the walls needed to be replaced due to aging plaster or something. Weston was paying for all of this, and since Nova and I owned the house, we didn't have to pay him back until we'd sold.

If we ever sold.

Weston was moving in with us once the remodel was done as well, and I didn't mind. I liked the idea of having a man around, not only to help me but to protect Nova and Toni.

Once my tumbler was filled, I secured the lid and went to the refrigerator. I wasn't hungry but bored. I sighed as I stood there.

"What are you looking for?"

"Nothing. Everything," I said as Toni laughed. "Why are there flowers in here?"

"Those are from Vera. She did Eleni's corsage."

I took the clear plastic container out and studied it. There were three roses. Two were white and one bright pink, with pink ribbon wrapped around it, making a bow.

"This is pretty."

"Do you think Eleni will like it?" Toni asked as she moved around the kitchen. I thought about sneaking a taste of the cream sauce but figured prom was far more important, and I didn't want to get into trouble.

"Yeah, she will." I put it back and reached for the pack of cheese slices, taking a few out and then closing the door. Toni's back was to me as she stared out the kitchen window. We were getting a new fence as well, some chickens, and maybe a dog. We had Scout, but he spent most of his time with Nova, and with my summer sports schedule, Toni wasn't sure if we should get one now or wait.

"Are you okay?"

She nodded. "Yeah, just thinking." Toni turned and wiped at her cheeks. She cried a lot, but I tried not to let her know I saw. It was hard for me to understand the connection she'd had with my mom. Like she was my mom, but she and Toni had been friends their entire lives, and now Toni didn't have anyone but us.

"I miss her too," I said.

"I know you do. I do as well."

I went to Toni and gave her a hug. I knew she liked these and needed them a lot.

The doorbell rang, and Nova yelled from the other room that she was going to get it. I followed her down the hall and smiled brightly when Eleni and her parents stood on the other side.

I welcomed them in, showed Eleni to Toni's room (where she would get dressed later), and then went to sit with her and her parents in the living room. I was thankful Weston was there to talk to her parents because they didn't say much to me.

Malik and his dad were next to arrive, then my grandparents, followed by Flinn, his date, and both sets of parents.

Our house hadn't been this full since my mom's funeral. That day had been somber, while tonight was a bit happier.

Toni and my grandma brought out trays of appetizers for everyone to snack on before dinner. Weston and my grandpa set up tables in the backyard under the strings of white lights Toni had put up, and I helped carry things out.

"If you'd all join us outside," Toni said shortly after everyone arrived. She led everyone outside and stood off to the side. I could tell she was still hurting from whatever memory had resurfaced earlier. I stood next to her, with my arm around her shoulders.

"Oh, this is magical," Eleni said. Everyone agreed.

"Thank you," I said quietly to her. "For making this special."

She nodded. "I wanted your mom to be a part of it too."

It hadn't occurred to me that that was why Toni had wanted to have everyone over to our house for dinner, but now it all made sense. Here, in the home my mom had loved so much, she'd be able to see everyone come together for prom.

After dinner, and after everyone had praised Toni on the delicious meal she'd made for everyone, I took my friends upstairs to get ready, while Eleni and Flinn's date, Wendy, got dressed in Toni's room. The girls had already had their hair done, and we were told they only needed to touch up their makeup. I thought Eleni looked perfect the way she was, but what did I know?

Malik, Flinn, and I came down first, dressed in our tuxes. One look at Toni, and I knew she was about to cry. She leaned into Weston and waved her hand in front of her eyes. I went to her.

"Do I look okay?"

She nodded and looked at me with watery eyes. "You look very handsome." Toni fiddled with my bow tie and then ran her hands down the lapels of my jacket.

The girls made their grand entrance, and I found myself breathless. Eleni looked gorgeous in her fitted gown. It had a low-cut V that accentuated her breasts. My mouth watered. We were getting so close to going all the way; we just needed privacy.

Toni reminded me about the flowers in the kitchen. I went in, with Malik and Flinn following.

"Damn, boy, no wonder you wanted the limo all to yourself," Malik said as he shook his head.

"I know." I sighed as the thought of Eleni grinding on my hand with her shirt off flashed in my mind. "I'm not sure how much longer I can hold out."

"Wendy and I aren't even dating, and we're doing it," Flinn added.

"Lucky. We get to touch each other and shit, but nothing more. Her parents are always home if I'm there, and same here. I'm so mad I didn't get my license when I turned sixteen. If I had, I'd be able to drive her places now."

"Whatever you do, use a condom." Malik shook his head.

I reached into my pocket, pulled one out, and shrugged. "Just in case."

"Of what?"

I jumped at the sound of Toni's voice and slipped my hand back into my pocket. My heart raced, faster than ever. How much had she heard?

She looked at me and then my friends. "Boys, can you excuse us for a moment?" Toni motioned for me to follow her outside.

Shit. Shit. Shit.

Toni walked toward the back of the yard, which I was grateful for because I didn't want Eleni's parents to hear us.

"Was that a condom?"

I nodded, knowing there was no point in hiding it.

"Jesus," she muttered as she pinched the bridge of her nose. "Do you know how to use it?"

The question caught me off guard and took a minute for me to answer. I slowly shook my head.

"Jesus," she said again. "Do you have another one?"

I nodded, reached into my pocket, and set it in her outstretched hand.

"You know your mom had you when she was a teen, and she wouldn't want this for you. I can't tell you not to have sex, although I wish you'd wait. I'd rather have you prepared." She ripped open the packaging and held it out for me to see.

"Do you see this edge?" She continued after I'd nodded and explained how this was the right way to put it on. She gave me a demonstration using her hand and arm, all while muttering "Jesus" every five seconds. She showed me how far one could stretch, which, honestly, I had no idea. Toni took it off and stuffed it into her back pocket, along with the wrapper.

"There is never an excuse not to wear one," she said.

"Do you use them?" I don't know why I asked such a personal question.

"Yes, I do," she said pointedly. "Sex changes things between people, Cutter. It's emotional and healthy, but it can be damaging. You respect everything Eleni says about how she's feeling, and when she says 'No,' 'Stop,' 'We can't,' or whatever else, you freaking stop. Do you hear me? You don't coerce her. You don't tell her it's going to make her feel good. Nothing. You get up and walk away."

I nodded.

"I'd really like for you not to have sex, but I can't stop you. However, tomorrow, we're having the talk and we're going to discuss everything because . . ." She looked at the house and shook her head.

"I know."

"If you don't want to talk to me, you can talk to Weston. Knowledge is power here, Cutter. This isn't something you do on a whim or because your hormones are driving you to it."

"I love her."

Toni nodded and pulled me into a hug. "You're going to be the death of me," she said to me. "Please be careful."

"I will."

We went back into the house. Weston stood in the kitchen, watching for us.

"Everything good?"

I nodded. "Yep." I didn't bother going upstairs to take another condom out of the box. Tonight wouldn't be the night, no matter how eager I was.

Once the corsages and boutonnieres were on, we stood for what felt like an eternity taking photos. When the limo finally arrived, we cheered. Toni had set it up so that it would drive us around town while we sipped on sparkling cider, and then drop us off at the dance. It wouldn't be a long ride, but it was a bright spot in my life since my mom passed away.

Chapter 36

Antonia

Summer blew by in the blink of an eye. I don't know whose eye, since I could barely remember it. If we weren't at baseball, we were in an overcrowded convention center for basketball with multiple games going on at the same time, with coaches yelling, parents cheering, and referees blowing whistles.

And when we weren't watching basketball, we were in the ballpark, under the lights, until all hours of the night. I told Weston that next year we were traveling with a pop-up camper because seeing Cutter sleep under the metal bleachers or under a tree—wherever he could find shade—didn't sit well with me. Not to mention, I hated that he ate poorly while we were on the road. The fast and processed foods drove me bananas. Cutter was a growing boy and needed proper nutrition.

Weston said there may not be a next year because Cutter could get an offer to play for a school, and then he wouldn't have to travel for exposure. I wasn't sure how I felt about that. Before, when Miri would tell me stories, I felt bad for her having to be away from home all the time. But now that I'd done it and was that mom in the front row, I sort of enjoyed it.

Maybe Weston would have to start coaching Nova in softball or something. I didn't even know if she wanted to play, but I was going to miss this.

Nova couldn't care less and had spent most of her time with my parents. She preferred to be pampered by Grandma and Grandpa than to follow her brother across the country for tournaments. Couldn't say I blamed her. My parents doted on her, and she had a good thing going with a horse trainer near my parents. Every weekend, my dad took Nova to the stables, where she learned to muck the stalls, ride, and care for the horses.

The Girl Scout horse camp had given Nova a sense of belonging. Her therapist said she'd seen a positive change in Nova, and she was smiling more. The research I'd done showed that horses had an innate ability to comfort their riders. Nova needed that. She still had nightmares, but they were less frequent, mostly thanks to Scout.

Ever since we moved into Weston's while the house was being remodeled, Scout had slept with Nova. She curled up with the dog like she had with her teddy bear. He didn't seem to care that she needed to hold on to him every night. Scout stayed and never left her side. He even went to my parents' with her.

Moving into Weston's when we did was the right thing to do. The day after we'd moved most of our clothing and necessities to his house, two pipes burst. One in the upstairs bathroom, which flooded the flooring and ceiling, and a sewer pipe in the basement. Both were a shitty experience. No pun intended.

I had already planned to replace the flooring but hadn't thought about the ceiling. By the time the house was scheduled to be done, it would be mostly brand new. The clapboard siding would come down in the fall, replaced with vinyl siding. A privacy fence was going up out back because I wasn't comfortable with Nova being out there by herself. After I'd gotten through the dead brush and shrubs, I found a dirt road leading into the woods not far from the house. That was enough of a nope for me. Miri had always wanted a white fence, and that was what it was going to be.

The kids and I had gone through Miri's stuff over the past few months. We weren't ready to get rid of anything yet. Her belongings would go into totes and into a protected storage unit until the kids were ready. I knew I'd never be ready to part with her stuff. After the remodel, her room would become mine, and the guest room would go back to being an office and where my parents stayed when they visited.

I was still unsure about sleeping in there because it was Miri's space, but the kids were insistent, especially with Weston moving in. They wanted this to be a home where we were all happy and feeling welcomed.

In our search, we'd found hand-sketched drawings of how she'd wanted the house to look. The kids asked if we could do what their mom had planned, and I immediately said yes. This was their house, and that was something I held on steadfastly to. Regardless of the impending adoption, when they were ready to sell or do whatever, it was theirs.

What hurt was when Cutter said he didn't want the baseball diamond on his wall anymore. I didn't fight him about it, but told the contractors to preserve the wall as best they could and put it in the garage. I didn't know what I'd do with it, but it would be there if Cutter ever wanted to see his mom's work.

Nova followed Cutter's decision as well, but she left her room purple because it was her mom's favorite color. The hand-painted solar system would go in a frame, on Nova's wall.

One of the things I planned to do next spring was buy and raise chickens. I had no idea what possessed me to even consider this, but being as it was something Miri had wanted to do, the idea had grown on me. Weston and I mapped out a space for the chickens and found the perfect coop online. He volunteered to rebuild the one we had already, but by the time the chicks would be ready, he'd be in full baseball season and wouldn't need the hassle.

Today, we were visiting the University of Richmond. The coach had reached out to Cutter about a visit to campus. Normally, they'd fly prospective members of their team to Virginia, but Weston had told the coach we were traveling and could swing by. This way, both of us were there: me as Cutter's mom and him as Cutter's coach.

Cutter was excited, and honestly, so was I, even though I missed Miri terribly and wished she were here to see her boy shine. He'd grown a couple more inches since her passing and had somehow maintained his honor roll status despite losing his mom.

Weston drove through campus, but not before I could snap a photo of the Spider mascot on the gates. I hadn't paid attention to many colleges until March Madness, when Cutter made me fill out a bracket, but the Richmond logo with the Spider mascot was pretty cool.

"We'll have to go to the school store," I said as we looked for a parking spot. "Cutter will want something."

"Cutter's right here," he said, laughing. When Miri died, I thought he was going to turn into an unruly teen, defying me every chance he could. He hadn't. For a while, when I'd first arrived, things were touch and go with his attitude. I thought that was probably normal for any teenager experiencing a change in hormones.

He added, "Yeah, yeah. I want something from the store. Is that better?"

I glanced over my shoulder and smiled. He was such a bright spot in my life. I couldn't imagine not having him or Nova filling my days. I was so grateful to Miri for asking me to become their guardian, and then the kids for asking me to adopt them. They had completed my life.

Well, and Weston. He was a pretty amazing addition.

Weston parked near the baseball facility, and we got out. Cutter and Weston walked a pace ahead of me and my short legs. I took the opportunity to look around as I trailed behind. The campus looked beautiful. I'd gone to a city school, and we had very little green space unless we went downtown to the park. Here, there was rolling green, lush land.

"Weston, thanks for coming."

The voice of a man dressed like he was about to play baseball bro-hugged Weston. "Cutter, I'm Coach Sisto," he said as they shook hands.

"This is my mom, Toni," Cutter said, introducing us. He referred to me as Mom because it was easy, but I'd always be Toni at home, and I was more than okay with it. I didn't need the title because I had his and Nova's love and affection. They treated me with respect and kindness, and they came to me with any issues.

One of those issues was Eleni. I liked her. A lot, actually. She was very nice to Nova, which was important to me, and extremely respectful and polite. She reminded me a bit of Miri when she was seventeen and in love with the wrong guy. Not that Cutter and Eleni were wrong for each other; there were things like college, sports, and discovering who he was that I wanted to see Cutter excel at.

Ever since prom, Eleni had mentioned a couple of times that she planned to follow Cutter to college so they could be together forever. This worried me. If he earned a scholarship or even a spot on a team to play either basketball or baseball, that was where his focus would need to be. Not on his high school girlfriend.

Coach Sisto held the door open and waited for me as I lagged, lost in my thoughts. I vaguely remembered getting a tour of Boston University all those years ago but couldn't tell you a dang thing about it. I'd opted to live off campus with Miri and Cutter. They were far more important.

The tour started with Coach Sisto showing us one of the dorm rooms. It was as big as Cutter's room but made smaller by another bed, dresser, and desk. I watched him for a reaction to see if I could gauge where his mind was. He kept his face stoic, asked questions we had prepared earlier, and listened intently. I was proud of him.

After a quick stop in the cafeteria, we made our way to what Weston and Cutter deemed the important stuff: the athletic facilities. All the state-of-the-art gizmos and gadgets were lost on me. The tour included methods and tools to keep Cutter healthy and safe, the "newest" in technology for this and that, a weight room to rival every other school in the division . . . the list went on and on and didn't interest me as much as it did my guys.

Two hours later, we were back on the road and heading north. Cutter talked excitedly with Weston about the school and filled me in on the process of applying. He would still play in his high school season next year and would have to make a decision by the first of May, which was national signing day.

All I knew was that if Cutter could land a scholarship to play ball—that would be the best thing for him. It would give him purpose, something to live for, and the ability to chase his dreams.

We stopped in Boston for the night, for no other reason than to check on my penthouse. I hadn't given it up yet and wasn't sure I planned to. It was a nice little getaway, albeit a rather expensive one. We made it a point to get here at least one weekend a month. Although with it being this close to the water, the kids now wanted a boat.

"Can I sleep on the balcony?" Cutter asked as he opened the sliding door. He let in the hot, sticky air.

"It's not safe," I told him as I stood next to him. My phone pinged in my hand. I looked at the notification and my heart sank. We'd waited, for what felt like an eternity, for the adoption to be final. The judge assigned to the case had suggested I reach out to the kids' father at his last known address. I'd sent a letter, which had gone unanswered, probably because his last known address was the house he'd lived in when he was seventeen, and his father no longer lived there.

Miri's parents were still asking for visitation, which I suspected they would get. Cutter, speaking on behalf of his sister as well, had informed the GAL that he wasn't ready to have a relationship with them. The Vaughns were upset, and rightly so, but they'd had years to fix their relationship with Miri and had chosen not to.

I opened the email from the clerk and read, reread, and reread again.

"What's wrong?"

I shook my head and looked at him with watery eyes. "The judge approved my petition for adoption. You and Nova are officially mine."

Cutter pulled me into his strong arms and held me tightly. We both cried, happy tears, and shared our news with Weston when he came onto the balcony.

"So, are you going to be Cutter Bernardi?" Weston asked.

We both shook our heads, and I looked at Cutter to answer. With a small lift of his lip in a shy smile, he said, "Nova and I are going to keep Vaughn to honor our mom. But Toni is now M—"

He couldn't say the word, and that was okay.

I gave him a slight jab in the ribs. "You can still call me Toni."

Cutter sighed happily and hugged me again. "Thank you for being our person."

Being his and Nova's person was going to be the best damn thing I had ever done in my life.

Epilogue

Weston

One year later

Antonia and I dropped Cutter off at the University of Richmond. The current senior class helped us carry all his things to the third floor. Antonia made Cutter's bed while he and I unpacked his belongings. She hadn't said much on the trip, and I figured it was because her heart was breaking. For over a year now, he'd been her rock, and I expected he didn't even know it.

While she had Nova, who was Miriam's spitting image, Cutter was Antonia's first true love, she had once told me. She'd been there from the second Miriam had found out she was pregnant, through her pregnancy, and in the delivery room when Cutter was born.

What I didn't know until after we'd started touring colleges was that Antonia had never lived in the dorms at Boston University, because of Cutter. She didn't want Miriam to struggle raising her son, so they had an off-campus apartment together. It wasn't until Miriam had bought the house in Grove Hill that they all stopped living together.

I had wondered how it was so easy for Antonia to become the guardian of her friends' kids, but once I heard the entire story, it all made sense. There was no one else more capable of raising Miriam's children than Antonia.

"Do you want to raise your bed?" she asked Cutter, her voice pulling me from my inner musings.

"Should I?" He looked at both of us for the answer.

"Let's try it and see."

Antonia finished putting the bottom sheet on the bed and then stepped back so I could raise the bed. The mechanism was something we had asked for before school started and allowed Cutter to have his bed at three different heights. The tallest would give him a ton of storage space under his bed and allow for a beanbag chair or one of those small dorm room couches.

Once I had the platform spring in place, Cutter and I slipped the mattress back on. He had to heave himself up there, which wasn't much of a challenge, considering he'd grown another two inches this year. As soon as he was up there, though, I knew this would be a no-go. He was going to smack his head on the ceiling.

"Let's try the next level, bud. I'm afraid you're going to knock yourself out."

"Yeah, you're probably right."

The mid-level seemed to be the winner. He still had ample storage underneath and could easily sit on his bed. Antonia went back to making it even though we all knew he'd leave it a mess by the morning. She had focused on a lot of the milestones a teenager needed to hit but rarely worried about those of a mother. This was one of them.

After we'd unpacked and put everything away, we drove Cutter to the nearest box store and stocked him up on snacks. Because he had a full athletic scholarship to pitch, he could go to the cafeteria and eat whatever, but the boy was growing and had all but eaten us out of a home this past year. He was liable to eat a tree on his walk to the café if he didn't have something to snack on.

Back at campus, we parked and walked him to his dorm, even though he'd been here plenty of times to meet with his coaching staff. We paused at his dorm, and I watched Antonia struggle.

She smoothed his shirt over his shoulders and sniffled. "Remember, top grades. Don't fall for the peer pressure of drinking and partying. You're here to represent your school and community. I have a meeting set up for you next week with a national company that does a lot of business here. They want to do some commercials with you."

"I remember."

"You don't take money from anyone unless you run it by me first, got it?" she said as she looked at him. I had to give her credit; when I'd explained the Name, Image, and Likeness situation to her, she'd taken it upon herself to protect Cutter. There was still a policy to follow, and he couldn't take money from just anyone.

Antonia had put her knowledge to work and represented Malik and Jayden as well. Malik was now the proud father of a little girl and attending the University of Richmond on a full basketball scholarship. He and Janelle were coparenting, and she'd been extremely supportive of him moving to Virginia. He was paying child support and had already started a trust fund for his daughter with the help from Antonia. She refused to take a fee from the boys, stating they needed someone in their corner who cared about them and not their bank accounts.

"Don't forget, you're throwing tomorrow," I reminded him. He had a strict schedule to adhere to, and it was important he do so.

"Coach already texted me. I'm going to go see him after you two stop hovering." He winked at Antonia. Their relationship could be a lot different from what it was, and at times I'd feared Cutter would lose who he was after his mom died, but he hadn't.

"Okay, we'll leave you. We're heading to the beach, but it's just a couple hours away. If you need us, call." Antonia gave him a quick hug and then stepped back.

"I'll be fine."

Cutter and I hugged, and then something told me I needed to encourage Antonia to say what she needed to say. I placed my hand on her hip and leaned in. "Tell him what's on your mind." She nodded against my scruff.

Antonia cleared her throat, not that it did anything for her. She tried again. "Cutter, I—"

"I love you, Mom," he said before she could get the words out. He crashed into her open arms and held her tightly. My eyes watered, watching the two of them.

"I love you too. Do good, okay? Don't squander this opportunity. Your mom would've wanted this for you."

"I know, and I won't. Tell Nova I'll call her every Sunday."

Antonia nodded and released him, wiping her tears. Cutter and I hugged again, and then he jogged off.

A lot had changed in the last year and a half, except for how I felt about Antonia. I reached for her hand and held it tightly. "It's going to be okay. He'll come home at Thanksgiving and eat us out of house and home."

"I'd like to come for Parents' Weekend," she said as if it weren't already on our family calendar. "It's important he knows he has a support group."

"He knows, but yes, I'll take the time off, and we'll fly down."

In the car, she didn't say much as I drove to our hotel. We'd decided to spend a couple of days at the beach as a mini vacation before driving back to New Hampshire. The southern weather in August was still warm and relaxing.

We checked in, set our stuff down, and set out to explore the quaint town. We shopped, taste-tested samples of fudge, and roamed the streets until it was time to head back to the hotel and change for dinner.

"We could order in," she said as she pulled her belt tight around her waist.

"We could, but we have a reservation, and while our once-a-month weekend in Boston is nice, I'd like to take my girlfriend out."

She rose onto her toes and kissed me. "You know the house is going to be quiet."

"Not by much," I told her. "Nova's social calendar is filling up, and she told me she wants to play soccer."

"She mentioned it. I don't know anything about it."

"Shocker," I said teasingly. "Everyone is learning at her age; she'll be fine. I'll take her and get her signed up next week."

"You're the best."

My eyes fluttered. "I try."

The restaurant where I'd made our reservation abutted the beach. I'd asked for a coastal view and wasn't disappointed with where they sat us. We were so close, there was sand under our feet.

We ordered a bottle of wine and perused the menu. When she told me she planned to order a salad, I knew we should've come here tomorrow night. Sometimes she made herself sick with worry, and having dropped Cutter off, she most likely wasn't feeling well.

"Do you want to go back to the room?"

"No, this is lovely."

I reached for her hand. "He's going to be okay, and if he's not, he's going to call you."

"I know. It's silly, but I'm going to miss him."

"And you can see him whenever you want. Thanks to modern technology, you can video chat by pressing a button."

Antonia relaxed. "Easier said than accepted."

I didn't even want to think about when Nova left for college. Antonia was going to be a nervous wreck.

After dinner, we walked along the beach, watching as the waves came ashore and the sun went down.

"I think this is a good spot," she said as she dug into her handbag. "Miri would want to be where her son is."

She opened a small bottle and shook out some of Miri's ashes. The slight breeze in the air helped push them all around.

We were silent for a moment, standing there, watching the ashes disappear. I pulled her close, and she rested her head on my shoulder.

"It's nice here."

"It is," I said. "We'll have to make this an annual trip."

"Next year, he'll want his car."

This time I was going to be the voice of reason. "I don't know if I'll be comfortable with him driving this far without someone with him."

Antonia raised her head and looked at me. "You could always drive down with him and then fly back. Malik may want to ride with him as well."

"Definitely a possibility." I kissed the tip of her nose, and she sighed. I was madly in love with her and had been since the day I'd met her. I'd been there at her worst, and when she could've pushed me away, she hadn't. Instead, she'd invited me in, folding me into her chaotic life as a new mom. There wasn't anywhere else I'd rather be.

Slowly, I got down on one knee and fished the ring I'd bought for her out of my pocket. Antonia stepped back slightly and covered her mouth with her hand.

"Weston." Her voice was barely above the sound of the waves, but I heard her clearly.

"Somewhere around the three-week mark of knowing you, I said I was going to marry you. I've never felt this way about anyone, Antonia. Ever since you walked into the gym, and still to this day, I go to sleep and wake, thinking about you.

"When we all moved in together, you gave me the family I'd always wanted. Together, we're raising two amazing kids, and I'm so thankful to be on this journey with you."

I held the ring between my two fingers and then held it a bit higher. "I know we haven't talked about taking this next step, but I'm hopeful you want to be my wife. Will you marry me, Antonia?"

Antonia crouched to my level and held my hand in hers. "Weston, you've been my guiding light since I arrived. You were there, a constant in my life, waiting for me to notice you. I noticed and continue to do so every day that we spend together. Saying yes to you would be . . ." She paused.

"But?"

"No buts," she said and cleared her throat. "Can I finish?"

I nodded.

"Saying yes to you will be the easiest thing I've done in a long time. Yes, I'll marry you. Under one condition."

"Name it."

"We get married at Christmas, when Cutter's home. Just us and our friends and family, in our home where Miri's watching over us."

"Sounds like the perfect wedding for me. Before I slip this ring on your finger, you should know, Cutter gave me some of Miriam's ashes. I had the diamond created with them."

A single tear slipped down her cheek. I wiped it away, never taking my eyes off hers. "I knew you'd miss sharing this moment with her, so I did what I could to make sure she was here." I slipped the ring on her finger and then caressed her cheek with the back of my hand.

Antonia held her hand out, allowing the setting sun to cast a prism in the diamond. She beamed.

"I'm sure you can figure out that I asked Cutter for permission, but I asked your father as well."

"He said no, didn't he?" Antonia laughed.

I couldn't help but laugh right along with her. "It was your brother. I'm going to have to work on him."

She cupped my cheek and looked into my eyes. "I love you. I know our lives are hectic and I don't say it enough, but know that I do. Aside from the kids, you're the best thing to happen to me."

"I love you more," I said as I pulled her to me and sealed our lips together. We'd already become a family, and now we were going to make it official.

Acknowledgments

This story had been playing in my mind for a while, but it didn't fully take shape until my daughter and I went to visit a friend—who happened to be vacationing just a few towns over—for coffee. What should've been an hour-long visit turned into an amazing, all-day adventure.

And that's how the character of Antonia was born.

So, Cara—thank you. Thank you for being a constant in my life and in the lives of my girls. And thank you for introducing us to your sister, Toni. I adore you both more than words can say.

To Lauren and Lindsey—my favorite Ls. I appreciate you so much. You always know how to make my words shine and keep me grounded. This was, by far, my most favorite development letter ever received. I'll save it forever!

To my incredible team at Montlake—being part of this family is a true blessing. Thank you for believing in me and in my stories.

To my bestie, Yvette—sometimes I loathe your imaginary red pen, but truthfully, I wouldn't want to do any of this without you. Your insight, patience, and brilliance mean everything.

To Erik, Madison, and Kassidy—I love picking your brains about titles and cover options. Your input is invaluable, and I'm so lucky to have your support.

To JiLL, Racicot, and Rugby—you're the best writing companions ever.

To Michelle D.—our daily and nightly sprints have been a game changer. Your wisdom, guidance, and friendship continue to be a constant in my life, and for that, I am forever grateful.

To Taylor D.—all is well. Always.

To Karrie O.—thank you for the encouragement and the constant "Is it done yet?" messages.

And finally, to Trudy—I cherish you.

About the Author

In 2012, Heidi McLaughlin turned her passion for reading into a full-fledged literary career. She is now the *New York Times*, *Wall Street Journal*, and *USA Today* bestselling author of The Beaumont Series, The Boys of Summer, and The Archer Brothers. McLaughlin has written more than twenty novels, including her acclaimed first novel, *Forever My Girl*, which was adapted into a 2018 film starring Alex Roe and Jessica Rothe.

Visit the author at www.heidimclaughlin.com, and keep up with her latest releases by subscribing to her newsletter.